ROUGH EDGES

Rough Edges

By
Jannifer Hoffman

Resplendence Publishing, LLC
http://www.resplendencepublishing.com

Resplendence Publishing, LLC
P.O. Box 992
Edgewater, Florida, 32132

Rough Edges
Copyright © 2009, Jannifer Hoffman
Edited by Chantal Depp
Cover art by Rika Singh
Print format ISBN: 978-1-934992-64-7
Electronic format ISBN: 978-1-60735-010-1

Electronic release: January 2009
Trade paperback printing: April 2009

Dedication:

Cherie Hoffman
(who loves my son as much as I do)
And
My beautiful second family
Jeanne Christie
Mike and Holly Christie
Jackie and Erik Madsen

Acknowledgements:

As always my loyal critique partners
Kelly Kirch, Terri Schultz, and Bonnie Barrett
You guys are the greatest.

Special thanks to my reading buddy, Mary Bender

And
Many, many thanks to my editor, Chantal Depp

CHAPTER ONE

Colorado rancher seeking live-in
Nanny for energetic four-year-old twins.
Basic first aid a necessity.
Skilled in piano, swimming, and
horses a plus. Good wages, time off,
and private living quarters.
Minimum three references required.
Zero tolerance for dishonesty.
Contact Dirk Travis,
Fax #388-761-9206

Julia Morgan finished reading the ad and turned hostile green eyes up to glare at her sister. "What is this, Katie, some kind of a joke?"

"Not at all," Katie said. "That ad was written with you in mind. You swim, you play piano, and well, I'd say you can handle basic first aid."

"I didn't study medicine for eight years to be a nanny."

Katie grunted. "You also speak three languages and play a mean piano, yet you haven't touched the keys or seen a patient for eight weeks. Are you planning to sit around and mope for the rest of your life?"

"I'm not moping, dammit, I'm depressed. You're the psychiatrist; can't you recognize depression when you see it?"

"Sure, I also recognize self-pity. And, Julia, you're up to your ears in it."

"I have good reasons."

"Well yes, I'll grant you that. You divorced your no-good cheating husband, and since he was the chief-of-staff at the hospital, he made it impossible for you to stay on. What can I say, Geno Campanili is an ass, I'm glad you took your maiden name back. I wish I had. You know, County Med isn't the only hospital in Minneapolis. Surely with seven years practicing medicine behind you—"

"You're way off base and you know it."

Katie took a deep breath. "Okay, I know it's more than the divorce and losing your job. I'm sorry, but you need to deal with this."

Scalding wet tears welled up in Julia's eyes. "I lost my babies; my precious twins. Do you really think taking care of somebody else's twins will make up for that?"

Katie sat down and put an arm around her sister. "Julia, you're three years older than me and I've always looked up to you. With Mom and Dad gone, we're the only family we have, there's nobody on this earth I love more than you. That's why I'm telling you it's time to get on with your life. I know that sounds cliché but I don't know any better way to say it. Get out there and start living again. Look at you—every time I come over here you have that same old gray sweat suit on. For God's sake, it's the Fourth of July, get out and do something."

Julia pushed a hand through her shoulder-length auburn hair and brushed a tear from her cheek. "I'm not ready."

Katie hesitated a moment, then sighed. "You've never told me what happened that night you miscarried a perfectly healthy five-month pregnancy, but if I ever find out Geno had anything to do with it, I swear I'll personally kill him."

"People go to jail for murder, Katie."

"Yeah, well we both know that doesn't always

happen. Are you afraid of him, Julia?"

"Can we change the subject?"

Katie gave Julia a sad smile. "Of course, I didn't want to talk about bygones anyway. You need to start creating a new past."

Julia blinked away her tears and smiled. "Spoken like a true professional."

Katie grinned. "Okay, let's get back to the ad. I think it's an omen. I had nothing to do during my three-hour layover in Denver, so I picked up a paper lying on the seat beside me and here's this ad right in front of me with a big yellow highlighted circle around it. I knew immediately that 'rancher' was looking for you. His requirements fit you perfectly."

"You're hallucinating, Katie, I've never sat on a horse in my life."

"Three out of four isn't too bad. Besides, it's a lot easier to learn to ride a horse than it is to play piano."

"I told you, I'm not going to waste a medical degree being a nanny."

Katie rolled her cocoa colored eyes. "What have you been doing with your degree for the last two months? You wouldn't have to do it forever. Just promise you'll think about it. Don't worry about the references. I have more than three friends whose children you've treated, and any of them will be happy to put in a good word for you."

Julia finally laughed. "You're actually taking this seriously, aren't you?"

"Like I said, it's an omen." Katie grinned. "And the best part of all, it's nine hundred miles away. You can just disappear and Geno will never know what happened to you."

* * * *

The next morning Julia was in the middle of typing her resume when the phone rang.

It was Geno.

"Hi, honey. How are you?"

Julia's stomach lurched. "What do you want, Geno?"

"Meet me for lunch. I'd like to talk to you."

It had taken all the fortitude she had to divorce him, and she couldn't back down now. Geno would hound her forever if she didn't stand up to him. "We have nothing more to say to each other. Our divorce is final and so is our life together."

"The divorce was a mistake, Julia. We belong together. I still love you, sweetheart."

Julia gritted her teeth. "Did you love me when you were screwing Lana Becker in your office?"

"I told you, Lana means nothing to me. You're the one I love. Let's at least talk about it."

"That might be possible if it were the first time. You and I both know there've been others." Julia drew a deep breath letting it out in a rush. "I shouldn't have been surprised, I guess. After all, I used to be one of those interns."

"You were different, I loved you."

"Did you also love Danielle and Mandy?"

"They were trash, Julia."

"Is that why they both lost their jobs?"

"Julia—"

"I'm through, Geno. I'm going on with my life and you aren't in my plans."

Julia was about to hang up when Geno's chilling voice bit into her. "I hope your plans don't include practicing medicine. I can make that a little difficult for you."

"You can't stop me. County Med isn't the only hospital in town."

"No, but with your record, you won't get taken on anywhere else either."

"My record is impeccable."

"What about that little incident with the Nelson baby?"

Pain wrenched Julia along with the memory of a seven-month-old baby boy dying in her arms. "I couldn't have saved that child and you know it."

"No, but you might have been able to prevent it from happening."

"I had no way of knowing his father was abusing him. Besides, I was already cleared of that."

"Just between you and me, honey, records can be changed. There's likely to be a new development in that case."

"You bastard! Stay out of my life!" Julia slammed the phone down. Closing her eyes, breathing heavily, she pressed cold shaking hands to her warm face. She knew Geno all too well. He had the power to save lives, but he also had the power to destroy them. She'd seen him do it before.

Geno was one of the most sought after and respected surgeons in the city. Minneapolis was a big community, but when it came to the medical field, it was like a small town—everybody knew everyone else—at least those who'd made a name for themselves. Geno Campanili was at the top of that list. It was futile to try to explain her side of the story. Who would believe her? Who would believe that the renowned Dr. Campanili had a dark side that he kept hidden from the public? He didn't know where she lived, but he had too many connections, he could find her if he wanted too.

After two hours of pacing her small apartment, Julia called her sister's office.

The receptionist must have been out because Katie answered the phone. "This is Dr. Katie Benson."

"Katie, it's—"

"Julia! You changed your mind about the ad. You want to go to Colorado."

Julia shook her head. "What? Have you changed professions? You're a mind reader now?"

Katie shrugged. "I just know you, sis. Colorado could be good for you, and this rancher might be a handsome stud."

"After Geno, I've sworn off handsome studs. In fact, I'm not interested in men period. It's the children that intrigue me. I've always enjoyed kids; that's why I chose pediatrics. I think maybe it is time for a change of scenery, and while I'm there I can check out the local clinics in Denver."

"That would be great," Katie said. "I go through Denver regularly. I could see you almost as often as I do now."

"I'm going to think of this as a vacation. How hard can it be to take care of two four-year-olds? I don't even care about the money. Fortunately, Geno and I kept our finances separate. Since I was the saver, I don't have any financial worries."

"Plus you still have your trust fund."

"That's the only bright spot in this whole mess," Julia said. "I never told him about the clause. Ironic isn't it? The only way he could get his hands on Dad's money was if we had children together."

What Julia didn't tell Katie was that she hadn't been ready to have children with Geno. Even though he'd brought the trust fund up a few months before she'd actually gotten pregnant. There was a lot about Geno she couldn't tell her sister, even now after the divorce was final. Katie wouldn't understand—no one would understand why an educated successful woman would stay married to a man like Geno if they knew the full truth about him.

"I know he didn't want you to get pregnant, he used to say some baloney about you being all he needed. It was always about what he needed, wasn't it?"

"I don't want to talk about Geno," Julia said.

"That restriction Dad put on us has always teed me off. It's like he's trying to control our lives from the grave. I swear he left his money to us only because he had no one else to give it to. God, he was such a tightwad."

"He paid for our education. He expected us to use it

to support ourselves."

"Stop making excuses for him, Julia. You're in denial. You know as well as I do what a control freak he was. I don't believe you'd ever have married Geno if Dad hadn't coerced you into it"

Julia's fingers squeezed down on the receiver. "That's a closed subject. Now stop psychoanalyzing me. Save it for your patients."

A heartbeat of silence hung between them before Katie spoke again, more softly. "I'm sorry. It's just that I want you to get out and start living again."

"All right, how do I go about answering this ad?" Julia asked, wanting to end the subject of both Geno and their father.

Katie's tone brightened immediately. "It's already done. I faxed your qualifications out yesterday."

"Katie, for an educated person, you can be such a twit. What if I hadn't wanted to go?"

"Ah, but I knew you would."

Julia bit back a frustrated reply. "Just what did you tell him? What about the references? And—"

"All taken care of."

"Katie, did you tell him I'm a doctor?"

"Of course not. He'd know you're grossly overqualified and he'd never hire you. Here's the fun part. I got a response back this morning. Stay put; I have two hours before my next appointment. I'll be over in fifteen minutes. Bye."

A resounding click echoed in Julia's ear. She stared at the phone a moment before snapping it firmly back in its cradle. Her hands were shaking.

Damn, her take-charge sister.

As much as she loved Katie, sometimes her sister went too far. Julia had wanted a few days to get used to the idea of going to Colorado. Maybe by then the position would have been filled—or she might have had time to change her mind. Of course, she still could, she told herself. Let Katie explain to the rancher what she'd done. It would serve her right.

Julia was still annoyed when the doorbell started ringing non-stop, Katie's signature announcement. She knew before she answered the door she couldn't stay angry with her overzealous younger sister. She loved Katie too much. She did manage to put a grim, disapproving expression on her face.

Katie burst into the house, ignoring Julia's stern look, waving a handful of papers. "You really did a good job writing this up, Julia. I couldn't have done it better myself."

"You *did* do it yourself. So help me, if you fabricated a ton of lies about me, I'm not going, and I may never speak to you again."

Katie handed Julia one of the papers. "Here, read it and tell me if everything isn't true."

Julia gave her sister a sideways glare, snapping the paper out of her hand. It held no more than a few scant lines of Katie's exquisite cursive penmanship.

In response to your ad for a nanny: I am very adept at handling children of all ages. I was on a swim team for three years and helped finance my way through school by giving piano lessons. My first aid skills are current and I have spent most of my adult life being a caregiver to children. I fear my knowledge of horses is limited, but I'm always open to learn new things. I also have a special interest in twins. I look forward to hearing from you.

Respectfully,
Juliana Morgan

Julia read it twice, looking for a flaw. She finally looked up at her self-satisfied grinning sister. "I don't remember ever being interested in horseback riding. I don't even think I like horses."

"You've always had a compulsion to learn new

things. That's why you took language courses that weren't required, and practiced piano until your fingers swelled. I had the same number of lessons you did, and I barely managed Chopsticks."

"That's probably because you were more interested in painting and dance classes."

"Exactly." Katie explained. "That's why Mr. Dirk Travis is looking specifically for you."

"You're so full of it Katie—let me see the references you conned out of your friends."

Katie handed Julia three typed and signed letters.

With a skeptical glance at her sister, Julia quickly read the neatly typed references. The first one explained that Julia was *instrumental* in helping her son when he broke his arm. *She took charge during an emergency situation, and saw to it that my son got the medical treatment he needed*

Julia remembered that case. Her patient had a compound fracture. He came by ambulance, his mangled arm hanging loose, the bleeding stopped by paramedics. She'd prepped the boy and sent him into immediate surgery to straighten the arm and install a pin. The letter avoided the details but stuck with the truth.

The second, a two-year-old child had swallowed a hard candy. Julia worked ER duty the night he was brought in barely breathing. The letter gave her credit for saving the boy with fast thinking—no mention being made of her treating him as a physician.

The third letter written by Katie's next-door neighbor explained how she had come running over hysterical, screaming that her husband was having a seizure. It turned out to be a heart attack. Julia kept him breathing until the paramedics arrived to take over. It was something anyone with cardio pulmonary training could have done.

Julia released a long, heavy, sigh when she looked up at Katie. "What if he calls these people?"

"Not to worry. They all know the situation. I helped them rehearse their answers."

"You are an obnoxious brat, Katie. It's a good thing I love you anyway." Then Julia noticed that Katie had another paper in her hand. "Okay, what's that one?" she asked.

Katie held up the paper. "What this?"

Julia bristled. "What is it, Kate?"

"Oh, just Mr. Travis' reply."

"You got a reply already?"

Katie grinned, handing over the fax.

"I don't even want to know how you managed all this in such a short time," Julia said taking the letter.

Ms. Morgan,

My father has always warned me about something looking too good. Your qualifications are too perfect to believe, but I'm going with my own gut instinct on this.

This is extremely important to me, so rather than have a long distant phone conversation I'd prefer to meet you in person. Can you fly to Denver for an interview on Saturday? Come prepared to start immediately. If I decide you are not right for the job, I will pay you for your time and reimburse your expenses. I will do likewise if you find you are not up to the assignment.

I trust everything you have told me is truthful.

If this plan works for you please fax your ETA so I can pick you up at the airport.

My children and I look forward to your arrival.

Respectfully,
Dirk Travis

CHAPTER TWO

Julia was on a plane to Denver two days later. She had nearly gone into a panic when she realized she had such a short time to get ready.

She went back and forth between telling herself she was crazy for attempting this radical change in her life, to looking forward to having a hand in raising twins. She wished she knew if they were boys or girls, or maybe one of each. Her twins had been girls—identical twin girls.

The memory washed over her in a wave of grief so intense she had to fish in her handbag for a tissue.

She still couldn't understand Geno's reaction when she had told him she was pregnant. His words continued to haunt her. "How could you let this happen? You're a doctor for God's sake. I suppose you conveniently forgot to take your pills".

She was certain she hadn't forgotten to take her pills, deliberately or otherwise, and by the time she realized she was pregnant, the pill container was empty, making it impossible to have them analyzed.

When she'd reminded him that he'd mentioned having a baby only a few months earlier, he'd gotten even angrier. "Yeah, I remember. You said no. You're just like your father, you have to take charge, make your own rules."

Those words cut to the core. He knew exactly how comparing her to her authoritarian father hurt. As usual she'd slinked away in tears, hiding from him until his anger subsided. Even after that scene she naively believed he'd eventually come around and be as happy about the baby as she was. It had seemed for a while he was happy. He even suggested she lighten her workload and see fewer patients.

In her third month she found out there were two babies. When she sprang that bit of information on him, he stormed out of the house and didn't come back for twenty-four hours. Later he apologized, brought her flowers, said he'd just needed some time alone to get over the shock of having twins.

Near the end of her fifth month, she rushed into his office, excited to show him her latest ultrasound, and found Lana Becker on his lap with her skirt hiked up to her elbows.

Julia raced home and started to pack. Fifteen minutes later, Geno walked into the room and tried to put his arms around her.

"What are you doing, Julia?" he'd asked.

Julia twisted out of his grasp. "I'm getting a long overdue divorce."

His face reflected utter disbelief. "Just because of Lana? That was trivial. You can't throw away eight years of marriage because of one little slip-up. And what about my babies?"

His babies? What about his babies! A rage so intense came over her she could feel her throat squeezing shut, and a black haze crowding her brain. If she'd had a gun in her hand she'd surely have shot him. She swung her arm to slap his face, but he sidestepped her swing. Awkward and off balance with the weight of her pregnancy, she fell, hitting her head on the nightstand. The room went black. When she regained consciousness, everything was a blur—the ambulance ride, the pain wrenching hours afterward. The worst pain came when finally coherent, she found out she had miscarried the babies.

She still had nightmares that Geno had done

something to her while she was unconscious.

Geno Campanili was now in her ugly past. She had to keep him there.

At three o'clock her plane landed in Denver. When she arrived in the baggage area she spotted a tall, lanky man much older than she expected holding a sign with her name on it. His faded jeans and dusty boots looked to be as old as he was and there was no mistaking the scowl on his weathered face or the malice in his unsmiling, penetrating gray eyes. Those eyes deepened in color as she approached him.

"Ms. Morgan?" he asked in a gravelly voice.

Julia nodded. "Yes, and you are?"

"Gus Travis, Dirk's father. You got bags?"

"Yes. They should be coming shortly."

This was the man who'd warned his son about anything that sounded too good. At least that explained his sour disposition. He was looking out for his son.

As they waited for the bags, his assessing gaze traveled the length of her five-foot-seven-inch frame, from neatly groomed hair to kid leather shoes. His down turned mouth, made it clear she didn't pass his inspection. Since she'd taken great care winding her thick chestnut hair into a loose French braid and dressing conservatively in a green linen skirt and white silk blouse trying to look like what she thought a nanny might wear on an interview, this odious man's disapproval annoyed her.

Except for an occasional grunt, he didn't speak at all while he led her to an ancient pickup with duct-taped fenders. He flung her two large bags, with surprising ease, into the back of the truck while she got into the passenger side clutching her carry-on bag and purse. The inside appeared to be in no better shape than the exterior. The straw on the floorboards could have lined a pigsty. She half expected chickens to fly out from beneath the tattered seats.

"Nice truck," she mumbled as he got in behind the wheel.

He snickered. "Gets me where I need to go."

After a half hour of driving in uncomfortable silence, she made an attempt at conversation. "How far is the ranch from Denver?"

"A ways," Gus replied.

She gave him a sidelong look wondering if he had some particular reason for not approving of her, other than her credentials being "too good to be true", or if he was just naturally crabby and preferred to be left alone.

"I get the feeling you don't approve of me," she said finally.

His only comment was an inaudible mumble.

"Can I ask why?" she persisted.

His gaze flicked over her then went back to the road. "I'd answer that, but I'm not good with fancy words. I might be a little too blunt for a refined lady like yourself."

"Please, be blunt. I'm an adult."

"I don't take much to Easterners."

Julia gave a raspy laugh. "Mr. Travis, Minnesota is in the Midwest, not the east."

"It's east of Colorado."

"If that's how you see it, I guess I can't argue that point."

"Dirk had twenty-eight answers to that ad. All instate women, except you."

"So why didn't he hire one of them?"

"Seems the young ones were looking for a rich husband and the older ones couldn't keep up with two four year olds. They could all ride a horse, but none of them could play piano—except you."

He stopped talking, but Julia sensed he had more to say so she just stared out the window and waited.

She was right. When he turned off the highway and headed southwest toward the mountains he started up again.

"You don't strike me as a woman looking for a rich man—and you look fit enough to handle younguns. That brings up the curious part. Why is a good looking, educated, according to your letter, woman willing to come out here to live in the sticks to take care of somebody else's kids? Why ain't you married and raising a brood of your own?"

"Maybe I'm gay."

That brought a crack of laughter from him. "Not with legs like that you ain't."

Julia could only guess where he got his criteria for lesbians.

"Look at your fingernails," he went on. "I swear, I ain't never seen nails that perfect that weren't covered with six coats of red polish."

She could have told him that polish wasn't sanitary or acceptable when treating patients. Instead she curled her perfect nails up into her palms and stared out at the breathtaking landscape. To the northwest, the Rocky Mountains loomed, a deep purple haze. At the higher elevations she could see snow lingering in spite of the warm July temperatures.

As they enter the Pike National Forest, she compared the lush greenery to Northern Minnesota.

"You strike me," Gus Travis said suddenly, interrupting her thoughts, "as a woman born with a silver spoon in her mouth looking for a little adventure. If that's the case, you'd be better off, and so would my grandkids, if you admitted it right now so I could turn around and get you back on a plane to your cushy life."

For a man who spent the first half-hour of their trip grunting, he certainly had a lot to say. It amazed her at how observant he was—maybe she shouldn't have worn the kid leather shoes and silk blouse, but she hadn't expected a man to notice such things.

Well, she'd observed a few things of her own.

"Tell me something, Mr. Travis. Did you drive this decrepit old truck deliberately today to try to turn me off?"

He didn't answer, but his twitching lips spoke

volumes.

Twenty minutes later, he turned onto a gravel road toward a fenced area. The truck rattled over a strip of ribbed horizontal poles imbedded in the ground. She guessed it was some sort of gate to keep the livestock from wandering. A *Rocking T* sign decorated with antlers hung above it.

A few minutes later, they crested a hill and started down into a lush green valley. Here she got her first look at the ranch. Nestled below the timberline with the mountains in the background, it looked like it belonged in a scenic painting. She saw numerous buildings, encircled by trees, painted red with white trim and green shingles. They all seemed connected by log corrals with the large barn being in the center. A modern four-level house set apart from the other buildings surprised her.

Gravel crunched under the wheels as Gus pulled up in front of a barren flowerbed near the front door. "You go on in," he said. "I'll bring the bags."

She heard angry shouting even before she stepped out of the truck. Her stomach clenched. She walked up to the front door and knocked hesitantly, doubting it would be heard.

Gus, who seemed oblivious to the dispute going on in the house, called from behind her. "Just go on in."

She raised her hand to knock again only to have Gus reach around her and swing the door open. With him directly behind her she had no choice but to step inside. Gus followed her.

He set her bags inside the door, turned and smirked at her. "Well Missy, you're on your own." That said, he walked out, pulling the door shut behind him.

Standing in the kitchen, Julia heard the angry male voice coming from the next room.

"Dammit, Jason, come out of that bathroom! I don't have time for this crap. Either open the door or I'll break it down and then you'll really be in trouble!"

Julia suspected Gus was waiting outside to take her back to the airport. Right now it seemed like a good idea. Knowing that was exactly what he expected her to do gave her courage. She dropped her handbag and carry-on beside the suitcases and walked toward the noise.

A towering man in well-worn jeans and a red plaid shirt pounded a fist on a door. Water soaked towels lay on the floor in front of it. On the sofa, a small girl huddled, clutching a white Scottish terrier. Both looked as though they'd much rather be someplace elsc. On the short open stairway to the left, another girl about eleven-years-old sat on the fourth step. Julia had the feeling the dog wantcd to bark at her, but the small girl had a choke hold on its neck. Both girls were watching the man who went from shouting to pleading and back to shouting.

Julia took a deep breath and walked up to the closed door.

"Could I help?" she asked.

Dirk Travis, a younger version of his father, turned to stare at her with startling gray eyes. With his dark hair rumpled from running frustrated fingers through it, he reminded her of a wild animal—a very male animal with a two-inch scar on his left temple.

He gave her what might have been a sympathetic look.

"We have a situation here, Ms. Morgan. My son, Jason, locked himself in the bathroom and refuses to open the door. Probably because he's flooded the whole damn thing along with half the living room." He indicated the wet towels on the carpet.

"Would you like me to talk to him?" Julia asked.

Dirk stepped aside. "Please, be my guest. My next move will be to break the door down."

Julia moved close to the door where she heard a small whimpering sound from the other side.

"Jason," she called. "Can you hear me?"

The whimpering stopped. A moment later a timid "yes" came from Jason.

"Jason, why won't you open the door?" she asked

"I maked a mess," he said.

"Why don't you come out so we can clean it up?"

"I can't."

"Why?"

"Daddy's mad. He's gonna spank me."

Julia cast a sharp glance at the boy's father.

Dirk threw his hands in the air and rolled his eyes skyward. The preteen on the stairs snickered.

Julia turned her attention back to Jason. "Has your father ever spanked you before?" she asked.

The reply was slow to come. "No."

"How do you usually get punished?"

"I get time out."

"How long is your time out?"

"About a hundred hours."

Julia suppressed a smile. "Would you like to stay in the bathroom," she asked, "and have your time out in there?"

"No."

"Then why don't you come out and go to your room so you can get your time out over with sooner?"

Jason didn't answer.

"Would you like to do that?" she persisted.

"I can't"

'Why can't you?"

"I don't have any pants on.

"Where are your pants?"

"In the sink… I had…an accident."

Julia glanced at Dirk Travis. He raised his brows in surprise.

"Can we get him a pair of pants?" Julia asked.

Dirk turned to the girl on the stairs. "Megan, run up and get him a pair of pants."

Megan gave him a sullen look, but got up and went upstairs. She came back a minute later, handed the pants to Julia, then returned to her seat on the steps.

"Okay, Jason, open the door and I'll hand you your pants."

A shuffling sound came from behind the door, then the soft click of the lock. When the door opened a couple of inches, Julia pushed the pants inside. They disappeared from her hand. A moment later the door opened and a dejected Jason shuffled out, his eyes fixed on the floor. He walked gingerly until he was past his father then bolted for the stairs. The dog tore free of the girl, leaped off the sofa, and raced after Jason. When the dog deserted her, the girl jumped off the sofa and ran for the stairs.

"I want my Mommy," she cried as she disappeared at the landing.

Dirk swore, and looked in the bathroom with an audible groan. There were water soaked towels everywhere." Megan, would you please clean this mess up? I have to get back out to the stable."

"What do I look like," Megan grumbled, "your slave?"

Dirk gritted his teeth. "Megan, this is not a good time to be giving me any lip. Or maybe you want a hundred hours of time out, too, or a beating, your choice. You were supposed to be watching them."

Megan got up and started toward the bathroom. "I'm only eleven. I'm just a kid."

"Remember that the next time you try to wear makeup."

"Why don't you just send me to an orphanage?"

"Don't tempt me with that just now!" Dirk said. He turned to Julia. "I'm really sorry you walked in on all this, Ms. Morgan. Things usually aren't this hectic around here."

A resounding "Hah" came from the bathroom.

Julia couldn't help but smile. She remembered all too well the turmoil of being eleven. "Please call me Julia. I didn't realize you had three children."

"I'll explain later. Right now I need to get back to the stable. I have a mare trying to foal." His serious face broke into a dazzling, but strained smile as he extended his hand.

"Welcome Julia, I'm Dirk Travis, in case you wondered. You can call me Dirk."

"It rhymes with jerk," Megan mumbled under her breath as she walked by with an armload of dripping laundry.

Dirk scowled at her back. "Meggie, be a dear and show Julia where her room is. Then you can put the casserole Rosie left in the oven. We'll eat in an hour," he said to Julia. "Sorry to abandon you like this, but I really need to go tend to that horse."

"Can I watch?" Megan asked.

"No, you're just a kid," Dirk answered as he stomped out the door.

After Dirk left, Megan cast a glare at Julia, as though daring her to make a snide comment. "Your room is down there," she said pointing to a short stairway to the right of the bathroom. "There's only three doors, the one on the end is the garage, one is Dirk's office, the other one is your room. I trust you can find it by yourself."

Julia smiled. "I'm sure I can. You want me to help you with the casserole?"

"No, I'm almost twelve and very grown up for my age in spite of what the jerk thinks. And don't get the idea I need any nannying. You're here for the brats, not me."

Without giving Julia a chance to reply, Megan whirled around and disappeared through a room off the kitchen that Julia assumed was the laundry facility.

Julia shook her head, and went to the kitchen to retrieve her bags. Coming back through the mammoth living room, she noticed her surroundings for the first time. Decorated with a western motif, the cozy room included rustic tables, a large pine sofa, and two massive chairs in colorful Native American fabric. Numerous De Grazzia prints decorated the earthy sponged painted walls. A baby grand piano dominated one corner of the room, sticking out like a ballet dancer at a hoedown. She paused to admire the black lacquered finish.

She lugged her bags the five steps down to the lower level, found the two rooms across the hall from each other and located hers on the first try. It was larger than she'd expected with its own bath, a cozy sitting area, and mini kitchen complete with a sink and small refrigerator. She opened the curtains that covered sliding doors leading to the back porch and saw a spectacular view of the mountains. It was the first encouraging thing she'd encountered.

She could have unpacked, but decided against it. What if she wouldn't be staying? Instead she decided to take a shower to wash away the dust she'd accumulated riding in Gus's old truck.

While the hot steamy water poured over her, she thought about Dirk Travis. He wasn't strikingly handsome, but he had a rugged animalism about him and gray wolf like eyes that devoured with a simple look.

Katie would have been delighted. Julia was not. The last thing she wanted was to be attracted to this man. She had to make it clear right from the onset that she had no interest in Dirk Travis other than as an employer.

Looking out her window, the view was enough to tempt her to stay, and she was more than a little curious about the children. The little girl mentioned her mommy. Where was she? Was Dirk still married? And where did Megan fit in?

* * * *

Dirk made long strides toward the stable. He felt frustrated and angry and a whole lot of other emotions he didn't have time to name at the moment. He only hoped that unfortunate scene inside didn't have Julia Morgan running for cover before he got a chance to explain why he was such a piss-poor father. He loved those kids, but he didn't have a clue how to handle them. In the seven weeks since Gloria dropped them in his lap, it had been one disaster after another with Rosa Gravera, his cook and housekeeper of three years, threatening to quit if he didn't get someone to take care of the twins. "I have grandchildren," she'd said. "I'm too old to chase four-year-olds."

It was an understatement to say Julia Morgan was not what he expected. She was too good-looking, too refined, too—everything. What had he expected? He wasn't sure, but whatever it was, she didn't fit the mold. Nannies were supposed to be—what? Homely and frumpy? They certainly didn't have exotic almond shaped eyes the color of emeralds and rich auburn hair that had no place in a matronly French braid, nor did they carry themselves like royalty looking like they just stepped off of a modeling runway. Why did he have the feeling her plain clothes, staid hairstyle, and lack of makeup were a disguise? He wasn't entirely sure why that should irritate him, but it did.

At least, and most important of all, she seemed to be able to handle kids. That alone convinced him he wanted her to stay—but it would have to be on his terms. On the top of his list of terms was no personal involvement. He would set her straight on that right from the start; if she had romance in mind, like ninety percent of the other applicants, she could high tail it back to the city, no matter how good she was with kids.

At the stable he greeted his right hand man, Charlie Mack, with an affable grunt. Mack was a tall, good looking ex-jock with more charm than sense and a prison record resulting from an unfortunate dalliance with the wrong seventeen-year-old girl. No matter he was barely twenty at the time and she was a willing participant; her daddy was a cop and they sent him up for seven years. He'd served four of them before he got paroled, swore he'd learned his lesson, and came to the *Rocking T* as a horse trainer. Dirk liked him; the man was good with animals and could practically charm the saddle onto the orneriest horse.

"That the new nanny?" Mack asked.

"I haven't hired her yet," Dirk said, his attention on the birthing stall and his prize mare. The beautiful chestnut thoroughbred was lying flat, breathing laboriously between bouts of moaning and fidgeting. "How's Evening Star doing?"

Mack, squatting in front of the animal rubbing her neck, shook his head. "I don't know. She's been in labor too long. I'm afraid you might have to go in."

Swearing softly so as not to upset the mare, Dirk opened the gate and stepped inside. "Try to keep her head down," he said, rolling his sleeves up. "And talk to her real nice like." He knelt behind the horse and put a hand inside the birth canal.

Evening Star started kicking, attempting to get to her feet.

"Keep her down, Mack," Dirk said with quiet urgency as he worked his arm, up to the elbow, into the mare.

Mack put gentle but firm pressure on the horse's neck. "Easy girl. Papa's here, he'll take care of you. Hang in there just a little longer."

While Mack kept his soothing words flowing, Dirk searched for a leg. He found it, then another along with a tailbone. "Damn, it's breach."

"Can you turn it?" Mack asked.

"No, it too late. I'm going to have to pull it." At that moment Evening Star decided to push, squeezing down painfully on Dirk's arm. He grimaced, pulling back bringing the hind legs with him. When the contraction ended, the hind legs were visible.

Dirk kept a firm grip on the legs to prevent them from slipping back in. "When she pushes again, make sure she stays down; use your body weight on her head if you have to. If she gets to her feet we could lose the colt."

Mack acknowledged the order as he continued murmuring encouragement, rubbing the panting mare's sleek wet neck.

When the next contraction hit, Dirk got into position. While Mack threw himself on the struggling horse, Dirk braced his feet on her rump and pulled, stretching every muscle in his body. It took three more contractions before the limp colt lay in Dirk's blood and amniotic fluid drenched lap. "It's a girl," he said working quickly to clear the newborn's air passage.

"Is she okay?" Mack asked.

Dirk didn't answer as he desperately tried to bring life to the colt. He gave it some jarring thumps on the backbone, massaging its throat. Finally it shook its head and started gulping ragged breaths of air.

A resounding cheer burst out of Mack.

Dirk came to his feet, grinning. "You can let Star up. It's her turn to take over."

"Oh, my God, she's beautiful," Megan cried from the top rail. When Dirk turned toward her, she said quickly, "I just came to tell you supper will be ready in fifteen minutes."

Dirk smiled. "You're right, she is beautiful—she looks just like her mama. I'll need to shower before I come in. I can use the one in the bunkhouse. You think you could get me a set of clean clothes."

Megan stared with wide-eyed distaste at his saturated jeans and shirt. "Yuck! I'll be right back." She jumped off the railing and disappeared out the barn door.

CHAPTER THREE

Supper was chaotic to say the least.

Jason spilled his milk, and Megan rushed to sop it up. Christa, Jason's twin, refused to eat casserole until Dirk, with semi-controlled patience, picked the tomatoes out of it. Megan complained about being the resident slave. Dirk suggested maybe she should be wearing chains. Jason spilled his milk again, this time in his plate. Megan replaced his plate grumbling about his clumsiness. The terrier, Pickles, sat by Christa's chair, whining for scraps. He refused to eat the tomatoes she handed him and dropped them on the floor. Megan picked up the tomatoes and locked Pickles in the laundry room, which brought a round of protest from both Christa and Jason.

Dirk looked apologetically across the table at Julia. "I wish I could tell you it's not normally like this."

Julia gave him a sympathetic smile. What she would have liked to tell him was that the activity surrounding the table was a heartwarming change to the environment she'd grown up in and the one she'd shared with Geno. Her father had demanded absolute silence at the dinner table—from everyone other than himself. It was usually the time of day when he aired his disappointments in life and the shortcomings of his wife and daughters. The only laughter in their home happened behind closed doors when she and Katie were alone, or with their mother, when their father was away on one of his many business trips. She'd had enough meals at friends' homes to know how active a normal family meal could be, and all her life she'd longed for it.

Meals with Geno had been different. Except for the first couple of years of their marriage, they said very little to each other. She kept her silence for fear of provoking one of his ugly temper tantrums, and when Geno talked, the subject was usually one or more of his many accomplishments in life. She'd nod or comment at the appropriate times while mentally planning her appointments for the next day.

"May I be excused?" Megan asked. "I have to call Trisha about her birthday party."

"Yeah, go ahead," Dirk said. "I'll take care of the dishes." As Megan rushed off, he called after her. "Remember your half hour limit, Meggie."

Megan made a loud exasperated groan, turning to face him from the doorway. "You do know her party Friday night is a sleepover, don't you?"

Dirk got up and started gathering the dishes. "Fine, as long as one of her parents is there—and no boys."

Megan rolled her eyes and stomped off mumbling. "Whatever."

Jason and Christa got up to race after her.

Dirk stopped them short. "Did you guys forget something?"

"May we be excused?" they asked in quick perfect unison.

"Yes, you may, and leave Meggie alone while she's on the phone," he called after them laughing.

Julia got up and started clearing plates and glasses, relieved to do something she felt comfortable with. "They are delightful," she said.

"Yeah, they are, but they're also a handful. The good news is we'll have thirty minutes of peace and quiet because they'll be sitting like church mice outside

Meggie's door, trying to listen in on her phone call."

"Megan is amazing for her age. She behaves more like a mother than a sister."

With practiced ease, Dirk scrapped plates and started filling the dishwasher. "There's a sad reason for that," he said. "Let's sit out on the back porch, so we can talk without little ears hanging around the corner. You go on out." He nodded toward a pair of sliding glass doors. "I'll finish up here and bring the coffee. How do you like yours?"

"Black is fine."

Outside, Julia took a seat on a cushioned chair by a small table. She breathed deeply of the fresh mountain air and stared into the brilliant orange sun, less than a hand high over the horizon. It was so peaceful without the sounds of car horns and traffic noise, and so removed from the demanding social calendar Geno's position had forced her to participate in.

Moments later, Dirk interrupted her musings when he set a Denver Bronco's mug in front of her and took the seat across the table. "It sure is beautiful here," she said looking out at the distant purple mountain haze.

"Yeah, I love it. Dad built the ranch in a rift where the Pike National Forest separates. It's one of the few places in the area privately owned. The mountains you see are the part of the Rockies where the ski resorts start. On a clear day, with a good pair of binoculars, you can actually see Breckinridge. We have the Tarryall River flowing on the north side and the South Platte on the south side."

Dirk stared into the western sky for a time without speaking. Finally he sighed. "I was born here, in the little cottage back in the trees by the barn. We use it as a bunkhouse now. I had this home built when I married Gloria, and since she didn't get on well with Dad, he stayed in the cottage."

"Gloria was your wife?"

"Is my wife,' he corrected.

The look on her face told Dirk she was surprised, and he knew before he went any further he'd have to explain. "I may as well tell you the whole story so you understand my position here and why I'm such lousy father."

"You're not—"

"Please, don't patronize me," he interrupted. It was bad enough he had to lay his disastrous marriage out on a table to be examined so she could understand his relationship with his children. He didn't want her to think he was doing it to gain sympathy.

"I married Gloria six years ago. Obviously Megan isn't my daughter. She's Gloria's child by her first husband. Meggie was two when we married—a sweeter little angel you never saw—and she loved the ranch back then. Gloria never did, too secluded for her, and too far away from the social whirlwind she craved. She wasn't happy when she found out she was pregnant and discovering she carried twins didn't help matters. She had this dream of traveling the world doing concerts. She was—is an excellent pianist. I guess she thought the babies would tie her to this ranch forever. She finally took off to pursue her dream, but the surprising thing is, she took all three kids with her. Since the twins were only eighteen months old, I believed they needed their mother, so I didn't fight for custody—not that I'd have gotten it anyway. She moved to New York and, as talented as she was, I wasn't surprised she managed to earn a living playing piano." He didn't add that her income was supplemented by hefty support payments from him.

"Did you get to see them?" Julia asked.

"Once, I flew to New York for the weekend. They were almost three at the time. It was a disaster. They barely remembered me, wouldn't speak to me, and either hung on their mother's leg staring at me as though I were a storybook villain, or hid out in Megan's room the whole time I was there. They'd gotten used to a different life and

I was an unwelcome intrusion. Even Megan, who did remember me, kept her distance. She made it quite clear that I had deserted her. It broke my heart, but there was little I could do short of totally disrupting their lives. They seemed to be well cared for so I came back home intending to file for divorce."

"But you didn't."

"No. I started proceedings, but then she called, all excited about a tour through Europe—the chance of a lifetime, she said. She wanted to take Meggie, but couldn't handle the twins and would I keep them while she went? As angry as I was with her for putting her own life ahead of theirs, it gave me a chance to get reacquainted with my children, so I readily agreed. That was two months ago."

Julia's finely shaped brows shot up. "Oh, my gosh."

"Yeah."

"But you have Megan too."

Dirk took a deep breath, releasing it slowly. "For that I could have strangled her. Not because she left Meggie, but because she didn't tell her. She had some guy drive them all here from New York—her agent, she said. Meggie was so excited about going on the trip."

Dirk paused, turning to gaze at the darkening shadow of mountains, swallowing the thickness in his throat. "She stayed less than an hour then just drove off, leaving Megan behind with Jason and Christa. She didn't even bother to say goodbye. Megan sat by the window for two days waiting for her mother to come back for her."

"How could she do a thing like that?"

Dirk shook his head. "It's beyond me."

"Did she at least call to explain?"

A cynical laugh escaped Dirk. "We haven't heard one word from her."

He watched her silently for a moment, noting the tear swimming in her eyes before she turned away.

"Sorry to lay all this on you," he said, "but I felt it was important to help you understand what the twins and

Meggie have been through."

She nodded. "Yes, thank you for that."

"I'm prepared to pay you seven hundred a week. You can have Sundays off, and any other time you think you need, we can work around it. Carrie and her husband, David Masters, live a trailer home back in the trees on the other side of the corral. Dad and Charlie Mack live in the bunkhouse. David and Mack work for me. I'll introduce you tomorrow. Anyway, Carrie has been willing to step in and help out, but she's eight months into a difficult pregnancy so she hasn't been able to do much lately. Rosa Gravera comes every day to do the housekeeping and the cooking during the week. On weekends I take over and Meggie, as you've seen, is a big help—when she's not sulking. Her capability leads me to believe it was Meggie who took care of the twins while her mother ran around. I'm hoping your being here will relieve her of that responsibility. In spite of her constant complaining about being a slave, don't be too surprised if she balks at giving it up."

"It would surprise me if she didn't."

Her insight pleased him. "I'm glad you understand."

"I guess then, my tenure would only last until Gloria returns."

He drew air into his lungs, staring at the sinking sun, drumming his fingers on the glass table. "I have no intention of letting Gloria take Jason and Christa away from me. I'll fight her tooth and nail with every dime I have. Unfortunately, I can't stop her from taking Meggie."

Dirk stared into his empty coffee cup, knowing there was more he had to say. He hadn't arrived at the most delicate part of the interview. "Now that you've heard my story and before you tell me if you want to stay, there are a few questions I need to ask you. I'm not quite understanding why a woman like you would be willing to drop your life—whatever it was—and move out here to live. I don't mean to pry, I just want some security that you won't suddenly up and leave, go back to a husband or boyfriend."

"I don't know what you mean by 'a woman like me', but I can assure you, I'm not pining for my ex-husband and I don't have a boyfriend."

Dirk hesitated a moment. He knew he had no right to ask his next question, but right now his children were more important to him than protocol. "Legally you don't have to answer this, but are you by any chance pregnant?"

She turned away, staring into the sunset. "No, I'm not pregnant."

"Good. I just have one more thing to say. I had a lot of other applicants, a good share of them husband hunters. I feel it's only fair to warn you that if you have any thoughts along that line you may as well know right now it's not going to happen. Now do you have any questions?"

She managed a thin smile. "I'd say you've spelled out my feelings exactly in the romance department, in fact, I wouldn't have it any other way. I do have one question. In your ad you mentioned an ability to play piano?"

He smiled. "That's for Meggie. I think she has talent and maybe you could give her a few lessons. I asked about the swimming because we have a pond nearby where the kids like to swim. The first aid—we're fifty miles from the nearest hospital. There's a clinic in Danango, down the road about eight miles—that's where Rosa lives—but the doctor only comes every couple of weeks. That's no help in an emergency. Dad has a heart condition and with kids getting skinned knees and such, I'd just like to know somebody is around who can handle the basics without panicking. As far as horseback riding, I'm planning to get the kids started riding and if you're interested, you could learn right along with them. If you don't care too, I won't hold that against you."

"Okay, I'll get back to you on that. One other thing, I need to buy a car so I have some transportation."

"Not necessary. My wife's Land Rover is in the

garage. It wasn't classy enough for her liking. If you don't mind driving an SUV you're welcome to use it."

Julia smiled. "I appreciate the offer and don't mind at all driving it."

"Good." He held out his hand. "You can start tomorrow. We can just wing it for a few days until you get into the swing of things." He gave her a bodily once over. "Don't worry about a dress code. Most people are more comfortable in jeans out here."

* * * *

Dirk lay on his bed, fully clothed, staring up the ceiling. Julia Morgan confused him. He wished she'd given him some hint as to why she'd accepted the nanny position. He hadn't felt right questioning her about her personal life. After all, he'd called her three references and they'd all given her a glowing report, plus she was intelligent, well groomed, and more than qualified. Too good to be true? Why had she turned away when he asked her about being pregnant? So what if she had some secrets in her past. Hell, nobody knew about past secrets better than he did. Fortunately he wasn't the one who had to supply the references or explain why he couldn't fight for custody of his children.

CHAPTER FOUR

Julia spent the remainder of the evening unpacking and getting acquainted with her new living quarters. After ten weeks of vegetating, she looked forward to this new challenge though her stomach churned with nervousness.

She plugged in her cell phone so she could call Katie when she finished hanging up her things. Right now she could use a little boost from her overzealous sister.

She sat on the bed and opened her carry-on case, containing her emergency kit complete with medical instruments. On the flight she had turned it over to an attendant after showing her physician's license, but it was something she couldn't bear to leave behind.

When she thought about Geno, she experienced an overwhelming sense of relief to be this far away from him. How could she have put up with his brutality for so long—especially since she'd been required, as a doctor, to report abusive spouses and parents? Was she programmed by her own father to accept that lot in life?

She set the medical bag inside her otherwise empty suitcase on the closet floor, and picked up her cell phone to call Katie. The phone blinked *no service.*

* * * *

The next morning, Julia had barely finished showering and dressing when she heard scratching and whispering noises outside her door.

Smiling to herself, she quickly flung open the door. Jason and Christa lay on the floor, their ears pressed to the space that had been the door. They both stared up at her with wide blue eyes before scrambling to their feet and racing up the steps, Pickles close at their heels. Julia laughed at their childish antics; she would have to remember their penchant for listening at doors.

Oddly, their actions elevated her confidence. Still smiling, she left her room and walked up to the kitchen, where she found Dirk making breakfast. She'd expected Rosa. Then she remembered it was Sunday and Rosa had weekends off.

She took a deep breath, mentally chastised herself for lack of nerve, and managed a cheery, "Good morning."

Dirk turned to look at her, his eyes flicking over her loose-fitting jeans and lime pullover. He grinned. "Good morning to you. I see you're ready to face the dragons."

She wondered why she hadn't noticed his heart-stopping smile the day before and hoped it was something one became immune to. She shrugged. "I know you said I could have Sunday off, but since this is my first day, I'd really like to spend it getting to know the kids."

"Fine with me. This is usually the day they have me full time. I planned to take them on a hike and you're welcome to come along."

"I've never been hiking before but—sure, why not. What can I do to help here?"

He gave her a curious look then turned back to flipping pancakes. "You can call the troops down, everything's ready."

When they pulled out of the drive an hour later in Dirk's crew cab pickup, Julia caught a glimpse of Gus watching from the corral with a glacial stare that could have frozen stone. People disliking her made her uncomfortable, particularly when she'd done nothing to warrant their disapproval other than coming from the *East*. She wondered what she'd have to do to get in his good graces. Obviously going off for what appeared to be a pleasant family outing with his son wasn't going to do it.

Hiking in the Pike National Forest proved as enlightening for Julia as it was for Jason and Christa. Even Megan, who'd complained about being forced to go, seemed to enjoy herself, listening intently whenever Dirk explained some element of nature.

Jason and Christa were more interested in exploring. When Jason overturned a rock to examine the tiny wriggling creatures underneath, Julia went down on her knees for a closer look. It fascinated her to realize that a four-year-old could name more insects than she could. From her position on the ground, she smiled up at Dirk and found him watching her with a somber expression on his face. He immediately turned his attention to name the yellow and purple Columbines Christa clutched in her fingers.

At lunchtime they stopped by a crystal clear stream and snacked on cheese, crackers, and sodas. Soon thereafter they started the trek back to the trailhead. On the drive to the ranch, Dirk remained silent while the twins continued their chattering excitement, which Megan tried unsuccessfully to ignore. Julia rested against the seat trying to remember when she'd had a more relaxing and enjoyable day.

Dirk released an audible groan when he pulled up beside a white Mercedes in front of the house.

"What's she doing here?" Megan grumbled from the back seat.

Dirk admonished her. "Mind your manners, Megan, she just wants to see Star's new foal."

"Can we see it too?" Jason chimed.

"Of course. You can all come."

"What about Nanny?" Christa asked following her sister out of the car.

Dirk laughed. "Yes, Nanny too." He turned to Julia. "Nanny doesn't seem like a proper form of address. What do you prefer they call you?"

Julia thought for a moment then smiled. "When my sister was little, she couldn't pronounce Juliana, so she just called me Anna. How about that?"

Megan slammed the car door. "That's dumb. It sounds like an old lady, like grandmother or something."

"You can't tell she's not old enough to be a grandmother?" Dirk chided her.

Megan gave him a dark look.

"Well," Julia said. "Since you're older, I don't see any reason why you can't call me Julia if you like."

Megan muttered a reply low enough that Julia couldn't hear.

As they walked toward the stable, an exotic raven-haired woman dressed in red jeans and white sweater clinging to a body that belonged on the cover of Vogue sauntered their way. Julia was suddenly aware of her own soiled jeans and disheveled hair.

The Vogue cover rushed up to Dirk and planted a red-lipped kiss on his mouth. "Darling, where have you been?"

Megan gave the woman a look that should have been illegal for a child of eleven. "He went on a hike with his family and our wonderful new nanny, Julia."

Megan ignored Dirk's raised eyebrows and marched past him toward the stable with Jason and Christa close on her heels.

"Watch those two," Dirk yelled after her. "Just so you know," he said to Julia, "The twins aren't allowed in the barns or corrals without adult supervision. Most of our horses are thoroughbreds and they can be high-strung by nature." Dirk slipped an arm around Vogue-cover's narrow waist. "Julia Morgan, this is Melody Dupree. Melody is a close friend and has some mares here for breeding."

Julia could see that name on the cover of a magazine. "Is that what you do here—breed thoroughbreds?"

"Breed them, raise them, train them, among other things. I do have some cattle, but the focus is mostly on the horses."

"I was hoping we could go for a ride," Melody cooed in a voice that matched her name.

Dirk shrugged. "Sure, why not. You'll be all right with the kids for an hour or so, won't you?" he asked Julia.

"Of course." Why was she tempted to say, *no, it's my day off, and isn't it your day to spend with the children?* She didn't usually have catty thoughts.

They walked into the barn where Megan and Jason straddled the top rail of a stall. Christa bounced around on the ground. "Lift me up, Daddy. I can't see."

Dirk laughed and swung her up beside her brother. "Here you go, punkin."

"Is it true you had to help her get borned?" Jason asked, staring in awe at the new colt nuzzling mother's milk.

Dirk gave Megan an odd look. "Who told you that, Jason?"

"Meggie."

Megan groaned. "Any moron could have known that by the way you were all covered with muck and stuff."

Dirk shook his head. "Sometimes you amaze me, Meggie." Before Julia could figure out if that was a compliment or a complaint, he started to leave. "You guys can wait here," he said "I'm going to have Mack saddle a couple of horses."

"When can I start riding?" Megan asked.

For a second, Dirk looked like he wanted to say something more, then his features softened and he smiled. "Soon, Meggie, real soon."

Dirk regretted his decision to go riding with Melody even before they left the yard. In the past watching her curvaceous behind sway in the saddle had stirred his blood, but today it irritated him. When the kids came two months earlier, he'd called Melody to inform her that their little trysts were over. He couldn't have her spending nights at his place with his children sleeping in the next room.

It took less than ten minutes for her to sidle up to her favorite subject. "I brought a blanket along," she said. "Just in case we want to stop and…rest."

Dirk had noticed the blanket she'd tied to the back of her saddle. "That's not a good idea—"

"Are you getting your *needs* met elsewhere, Dirk?"

"Since when would that bother you?"

"Maybe the new nanny? She's quite a looker."

"Don't be ridiculous, Melody. In the first place, Julia just arrived yesterday, and in the second place, she's here to take care of the kids, not service my needs, as you put it."

Melody grunted. "She doesn't look much like a nanny."

"Will you get off of it?" He jabbed his horse in the flanks and galloped on ahead of her, hoping to put an end to the discussion. He didn't want to talk about Juliana Morgan, and he didn't want to think about the pleasant day he'd had with her. Julia had an aura of innocence about her. Observing her excitement in the woods was a delightful change from most of the women he'd known—even the bubbly exuberant Melody. Of course, Melody's mind had only one track: sex. That was good while it lasted, but as far as he was concerned it was over. His kids were now his main priority; they'd been neglected long enough.

Melody, an experienced rider, was beside him in an instant. She stayed with him until he slowed his horse back to a walk.

"Why don't you come to Denver for a weekend and stay at my place. I mean, now that you have a nanny and all…"

Dirk should have known Melody wasn't a woman who took subtle hints. He had to spell it out for her. "Melody, if we're going to have any kind of relationship it's going to be on business terms only. I just don't have time for anything else right now."

A sad smile settled on her face. "I suppose saying 'I

love you' won't help."

Dirk was certain Melody's 'I love you' meant 'let's have sex'. That's why he'd been attracted to her; she liked her freedom and wasn't looking for strings. Between his deserting wife, and a mother who left when he was ten, Dirk had learned a cruel lesson—city-bred women weren't satisfied with remote ranch living.

"No, it wouldn't," he said. "It only complicates things. Do you still want me to keep your mares? One is due to give birth any day now."

Melody turned wide blue eyes on him. "Of course, I want you to look after my thoroughbreds. You have top-notch stallions. I can't think of any place I'd rather have them. Besides," she said, kicking her mare into a gallop, "that way I have an excuse to come see you."

* * * *

Julia sat out on the pouch overlooking the mountains, nursing a cup of coffee. The twins were worn out and Megan had insisted they go straight to their room for a nap. Surprisingly, they gave her no argument.

With nothing else to occupy her mind, Julia's thoughts focused on her new boss and his lovely companion. It shouldn't have surprised her to see Dirk so eager to go riding with the exuberant Miss Melody. He'd been without his wife for three years; naturally he'd have girlfriends.

Julia did get a small measure of satisfaction from Megan's obvious dislike of the woman. Not surprisingly, Megan snubbed Julia five minutes after the riders had left.

Then there was Gus.

She'd observed him standing at the corner of the stable, watching his son ride off with Melody, and the look he sent after them went beyond hostile. Julia sighed. At least she wasn't the only woman on his disapproval list.

Before she'd left the stable, a man approached her, introducing himself as Charlie Mack, Dirk's right hand man. Charlie was friendly, charming, and witty with a disarming smile and dark hooded eyes that seemed too old and too observant for his twenty-some years. He'd offered to show her around the ranch, or drive her anywhere she needed to go on her time off. She declined the first, expecting Dirk to give her a tour, and the second explaining she had her own transportation. She was certain she'd seen him outside earlier and wondered if it was a coincidence he'd waited to materialize after Dirk and Melody had left.

Julia blew out a huff of air, wishing she understood exactly what annoyed her about the woman. She hadn't done anything to gain Julia's disapproval. Dirk said he'd be home to make hamburgers on the grill for dinner—or supper as he called it—so he wasn't planning to spend too much time with Melody, unless she stayed to eat. Julia shook that thought away.

She found it relaxing not having to worry about planning and preparing meals. Dirk had made it clear from the onset he didn't expect her to cook with the exception of fixing lunches for the children on Rosa's days off. Not that she disliked working in the kitchen, but Geno's peculiar tastes and demanding attitude had made it an unpleasant experience.

Tomorrow she would meet Rosa Gravera, the woman who tended to the meals and housekeeping from Monday through Friday. Julia hoped to find an ally in the Spanish-speaking woman since Julia was quite fluent in the language. A fact she hadn't shared with her employer since she thought him already too curious about her background.

More than once during their hike he'd asked subtle questions like why she had a special interest in twins and how, living in Minnesota, did she happen to see the Denver Post ad. She'd told the truth about the ad, but skirted around the twins inquiry saying most people were fascinated by multiple births. Even though it was a truth, she'd averted her eyes so he wouldn't see the pain his question caused her. He'd accepted her based on their interview so she saw no need to rock the boat, as her mother would say, when she warned Julia and Katie not to share any information they didn't have to with their father.

At dinner, Jason didn't spill his milk and Christa approved of everything on her plate. Dirk seemed to be in a good mood, good-naturedly teasing the twins, and even Megan cracked an occasional smile—until she hit Dirk with her latest gripe.

"Why is *that woman* always here?" she asked.

"She's a customer. I'm boarding and breeding mares for her. You know that, Meggie, so why do we have this same discussion every time she comes?"

"I don't like her." Megan grumbled. "She's such a phony."

"What if I said I didn't like your friends?"

Megan snorted. "If you didn't like my friends you wouldn't let me see them."

Dirk had trouble trying to hide his amusement. "I guess that's what makes me the adult and you the kid."

Megan took a bite out of her hamburger, rolling her eyes.

"What's a phony?" Christa asked.

Megan looked at Julia. "Why don't you explain to her what a phony is?"

Julia felt a trap being sprung. She glanced at Dirk, uncertain if she wanted to be involved in this conversation.

He nodded. "Go ahead."

Julia cleared her throat. "Well, a phony is someone who pretends to be something they aren't."

Megan grinned.

Dirk settled piercing gray eyes on Megan. "Tomorrow you start piano lessons," he said.

"When can I ride a horse?" Jason asked.

"Not until we get one your size," Dirk answered, chucking him under the chin.

* * * *

Julia managed to be up before the twins the following morning, and she found Rosa bustling about the kitchen making breakfast. Rosa, nearly as round as she was tall, had her graying hair bound in a tidy little bun, and dark Spanish eyes that twinkled when she smiled. She flashed a wide smile at the first sight of Julia.

Julia retuned the smile and extended a hand. "Hello, Rosa, I'm Julia."

Rosa grasped Julia's hand. "Me no speak so good English," Rosa said with a touch of sadness in her voice.

"Entonces es bueno que puedo hablar español."

Rosa's grin showed a full set of teeth. She reached out and clasped hefty arms around a stunned Julia. "You are answer to my prayers, sweet *señorita*. First I pray for someone to take over the care of those two *niños*—I am too old they wear me out—then I pray for someone to talk to."

Julia laughed. "I hoped to see a friendly face this morning. I guess we both have something to be thankful for."

"Yes," Rosa agreed, nodding. "Maybe you could please go bring the children to breakfast now. Mr. Travis left early and will not eat with us."

* * * *

That afternoon while Julia gave Megan piano lessons, Christa walked into the room with a doll plastered with bandages. She laid the doll on the sofa and proceeded to listen to its cotton heartbeat with a three hundred dollar stethoscope.

Julia's own heart did a triple beat. "Keep playing," she told Megan before she raced to rescue the stethoscope from Christa.

"Where did you get this?" she asked, attempting to stay calm.

Christa grinned. "From a bag in your closet."

Julia chastised herself for leaving the bag where curious little hands could find it. She knelt down beside Christa, pulled the device from her ears, and clasped it to her chest out of Megan's view. "You shouldn't be going into Anna's things, honey. Not without asking."

"I couldn't ask, you weren't there."

Obviously not, Julia surmised. "I'll tell you what. If you promise never to go into my room again when I'm not there, I'll buy you a doctor play set of your own when I get into town."

"Okay," Christa said, smiling. "Then when Joanie gets sick again I can fix her."

Julia touched the doll's curly yellow hair. "Is this Joanie?" she asked.

Christa nodded. "Mommy gave her to me before she went away." She looked up at Julia with tear-filled eyes. "When is mommy coming home?"

Julia swallowed the lump in her throat. "I don't know, sweetheart. I guess we'll just have to wait and see."

Christa blinked away her tears, sighed deeply, and gave Julia a sad smile. Suddenly tiny arms flew around Julia's neck. "I'm glad you're here," Christa said. She stepped back, grabbed her doll, and ran up the steps toward her room.

Julia stood for a moment staring after the little girl. When she realized the piano music had stopped, she turned to see Megan watching with inquisitive green eyes.

"Please, keep playing," Julia said. "I'll be right back." She hurried down the steps to her room, holding the stethoscope in front of her. She wasn't certain if Megan had seen it, but the piano started playing again a little louder than before.

Julia pulled the medical bag from the suitcase in the closet, replaced the stethoscope, and did a quick inventory of the contents. Satisfied that everything else was intact, she put the bag up on the top shelf in the closet, out of reach of searching little fingers, making a mental note to be more careful in the future.

Hours later in the twin's room, Julia read to Christa while Jason drew on a chalkboard. A sudden loud roar came from Dirk's office downstairs.

"Jason, get down here this minute!"

Jason looked up at Julia with large eyes. When his

father called again, he got up and sulked out the door. Julia and Christa followed.

Being the first time Julia had set foot in Dirk's office, she took note of the daunting room. An elk head sporting a large rack and two equally impressive deer mounts adorned one wall. Another wall held a display of marksmanship trophies, and more mounts including an antelope and two white, mountain sheep. An empty rifle cabinet dominated a far corner.

In front of the large window, looking out on the yard and stables, stood an L-shaped mahogany desk. On its polished surface sat, among other things, a computer and printer, and on the side table, a fax machine, beside that, a four-drawer file cabinet.

Dirk, his face dark, stood behind his desk, arms folded over his chest. Ignoring Julia and Christa, he fixed his angry gaze on his son. "Jason, what is the rule about being in my office?"

Jason kept his eyes on the floor. "We can't be in here without you."

"Since you know the rule, can you explain how this colored face got all over my desk pad?"

"I did it," Jason mumbled. "Sorry."

"You did it while I was gone this morning, didn't you?"

Jason nodded.

Some of the fight seemed to go out of Dirk. "I guess I should be thankful at least that you aren't trying to deny it."

Julia moved closer to look at the drawing Jason had made. She could see why Dirk knew it was his son's work. Jason's artistic talent, even at four, was apparent. It was the face of a woman with long, yellow hair and cherry red lips. One cheek had a spot resembling a beauty mark.

"What do you think your punishment should be?" Dirk asked his son.

Jason shrugged small shoulders keeping his eyes fixed to the floor.

For the first time Dirk looked at Julia. "Before I give him a hundred hours of time-out, I'm going to ask your opinion of Jason's behavior. You seem to be better at this than I am."

Julia glanced from Dirk to Jason to the drawing. "Who is the lady in the picture?" she asked Jason.

For the first time, Jason sniffed. He rubbed a hand over his eyes. "It's mommy."

Dirk's gaze flew to Julia's face, as though to say *you knew, didn't you?*

When Julia nodded, his shoulders visibly slumped.

He turned his attention back to his son. "Why did you draw a picture of your mother in my office, Jason?"

"If you saw how pretty she was, maybe you'd let her come back," he murmured.

"Jason, I didn't make your mother go away."

For the space of a few moments, silence hung like a tangible being in the room.

Finally Dirk spoke. "I'm not going to punish you for drawing the picture, son, but I am going to send you to your room for coming into my office. This is not a playroom. Understand?"

Tears slid down Jason's round cheeks onto his trembling chin. He nodded solemnly, turned and walked out, passing Megan who'd come to stand in the doorway. Megan spared Dirk a frosty glare before she grabbed Christa's hand and pulled her out of the room.

Julia's heart went out to Dirk until he let loose with a string of swear words.

"God damn that woman... If I ever get my hands on her, she'll fucking wish she'd never been born"

Julia cringed. When she attempted to leave he stopped her.

"Don't go. I need to talk to you."

Julia's heart began to hammer. She hated being such a coward. Though his angry words weren't directed at her, they brought too many bad memories to the surface.

"Look, I'm sorry," he said quickly. "This has been going on for two months now and I'm at a loss as to how to deal with it." He dropped into his chair and stared up at her. "How is it that you've been here less than one day and you already know those kids better than I do?"

Julia wasn't sure if he expected her to answer.

"What am I doing wrong?" he asked.

Her gaze fell to the empty rifle cabinet behind him. She wondered if he'd removed the weapons because of the children. "I don't know that you're doing anything wrong, but it's natural for them to miss their mother. You may just have to be patient and wait it out."

"I guess I'm not a very patient man. I always thought I was, but they're doing me in."

Julia managed a smile. "Kids can bring that out in even the best of parents."

He watched her for a moment. "How do you know so much about kids?"

"I—I took child psychology courses in college."

"You went to college to become a nanny?"

Julia didn't like where this conversation was headed. "Not exactly," she said. "Maybe you just need to spend a little more time with them."

Dirk ran both hands through his dark hair. "Yeah, I guess you're right. Look, I'm sorry I sounded off like that. I know I brought you into a mess, but I'm hoping things will start leveling out now that you're here. At least you can help me understand them. God, they're like aliens from another planet."

Julia laughed. "I never thought of it that way."

Dirk liked her soft, gentle laugher. She had a way of relaxing him and easing a taut situation. He'd noticed the anxiety in her eyes when he started swearing and wondered what was behind her fear, something that explained why she was willing to travel nine hundred miles to take a job she was obviously overqualified for. He wouldn't press her for information; after all, he too had a past best kept under wraps.

"I guess you can go," he said. "Thanks once again for your help. Oh, and please close the door when you leave, I have some work to do."

She smiled, murmured a quiet "no problem" and left, pulling the door shut behind her.

Dirk stared at the picture of his wife. It was a child's drawing, but if Julia, who'd never met Gloria and didn't know about the beauty mark, could recognize her, why hadn't he. Of course, his focus had been instant anger at Jason for disobeying a direct order.

An odd disturbing thought struck him. Gloria had a cousin in Minnesota. Did Julia know Gloria? Had the two of them possibly conspired to provide him with a nanny? He hadn't heard Julia play piano yet, but they could have met through a mutual love of music.

He shook his head and put that unlikely thought on the back burner. Picking up the name plaque his father had given him at his college graduation, he opened the complicated sliding panel beneath it and removed the key to his desk. It was basically childproof, however, he needed to reassure himself that the contents of his desk hadn't been tampered with. Specifically, Gus' 38 Smith and Wesson in the back of his top left drawer.

CHAPTER FIVE

During the next three days, Julia settled into a comfortable relationship with the twins. Jason continued his onslaught of little-boy pranks, like drawing red circles around Pickle's eyes with a permanent marker, and using the same marker to mutilate Megan's mirror with a dozen smiley faces.

Christa, on the other hand, was a sheer delight. The only major outburst came when Megan threw a verbal pout because Christa, after skinning her knee, said *thank you mama* to Julia for bandaging it.

"She's not your Mama," Megan had snapped with anger-laced venom.

Megan only seemed to accept Julia during the piano sessions. Her ability to take on something as difficult as Bach's Fifth symphony amazed Julia. By the second lesson, she'd managed some of the most complicated notes. Even more amazing, she readily accepted Julia's critique with minimal grumbling. At one point she slid over and demanded that Julia show her how to do a particularly difficult part. In the middle of the piece, Julia looked up to find Gus standing in the doorway watching and listening, frowning.

His craggy frown turned into a smile for Megan. "Your dad has a surprise for you, Meggie."

"What is it, Grandpa?" Megan asked.

"I can't tell you, but he wants you out to the corral right away."

Megan looked at Julia as though asking permission to end the lesson.

"Go ahead," Julia encouraged. "We were just about finished anyway."

Megan got up and rushed into the circle of Gus's waiting arm. "He's not really my dad, Grandpa."

Gus gave her a hearty squeeze. "Oh, really. Then how does that make me your Grandpa, Meggiebug?"

Megan giggled.

Gus turned back to Julia. "You're supposed to bring those other two rascals too," he said.

It wasn't the first time Julia had seen both of them transform into a loving duo when they were together. She wondered what it would take to gain Gus's approval. She wasn't sure why she wanted it, but people disliking her for no reason bothered her. Katie would probably give her some psycho-hoopla about looking for a father figure.

Julia really wanted to call Katie, just to talk and tell her about the ranch and the kids, but she didn't feel comfortable using Dirk's phone, not to mention Geno's storehouse of connections. If he wanted to find her, the first thing he'd do was start tracing phone calls. She'd wait until Sunday, when she could drive to an area where her cell phone worked, or find a pay phone.

Thinking about her sister lightened her mood as she went upstairs to fetch the twins from their playroom. She'd discovered the best way to occupy them while she gave Megan her lesson was to make it a special time when they could watch a video.

Outside, a large horse trailer hitched to a four-wheel drive pickup backed up to the corral gate. Megan perched on the top rail with Gus standing beside her. A young woman stood next to them. Inside the corral, Dirk, Charlie Mack, and another man were unloading the trailer.

Julia had to grab on to both Christa and Jason to

prevent them from climbing into the corral as three pinto ponies bounded from the trailer.

Megan's excitement couldn't be contained. "Who are they for, Grandpa? Are they for us?"

Gus laughed. "Why don't you ask your dad?"

When Dirk approached the fence, Megan squealed with excitement. "Are they for us? Are they?"

"You bet they are," Dirk said, ducking under the railing to pick up Jason. "What do you think, son? Would you like a pony of your own?"

Julia lifted Christa settling her on a hip so she could see.

"Is one for me too?" Christa asked.

Dirk reached over, tousled her blonde curls. "Sure is honey. We just have to decide which one."

Jason and Megan were suddenly shouting their choices.

"I want that one," Jason said, pointing to the largest of the three.

"Sorry, son, that's Meggie's. She's older and can handle a bigger horse."

If not for Gus's arm restraining her, Megan would have leaped off the corral amid the circling ponies. "Can I name him, myself? Can I?"

"Me too," Jason chimed.

"What about you, Christa?" Dirk asked. "You want to name your pony, too?"

Christa buried her face in Julia's shoulder. "I'm scared," she whispered.

"That's a funny name for a horse," Julia said.

Christa lifted her head and giggled.

They all watched as Charlie Mack threw a rope around Megan's brown and white spotted mare. He spoke softly to the animal as he drew it close to rub its neck and ears.

Megan squealed with delight. "I'm going to call her Victoria," she said.

A third man, someone Julia didn't know, walked into

the trailer and came out with three small saddles. This time Jason squealed too while Christa clung tighter to Julia.

Julia felt the little girl's fear. After watching Dirk ride off with Melody that day, she'd avoided telling her employer she was wary of large animals that weren't safely tucked in zoo cages

"It's okay," Julia whispered to her. "I'll tell you a secret, honey. I've never ridden a horse before either."

Christa's blue eyes widened. "Really?"

Julia laughed. "Really. And I promise you, nobody will force you until you're ready. Will you trust me?"

Smiling, Christa nodded.

The young woman beside Megan held out her hand to Julia. "You must be Julia Morgan," she said. "I'm Carrie Duncan and that's my husband David with the saddles. We got these ponies from the Indian reservation west of here."

Carrie looked to be in her late twenties, a petite woman—a good six inches shorter than Julia—with sparkling brown eyes and a pixie haircut.

Julia took the woman's warm hand, noting her heavy pregnancy. "I'm pleased to meet you, Carrie. I see you're getting ready for a blessed event."

Carrie patted her enlarged midsection. "Sure am. We made a stop in Denver to visit the doctor. He said it should only be another couple of weeks. David is trying to get me to stay at my mother's house in Denver until it's born, but I hate being away from him. Not to mention my mother can be tad overbearing."

They both had an understanding laugh at the obvious understatement and continued their visiting as they turned their attention back to the corral.

Dirk sat Jason on the rail, warning him to stay put, then grabbed a bridle and helped Charlie put it on the nervous Victoria so David could sling the small saddle on her back and carefully tightened the cinch. Dirk and David stood back watching Charlie Mack walk the pony around the corral murmuring gentle words of encouragement to the animal. Finally, he nodded to Dirk, who stepped forward and held the reins while Charlie vaulted into the saddle. The stirrups were too short, so his feet hung loose at Victoria's side.

Victoria pranced around the corral making only feeble attempts to misbehave. Tears sprang to Julia's eyes as she leaned forward to observe the look of rapture on Megan's face while Charlie continued the 'breaking in' of her long awaited pony.

After a few minutes, Charlie brought Victoria up to Megan, saluted with a grin, and hopped off.

"Are you ready?" Dirk asked Megan.

Nodding eagerly, Megan jumped off the fence and insisted she had to introduce herself to Victoria before riding her. With that formality taken care of, she put her foot in Dirk's hands to be hoisted into the saddle while Charlie restrained the animal by holding the reins at the muzzle.

"We're not going to give you control until we're sure he's ready," Dirk said as he adjusted the stirrups. "Charlie's just going to lead you around the corral for a bit."

"Okay," Megan said.

While Megan rode, Dirk walked up to Jason. "Yours is the black and white one with the brown star on his face. What are you going to name him?"

Jason lifted his shoulders. "I don't know."

"How about Champion?" Dirk said. "You can call him Champ."

An eager smile spread over Jason's features. "Okay. When can I ride him?"

"As soon as he's ready." Dirk took the lariat Charlie had used earlier and caught Champ with one easy swing. With David's help, he had the horse bridled and saddled by the time Megan made her third pass around the corral.

Charlie stopped Victoria by the fence while Dirk hopped on the smaller pony. With a full-grown man's weight on his back, the little paint didn't even want to walk much less buck. Dirk slipped off in front of Jason.

"I think Champ has been ridden before. Are you ready son?"

This time Dirk took the pony around giving Jason his ride. Charlie led Victoria keeping well behind Champ.

Carrie laughed. "I think I should run up to the house and get my camera to get some pictures of this memorable event."

Her husband stepped through the fence. "I don't think you should be running anywhere, except to lie down and rest." He put an arm around his wife and extended a hand to Julia. "Hi, I'm David Masters. You must be Julia Morgan?"

Julia shifted Christa to her left hip so she could clasp David's hand. "Yes, I am. Pleased to meet you. If you tell me where that camera is I'll get it," she said to Carrie.

"I can do it," David offered. "I'll be back in a minute. Christa, you want to come with me? Looks like you're getting a little heavy there."

As David led Christa away, Carrie looked after him, smiling. "He loves kids. It took us so long to get pregnant. He's a bit overprotective."

"You do look a little tired," Julia said. "Maybe you should go lie down. Dirk said you were having a difficult time of it."

"Yeah. Maybe I will go rest; my back is aching from the drive. We can chat later. I'm looking forward to getting to know you. I never was able to get friendly with Gloria; she was so standoffish. Can't say any of us liked her much." With a little wave, she walked away rubbing the small of her back.

A few minutes after Carrie left, a deputy sheriff's patrol car pulled up, parking in the middle of the yard. Julia watched as a fiftyish man sporting a crumpled blue uniform and the face of a bulldog got out of the car. He spat a brown wad of chew on the ground and walked up beside her.

He gave her a quick up and down appraisal. "You the new girlfriend?"

Julia hadn't noticed Dirk had turned Jason's pony over to Gus until he came up behind her. "What the hell do you want, Sanford?"

"I'm on official business, Travis."

"Why didn't Gunderson come out here himself?"

"He's laid up with an ailing knee."

"Yeah, well state your business or get off my property."

"I can see you didn't learn any manners in—"

"What do you want?" Dirk snapped. "We're busy here."

Sanford's gaze flicked over Julia once more before he hacked out another brown stream at Dirk's feet. "When's the last time you saw your wife, Travis?"

"Why?"

"How about I ask the questions, and you give the answers?"

"How about you explain why you're asking them first?"

"It seems your *wife* has gone missing." He gave Julia yet another once over. "This her replacement?"

"You have a foul mind, Sanford. Not that it's any of your business, but Julia is the nanny I hired."

"Oh right, I saw the ad."

Julia was starting to feel very uncomfortable. She waited for a signal from Dirk indicating she should leave, but he seemed to have forgotten she was there as he focused in on Deputy Sanford.

"Hey, boss," Charlie Mack called from the corral. "Want me to get a shovel to clean up the road apples in the yard?"

Sanford's face reddened. "Watch your tongue, Mack. You're on my list, too."

"What list is that?" Dirk asked.

"Never mind. Just tell me when you last saw your

wife."

"Almost two months ago when she dropped the kids off."

He took a note pad out of his shirt pocket. "What day was that?"

"May fifteenth, just before the school year ended."

"Do you recall what she was wearing?"

"A black and white polka dot dress."

"Any jewelry?"

"Hell if I know. Wait yeah, she had a large ying-yang pendent. Rarely took it off. When was she reported missing?"

Sanford scribbled something in his notepad. "A couple of days ago."

"Who filed the report?" Dirk asked.

"Not you obviously."

"Who?"

"Her agent, fellow named Tom Payton. He said she didn't show up for a concert."

"Maybe you should question him, he left here with her. They were going to do a European tour."

Sanford stared at Dirk as though deciding whether or not to believe him. "Anybody who can verify that?"

"No."

"All these people you got working around here and nobody else saw him?"

"It was a Sunday, everybody was gone."

Looking past Dirk toward the corral, the deputy scowled. "What about the kids?"

Dirk sucked in a breath of air grimacing as though he had a sudden stab of pain. For the first time he looked at Julia. "Jesus, I have to tell them."

"I want to talk to her," Sanford said, indicating Megan.

"The hell you will. Not until I've had a chance to break this to her."

"Guess I can understand that. Just don't go putting

any words in her mouth."

Julia had just started thinking maybe the odious man had a heart after all until he added that.

Dirks hands clenched into fists.

Sanford seemed unconcerned. "How long do you need? I'll wait."

"Come back tomorrow."

Sanford shook his head. "No can do, Travis. Either I talk to her today, or you bring her in to Danango with a court order."

Dirk swore.

Julia felt his pain and wanted to help. "What do you need to question her about?" she asked.

"Right now, I'll settle for verification that Gloria left here with Tom Payton."

"Just be careful you don't say anything to upset her," Julia said none too gently.

"You wait here," Dirk said to the deputy. He took Julia's arm and directed her over to the corral, talking in a voice low enough so Sanford couldn't hear. "You have any suggestions on how I should go about this?" he asked.

Julia sighed. "I wish I did. But you're going to have to explain why he wants to question her. She's too smart not to be suspicious."

Dirk nodded then called to Charlie. "Bring Meggie here."

Charlie led Victoria to the rail. "What does Butt Face want?" he asked.

Dirk murmured something about "Later" then stepped between the rails into the corral and approached Megan "He wants to ask you some questions, Meggie."

Megan frowned. "Me? About what?"

"It seems your mother didn't show up for her trip to Europe and they're looking for her."

Julia watched Megan's face closely. If the news disturbed her, she hid it well. She nodded, patting Victoria on the neck. "Okay. Can I ride some more?"

Dirk smiled. "Sure, but you're going to be stiff tomorrow." He lifted her down and opened the gate for her.

The three of them walked back to the sheriff who spat on the ground one more time apparently to clear his mouth.

"That's a disgusting habit," Megan told him.

Julia gave Sanford a warning glare even while she bit her lip to keep from grinning.

"Megan, this is Deputy Sanford." Dirk said.

Sanford cleared his throat. "All right, Megan, your dad tells me your mother left here with her agent, a man named Tom Payton. Can you verify that?"

Julia waited for Megan to correct him about calling Dirk her dad, but surprisingly she didn't. Instead she looked up at Dirk apologetically.

"I know she said he was her agent. But she lied and she told me not to say anything."

"If it wasn't Tom Payton, who was it?" Dirk asked.

Megan shrugged. "A guy from New York."

"Do you know who he was?" Sanford pressed. "Can you remember his name?"

Megan nodded. Her face took on color, and tears filled her eyes. "His name is Carl Edwards."

This wasn't the first time Julia had seen a child struggling to hide something. She recognized the signs. "What is it Megan?"

Megan stared at the ground.

Anger at the faceless Carl Edwards goaded Julia. "What did he do to you? Did he hurt you?"

Megan shook her head.

"What is it? What aren't you telling us?"

"He's my father."

CHAPTER SIX

Dirk stared at Megan as though she'd sprouted a second head.

"I'm sorry," Megan said. "She said if I told you, you'd be really angry."

"Damn straight!" When Megan flinched, he backed down quickly. "It's okay, Meggie. It's not your fault, and I'm not upset with you. Why don't you go on back and ride Victoria? Maybe Charlie can show you how to brush her. We can talk later." After the Sheriff leaves, he thought.

She nodded, gave the sheriff an accusatory look, and walked back to the corral.

As soon as Megan was out of earshot, Dirk rounded on Sanford. "Why the hell did Payton wait two months to report her missing?"

"How should I know? Maybe she just went missing a couple of days ago."

"Excuse me," Julia interceded. "I don't know much about the law, but isn't that information you should already have?"

Sanford's face reddened.

Dirk sneered. "I guess you didn't bother with facts in your rush to come out and harass me."

"Either way, she's missing," Sanford sputtered. "And you're the prime suspect. She had your kids and you didn't like it. You didn't like supporting her and her boyfriends in New York. And with your record—"

"You slimy piece of leftover buzzard bait," Dirk said moving up to within inches of the Sheriff's face. "How do you know what I like and don't like?"

"It's pretty easy to assume—"

"Git!" Dirk pointed to the patrol car. "Get your sorry carcass off my land and don't come back until you can back up your idiotic assumptions with proof."

Sanford looked as though he had more to say, but he gritted his teeth, spun on his heels, and stomped back to his patrol car. He got in, started the engine and brandished a threatening fist out the window. "This isn't finished, Travis, I'll see your ass back in jail if it's the last thing I do."

Dirk let out a hissing breath watching the patrol car leave spewing a trail of gravel. A heavy hand gripped his shoulder.

It was Charlie Mack. "Take it easy, boss. He doesn't have anything on you. I'll bet fifty bucks he's not even assigned to Gloria's case. Seems to me that would be a conflict of interest."

"Yeah." Dirk turned to find Julia staring at him with curious green eyes that held a spark of sympathy and something deeper—fear? Behind her he saw David returning with Christa. "Come on, Mack, let's get Christa's pony ready."

Mack laughed. "Maybe we should bring Black Lightening out so you could ride off some steam."

"Not a bad idea," he muttered, swinging his daughter up in his arms. "Are you ready to ride, Punkin?"

A jumble of emotions ran through Julia's head as she followed Dirk carrying Christa toward the corral. What exactly, she wondered, had the sheriff meant when he said he wanted to see Dirk *back* in jail? It seemed, given the earlier comment about his record, Dirk had done time. If so, what for?

Christa's face showed none of the excitement her siblings had as she watched Mack ride the energetic pony around the corral. She looked at Julia with sad eyes that said she would rather be in the house playing with her dolls.

"I'm scared, daddy. Can Anna be with me?"

Dirk gave her a squeeze. "Anna has to learn about horses first. Maybe we can give her a riding lesson tomorrow, but for today, I'll walk along beside you and if you want to stop we will. Okay?"

"Okay."

"What do you want to name your pony?"

"Anna."

Dirk laughed. "I don't think Anna would like to have a horse named after her. How about you call her Molly?"

Christa looked at Julia for approval. "Is Molly a good name?" she asked.

Julia nodded. "Molly's a wonderful name. You don't have to be afraid, your daddy will stay with you."

Christa gave Julia that same disarming smile she'd seen earlier from Dirk.

Julia felt a sudden tug at her heartstrings, followed by an uneasy stab of pain. Though she appreciated Christa's admiration, the little girl was becoming increasingly attached to her. Something Katie had said disturbed her. *You don't have to do it forever.*

* * * *

While Dirk took the twins to their rooms to get ready for bed as he insisted on doing every night, Julia sat out on the back porch to watch the blood red July sun dip toward the mountain peaks. She thought about Geno, Katie, and her practice left behind in Minnesota—and her babies. Meeting Carrie brought back bittersweet memories. Julia had to struggle against the urge to touch Carrie's stomach, to feel the baby kick, the way her twins had started kicking two weeks before she'd lost them.

It seemed like a lifetime rather than only five days

since she'd left her home and everything that was familiar to her. She had no qualms about leaving Geno behind, but she missed Katie.

Dirk stepped out on the porch, interrupting her musings. He held a bottle of wine he'd already uncorked and two glasses.

"I'm not much of a drinker," he said. "But I'm not in the mood for coffee tonight. I don't know if you like wine, but I brought an extra glass just in case. I was hoping I wouldn't have to drink this whole thing myself."

Julia quickly pushed aside a vision of Geno coaxing her to drink brandy on their first date. "Maybe just one glass," she said.

He sat down across from her, filled both glasses, and set one in front of her. "It seems," he said after emptying half his glass, "that you and I have a mutual love of watching the sun go down at the end of a long day."

"It certainly has been a long day, but a rewarding one, seeing how the kids, especially Jason and Megan, love their ponies."

"Yeah, they do, don't they. Meggie used to ride all the time, little tyke that she was, before Gloria took her away. She was cute as a button, still is." Dirk hesitated a moment. "I hope I wasn't speaking out of line when I told Christa I'd give you riding lessons tomorrow. That offer stands only if you're interested."

A picture of Melody Dupree flashed unsolicited through Julia's mind. She wasn't sure why, but the vision of Melody, at ease astride a horse, left an odd sensation of wanting to compete. She took a sip of the sweet, mellowing wine. "To be honest," she said, "I've always been a little leery of horses, but if Christa can do it, I'm willing to give it a try."

"Something else," Dirk said. "I have to drive Meggie to her party in Danango tomorrow night. They have a great taco place there and I thought I'd take Jason and Christa out to eat. They both love tacos—as long as they don't put tomatoes in Christa's," he added laughing. "Anyway, unless you're looking forward to having some time to yourself, you're welcome to come along. Danango is small but it's the closest thing to any kind of shopping this side of Denver, and I thought you might like to familiarize yourself with it."

Julia declined a refill on her wine. "I'd like that. It sounds like fun." *And maybe my cell phone will work there.*

They chatted for a time, sharing their thoughts on the kids, and their excitement over the horses, carefully avoiding the subject of Deputy Sanford.

Dirk polished off his second glass of wine, leaned back, stared out toward the mountains and sighed. His fingers idly slid up and down the stem of his glass. "I owe you an explanation about today with Sanford," he said finally. "But first I'd like to ask you something."

Julia stared at him saying nothing, waiting. When he didn't go on she became curious. "Go ahead, what is it?"

"I know this is personal but…are you afraid of me?"

The question took Julia by surprise, and she wasn't sure how to answer it. "What makes you think I'm afraid of you?"

"I can see it in your eyes…every time I raise my voice."

"I… I don't do well in—ah—aggressive situations, if that's what you mean."

"Yeah, I suspected that. I suppose I alienate the kids too when I lose my temper and spout off."

Julia managed a smile. "Children respond much better to a calm controlled voice than a thunderous blaring one." She shrugged. "Children do naughty things by nature."

Dirk returned her smile with a crooked grin. "I should know that from my own memories. My mother took off when I was nine and left me with Dad. To say I was bitter would be putting it mildly. I wasn't an easy kid to raise."

"It might help if you recall some of those feelings when you deal with your own son."

"As good as you are with kids," he said shaking his head, "you must have had one of those *Leave-It-To-Beaver* childhoods."

A memory flashed through Julia's mind of her father grabbing a fistful of her hair and yanking her off her feet because she forgot to close the front door. Her throat choked up, she couldn't answer him.

Dirk suspected he had sorely missed the mark on her ideal childhood when she dropped her gaze to hands clenched tightly in her lap. When she finally responded, she changed the subject.

"You mentioned explaining something about Deputy Sanford," she said.

"Oh yeah," Dirk said drumming his fingers on the table. "I'm sure you didn't miss his comment about sending me back to jail. I guess I owe you an explanation."

He plowed a hand through his nearly shoulder-length hair in an agitated manner. "I need to get a haircut," he muttered. "I wasn't trying to be deceitful by not mentioning this before, but I did four months in the Colorado Correctional Institute."

She gave him a surprised yet expectant look.

"It's not something I'm proud of, and I don't like talking about it. Rather than have you speculate, I'm going to tell you what happened.

"About a year after the twins were born, Gloria and I attended a barbeque at a neighboring ranch between here and Danango. To cut to the chase, one of the ranchers made a pass at Gloria. With hindsight I suspect she invited it, but at the time, I was still quite enamored with my lovely wife. He and I got into a shoving match, he took a swing at me and missed, I swung back. My fist connected with his jaw, he fell backwards, cracked his head on a fence post, and ended up in a coma for three days."

Julia's brow arched. "If what you're saying is accurate, he swung first, why would it even go to court?"

"Because the rancher's name is Sanford, Matthew Sanford."

"The same name as the Deputy Sheriff?"

"You guessed it. Raymond Sanford is Matt's father. I got railroaded, and sent up for five years on a felony charge."

"That's ridiculous."

Dirk smiled. "That's what the judge said in my appeal. He reduced my conviction to a gross misdemeanor and sentenced me to time already served, with three-years probation—that ends in thirty days. I was a free man, but I came home to an empty house, my wife had taken the kids and left."

* * * *

While the house was still quiet, Dirk sat at his desk trying to catch up on some paperwork. Pen in hand, he found himself not working, but staring out the window at the stables, his mind across the hall where Juliana Morgan still slept. For some reason, he couldn't get his mind off her, which was also why sleep eluded him through most of the night.

She was an enigma. Smart, sexy, great with the kids, but a strange shadow surfaced in her eyes whenever a conflict arose. And yet she'd stood up to Sanford, calling him out for his incompetence—protecting Megan.

Thanks to Sanford, Dirk was forced to tell her about his record. He'd had a nagging fear that she'd ask to be discharged when he told her. Instead she'd listened calmly and with far more understanding than he'd expected.

It disturbed him that no matter how much he shared about his own life, she remained firmly closed regarding her own. That alone lead him to believe she was hiding something. Did she have someone or something she feared? A traumatic experience? A boyfriend? An ex-husband. Her father? One thing she'd unwittingly revealed, her childhood was anything but rosy.

He'd finally decided to put her out of his mind and

get back to filling out papers when the fax machine started to whir. A few seconds later, a short handwritten memo appeared.

He shouldn't have read it, but it was so short a mere glance told him what it said.

To: Julia Morgan
From: Katie

Julia, call me ASAP. Use a pay phone. Keep your cell turned off.

Trouble with GC

Love you,
Katie

Dirk stared at the memo, not just at the words, but the perfect elegant penmanship. Something about it triggered a memory. He swiveled his chair to his file cabinet and pulled out the file he'd started on Julia. Fishing through the short stack of papers, he located the original note sent when she applied for the position as his nanny. He laid the note beside the fax he'd just received.

The handwriting was identical.

CHAPTER SEVEN

When Julia stepped out of her bedroom to meet the day, her eyes were drawn to Dirk's open office door. He was seated behind his desk and appeared to have been waiting for her. He motioned her inside with a flick of his wrist.

With a mind of its own, her heart increased its beat as she entered what she considered his sanctuary. She coveted the rich smelling cup of coffee setting in front of him.

"You received a fax," he said, holding a single sheet of paper out to her.

She took the paper, thanked him, and glanced at the short note. *Trouble with GC— Geno.* Heart rate tripling, her eyes lifted to Dirk, and she could tell by the crease in his brow that he'd read it.

"I'm sorry," he said quickly. "I didn't mean to read it, but it was so brief, I saw the words before I realized it was for you."

Julia had the feeling the honest-to-a-fault Dirk Travis was only telling a half a truth. He hesitated while she stared at the note. "Anything I can do to help?" he asked.

Julia shook her head. "No, thanks. It's nothing really," she lied. "Katie has a tendency to be on the dramatic side. I'll take care of it. I should have called her by now, but my cell won't work here."

"That's the reason I don't bother having one." When

she turned to leave, he called after her. "You're welcome to use my phone anytime you like."

"Thank you, I might do that sometime."

The note was branded in Julia's brain. *Use a pay phone. Keep your cell turned off.* That meant Geno could trace calls made to Katie's home, and probably her business as well. Not only that, he could trace the signal on her cell phone. To find a pay phone, Julia would have to wait until they got to Danango tonight.

After she left, Dirk stared at the empty doorway. She'd given him no clue as to who Katie was. A friend? A relative? A lawyer? Whoever she was, Katie had sent him the application for nanny, not Julia. One way or another, Julia had misled him, and that, he told himself, was justification to investigate.

The only phone number he had to work with was the one at the top of the fax. He could try dialing sequential numbers, hoping it was a small office. He picked up the phone and dialed the number on the fax, changing the last digit to one number higher. A busy signal beeped in his ear. He tried again using one number lower. A recording informed him the number wasn't in service. He repeated the process several times, always using a different last digit. On the fifth try a woman answered.

"Doctor Benson's office. May I help you?"

Dirk hesitated, trying to think. "Yes, I'm not sure if I have the right doctor. Is this Doctor Katie Benson's number?"

"Yes it is; are you calling to make an appointment?"

"Ah... I'm not sure. Can you tell me what field of medicine Doctor Benson is in?"

A gum popping sound filled his ear. "She's a psychiatrist. Is that what you're looking for?"

"No, I must have the wrong doctor. Thanks anyway."

"You bet. Bye now."

Dirk hung up the phone, trying to organize his

thoughts. The only conclusion he could come to was that Julia's psychiatrist had sent the application. But why? A number of reasons flooded his head, none of them to his liking. He tried to reason with himself, give Julia the benefit of a doubt. After all, he hated it when people jumped to unqualified assumptions. People saw psychiatrists for all kinds of reasons—that didn't necessarily make them dangerous or unstable. He recalled the look of deep sadness that sometimes filled her eyes. Maybe she had a loss, a death, she was dealing with—a parent, a child, a sibling—a husband?

Why had Doctor Katie Benson sent the application? Surely a doctor wouldn't have sent Julia to a nanny position if she were any kind of a threat to children. That thought relaxed him somewhat, and he released a huge sigh, determined to concentrate on his paper work.

When Julia was ready, she'd explain.

He'd had no business reading that fax.

Who or what was GC? he wondered.

* * * *

Knowing she couldn't do anything about the fax at the moment, Julia stuck it in her pocket, and went about her usual day. Unfortunately, putting the letter aside was easier than ridding her thoughts of Geno. She pictured him being livid and desperate when he found she'd disappeared.

Thankfully she'd had the foresight to forward her mail to Katie's house. Geno had too many connections, not only in the medical field, but also with the police department where he made huge donations every year. Nobody knew better than Julia just how tenacious he could be. As long as she didn't make a call to Katie from the ranch, Geno would not be able to find her. She'd been real careful about leaving no tracks.

Just before lunch it started to rain, so Julia's riding lesson was postponed. At two-o'clock she sat down with Megan for piano lessons.

"How would you like to try a duet?" Julia asked.

"I can't," Megan groused.

Julia frowned. "Why not?"

"Mom said I'm not good enough."

Julia wondered about a mother who would say something like that. Megan was a gifted eleven-year-old, and her mother was a concert pianist. Which probably explained why, with only a couple of exceptions, all the sheet music Julia found in the bench seat was classical— only a few light and entertaining pieces, and nothing modern that would appeal to kids.

"Well, we're not going to do a concert, so it's okay to make mistakes. Besides we're just practicing. I found the notes to Dueling Banjos this morning and thought it would be fun. What do you think?"

Megan shrugged. "Whatever. I don't care. Grandpa got that for me when I was little, but I never learned it."

In spite of Megan's lack of enthusiasm, Julia took that as a yes, opened the sheet music, and sat down beside Megan. "You want to do the first part or the second?" Julia asked.

"Whatever."

Julia reminded herself that Megan was a child, and had no idea how annoying that word was. On the other hand, maybe she did know.

"I've never played it before either," Julia said. "We can learn together."

She went through the first scales slowly, stopping when it was time for Megan's part. Megan's fingers flew over the notes with only a few mistakes. When she finished, Julia started again. After half an hour of practice, they had mastered the piece and were both fully absorbed in the music, fingers flying. Each time they finished, Megan's smile got broader.

Neither one of them realized they had an audience until Dirk clapped his hands. "Bravo. Bravo."

Julia looked up to find him leaning against the doorway, his rain dampened hair falling jauntily over his forehead. She had no idea how long he'd been listening, but his comfortable stance suggested he'd been there a while. His praise brought a merry stain of red to Megan's cheeks.

"That sounded real good," he said. "You should play that for Gus sometime. It's his favorite number. Sorry to disturb you, but I thought since it's raining outside we could leave for town a little early so I could get a haircut."

"Can I go straight to Trisha's house?" Megan asked.

"I don't see why not," Dirk said, smiling. "Can you both be ready to go in an hour?"

Megan blanched. "Omigod." She got up and dashed for her room, a string of frantic things-to-do echoing in her wake.

Dirk shook his head. "I hope that was a yes."

Julia laughed. "If you think an hour throws her into a panic now, wait until she's a teenager."

"Speaking from experience?"

Julia had a sudden vision of her father slapping Katie for taking too long in the bathroom. "You might say that," she said, closing the piano and gathering the music to put away.

Dirk pushed himself away from the doorframe. "I've been working in the stables all day so I guess I'll grab a shower. You don't have to dress up, it's just a taco joint, same with the kids. Megan's the only one who'll be presented to royalty."

After Dirk disappeared at the top of the stairs, Julia decided to change into a clean pair of black jeans and a sea-green pullover. Living out here, there weren't a lot of opportunities to go out—not that a taco joint was exactly "going out", but it was the closest she'd come to it since her miscarriage and she felt an odd sense of anticipation.

As she brushed the French braid out of her hair, leaving it hang loose at her shoulders, she reminded herself this wasn't a date in any way shape or form—still, she applied a pale shade of lipstick and touched her cheeks with a hint of blush, then went to check on the twins.

They were all downstairs waiting when Megan appeared wearing a short hip hugging jean skirt, a cropped-off pink top, red lipstick, and enough eye makeup to embarrass a raccoon.

Dirk went livid. "Get back upstairs and wash that gunk off your face, or you're not leaving this house."

Megan stamped her foot. "You're so mean. My friends all wear makeup."

Dirk pointed to the upper level. "Move!"

Megan's blackened eyes filled with tears as she whirled and ran for the stairs.

In the wake of Megan's crying, Julia gave Dirk a 'you're yelling again' look. He gritted his teeth and swore under his breath, thrusting a hand through his too-long hair.

Julia hurried to her room for her cosmetic bag before she followed the sounds of Megan's sobs to the upstairs bathroom where Pickles sat outside the door, hanging his head.

Julia knocked. "Can I come it?"

"Why?" came the belligerent, muffled reply.

"I want to show you something."

A moment later the lock clicked and the door opened. Megan, still sobbing, was furiously scrubbing her washed face with a towel. "He's horrible. I'm never speaking to him again."

Julia took a seat at the vanity table. "He's just concerned, Megan. He—"

"I hate him!"

"Don't hate him for caring enough about you, and protecting you from growing up too fast."

"He doesn't care about me."

"Of course he does. You need to understand about makeup though. It shouldn't overpower your natural beauty. Now, dry your eyes and come here. I'll show you how to do it."

Megan gave a colossal shuddering sniff before she moved in front of Julia.

Using her own makeup kit, Julia started with a pale rose blush on the high point of Megan's cheekbones sweeping it back to the corner of her eye. "You have beautiful green eyes," Julia said as she continued working. "Too much mascara and eye shadow will dominate the natural color. All you need is a touch of enhancement, but keep it subtle so no one will even guess it's there."

"I bet your father let you wear makeup." Megan said.

Julia's throat closed around a constricting lump. She swallowed it down, and shared with Megan a secret, dark side of her life. "First of all," she said, carefully keeping her voice steady, "my father wouldn't have allowed me to go on a sleepover, and if I so much as put lipstick on, he would've dragged me to the bathroom and scrubbed my face until it was raw." She didn't mention that she was fifteen the last time it happened. That's when she learned to apply makeup that couldn't be detected.

"Geez, he sound's worse than Dirk."

"Megan, you have to remember that Dirk is new at being a father to an eleven year old. He's still learning. Give him a chance. He loves you."

Megan made a soft snorting sound.

"Do you have a birthday gift for Trisha?" Julia asked, changing the subject.

Megan nodded. "I didn't have any money to buy something, so I'm giving her the African snow globe I got for my birthday in March. It's real neat with all these jungle animals, and when you wind it up, the animals go around in a circle and snow falls on them."

It sounded to Julia like the globe was something Megan treasured. "Don't you get an allowance?" she asked.

"No."

"I think I need to have a serious conversation with Mr. Travis. There, all finished. Take a look."

Julia stood up behind Megan as she surveyed the results. Megan patted the ribbon on top of her head that

Julia had used to sweep the hair back from her face. "It looks nice, real nice. I like it."

Julia gave Megan's shoulders a squeeze.

"Good, now let's go down and show you off."

Megan hesitated. "What about my clothes? Will he yell about them?"

Julia studied the short skirt and midriff baring top. She'd seen a lot of young girls coming to her office dressed like that. More than once she'd been tempted to voice her disapproval. "I think you look fine for a girl's party, but when you go to school, wear something a little more— conservative. You don't want to reveal all your secrets to everybody." She gently poked Megan's cute belly button.

Megan giggled and they walked down the stairs together.

Julia tried to catch Dirk's eye hoping to warn him about saying anything negative, but his gaze was fixed on Megan's face. Julia held her breath until he smiled.

"There you go Meggie. I knew you didn't need all that junk on your face to look beautiful."

Dirk's gaze lifted to Julia as he mouthed a silent thank you.

Julia felt the heat rise to her face as those striking gray eyes locked in on her. Her heart rate tripled, and the rush of blood to her head made her feel lightheaded and feminine.

* * * *

Sitting at the edge of nowhere, Danango was a small community of 2500 predominantly Hispanic people. As he continued to describe the town, Dirk showed her the focal point, a block square mercantile on Main Street claiming to sell everything from potatoes to paint to pharmaceuticals. The surrounding streets sported an equal number of bars and eating establishments, a combined beauty salon/barber shop, a hardware store, a bowling alley, and a number of miscellaneous hole-in-the-wall shops.

Dirk drove through the poorer section of town to get to

an elegant colonial house at the end of the street where Trisha Carson lived.

Julia noticed a sprawling home on the hill surrounded by a chain link fence and made a soft whistling sound. "There must be a few wealthy people living here."

"That's the mayor's house, the honorable Paul Chatterley."

"A mayor in a town this size can afford a house like that. It looks like it has a swimming pool in the back."

"Yeah, well, I guess I should mention he has his own law firm in Denver. The only reason he lives here is because his wife, Francesca, was born in Danango and she won't leave. He spends more time in Denver than in Danango, though."

Dirk parked the car in front of the colonial. "If you want to stay with Jason and Christa, I just need to confirm a time to pick Megan up in the morning."

While Julia waited in the car, she stared up at the big house. The design reminded her so much of her own home in Minneapolis, and she realized, as beautiful as it was, she didn't miss it at all. There were too many bad memories associated with it.

Dirk came back out to the car frowning. "I didn't realize it was a birthday party. I should have given Megan money to buy a gift. She had a wrapped present, but I have no idea how she got it."

"That's something we need to talk about," Julia said.

Dirk started the car, arching an eyebrow in her direction. "Do you know what Megan's giving Trisha?"

"Yes, it's an African snow globe."

"Damn, I sent that to her on her last birthday. I thought she'd love it."

"She did. But she didn't have anything else to give. Which is exactly why she needs to have an allowance."

"Sh—" Dirk glanced in the back seat. "Shoot. I guess I screwed that up."

"Uh huh."

Dirk backed out of the drive, grinning at her. "I'm not going to get any sympathy from you, am I?"

"Nope."

"All right. How much should I give her?"

Julia tried to recall what girls Megan's age were getting. "I guess anywhere from five to seven dollars a week would be appropriate."

Dirk made a pained face. "I'm going to have to sell a cow."

"Plus a clothing allowance," she added.

"That's another thing," Dirk said quickly. "I didn't have the heart to scold her again, but I'm not letting her go to school dressed like a teenage vamp."

"I've already talked to her about that."

Dirks brow shot up. "How have I survived these last two months without you?"

Julia tried to conceal a grin. "That was going to be my next question."

"What's a vamp?" Jason asked from the back seat.

"Lord," Dirk whispered. He glanced in the rear-view mirror at his son. "Look it up in the dictionary," he said.

"What's a dickshary?" Christa asked.

Dirk grinned "I'm forever talking myself into a corner with those two." To the twins he said. "Anna's going to explain it while I get a haircut."

"Oh, thanks a lot," she said, laughing. "While I'm at it, I'll explain what *copout* means."

Instead of heading back along Main Street, Dirk turned onto a side road. "There's Megan's school," he said pointing to a sprawling brick building surrounded by fences. "All twelve grades go there, along with kindergarten."

From the back seat came in unison, "Can we go to school there too?"

"Not this year," Dirk told them. To Julia he said, "They won't be five until next May. Did I mention that you'd be teaching them preschool at home?"

Julia smiled. "I think it might have slipped your mind."

"I've ordered some pre-school computer disks to help out—by the way, there's the clinic next to the school."

Julia stared in shock through the rain-spattered windshield at the tiny frame building. The hospitals she'd worked in had supply closets that were larger. "I'm surprised a town this size doesn't have a hospital."

"Take a look around. Except for that street where Trisha lives, this little town is pretty impoverished. Probably half of the people don't have health insurance, and the medical staff that comes every couple of weeks basically works free. It's not much, but it's all they have. Any emergencies get treated in some of the larger neighboring cities, or they go to Denver."

Back on Main, Dirk pulled up in front of Manny's Taco Town. He pulled out his wallet and handed Julia two twenties. "You can take the kids inside, they have a youth section with video and skill games for all ages. There's a monster bin full of plastic balls they like to play in, you just need to buy a handful of tokens. I shouldn't be very long at the barbershop. Okay?"

Julia nodded. "Sure, I can handle that."

By the time Julia got the kids out of the car, Dirk had already disappeared inside the barbershop. She reached the entry to Manny's when she realized she'd forgotten to lock the car door. Jason and Christa waited anxiously while she hurried back to flip the lock, as she did so a sheriff's car rolled by and she recognized Deputy Sanford at the wheel. He looked straight at her, then parked across the street in front of the mercantile.

Dismissing thoughts of the deputy sheriff, Julia followed the kids into Manny's where they headed straight for the plastic ball bin. Three other children were already bouncing around in the multicolored balls. Jason and Christa removed their shoes while Julia went to the token booth, bought ten dollars worth, then handed six tokens to the teenage girl attending the booth.

With the children safely tucked in the netted bin, Julia looked around for a phone where she could talk and still keep an eye on the twins. She spotted one a few feet away. Giving the attendant another six tokens, Julia explained that she was going to use the phone, and requested that the kids be in the bin as long as they wanted. She would give additional tokens if needed when she finished on the phone. The girl waved her off with a nod and a smile.

Julia's hand shook as she dialed Katie's apartment number, hoping that with the time difference, she would be home by now. On the fifth ring, Katie answered, breathless.

"Hello."

"Katie, it's Julia."

"Oh, thank God you caught me. I just walked in the door. How are you?"

"Good. Fine. What's happening there?"

"Oh, Geno's being his prick of a self—it comes so natural for him. He's positively irate that I won't tell him where you are."

"Has he threatened you?"

"Don't I wish. I have my phone calls taped. If he so much as hints a threat I'll have his tail in a vise so tight he won't know what hit him. We have some great laws in this state. I'm sure he's too clever to make a dumb mistake like that though. I do know he's called at least two of my acquaintances, and possibly more, looking for you. These are people I've talked to in the last week, one in Boston from my work phone and one in Texas from my home phone. That's why I wanted to make sure you don't call from Dirk Travis' home—and thank goodness your cell is out of range because that can be traced by the tower signals. Keep it switched off." After a moment Katie added, "I just wish you'd gone with me when I took those gun safety classes."

"For goodness sake, Katie. I've never even owned a gun and I don't want to. Besides, Geno wouldn't hurt you."

When Katie didn't answer, Julia became alarmed. "Are you sure you're all right? Is there something you aren't telling me?" Julia asked.

"Don't worry about me. I can take care of myself."

"Katie—"

"I'm peachy fine. How's the nanny business? Is Dirk Travis as dreamy as his name?"

A half smile tickled Julia's face as she remembered Megan saying Dirk rhymes with jerk. "The twins, Jason and Christa, are darling. He also has an eleven-year-old girl, Megan. She's a treasure. You'll be happy to know I was supposed to start my riding lessons today—I was spared because it's raining."

"What about Dirk?" Katie urged.

Julia debated whether or not to tell her sister about Dirk's prison record, and then decided against it. "Dirk is okay. He's been all business and he has a girlfriend." She wasn't sure if Melody was actually a girlfriend, but she wanted to get Katie off the romance track.

"Oh well, bummer. Before I forget, I need your address so I can forward your mail, and your phone number at the ranch so I know where to reach you if I need to. It's best if I call you. I can do it from a phone booth. Would Dirk have a problem with that?"

"No, not at all." She gave Katie the address and phone number. "I have Sundays off so I can drive into town and call you from here."

"Maybe it's best if you don't, let me call you unless it's an emergency. Too many calls from the same number or area might raise a flag. I don't know who Geno's in bed with to get a list of my phone calls, but I'm going to try to find out."

"Did I mention Dirk is married?"

"No. You must have forgotten that little detail. If he has a wife *and* a girlfriend, why does he need a nanny?"

Julia looked up to see Dirk walk in the front door. She gave him a small wave and a smile. He acknowledged her with a nod and headed toward the bouncing ball bin. "He's been separated from the wife for a couple of years and now she's gone missing."

"Missing!"

"Look, sweetie, I need to go now."

"Okay, keep me hanging. I'll catch you later, and don't worry about Geno, I'm starting to enjoy watching him dangle."

Julia hung up, took a deep breath to compose herself, and walked over to Dirk. He was talking to the kids, laughing. Julia asked the attendant if she needed more tokens.

"No ma'am. They still have a couple more minutes to go."

"They aren't ready to come out," Dirk said. "Give her another handful of tokens and we'll go grab a table where we can see them. They don't get to do this sort of thing very often."

Julia handed over twelve more tokens, stuck the last one in her jeans pocket, and then sucked in her breath as Dirk's hand rested on the small of her back as he directed her to a table.

She knew it was probably just a reflex on his part, but his hand felt like a fire iron spreading a strange heat throughout her body. It wasn't an altogether unpleasant feeling. It was a gesture Geno had never used.

They sat down across from each other at a square table, and the waitress handed them menus while Dirk ordered a pitcher of root beer. Julia noticed his shorter hair. It gave him a totally different look, less reckless and more handsome, if that was even possible. Katie would have a field day if she could read Julia's thoughts right now.

"You approve," Dirk asked, startling her out of her musings.

She managed a casual smile. "You lost the pirate look."

Dirk laughed. "That's good, I guess." He picked up the single page price sheet. "Everything go all right with your phone call?" he asked without raising his eyes from the menu.

Julia's heart rate kicked up, and for a fleeting moment she wondered if she should tell him about Geno. Confident that Geno couldn't find her, she rejected the idea and pasted a smile on her face. "Yeah. All's fine on the home front."

Jason and Christa saved Julia from answering any further questions when they arrived, circling the table like two small whirlwinds.

Jason leaped up on one of the empty chairs. "Can we go again?"

Christa climbed onto the opposite chair. "Daddy, it's so much fun."

"How about you go again after we eat?" Dirk said.

"Okay," Jason replied, then whispered across the table to his sister, "Let's eat real fast, Christa."

After they placed their order, Jason and Christa settled down to color the place mats set in front of them. Julia started pouring root beer into their glasses. She asked Dirk if he wanted some. When he didn't answer, she looked up to find his attention fixed on the front door.

She followed his gaze and saw Deputy Sanford and a younger man, who resembled the deputy enough to be his son, take a seat at a booth not twelve feet away. She doubted it was a coincidence they had come to Manny's Taco Town to eat.

She cleared her throat loudly enough to get Dirk's attention. "Do you want root beer?" she asked a second time.

He gave her a sheepish grin. "Yeah. Sorry."

"I take it that's his son, Matthew."

Dirk nodded. "Yeah."

"I saw them outside earlier. You do understand they're here to antagonize you?"

Dirk glared toward their booth. "Yeah."

"Are you going to let them get by with that?"

Dirk tore his eyes from the Sanford's and gave Julia a hard look. He opened his mouth to say something, then quickly closed it and grinned. "No, I'm not. Jason, would you like to trade seats with me so you can sit beside your sister?"

Jason's face lit up. "Okay."

Dirk picked Jason up and exchanged seats with his son. He sat down again with his back to the offending booth. Raising his root beer to Julia in a toast he smiled. "Here's to a pleasant family evening."

Julia clinked his glass with her own, a warm feeling settling in the pit of her stomach.

"Can I have a 'lowence too," Jason asked suddenly.

"Me too," Christa echoed.

Dirk burst out laughing. "Do you guys hear everything you're not supposed to?"

They both nodded, giggling.

They were just finishing their meal when out of the corner of her eye, Julia saw the younger Sanford get up and approach their table. The kids saw him coming before Dirk did, and watched him with wide eyes. Julia could see why they stared at him. One side of his face was streaked with four long, recently healed, scratches; his nose twisted wickedly where it had obviously been broken. Other scars on his arms and face made him look like he'd tackled a large cat and lost.

Julia hoped he'd keep walking.

Of course he didn't.

He stopped directly behind Jason. A white knob scar on his lower lip flattened when he smiled. "So, Travis, rumor has it you misplaced your wife."

Julia had heard of people saying they got so angry

they saw red. She never believed it was true—until that very moment.

"You ignorant fool," she gritted. "Do you have any concept of what you're saying in front of these children or does your brain, providing you have one, only reach to the center of your rear cheeks?"

Both Dirk and Sanford stared at her, speechless.

She hadn't finished. Her fingers curled in her palms, itching to dig into his face. "Why are you still standing there? Leave this table immediately or I'll be happy to add to your fine collection of scars."

When Matthew Sanford whirled around and stomped away, Julia felt a rush of heat rise to her face, she closed her eyes trying to control the dizziness that threatened to overwhelm her. Never in her life had she spoken to another human being like that. Never. Not to her father, not to Geno.

She dropped her face in her hands gasping, breathing deeply, choking back the tears that threatened her composure. From somewhere she heard Christa's frightened voice asking "What's wrong with Anna?" and Dirk answering, "Don't worry, Anna's fine. She's just resting. Do you want to go play in the balls again?" They must have said yes because Dirk asked if they knew how to buy tokens. They both said yes and raced off.

A firm hand came to rest on her shoulder. "Julia? Are you okay?"

Keeping her hands over her face, she nodded vigorously. "I'm so sorry. I don't know what came over me. I've never done anything like that before."

"I bet you wanted to," he said, a touch of humor in his voice.

Again she nodded, but she thought she heard him chuckling. She brought her hands down and looked up at him. He had slid his chair over beside her and he was grinning.

"It…it's not funny. I… I was horrible."

"I guess you didn't get a good look at his face. From where I sat it was hilarious. He deserved every word you said and more."

"Are they gone?" she asked not wanting to risk a glance in that direction.

"They both hit the exit like their tails were on fire."

"That was awful to do in front of the children."

"Believe me, it would have been worse if I had stood up and popped him into the next county, which is exactly what I was set to do before you stepped in."

"Wouldn't that have been a violation of your probation?"

Dirk snorted. "Why do you think he came over here? So you see, you not only defended the kids, you saved me from explaining myself to a judge." He slipped an arm around her shoulders and gave a light squeeze. "You okay now?"

"I guess, as long as you're not upset with me." When she turned to face him, they were so close she could smell his earthy aftershave and feel his heat.

"Not a chance," he said leaning over to kiss the tip of her nose before he slid his chair back. "Can you honestly tell me it didn't feel good to set that arrogant piece of trash in his place?"

Julia thought for only a moment before she laughed. "As a matter of fact, it felt great."

"Why don't you collect our ball jumpers while I go pay the tab?"

* * * *

His words stuck with Julia as she brushed her teeth and scrubbed her face getting ready for bed that night. He had said "our ball jumpers" as though she was actually part of his little family. She knew it was just his way of talking, but still, it felt nice.

She gave herself a sharp mental shake. Starting to think of those kids as her own was a grave mistake. As comfortable as she was living on the ranch, she knew the time would come when she'd have to take up her profession again and leave. Maybe sooner would be better than later. She'd known from the onset that one didn't just disregard eight years of medical training to become a nanny. Detaching herself, however, was going come with extreme emotional pain.

Sleep eluded her as she snuggled into her warm bed. Spouting off at Matthew Sanford had felt good—damn good. How often had she wanted to do that to Geno—and even to her father, which was unthinkable? She didn't even want to consider what he would have done to her in retaliation.

She finally slept with the memory of Dirk's arm around her shoulders, and the scent of his aftershave. That kiss on her nose, however odd, was just a reflex on his part, she'd seen him do that to Christa on numerous occasions.

* * * *

Dirk tossed and turned, trying with little success, to get comfortable. He shouldn't have touched her, even something as minor as putting a comforting arm around her. Theirs was a business relationship, nothing more. She was his employee, nothing more.

He'd just been so damn proud of her when she stood up to Sanford, protecting his kids like an enraged mama-bear. Her actions saving him from a court appearance and probation violation hadn't even entered her mind—she was protecting her cubs.

What about that kiss on her nose? What he really wanted to do was gather her in his arms and kiss her proper-like, take care of the ache in his groin that was making an appearance every time he got within ten feet of her. He wondered what it would be like to spread her legs and bury himself in her soft heat.

Groaning, he put a quick check on his thoughts and wondered if maybe he'd have to make a trip into Denver to see Melody. Somehow, that thought didn't pacify him.

He turned over one more time, punching his fist into his pillow, wondering how many sheep he'd have to count to get some rest.

CHAPTER EIGHT

The rain had stopped, but Julia's riding lesson was again postponed when one of Melody's mares went into labor.

Dirk looked exhausted when he came into the house at three o'clock to announce he was taking the kids to a swimming park on Sunday. They all cheered when he said Gus was going to go along. Instead of suggesting that Julia join them, he handed her the keys to Gloria's 4-wheel Land Rover and asked if she needed a briefing on how to drive it.

She declined, shrugging off her disappointment at being dismissed by telling herself it was for the best. Maybe they had been spending too much time together and it would be good for her to venture out on her own a bit. Recalling her plan to investigate the hospitals in Denver, asked if he had an Internet service that she could use.

He hesitated a moment. "Sure, the computer in my office is hooked up, help yourself."

"Do you have a Colorado map?"

"There's one in the car—in the door panel pocket. Most of the back roads don't appear on it, but you know the way to Danango and that's on the map. Just keep your bearings straight and don't veer off too far from the main highways." He looked as though he wanted to say more on the subject but apparently changed his mind. "I'm going into town to pick up Meggie and I'll bring back some carry-out for dinner."

* * * *

It didn't take Julia more than five minutes to decide she didn't like being alone in the house. She'd become too accustomed to the activities of the children. Before he left, Dirk promised her a whole day of peace and quiet since he planned to take the kids out to eat after spending the day at the park. She didn't want to admit, even to herself, how much she wanted to be with them.

With that thought pressing on her, she walked down to Dirk's office, took a seat in his cushy brown leather swivel chair and booted up the computer on his desk.

Julia spent the next hour researching hospitals and clinics in the Denver area, writing down the pertinent information, and printing out route maps. Since it was Sunday, the clinics wouldn't be open, so she settled on two hospitals to visit on the west side of the city. It was unlikely she'd actually get to talk to anyone, but she needed to occupy her time anyway. Maybe being in the familiar atmosphere of a hospital would lighten her mood and make her start thinking about practicing again. That finished, she brought up a site that sold African snow globes.

The drive to Denver took less than an hour. Apparently, Gus had taken some decrepit side road hoping she would beg to be taken back to the airport. She had to admit he was a crafty old goat. Certainly he could have used Dirk's truck or the Land Rover to pick her up instead of that fifty's something pickup.

Hoping she would find someone on duty to talk to, she'd worn an off-white wool skirt and matching blazer over a royal blue silk blouse.

The first hospital was right off the freeway and she decided to walk the halls a bit then go to the cafeteria for lunch. It wasn't a coincidence that her meandering took her to the maternity ward on the fourth floor. The nursery had several empty bassinets, as most of the babies were in the rooms with their mothers. One premature infant slept fitfully under the protective hood of an incubator.

As Julia stood there staring at the tiny human being, an overwhelming wave of grief hit her, tightening her chest, cutting off her breath. She would have been in her eighth month by now, nearing full term. Through tear-clouded eyes she watched a nurse enter the room and, noticing Julia's anxiety, assumed she was there to see the baby. The nurse came up to the window.

"Would you like to come inside," she said with a smile and a motion to the side door.

Julia shook her head a bit too vigorously and scurried away.

The nurse's stations were clean, quiet and well managed, as were the rooms Julia passed. Satisfied, she found her way to the cafeteria, ordered an egg salad sandwich, and moved to the end of the line to wait for her order. A weary looking woman in her late thirties, wearing battle-worn scrubs, walked in, ordered a cup of coffee and passed by Julia to the cashier. Her nametag identified her as Margaret Jenson M.D. She moved slowly to an empty corner table. Julia paid for her meal, picked up her tray and approached the woman.

Margaret Jenson looked up with interest in her eyes.

"Excuse me, Dr. Jenson," Julia said, thankful that this was the one area of her life where she felt confident and in complete control. "I wonder if I could sit and talk to you a moment."

The woman's tired brown eyes did a brief assessment of Julia. "If you want to inquire about a family member, you're better off going to the nurse's station. I've been in emergency for five hours and frankly I'm beat."

Julia smiled. "I can sympathize with you. I'm a pediatrician, visiting from Minnesota. I was thinking about making a move to Denver and wondered about the physician status here."

Margaret waved a hand to an empty chair and smiled. "Please sit, as long as I don't have to report on the condition of your husband or your brother or anybody else, I'd actually appreciate the company." She held out her hand. "I'm Margaret Jenson, everybody calls me Margaret."

Julia shook Margaret's hand and sat down. "I'm Julia Morgan. It sounds like you've had an exhausting day?"

Margaret laughed. "Believe me, that's an understatement. There were two of us on call today and we had three emergencies with multiple injuries."

"Sounds like a war zone. Are you finished for the day?"

"Thank goodness, yes. The replacement troops have arrived." Margaret added cream and artificial sugar to her coffee, took a sip and sighed. "Now what can I help you with? Did I understand you were looking for a position?"

Julia decided the best approach was honesty. "Possibly. I have an ex-husband in Minneapolis; he was chief of staff at County Med where I practiced."

Margaret laughed. "Say no more. I can relate to that scene. I moved here from Seattle three years ago under similar circumstances. Truthfully, you'd be better off coming back on a workday and talking to the administrator, Greg Paris. I can tell you one thing, if you have a clean record, you've come to the right place. Pediatricians are in short supply in Colorado."

Julia's heartbeat kicked up. "Well... I just don't know what I'm going to do." Julia hesitated, she wanted to be honest but she wasn't ready to bare all to a stranger. "I'm still dealing with a tragedy in my personal life and I'm not sure I'm ready."

Margaret reached out and put a sympathetic hand on Julia's wrist. "Well, Hon, when you're ready, come back and see Greg. You'll need to contact a clinic first of course, but I'm sure you know the procedure. I'd recommend Health Central for starters. And do it now because it takes a couple of months to get insurance approvals. When you get that taken care of, come back and talk to Greg because as far as I'm concerned this is the best hospital in Denver, and the staff is terrific—and a good number of them are single men."

Julia smiled, she knew Margaret expected her to. "I'll keep that in mind," she said, taking a bite of her sandwich.

"I just had a thought," Margaret said a moment later. "In case Health Central isn't in the market for a pediatrician, I have a copy of the latest Colorado AMA Magazine, that will tell you who is looking to hire. Wait here, I have one in my carryall bag you can keep."

"I'd appreciate that. Thank you."

* * * *

By the time Julia visited the second hospital on her list, did some shopping for the kids, and grabbed a quick dinner, it was time to head back to the ranch so she could drive the unfamiliar roads in daylight.

When she pulled into the ranch yard at nine o'clock, a wonderful sense of coming home hit her. The cheery lights shining through the windows were like a welcoming beacon.

She found Dirk on the sofa reading to Christa, with Jason asleep on his lap. Christa leaped up and ran toward Julia, her arms stretched wide.

"Anna! Anna! You came home!"

Laughing, Julia dropped her parcels and picked the little girl up for a heartwarming hug. "Of course I came home, sweetie. I missed all of you."

Out of the corner of her eye, she caught Dirk appraising her wool suit, his expression indiscernible, at the same time she saw Gus sitting across the room. His frowning disposition hid nothing. Gus got up to leave and walked past her, speaking low enough so Dirk couldn't hear.

"Dressed for an interview?"

She felt her face grow warm. Not for the first time, she had the feeling Gus Travis could see into her soul. Before she could comment, he was gone. He had a most annoying habit of doing that. Just as well though, after all what would she have said? She wasn't actually looking for an interview today, but what she did bordered on it.

"We had lots of fun today," Christa said, interrupting Julia's thoughts. "We went swimming in a lake and got to go on rides. Why didn't you come with us, Anna?"

Julia hadn't intended to look at Dirk, but her gaze seemed to glide in his direction of its own accord. His face remained stoic.

"Because," she told Christa, "Anna had other things to do today."

Dirk stood up with his sleeping son in his arms. "Come on Christa, time for bed."

Christa made a small pouty face. "Can Anna put me to bed, Daddy?"

"I guess that's up to Anna," Dirk replied.

"Of course," Julia said, putting Christa down. "Why don't you help me carry my bags to my room then we'll go up and get your pajamas on." To Dirk she said," Could we talk afterwards?"

Something that might have been surprise registered on Dirk's face. "Sure, meet me in the kitchen. I'll put the coffee on."

Carrying his son up the stairs, Dirk wondered if she was finally going to let him in on what was going on in her life. GC? Katie? Why she'd gone out on a Sunday, supposedly not knowing anyone, dressed to kill in an outfit that certainly didn't come off a discount rack. Damn, but she'd looked good, too good. He knew his father hadn't meant for Dirk to hear that little slur about an interview, but the thought had crossed his mind, too. Where had she gone? Shopping? Dressed like a CEO?

He wasted no time tucking Jason in and heading for the kitchen. Thoughts of his father played on his mind as he spooned coffee into the filter. Gus didn't like Julia, he'd made that clear even before she'd come, and again today. "She won't stay," he'd said. "I know the type." Dirk had explained that Julia was in fact *a nanny—not his wife.* "Yeah?" Gus had said. "Tell that to Christa. She's going to be heartbroken when Julia leaves, and mark my words, that woman will be gone as soon as something better comes up."

Dirk hoped his father was wrong. Julia Morgan was just about the sweetest person he'd ever met. And he liked her—a lot. Too much. All day long, he'd chastised himself for not asking her to come along with them. He could tell she'd wanted to.

The rich aroma of decaf coffee, steaming from two mugs on the table, filled the room by the time she walked in. She'd changed back into jeans and a forest green sweater that matched the color of her eyes. Her hair hung loose, softly framing her face. Why did he have the feeling she was more at home in her other clothes, with her hair bound up? Was it because every pair of jeans she owned looked like they'd never been worn before, and she continually shoved her heavy locks behind her ears?

He tried not to appear anxious as he shifted in his chair, motioning to the one across from him. "Have a seat. Coffee's good, if I do say so myself. Are you hungry?"

Julia shook her head. "No, just coffee is fine." She took a seat and cradled her mug with long delicate fingers.

He hadn't noticed before how perfect her hands were, her nails well groomed, clean and rounded, as though she cared for them daily. Was it because Gus had pointed it out?

"Did you have a good day?" he asked.

She smiled and nodded. "Yes, I went in to Denver. I— I've never been there before—except at the airport, of course."

When she sipped coffee for a time without further comment, Dirk's curiosity got the best of him. "You wanted to talk," he said.

Her smile faded and she fidgeted with the mug, tracing the rim and the handle as though she was trying to memorize it for sculpting later. "I'm having a difficult time with something," she said finally, "and I was hoping you could explain it to me."

Dirk raised his brows in question and waited.

"Why doesn't Gus like me?" she blurted.

The question shouldn't have taken him by surprise, but it did. Probably because it wasn't even remotely close to what he'd expected her to say. He had to regroup his thoughts…quickly. Denying his father's feelings toward her didn't enter his mind. However, telling the truth bared yet another corner of his soul, while he still knew little or nothing about her.

Dirk signed. "I wish I could say it's a long complicated story, but it isn't. It's short and simple. My father married the wrong woman. He loved it out here; she hated it. After ten years of marriage, she packed up, took my little sister and left Dad and me on our own. End of story."

Julia's eyes widened. "My God, that's awful. How old were you?"

"Nine, Tanya was seven. My mother said I was too much to handle."

"Did you ever see her again?"

"Oh, sure, she lives in L.A. She came every summer, stayed a week, then flew off into the sunset again."

"Did your sister come too?"

"Yeah, until about five years ago."

Julia's fine copper brows rose. "You haven't seen your sister in five years?"

"Just once since I married Gloria." Tanya had come to his trial. "Tanya didn't get on with her very well—neither did my mother for that matter."

"But your mother continued to come."

"The last time she was here, Jason and Christa were three months old. I swear it was the first time I'd seen her happy. I had the feeling, if it hadn't been for Gloria, she would have stayed longer."

"Did she come the next year?"

Staring into his empty coffee cup, Dirk stalled. It wasn't something he liked to talk about. "No," he said finally, "I was in prison."

"And when you came home, Gloria had left with the children," she finished for him.

Dirk nodded. "That pretty much sums it up in an ugly nutshell. Gloria's leaving just added to Dad's distrust of city women."

"Now he dislikes anyone who reminds him of his ex-wife."

"Wife. They never divorced."

"Religious reasons?"

"No, he'd deny it until the moon turned to cheese, but they still love each other."

"Is that why you didn't divorce Gloria?" Julia's hand flew to her mouth. Her face turned a bright shade of red. "Oh, my gosh. I can't believe I asked that. I'm sorry, it's none of my business."

Julia was horrified that she'd pried into his personal life. She wasn't even sure why she wanted to know if he still loved Gloria. When he stared at her with those piercing gray eyes, she thought she had, rightfully so, angered him.

She opened her mouth to continue her apology only to be cut off by his icy words.

"It's no secret that I stopped loving my wife when she came to testify at my trial. In her own wicked little way, she had the jury believing that I had an uncontrollable temper and was insane with jealousy. Now ask me if I wanted to kill her."

Julia clasped her hands on the table in front of her and gathered her courage to meet his stony gaze. "I can imagine you did feel that way, but I don't believe for one minute you would harm the mother of your children."

"You say that like you mean it."

"Of course I mean it. You love your children very much, including Megan. I can't see you doing anything to disillusion them."

Dirk gave her a lopsided smile. "Those were the exact words my sister used when she called after hearing that Gloria was missing."

Julia was relieved to get off the subject of his wife. She thought of Katie and couldn't imagine going for years without seeing or talking to her. "Then you get to talk to Tanya, even though you don't see her. I can't imagine having a sibling you didn't talk to."

"I don't talk to her often. She's an undercover cop for the LAPD, so she's not very accessible. Do you have any family back in Minneapolis?"

Somehow, Julia knew that eventually he would get around to asking, and she'd left herself wide open by questioning him. "Just a sister," she said. "There's no one else left."

* * * *

Dirk went down to his office and booted up the Internet, hoping to find out once and for all what Julia was hiding. He brought up a log of the last sites visited then leaned back staring at the screen, scratching his head. Four Denver hospitals and six clinics popped up along with an African glass manufacturer.

Frowning, he leaned back in his chair, rubbing his chin, concentrating on the medical facilities. He had no way of knowing why she'd researched them, and the first thought that came to mind was an unpleasant one. Was she sick? She certainly didn't look sick—in fact she appeared to be the picture of health. Nobody he'd known, including his mother and Gloria, dressed to the nines for a doctor's appointment. He didn't dare question her about it without admitting that he'd been following her tracks.

He refused to go down Gus's alley and believe she was looking for work. It didn't make sense that she'd take a nanny position then go looking for a job one week later. She didn't appear to be unhappy working for him. In fact she seemed more than content, and she'd taken to the kids far better than he expected, even managing to get Meggie on her side. Not to mention Christa, who positively adored her new nanny. Every time Christa asked for *Anna* throughout the day, Dirk had to endure those annoying looks from his father. Gus had gone so far as to suggest maybe Dirk was lusting after his shapely employee.

He shoved that thought aside rather quickly and pulled up the web site for Gloria's agent, planning to do some investigation of his own into the disappearance of his wayward wife. After writing down the New York phone number, he punched in the name Carl Edwards. The name popped up several times, but none appeared to be Megan's long lost father. From there, he went into public records where, for a small fee, he could bring up any possible criminal record on Edwards. A long list of arrests filled the screen, all petty violations resulting in only one conviction. He'd pled guilty to leaving the scene of an accident and spent six months in a Wisconsin county jail. His last known address came up as Madison, Wisconsin and that information was two years old.

Dirk called information in Madison and asked for a number on Carl Edwards. They had no listing in that name—dead end.

Would he dare question Meggie about where Gloria first met up with Edwards to drive to Colorado? Had Gloria been seeing him in New York?

Rubbing a hand over his tired eyes, he decided he'd start tomorrow, making calls that included Gloria's sister, Connie, in Minnesota. *Why hadn't she been the one to report Gloria missing?* Right now he was going to bed.

As Dirk walked past Julia's room, he noticed light under the door. She was still up. He resisted the urge to knock on the door and question her about the hospitals and clinics. Ask if she was sick. Ask why she needed a psychiatrist and why he saw fear in her eyes along with love when she mentioned having a sister in Minnesota.

At midnight, Julia heard Dirk close his office door then hesitate outside her room. Her heart began a war dance that continued even after he mounted the steps to his own bedroom. She'd been going over her notes on the two hospitals she visited and the phone numbers of the clinics she intended to contact. She'd make an excuse to drive in to Danango that week to make her calls. Taking that step didn't mean she was ready to leave the *Rocking T* any time soon. The process to start practicing in a new clinic could take three to four months. She just wanted to be prepared when the time came.

* * * *

The next morning, Dirk walked in the front door to discover Julia in the kitchen conversing with Rosa in perfect Spanish.

He raised an eyebrow at his ever-surprising nanny as he took a seat at the table. "You didn't tell me you could speak Spanish."

Megan walked in with her siblings in tow as Julia took her seat at the table. "You didn't ask," she said.

"She talks French too," Megan said, helping Christa onto her chair. "She taught me some words while we played piano."

Dirk shot Julia an incredulous look. "French?"

Julia shrugged. "It's no big deal, really. It was required in school."

Dirk didn't recall two languages being required where he went to school. He was about to ask her where she attended college, but Julia closed their conversation by asking Jason about his day at the park. That put both Christa and Jason into animated overdrive.

He couldn't get another word in until Rosa set their food in front of them, by then the moment was lost. He decided to let it drop for the time being. "Meggie, can you keep an eye on the twins while I give Julia her riding lesson this morning?"

"Can we watch?" Megan asked.

Dirk sliced Christa's pancake. "I don't see why not. Unless Julia objects." He glanced at Julia.

Julia held the syrup while Jason squeezed a generous amount on his plate. "Fine with me, but I've never even touched a horse that I can remember, so don't expect too much."

"It's easy," Megan chirped. "You'll see."

"Just remember," Dirk told her, "you're in charge of the dynamic duo—and no, you're not getting paid extra. Seven dollars a week allowance includes babysitting, dishes, and cleaning your room."

"I bought some petunias yesterday," Julia said to Dirk. "You don't mind if I plant them in the flower beds out front, do you?"

Dirk felt a sudden jerk on his heartstrings. He'd put the beds in because Gloria asked for them, but she never got around to planting anything. "Have at it," he said. "You'll probably find gardening tools in the garage. I have some calls to make after breakfast so, you should have plenty of time before you ride."

"Can we help?" Christa asked.

Julia laughed. "I was hoping you would. You too, Megan, if you like."

* * * *

Dirk found himself more interested in the activity outside his window than making his calls. Jason and Christa were on their knees setting out flowers while Megan raked the soil after Julia turned it over with a spade. Funny, he never pictured Julia with her perfectly manicured hands working in dirt. Gloria loved flowers, too, but she wanted someone other than herself to tend to them. Gus was wrong. There were a lot of differences between Julia and Gloria—and his mother for that matter.

Setting that thought aside, Dirk picked up the phone and dialed Tom Payton's number. His secretary answered.

"Music Man Agency."

"Is Tom Payton in?" Dirk asked.

"May I tell him who's calling please?"

"Yeah, Dirk Travis."

After a couple of clicks and a buzz, Tom Payton's voice came on the line. "Dirk Travis, good of you to call. Are you a relative of Gloria's?"

Dirk slowly sucked in his breath. "I'm her husband."

A moment of silence followed. "I'm sorry, I… I didn't know she was married."

Dirk grunted. "I guess that explains why you didn't call me before you reported her missing."

"Certainly… I had no idea. I became concerned when she didn't show up for a concert at Bellamy Hall. She loved to play and would have to be on her death bed to miss an opportunity like that."

"I thought the two of you were supposed to be touring in Europe."

"Excuse me?"

Dirk sucked in another breath of air. "Apparently there was no European tour."

"Not that I'm aware of. So…do you know where she is?"

Dirk gritted his teeth. "I wish I did." He wanted his hands around her throat. "Why did you wait two months to decide she was suddenly missing?"

"I had no reason to suspect anything before. She was always very religious about reporting in to confirm the schedule before she played."

"She hasn't performed in two months?"

"No, her last concert was May fifth. She said she was going to take a vacation and she'd be back to New York by July first to play at Bellamy Hall on the tenth. We had a contract and I needed to fill her spot if she wasn't available. It just wasn't like her to leave me hanging, so I went to her apartment and found out she'd lost it for non-payment of rent. They'd already sublet it."

"When exactly did you go to the police?" Dirk asked.

"I… July eighth. It was two days before the concert and I had to find a replacement. I didn't know what else to do."

"And you could justify breaking the contract if you had proof you tried to find her."

"Well…yes…but you have to understand. I have a reputation to uphold."

"Did she leave anything behind in her apartment?"

"Yes, by law they had to hold it in storage for two months."

"Christ. She had a seven thousand dollar baby grand piano. There must have been a lot of the kids' things. What happened to everything?"

"Kids? She had children?"

Dirk clamped down on the receiver, attempting to squeeze the life out of it. He had to remind himself that Gloria was the culprit here, not Tom Payton.

Payton interrupted his dismembering thoughts.

"Mr. Travis, if she was your wife, and had your children, why didn't *you* report her missing?"

"She told me the two of you were going on a three month tour through Europe."

"I see… I guess she duped us both."

CHAPTER NINE

Dirk reached over and swung his window open so he could hear the chatter of activity going on outside. He had a peculiar longing to be out there with them. He quickly abandoned that thought and dialed the Minnesota number for Gloria's sister, Connie Goodwin. He'd never met Connie, but had spoken to her on the phone twice. Both times she'd been rude and abrasive. He knew she lived in a trendy downtown apartment with a long time female friend.

Connie's husky voice came on the line. "Yeah, hello."

"Connie, it's Dirk."

"My less than sainted jailbird brother-in-law. What a pleasure." As usual, Connie pulled no punches.

Dirk gritted his teeth, forcing himself not to return her sarcasm—at least not until he had some information from her. "Sorry to bother you, Connie, but I was wondering if you've heard from Gloria recently."

"What, you misplaced your wife again?"

A rush of anger washed over Dirk. The last time he'd called Connie was when he got out of prison and found Gloria gone. The sound of Christa's giggles filled his ears as he took a deep, calming breath. "She came here about two months ago and left the kids. I haven't heard from her since—her agent is looking for her," he added hoping to get across that he really didn't give a rat's ass where Gloria was.

A disgusting sound came over the line. "I suppose he's got a gig for her at Carnegie Hall." A loud burp followed. "She was here all right, must have been on the way to Colorado cause she still had the kids with her—and a worthless piece-of-trash man." At least Dirk could agree with her on that. "She boasted about how much money she was making in one breath, and asking to borrow two thousand dollars in the next. Said she had this fancy tour in Europe and she'd pay me back in two weeks when she got her advance. Hah! Haven't seen hide nor hair of her since. If you do see her, remind her she has a loving sister who is quite anxious to hear from her. Actually, I was thinking about calling to see if you wanted to settle the debt for her—after all, she is still your wife."

When it snows in hell. "I'll be sure to give her your message if she shows up. Have a nice day and thanks for your time." Dirk hung up before he said something he'd regret.

Looking back out on the flower planting scene, Dirk saw Jason digging his fingers in the soft dirt and Christa pressing her nose into the still-potted purple and white Petunia's. Dirk turned to his desk and quickly fished for the digital camera Gloria purchased when the twins were born. It was one of the few things of value smaller than a breadbox that she'd failed to take with her. Rosa had found it stashed between the mattresses when she was cleaning.

Switching the flash off, he wound the window open a bit to get an unobstructed view. He caught Jason holding up a fat angleworm in his chubby fingers, and Christa rubbing her button of a nose on the velvet softness of the flowers. When Christa held the flowers up for Julia to smell, he got one of Julia bending forward with her hands on her knee breathing deeply. He could hear the loud moan of pleasure she made.

He stopped and moved back a bit when Carrie ambled up to them. She had her hands wrapped around her protruding belly as if it were a heavy weight to bear, and a smile on her face that was cheery, but strained.

Dirk's window was at least fifteen feet from where they were standing so he couldn't make out all they were saying, but he enjoyed watching. Julia stopped working to talk, and while they chatted Carrie suddenly laughed and grasped her abdomen. Moments later, Julia was stooping in front of her. Dirk had a side view of Julia framing her hands around the baby. A lump rose to his throat as he remembered doing that to Gloria. Julia was feeling the baby kick.

Julia beckoned Megan forward and the wide smile on the young girl's face when she felt the movement of secret life in the womb made Dirk think maybe she was old enough to watch a horse give birth. Very quickly he leaned forward and captured her smile on camera.

After a few minutes, Carrie left and Julia went back to planting. When Julia paused to rub the back of her hand over her cheek, Dirk realized it was tears she was brushing away. Dirk swallowed down a wave of emotion as a sharp pain settled in his chest. He turned back to his desk, attempting to put a rein on his thoughts but they flooded his mind unbidden.

Julia Morgan was a woman like none he'd ever met. She was sweet and kind, and sensitive with an easygoing, laid-back personality. The only time he'd seen her lose her cool was when she was protecting her charges against Matthew Sanford. A whole lot of other words came to mind to describe her, like talented, smart, and sexy. He hadn't touched her skin, but he knew it would be as soft as the petunia Christa had put to her face. It wouldn't take a whole lot to fall in love with a person like that. She was the kind of woman that could smooth a man's rough edges.

Dirk gave himself a sharp mental shake. Somewhere, she had hidden flaws. She had to—everyone had faults. He'd only known her a little over a week. You can't really know someone in that short of a time. Gloria had appeared to be a gift from God when he'd first met her. She was talented, smart, and homecoming-queen beautiful. It wasn't until after he'd married her that her more dominant traits appeared. She turned out to be selfish, self-serving, flirtatious to the point of embarrassment, and she had a unique ability to alienate anyone he was close to, including every person living on the ranch as well as his mother and sister. That brought him to one conclusion; it took a wedding ring to really get to know a woman. He had to cool his heels when it came to thoughts of his *perfect* nanny.

He got up, stuck the camera in his pocket, and headed for the stables to snap some pictures of Evening Star's colt. Stopping at the flowerbed, he planted a kiss on top of Christa's head then looked down at Julia, who was kneeling on the ground. She'd found a pair of work gloves to protect her hands and was setting plants in the holes Jason made while Megan laid out the design.

"Nice work you're all doing," he said, tousling Jason's hair. "When you're finished," he said to Julia," we'll get to your riding lesson if you aren't too tired."

Julia gave him a brilliant smile that said she loved what she was doing. "Sure, I have so much help we'll be done here in about half an hour."

"Good, I'll have Black Lightning saddled for you."

Both Megan and Julia looked up at him with wide eyes.

"I'm kidding," he said laughing. "You'll be riding Seminole, she's a pussy cat."

"Can we ride again, too?" Megan asked.

"Sure, you can. I'll see if I can get Grandpa or Mack to help us."

Dirk headed toward the stable with a spring in his step and a soft whistle on his lips. Inside he found both Charlie Mack and David. They'd just finished collecting semen from Black Lightning to artificially inseminate two fillies.

David met Dirk with a grin. "Quite a production line they have going on that flowerbed over there. I was afraid for a minute I'd see Carrie down on her knees helping."

"Looks like she's just about ready to pop." Dirk said. "Have you talked her into going to Denver to her mother's to wait for her labor to begin?"

David laughed. "I wish. I think she'd rather have it in the car on the way than deliver without me being there. Something about me experiencing the pain along with her."

Mack grimaced. "Ooh, that's brutal."

Dirk followed them into the small lab where they were setting up to inseminate the mares. "Can I ask you guys something?" Dirk asked as he pulled the breeding pipettes and shoulder length plastic gloves from the cabinet and handed them to David, who was the inseminator.

David measured semen into a vial. "Sure Dirk, what is it?"

David Masters had worked for Dirk since before he married Gloria. He'd met Mack while in prison. They'd spent two months together before Mack got paroled and in that time, Dirk learned about Mack's love of horses. When Mack left for the outside, Dirk had sent him to the *Rocking T* along with a letter to Gus, requesting that he give Mack a job. Dirk respected and trusted both of his key employees. Questioning them about his wife wasn't something he particularly wanted to do, but he needed to gather as much information as possible in case she wasn't found, and the authorities tried to pin her disappearance on him.

"Since you were both here when Gloria left, I wondered if there was anything you could tell me about her activities in the months I was gone. The authorities will probably get around to questioning both of you and I'd rather not have any surprises."

Both men immediately stopped what they were doing and exchanged a look that spoke volumes.

Mack spoke first, a little too quickly. "You know I'd never say anything to incriminate you, boss. You took me in when I was down and out. Just tell me what you want me to say and I'll swear it on a stack of Bibles."

"Same goes for me." David said. "You hired me when I was a green kid, you sent me to school to learn the inseminating business. This isn't just a job to me; it's my home, my life. It was pretty depressing here while you were gone."

Dirk shook his head. "I'm not asking either one of you to lie for me. I just want to know what Gloria was up too. It seemed like she took off the minute she found out I was coming home, and I'd like to know why."

That same look passed between them and this time it angered Dirk. "God dammit you two, you're not very good at poker. Now, I don't care if she was slutting around. I just want to know who the guy was so I can try to figure out where she is."

This time David's gaze settled on Mack, and his face turned a bright shade of crimson. "I didn't touch her boss. I swear it. She came on to me something awful, but my loyalties are to you."

Dirk was having trouble digesting Mack's words. He looked to David, hoping for answers.

"I believe him," David said. "Gloria threw herself at him every chance she got. I overheard him yelling at her to stay the hell away from him. That's when she started driving off and staying away overnight."

Dirk shot a hand through his hair, swearing savagely. "What did she do with the kids?"

"They stayed with us," David said quietly. "Carrie and I both love those kids. Rest assured, they were well cared for."

Dirk wanted to smash his fist in something. "Are you saying she left because she was afraid I'd find out?"

Mack glanced at David before he stared at the wall behind Dirk's head.

"Why did she leave?" Dirk demanded.

"She's gone and good riddance," David said. "Just leave it at that."

Dirk's hands clenched onto fists. "I don't give a flying fart about Gloria, but you two are really starting to piss me off. Right now I need to pound something. Who wants to be first?"

Mack stood in front of Dirk with his hands at his side. "Go ahead, if it'll make you feel better. I'd rather take a beating then rip your heart out."

"I told you I don't give a damn about her, so nothing you say is going to hurt me."

"You're wrong," David said.

"You're both hiding something and you know I'm not going to let it go, so you may as well fess up right now and save us a lot of time."

"She was pregnant!" David blurted out.

For the space of a few mindless moments it took all Dirk's energy just to breathe. His angry glare swiveled from David to Mack. "Whose baby was it?" he asked in a forced whisper. "Don't worry, I won't kill him. Nobody she screwed around with is worth going back to prison for."

David rubbed a hand over his brow. "I only know because in one of Gloria's rare moments she confided in Carrie. Gloria said she had to leave because you wouldn't allow her to have an abortion if you found out."

"She's right," Dirk ground out. "I might have killed her, but I wouldn't have condoned killing a baby, I don't care whose it was."

A profound sadness entered David's eyes. "She was five months pregnant—the baby was yours."

* * * *

Julia stood up to stretch the kinks from her back and survey their work while Megan sprayed the flowers with water. It was late in the year to plant annuals, but even so, they enhanced the front of the house, and the children had fun doing it.

A ruckus from across the yard drew her attention. She looked up in time to see Dirk burst from the stable on the back of Black Lightning. Seeing the large forbidding horse always sent shivers up her spine, and seeing Dirk on top of him didn't help matters any. She knew Black Lightning was the *Rocking T*'s prime breeding stud, but she'd never actually seen anyone ride him.

Once cleared of the stable, the stallion burst into full charge, racing through the yard. Julia felt the reverberations of pounding hooves shake the ground, and within seconds, horse and rider disappeared into the trees.

Megan stared in awe. "Oh, my gosh. Dirk is really teed off about something."

Across the yard, Julia caught sight of David and Charlie Mack as they watched the road that seemed to have swallowed up Dirk on the black stallion. Neither one of them had a particularly happy look on his face.

"Well, I guess we won't get to ride our ponies today," Megan grumbled.

"Why can't we?" Jason asked.

Megan made a face. "Because your father has a major mad-on."

Julia cleared her throat. "I tell you what we'll do instead. I bought you each something yesterday when I was in Denver."

Christa's face lit up. "You got us presents?"

Julia laughed. "Uh huh. You can have them as soon as you all wash up."

At that moment, Rosa stuck her head out the door to announce lunch would be ready in fifteen minutes. Julia ushered the children inside, keeping an eye over her shoulder thinking Dirk might be coming back, but there was no sign of him or the insane stallion he was riding.

After they'd eaten, Julia brought out the doctor kit she'd bought for Christa. It was complete with a toy stethoscope and a large supply of band-aids. She immediately dragged out her dolls and lined them up on the sofa for examinations.

For Jason, Julia found a standing easel with drawing paper larger than Dirk's desk pad, washable colored markers and drawing pens. Megan clearly hadn't expected to get anything, and her face lit up when Julia brought out a pink floral makeup kit that held an assortment of pale lipsticks, blush, and a tube of blemish cover up.

Rosa became flustered when Julia presented her with a colorful silk scarf.

With the kids absorbed in their gifts, Julia once again glanced out the window, hoping to see some activity in the still quiet yard. Her heart gave a sudden leap when the phone rang. Rosa answered it, talked for some time and when she hung up she dabbed a tissue to her eyes, sniffling.

Julia rushed to her side. "What is it, Rosa? Did something happen?"

Rosa blew her nose into the tissue. "It's my grandson. My daughter just started working at the mercantile a week ago so she had to put him in daycare. This is the second time she had to pick him up because he got ill. She's afraid she'll lose her job."

"Has he been sick?" Julia asked.

Rosa shook her head. "No, he's very healthy. She doesn't know what to do. He's fine when she takes him in the morning, and right after lunch they call her to come and get him. Last Monday and again today."

"Did she say what his symptoms were?"

"He breaks out in a rash all over his face and he gets all feverish. Last time he was fine after a couple of hours. She doesn't know what to do. The doctor doesn't come to town until Wednesday."

How old is he?"

"Not even two. He is so little."

"Call your daughter," Julia urged, "and have her find out what they fed the kids for lunch today."

Rosa didn't hesitate. She picked up the phone and dialed her daughter's number. After a moment she turned to Julia. "They have a weekly menu," Rosa said holding the phone aside. "Today they had peanut butter and jelly sandwiches, green peas and a cookie."

Julia frowned. "Ask her if—wait, can I talk to her?"

"Of course." Rosa handed Julia the phone. "Her name is Sonja."

Julia put the phone to her ear. "Hello Sonja, this is Julia Morgan. I was wondering if your son has ever eaten peanut butter before?"

The distraught young woman answered in English. "No, I don't like it so I don't even have any in the house."

"It's my guess," Julia said, "he's probably allergic to peanuts."

"My goodness, I've been so worried, we can't afford any more time of off work," Sonja said choking on a sob. "It could really be something that simple?"

"That's what it sounds like. Does he have trouble breathing?"

"No, just the rash and fever—and coughing a little. What can I do for him?"

"Go to the drugstore right away and get some children's liquid antihistamine, like Benadryl. Give him the dosage recommended on the bottle. Be sure to tell your daycare not to feed him anything with peanuts in it, including cookies."

"Thank you, thank you," Sonja gushed.

Suddenly reminded why she liked being a pediatrician, Julia smiled. "I hope the medication helps, but please call back if his symptoms don't go away. If he starts having trouble breathing, you rush him to an emergency room immediately—understand?"

"Yes, Doctor Morgan, Thank you again. Please tell Mama I will call her later."

Before Julia could respond, Sonja hung up. Just as well, what could Julia have done—lied and said she wasn't a doctor? Julia laid the phone back in its cradle and related Sonja's message to Rosa. Then she asked Rosa not to make a big deal of the incident to Dirk.

* * * *

By nine o'clock that evening, Dirk still hadn't come home. The twins were in bed and Megan was in her room reading. Julia paced the floor wondering where he could be this late. Surely he wouldn't be out riding in the woods after dark. Maybe he'd ridden in quietly and was in the stable, though she couldn't see any light out there.

At a loss as to what to do, she sat down to the piano. Her fingers slid over the keys doing some soft soulful jazz. The music wasn't exactly cheering her up, but it did relieve her tension. She'd been playing about a half hour when she realized Gus stood in the kitchen doorway staring at her. Even though she'd gotten accustomed to his sudden appearances, he still startled her. Her fingers slammed down on the keys and the music came to a resounding stop.

Gus stepped closer. "Any chance you know what set Dirk off in a snit today?"

Julia could tell by his tone he blamed her. She had two choices. She could duck her head and cower like she'd been doing most of her life, or she could stand up to yet another domineering male who had no respect for her.

She was sick and tired of cowering.

"I'm not his wife. If I had caused his anger, he wouldn't have needed to risk his life on a devil horse, he could simply fire me—or have you forgotten that?"

Gus's gray eyebrows rose. He was silent for a moment while he stared at her, one side of his mouth lifted. "I guess I just expected you to high-tail it out of here as soon as something better came along."

Julia steeled herself with a deep breath. She's gone this far, she wasn't about to back down now. "It seems to me I'd have the right to do that if I so choose."

Gus made a harrumphing sound, but before he could comment, the door from the garage opened. Julia swiveled in her chair in time to see Dirk enter the lower hall and stomp into his office. The door slammed behind him.

"Well," Gus said, "at least he's home safe. I better go try to talk to him."

Julia watched Gus walk down the steps to the office. He hesitated a moment, announced himself and knocked on the door. Even from where she sat at the piano she could hear Dirk barking at Gus to leave him alone. Gus said something she couldn't hear, then Dirk shouted again.

"I don't want to talk! Go away!"

Gus persisted until Dirk quit answering. Gus's shoulders slumped when he finally gave up and came back to Julia.

"I just don't know what set him off," Gus said. "I haven't seen him like this since he came home and found that witch gone with his kids. I'll lay you ten to one odds it has something to do with her. What do you think got him going?"

Julia was taken by surprise. For the first time since she arrived, Gus was actually talking to her, asking her opinion. She wished she had an answer. "I don't know," she said. "He was fine when he left the house, but he must have had some conversation with Mack and David because they didn't look too happy when they watched him ride off on Lightning."

"Maybe you could talk to him," Gus said, again surprising her.

"Why would he talk to me if he won't talk to you?"

Gus shrugged. "I'm not sure, but he likes you, and you've got spunk. You might be able to get to him."

Julia's heart took a giant leap to her throat. It was the first time in her life anyone had ever said she had spunk, not her father, not Geno, not even Katie. For some reason that overwhelmed her, endearing her to Gus as no other words could have. It brought a smile to her face.

"I'll give it a try," she said.

"Good enough. And good luck. Be persistent, he's pretty stubborn."

"Takes after his father, I guess."

Gus's craggy wrinkles rearranged into a grin. "You appear to be a good person. I hope I'm wrong about you."

Julia's inner smile faded as she watched Gus walk away. He wasn't wrong about her. In fact, he'd been right on target. Just as she'd told him, she wasn't a wife, she was an employee.

Sighing, Julia put her music away and closed the piano. Before she knocked on Dirk's door, she decided to look in on the kids. Maybe she was stalling.

Jason and Christa were asleep. She walked in their room, tucked the covers around them and for a moment watched their sleeping faces. This was something she didn't normally do since Dirk always put them to bed.

She hesitated a moment outside Megan's closed door. Then tapped lightly.

"Yeah?" Megan called from inside.

"It's Julia, I just wanted to say goodnight."

"Sure, come on in."

Megan was sitting on her bed with a Boxcar Kids book in her hand. She looked adorable in an oversized New York Yankees tee shirt.

"I heard voices," Megan said. "Did he finally come home?"

"Yes, he's home, but he's locked in his office. The voice you heard was Gus. He's concerned."

"What do you think got him all worked up?"

"I don't know, but Gus seems to think I should try to talk to him."

"Good idea," Megan said. "If he talks to anybody it'll be you. I think he has the hots for you."

Julia's eyes widened. "Why would you say that?"

Megan grinned. "Because he watches your backside a lot."

"You're hallucinating," Julia said, laughing. She walked over to the bed and gave Megan a kiss on the top of the head. "Goodnight, honey. I'm glad to see you reading. It's good for you."

When Julia started to leave, Megan said, "I like having you here, Julia."

Swallowing the lump that rose to her throat, Julia turned to give Megan a misty smile. "I like being here."

Downstairs, Julia gathered her courage and knocked on Dirk's office door.

"Go away! I told you I don't want to talk."

Julia summoned the spunk Gus seemed to think she had.

"It's Julia."

After a brief moment of silence he spoke again, softer this time. "What do you want?"

"May I come in?"

Another pause. "The door's not locked. Enter at your own risk."

Heart pounding, Julia turned the knob and opened the door. The only light in the room came from the window. Dirk was sprawled on the leather sofa, a drink with amber liquid held in his hand. The strong scent of bourbon permeated the room. It was an unwelcome smell she remembered from her childhood.

"Are you drunk?" she asked, contemplating whether or not she should flee.

"Not yet," he mumbled.

Julia closed the door behind her, not wanting Megan to hear him like this.

"Gus sent you in here, didn't he?" Dirk accused.

Julia approached him cautiously. "He's worried about you."

"Yeah, well he should have thought about that a few months ago."

"I don't understand," Julia said.

Dirk waved his half empty glass at her. "They were hiding pertinent information from me. David and Mack knew, so I'm sure Dad did too. They had no right."

"What information?" she asked, not really sure if she wanted to know. When he didn't answer, she walked over to the desk and switched a small lamp on. She turned back to him noticing how ragged he looked. Where he was usually quite neat about his appearance, his shirt and pants looked like they'd been slept in, and his hair was tousled from his wild ride.

"She was pregnant," he whispered, "with my baby."

That word always caused Julia a stab of anxiety to her heart. She walked over to him and sat down, perching on the far end of the sofa. She longed to reach over and brush the wayward hair back from his forehead. "Who was pregnant?" she asked.

"Gloria. That's why she left in such a hurry when she heard I was getting released from prison. She knew I wouldn't have allowed her to get an abortion."

"You think she aborted your baby?"

Dirk tossed down the remainder of his drink. "Without a doubt." His gripped the empty glass as though he wanted to hurl it someplace.

Julia didn't know what to say. She felt his pain. He loved his children just as she had loved her unborn babies. "I'm so sorry," she whispered.

He looked at her with eyes that suggested he could see into her soul. "You've lost someone, haven't you?"

Tears clouded her vision and she wished she'd left the light off. She nodded, knowing if she spoke her voice would start breaking up.

He stared at her quietly for a moment. "You lost a child, didn't you?"

A shudder racked her body and she couldn't stop the tears from trickling down her face. When she didn't answer, he moved next to her and put an arm around her sagging shoulders. His comfort broke down the last of her resolve and she put her hands to her face and cried, wondering how she had allowed her torment to surface.

"My poor sweet Julia," he said gathering her into his arms.

She pressed her face into his shoulder and let the tears come. "I'm—I'm sorry," she hiccupped, feeling guilty and selfish. "I came in here to comfort you, not the other way around."

"Don't be sorry," Dirk said. "There's an old saying about misery loving company. I never realized how true it was. Tell me about your baby?"

She slumped against him. "Babies," she managed to say. "I was five months pregnant with twin girls. I lost them three months ago."

His soothing arms were around her, rubbing her back, her neck, her arms. Then he was kissing the tears from her cheeks. His soft lips on her face began stirring emotions in her she'd thought long dead. She lifted her face and his mouth covered hers in a kiss so tender it made her want to start crying all over again. His hand went to the side of her face, brushing away the tears as his lips moved over her mouth. She tasted the sweet aroma of bourbon on her tongue, and she wondered how she could have ever thought it was an unpleasant scent.

His kiss was no comparison to Geno's greedy lusting. Julia eagerly responded to Dirk's gentleness, while somewhere in the back of her mind she knew it was wrong. She resisted the urge to put her arms around him.

Suddenly he froze. He pushed himself away from her. "My God, Julia, I'm sorry."

Julia put her hand to her mouth, where his lips had been burning a trail of desire though her body. She charged to her feet and fled to her own room. She barely had the door closed when she heard his knock.

"Julia, please open the door. I want to apologize. I took advantage of you at a time when you were vulnerable.

I should have been comforting you. I swear that's all I meant to do… Please."

Julia leaned her head against the door. She had started to shake. "It's…it's all right," she whispered just loud enough she hoped he could hear. She was afraid if she opened the door he would see that she didn't want him to stop, that somehow he'd read it in her eyes.

"Are you okay?" he asked.

"Yes," she said louder this time. "I'm fine. I guess we were both a little overwrought in there."

"Julia?"

"Yes?"

"Please don't think about leaving because of this. I— we need you."

Julia breathed a sigh of relief. "I won't leave. We're both adults. We can get past this. Good night. I'll see you in the morning."

Dirk walked to his room, a mixture of emotions crowding his weary mind and body. He'd practically ridden Black Lightening to the point of abuse. Now he'd done this. He wasn't happy with himself. But, damn, he liked kissing her. She was so sweet and soft. The kiss wasn't even sexual. It had started out innocent enough. She was so heartbreakingly sad he just wanted to comfort her. Things kind of got out of hand. He just hoped she would keep her promise about not leaving. He really did need her—and now he needed her in a yet another way.

CHAPTER TEN

Julia summoned her newfound *spunk* to leave her room and walk into the kitchen the next morning. She should have been relieved to find Gus sitting in Dirk's place sipping coffee and talking to Megan, but somehow, she was even less prepared to face him.

She felt like a total coward avoiding his direct look, heading for the coffeepot on the stove. Unfortunately, after saying good morning to Rosa, who was busy flipping pancakes, she had nowhere to go but the kitchen table. She sat down across from him unable to stop the heat rising to her face. No wonder Gus was able to read her mind.

Gus tweaked Megan on the cheek. "Why don't you run upstairs and get the rascals for breakfast."

Megan passed a questioning glance at Julia and left to get the twins.

Gus gave Julia a cordial nod. "I don't know if you got through to Dirk last night. But I talked to Charlie. He told me what set Dirk off."

Julia gave a slow nod. "Had you known about the baby?" she asked.

Gus shifted in his seat, avoiding her curious gaze. For a moment she thought he wouldn't answer. "Yeah," he admitted finally, "I knew. I couldn't tell him though. He loves kids. I never saw him so happy as when those twins were born and he always treated Meggie better than most men treat their own kids. I just couldn't tell him what that crazy witch had done."

"He was real upset about it last night. How is he this morning?"

"Gone. He had a good excuse. One of the neighbors called about a cow having birthing difficulties. Dirk's the closest thing to a vet around this area. People call on him all the time."

Julia wasn't sure why but she was taken aback by that revelation. "Did he go to school to be a vet?" she asked.

"He did until I had my heart problem. I needed to have open-heart surgery and was laid up for a couple of months. We didn't have any hands then, except for old Choctaw, a Cherokee Indian who was even older than me. Dirk came home to run the ranch. He's the one who really got it going. He took on breeding mares to board, and hired David to oversee it. Then when Mack came, we started training them. When Choctaw died, Dirk took over the vetting. He probably learned as much or more from Choctaw as he did in that fancy vet school."

"Some of those old medicinal remedies were very effective."

Gus made a grunting sound. "Frankly, I'm a bit surprised you'd think so."

Had Gus just given her a compliment? "Did Dirk talk to anyone before he left?"

"Just Rosa. He asked her to help out if you ran into any trouble with the kids, or if you had to leave for any reason."

That gave Julia pause. Did Dirk not trust that she'd stay after last night even though she'd promised she would? Clearly, he was giving her an out if she'd changed her mind. Little did he know that leaving was the last thing she wanted to do—especially after last night.

* * * *

When Dirk hadn't returned by noon, Gus came in and asked the kids if they wanted to go riding. Megan and

Jason leaped at the chance, but Christa begged to stay with Julia.

An hour later, Christa fall asleep on the sofa while Julia played piano for her. When the phone rang, Julia's fingers froze on the keys. Hoping it was Dirk calling, she listened while Rosa answered. A moment later, Rosa appeared in the doorway. She glanced at Christa's sleeping form, then summoned Julia to the phone.

Julia's heart kicked up a notch as she contemplated what she would say to Dirk. However, it wasn't Dirk. It was Rosa's daughter-in-law, Maria, in Danango.

Between broken English and tearful sobs, Maria explained she was eight months into her first pregnancy and she was having contractions. A week ago the same thing—and the week before that. Both times her husband left work so they could rush to the hospital in Denver but the doctor said it was false labor and sent her home. They couldn't afford another such trip. Would Julia please come and help her. Maybe tell her if it was truly labor this time.

Julia stared at Rosa, standing nearby franticly trying to wring water out of a dry dishtowel. "Did you tell her I was a doctor?" Julia asked.

Rosa shook her head. "No. No. I tell her how you helped Sonja's boy, and maybe you can help her. It's only eight miles. Can you go? Christa will be fine with me. Dirk said it was okay if you had to leave."

On the way to Danango with Rosa's directions in hand, Julia wondered what to say to Rosa to convince her it wasn't a good idea for her relatives to depend on Julia for medical care.

Julia found the house in the poorer section of town on a street of unkempt lawns, peeling paint, and cluttered yards. Maria's house, though tiny, looked better than most of the others. Inside she found a distraught Maria well into the final stage of labor. She'd been having pains for the last six hours, and still hadn't called her husband at work. Her water had broken and she was already dilated to ten. By the time her husband got home, it was too late to send them on the road to Denver.

Fortunately it was a routine delivery, and Maria had a small but healthy looking baby boy barely an hour after Julia arrived. By three-thirty, Julia had Maria and the baby nestled in the back of their old Ford station wagon with her husband at the wheel heading for Denver.

On her way home, Julia reflected on two other babies who hadn't been as lucky as Maria's son. It didn't matter that their parents lived in a six thousand square foot house in the middle of a high-end neighborhood, and it didn't matter that their own father, a skilled surgeon, was at the scene.

A tear slid down Julia's cheek as she drove into the yard. The first thing that caught her eye was a white Mercedes in front of the house. Melody Dupree. Gus was in the corral with Megan and Jason. The spot by the barn were Dirk usually parked his pickup was empty.

Julia pulled Gloria's SUV into the garage, grabbed her bag, and walked though the inside door leading to her room and Dirk's study. She stashed her bag inside, changed her shirt, and headed up the five steps to the sitting room in search of Rosa and Christa. A wonderful chocolate aroma came from the kitchen where Julia found them baking cookies.

Rosa stared up with wide questioning eyes, and Christa jumped up from her chair and ran to Julia.

She picked up Christa and smiled at Rosa. "Maria had a fine baby boy and they're on the way to the hospital now."

Rosa crossed herself and gave a prayer of thanks. She grabbed Julia's face, stood on tiptoes, and gave her a kiss on each cheek, tears of gratitude spilling from her eyes.

"Is Dirk home yet?" Julia asked.

Rosa shook her head. "No."

Julia put Christa down. Maybe she could avoid telling

him where she'd been—if she could get past Gus questioning her.

"Did Gus ask where I was?" she asked.

"He hasn't been back in the house since he took the other two riding."

Julia hesitated. "If you can avoid it, I'd just as soon nobody knows where I went."

Maria smiled. "It will be our secret. Thank you, so much. It is so hard without a regular doctor in Danango—"

"Can we go outside now?" Christa asked, tugging at Julia's arm.

Chancing a meeting with Melody Dupree was the last thing Julia wanted to do, but since she'd been gone all afternoon, she felt she owed some time doing what Christa wanted to do. Besides, it was a beautiful day. Maybe they could water the flowers.

No such luck avoiding Melody. Julia was barely out the door when she came out of the barn, followed by Mack. She wasted no time approaching Julia.

"Do you happen to know where Dirk is?" she snipped. "Nobody around here seems to know."

Julia gave Mack a look and found him rolling his eyes skyward, whistling through his teeth. Julia shrugged. "I haven't seen him since last night. Why don't you ask Gus, he talked to Dirk this morning."

"Gus seems to have developed a hearing problem."

Christa let go of Julia's hand and ran toward the corral where Megan and Jason were grooming their horses. "Sorry," Julia said. "I have to stick close to Christa while she's out here in the yard."

Melody threw her hands on her designer jeaned hips and made a grumbling sound, which Julia ignored, and hurried to catch Christa before she climbed in the corral.

Gus gave Christa a huge grin, plucked her over the corral, and carried her over to where Jason and Megan were working on their horses. Julia had no desire to answer any more questions for Melody, so she climbed into the corral and followed.

"Best be careful where you step." Gus mumbled, glancing down at her spotless white sneakers.

When she heard Megan starting to giggle, Julia realized it was already too late. She grimaced. "Guess I haven't spent much time around horses," she said. She didn't go so far as to say she'd never even touched a horse in her life. Instead she mustered her courage and walked up to Jason's horse to pat him on the nose.

"His name is Champ," Jason said proudly from where he stood on a step stool brushing the animal's back.

Champ immediately nuzzled at Julia's hand. She jumped back with a shocked squeak.

It was Jason's turn to giggle. "He wants a treat." He reached into his pocket and held out a small crabapple. "Here, Anna. Feed him this and he'll really like you."

Julia gave Jason a doubtful frown, but took the tiny apple between her thumb and index finger and held it out to Champ.

Gus let out a loud snort. "You feed him like that and he'll have your fingers for lunch."

"Lay it in your open palm," Megan said. "Don't be afraid."

Still wary, Julia did as she was instructed, and Champ, with surprising delicacy, plucked the apple from her hand.

"Can I feed him one?" Christa asked.

This time Gus pulled a tiny apple from his pocket. He handed it to her and set her on her feet. "Here you go, Squirt. Have Anna help you."

Julia stared at him wide-eyed. "Her hand is so little."

Gus made a sound that might have been laughter. "Just lay her hand flat on top of yours, Champ will know what to do."

Christa was still giggling when Dirk's truck pulled into the yard. He parked beside the barn, stepped out, and headed straight toward the corral. Before he could take four steps, Melody dashed from the barn and hopped in front of him.

Julia couldn't hear what they were saying, but Dirk appeared tired and agitated. His sleeves were rolled up past his elbows and his clothes looked in need of a washing. He glanced past Melody looking straight at Julia. Their eyes locked until Melody, in an obviously deliberate maneuver, stepped into his line of vision.

Julia wasn't sure why she glanced a Gus, but she did, and too late realized it was the wrong thing to do. The man didn't miss a thing, and Julia couldn't stop the heat from rising to her face.

Christa came to the rescue by calling out to her father. "Come on, Daddy, watch me feed Champ."

Dirk said something to Melody, touched her on the upper arm and walked toward the corral. Melody sent a deep frown in his direction before she headed back to the barn. As he let himself in the gate, Christa flew into her father's waiting arms. Some of the hard weary lines around his face softened when he picked her up.

"Anna fed Champ an apple and then I fed him one too…" She continued to chatter while Dirk walked over to his son and tousled his hair. "… and I baked cookies with Rosa cause Anna went away, and I was scared."

"Why were you scared?" Dirk asked.

"I thought Anna left like Mommy did, and wasn't never coming home again."

Dirks gaze flicked to Julia. "Well, it looks to me like she came home."

Christa smiled and nodded. "Uh huh."

Dirk grinned at her. "Sometimes Anna might have other things to do. Do you think we should lock her in her room so she can't leave again?"

Christa giggled. "No, that wouldn't be nice."

Julia groaned. So much for keeping her trip a secret. "Sorry," she said to Dirk, "I did have something I had to do."

"Not a problem. Rosa's perfectly capable of looking after the kids; she did it for two months until you got here."

"Anna stepped in stuff," Jason said, his mischievous laughter tingling.

Dirk looked down at her stained sneakers, laughing. "Yup. She sure did." He passed Megan a wink. "Okay, you guys, I've had a rough day. I need to have a talk with Miss Dupree, and then I have to get in the shower and clean some of this crude off me. You have things under control here?" he asked Gus.

Gus nodded. "Yup—everything that's in my control is under control."

CHAPTER ELEVEN

"Is Rosa a grandma now?"

Christa's question startled Julia. Supper had been going along smoothly until then. It amazed her how perceptive a four-year-old could be.

Of course, Dirk looked to Julia for an explanation. Julia managed a smile. "Rosa's son and his wife, Maria, had a baby boy today."

"I'll have to remember to congratulate her," Dick said. He grinned at his daughter, "You're pretty smart, Christa, how did you figure that out?"

"Rosa told me she was going to be a grandma when Maria had her baby."

"The kids know Maria," Dirk explained to Julia. "She's been here a few times."

A thoughtful frown covered Christa's face. "Why don't we have a grandma?"

Dirk cleared his throat "Well, actually you do have a grandma. She lives in California."

"Is she nice, like Rosa?" Christa asked.

"No, she's mean," Jason replied.

Dirk raised an eyebrow at his son. "Why would you say that?"

"Mama told me."

Dirk looked at Megan. "Is that true?"

Megan grabbed a pickle, bit it in half, and began chewing.

"Megan?"

Megan shrugged. "Yeah, I guess."

"Why? Why would she say that?"

"I don't know. I suppose it had something to do with the money."

Dirk's brow lifted another notch. "I hope you're going to explain that."

For a moment Megan didn't answer, finally she heaved a deep sigh. "Grandma Travis always sent us each a hundred dollars for our birthdays and Christmas."

When Megan stopped, Dirk prompted her. "Just how does that make her a mean grandma?"

Tears sparkled in Megan's green eyes. "Mama said the checks bounced."

Silence hung in the room until Dirk spoke. "Do you believe that, Megan?"

Megan hung her head. "No."

Julia swallowed the lump in her throat and looked around the table at all the sad faces. She wanted to say something, but she didn't know what. The whole scene reminded her entirely too much of her own childhood.

"It appears to me," Dirk said, "like your grandma owes us a visit. I know she loves you all very much, but I think she needs to come and say it herself. How does that sound?"

Christa and Jason, their faces back to smiling, both nodded vigorously.

Dirk smiled. "Now that that's settled, Meggie why don't you round up some of those cookies Christa made today."

After the kids had gone upstairs, Julia helped Dirk clear the dishes. She didn't like the uncomfortable silence between them and felt a need to break it. "I hope you realize that, considering what those kids have gone through, you really are a terrific father."

Dirk stopped with his hands full of dirty plates and looked at her. "Julia, that's just about the nicest thing anyone has ever said to me."

Julia shrugged. "It's true. A lot of fathers would have made a big scene just now. In spite of what you must have been feeling you handled it with amazing calm."

"You mean because I didn't tell them I wanted to kill their mother."

Julia laughed. "Yeah, especially that."

"Maybe your influence is sanding my jagged edges.

Julia placed a stack of empty glasses on top of his plates. "Let's hope."

Together they filled the dishwasher in companionable silence. After he'd closed the door and punched the start button, he leaned against the counter and looked at her. "Julia, about last night," Julia's heart started an immediate a thumping dance. "If I told you how sorry I was about that kiss, I'd be lying."

"It's all right...maybe we were both in need of comforting."

He gave her a sheepish grin. "Yeah, maybe, but the point is, Julia, when Christa said she got scared when she thought you weren't coming back it concerned me, because that's how Gloria left. I have no right to ask you this, but I'd appreciate it if you'd promise never to leave that way. I don't mean leaving for a couple of hours or even a day, but leaving with no intentions of coming back. I'd like you to be honest about it and tell me. I don't ever want Christa, or anyone else for that matter, to ask me if you're coming back and I have to say *I don't know.*"

"That's a reasonable request, Dirk, I would never do that to them—or you."

Dirk reached up, and traced his fingertips down her cheekbone. "Thank you, Julia. I realize you won't be here forever, but I want you to know I appreciate you and what you've done for the kids in the short while you've been here."

His touch sent heat racing through Julia's veins, and for a moment she thought he was going to kiss her again, but he suddenly dropped his hand. "I'm going to put the munchkins to bed and hit the sack early. I had a rough night last night." He smiled. "While birthing stubborn calves is rewarding, it's extremely exhausting work.

Julia smiled as she watched him walk toward the stairs. *So is birthing babies.*

* * * *

As tired as he was, Dirk couldn't sleep. He kept seeing Julia's mouth, and he wanted to kiss her so bad he ached. All day he'd been thinking about her. Knowing she'd eventually leave was torturous, but it was inevitable. She was running away from a depressing miscarriage, and when she recovered she'd want to move on—have her own kids. She'd said she didn't have a husband but she probably had a life, a career, and maybe family in Minnesota. He needed to keep that in mind and be thankful for the time he'd have with her.

What he didn't need was to take advantage of her vulnerability, her total sweetness, her kissable mouth.

Damn, he had to call his mother tomorrow.

* * * *

Three times in as many hours, Dirk dialed his mother's Los Angeles number, and each time received the same monotonous recording asking him to leave a message. He felt bad enough he had to actually look up her number and she'd probably think somebody died if he left a message. Frustrated, he tried his sister, Tanya's cell phone. No answer there either.

For the fourth time, he shifted through the glut of paperwork on his desk, paid some bills, filled out the forms on Star's colt and Melody's latest arrival. In doing that he was reminded of her visit the day before. He'd been in a foul mood anyway, and her appearance unannounced didn't help it any. She kept insisting that nothing should be changed in their relationship, and wouldn't take the hint that he no longer had time for or wanted to see her other than on a business basis. He'd finally had to spell it out for her, and she'd left in a snit.

The sound of laughter outside his window drew his attention to where Julia helped Jason and Christa water the flowers. Across the yard, Megan was in the corral bonding with her horse. *She going to brush that critter bald*, he thought chuckling to himself. It suddenly occurred to him that Julia hadn't had her riding lesson yet, and for the life of him he couldn't think of anything he'd rather do.

* * * *

Julia stared, with more than a little trepidation, at the rusty-brown horse Dirk called Seminole. She kept a safe distance away as Dirk saddle the little mare, explaining the process as he worked. She doubted she would ever have a need to actually saddle a horse, but she did her best to pay attention anyway—first the blanket, then the saddle, throw one stirrup over the saddle, do a little loopy loop with the strap. First he'd had to practically crawl under the animal to reach the strap from beneath the horse's belly. A move that sent shivers up Julia's spine. She could almost hear Katie laughing

"Are you ready?" Dirk asked.

No. "Sure, okay. What do I do?"

"Walk up and introduce yourself first."

She gave him a wary glance, wondering if he was kidding. She'd feel foolish doing it if he'd meant it as a joke, but he just stood there patiently waiting, so she had to do something. Oh, well. Even if it was a joke she could humor him. She took a couple of steps forward until she could pat the mare on her nose. Seminole immediately tried to nibble at her hand, and she jumped back, squealing. "I think she wants an apple," she said, remembering Champ.

Dirk laughed, as did all three kids from the other side of the railing. She groaned when she saw Mack, David, and Carrie—with a camera in her hand—coming to watch her riding debut. The only one missing was Gus. She barely had the thought in her head when she noticed him coming out of the stable.

Dirk motioned for her to come up beside him. "You always mount on the left side. Put you left foot in the stirrup and grab onto the horn."

"What if she starts walking," she asked."

"She won't."

"Seminole's as harmless as a puppy," Megan supplied from the rail.

It was time to summon a little guts, Julia told herself as she clutched the horn and placed her foot where Dirk directed it.

"Okay, mount up and swing your other foot over," he said.

Before she knew what happened, Dirk's hands cradled her buttocks, and she was seated in the saddle. A volley of applause drowned out the rapid beating of her heart.

Dirk walked around, adjusting the stirrups. "We're going to have to get you some boots," he said grinning up at her. "You okay?"

"Wonderful," she lied. "It's a piece of cake."

Chuckling, Dirk reached around Seminole, gathered up the reins and handed them to her. He showed her how to hold them, explaining how to make the horse turn. Using what he called a halter strap, he led her around giving her time to get comfortable.

"You look good up there," David said.

"Just don't do any sudden jerking back on the reins," Mack warned. "She has a tendency to rear."

Julia laughed at his joke, took a deep breath, and started to relax. She released her death grip on the horn—at least with one hand—and managed a smile. When she caught a glimpse of Gus's dubious frown, she sat up straighter and pretended to enjoy it.

Surprisingly, after about fifteen minutes, she *was* having a good time. Feeling the powerful muscles of the animal moving beneath her was both venerating and exhilarating. When Dirk set her free to ride on her own, she wished Katie could be there to see. Thinking of sharing the moment with her sister, Julia turned Seminole so Carrie could get a picture of her monumental accomplishment.

But Carrie had dropped the camera. Hunched over in David arms, she clutched her enlarged belly, a wet stain creeping down her denim maxi skirt.

CHAPTER TWELVE

Dirk watched Julia ride around the corral with something akin to pride. Pride, however, had nothing to do with the tightening in his groin. So engrossed was he observing her fine derriere sway, his heart skipped a beat when she suddenly leaped from the horse with the agility of a cougar and charged for the sidelines. That's when he noticed Carrie, doubled over in David's arms. He reached the coral gate in time to swing it open for Julia and hurried out behind her.

Carrie gasped in pain. "We have to get to the hospital,

"Somebody, quick, get her a chair or something," Julia ordered. "David, you better bring your car around."

Mack ran for the barn and produced a short stool in a matter of seconds. David eased Carrie onto the stool, and ran for his car, barely hearing his wife's call to bring her packed bag.

"It's too early," Carrie sobbed. "I shouldn't be in labor yet. I'm not due for another three weeks."

"Trust me." Julia said. "Your water broke. You're in labor. Three weeks isn't too early. You can have a perfectly normal delivery."

Tears flowed down Carrie's face. "It's going to die, isn't it? Just like the other one?"

Julia looked up at Carrie. "What other one?"

"A year ago. I carried my baby eight months and it died because the cord was wrapped around its neck."

"Oh, my God," Julia whispered. "This is your second pregnancy?"

Carrie gave a pitiful nod.

"How long were you in labor before?"

"About five hours, I think. Is it going to die, Julia?"

Julia put her arms around the young woman. "Of course not, honey. Your first baby's death was a rarity. There's no reason you shouldn't have a normal, healthy baby. You did say your doctor gave you a clean bill of health, didn't you?"

Carrie nodded, doubling over when another spasm hit her, just as David pulled up with the car.

"You need to drive fast but carefully," Julia told David. "This baby isn't going to waste any time appearing."

"Come with us," Carrie pleaded. "Please."

Julia looked up at Dirk.

"By all means go," he said, picking up an anxious Christa. "We'll be fine here."

"I need to get some things," Julia said, racing for the house. She returned with a small overnight case, an armful of clean towels, and a couple of pillows. By the time she got back out to the yard, they had Carrie loaded in the back seat of David's Suburban.

"Do you know what hospital we're going to?" Julia asked Dirk.

"Yeah, Westgate General, I'll call and let them know you're on the way."

Julia gave him a heartwarming smile. "Thank you."

As David sped out of the driveway, Julia wasted no time. She placed the pillows against the far door, giving thanks it was a large vehicle, and laid Carrie back with her knees up. Julia sat at the end, tucking a towel beneath Carrie's hips. Fortunately, the frantic woman took instructions without question. David, however, was another matter.

"Get a grip, David. You won't accomplish anything driving like a crazy person except to get us all killed. Just slow down to the speed limit and relax, there's nothing to worry about." Julia sincerely hoped it was the truth.

Deciding this wasn't the time to worry about her medical status, Julia pulled surgical gloves and her stethoscope from the makeup case where she'd stashed her medical bag.

Carrie watched with wide, questioning, eyes as Julia put the stethoscope to her hardened belly.

"The baby has a strong heartbeat," Julia said smiling.

Another intense contraction hit Carrie. She clutched her belly, crying out in pain. Julia once again reminded David to pay attention to the road in front of him.

She removed Carrie's soaked underpants and slipped on her gloves to do an examination. It wasn't good. She'd already dilated to ten and the pains were coming less than three minutes apart. With nearly forty miles to go, it was doubtful they'd make it to Denver in time. She had no choice but to let nature have its way.

"Had you been having pains before your water broke?" Julia asked.

Carrie took a deep gulping breath. "Just cramps. They've been coming and going all week, but they were only a little stronger than others I've had off and on for the last two months."

Telling an already distraught woman that she'd probably been in the first stages of labor and should have gone to the hospital hours earlier would accomplish nothing. Julia could do little more than hold Carrie's hand, continue reassuring her, and monitor David's erratic driving.

They'd reached the interstate and were about thirty miles from Denver when another cramp gripped Carrie.

"Do you feel like bearing down," Julia asked.

"Yes," Carrie gasped. "I think it's ready to come."

"Hang on," David shouted, even as he slammed the brakes. "There's backed up traffic."

Julia threw her body between the seat and Carrie to keep the spasm-clenched woman from slipping on the floor as they came to a sudden crawling pace.

"What is it?" Julia asked, taking her place back on the seat.

"I'm not sure. I think it's an accident. It must have just happened; I don't see any patrol cars yet." David's voice sounded shaky and clipped.

Julia wished they'd brought Dirk along to drive. "Put your flashers on and see if you can go around it. Be careful though. And don't worry. Babies are born in cars every day."

"My baby is going to die just like the other one!" Carrie wailed.

Julia glanced at David. His white knuckles had a death grip on the steering wheel as he crawled along the shoulder amidst the angry honking of horns.

Six precious minutes and three contractions later, they cleared the crumpled trailer of a rolled-over Cosco semi. Scattered merchandise littered the highway.

David kept the lights flashing as he dodged the debris and raced free. At the same time Carrie shrieked. "It's coming. I can't stop it."

Keeping her voice calm, belying the turmoil that churned in her belly, Julia tried to reassure her. "It's all right, let it come. I'm right here. I'll take care of it."

"But we're only twenty minutes from the hospital," David remarked as though that would alter what was happening in the back seat.

Julia didn't answer. The tiny dark head popped through the birth canal.

Carrie gasped, helplessly drawing deep gulps of air.

"Just one more big push," Julia said, her tone level in spite of the frantic pounding in her chest. She knew what this baby meant to Carrie and David. They'd already lost one child. She was confident in her skills, but this wasn't the best of conditions. She reminded herself that babies were born regularly in cabs with taxi drivers delivering.

The final push came and the little body slipped out into Julia's waiting hands. Limp and not breathing, the newborn baby girl laid in Julia's lap. She ignored Carrie's frightened cries, and using a suction bulb from her medical bag, Julia quickly cleared the infant's air passage. She sat the baby on her leg and supporting its head, leaned it forward and started rubbing its back and the soles of the feet. When that didn't bring her around, Julia rolled her to her back, bent over and placed her own mouth over the baby's mouth and nose giving it small puffs of air.

Carrie's wretched sobs permeated Julia's mind as she continued to work on the baby. Suddenly the tiny creature gave a lusty angry howl, her arms immediately flailing.

Julia felt hot tears slip down her cheeks as both Carrie and David burst out with blissful cheers. David swiped a sleeve over his eyes while Carrie tried to sit up to see her baby.

"It's a girl," Julia announced with a prayer of thanks. She cleaned the squirming infant as best she could before wrapping the baby in a towel and handing the little miracle over to her mother.

"It's best if you start nursing her right away," Julia explained. "It will contract your uterus and slow down the bleeding."

"What about the cord?" Carrie asked as she opened her blouse with Julia's help and got the baby suckling at her breast.

"The cord will be fine until you get to the emergency room. Just sit back and relax. Your baby's going to be fine."

Julia's heart swelled with an overwhelming mixture of happiness for Carrie, and grief for two other babies that didn't survive.

At the hospital, Julia went inside while David and Carrie waited in the car. Moments later, two interns came out with a gurney and gently assisted Carrie, still clutching her baby onto it. Julia provided a rundown on what she'd done and followed them inside. David, less shaken than when he'd been driving, hurried after them, but had to turn back when one of the attendants insisted the suburban be moved from the emergency entrance.

Julia breathed deeply of the familiar hospital smells. Antiseptics, drugs, and blood might have been an unpleasant aroma to most, but to Julia, it was like coming home. She admired the cleanliness of the rooms and the efficiency of the team on duty.

They whisked Carrie behind a curtain and an orderly directed Julia to a small lounge. David burst through the swinging doors breathing as though he'd just run a marathon.

"How is she? Where is she?"

Julia put a hand on his arm. "She's fine. They're both fine. They're being examined and I'm sure you can see them in a few minutes."

David gave a shaky laugh. "The baby is beautiful, isn't she?"

Tears clouded Julia's eyes. "Yes, she is."

"How long do you think it will take them?"

"Not long. Come on; let's go have a seat. If you don't calm down, you're going to end up in a bed yourself." Julia directed him to the waiting room but he didn't sit. He paced. Julia laughed. "Sit down, David. Wearing out the carpet won't make them work any faster."

David dropped into the nearest chair. He sat quietly for a long moment then suddenly looked up at Julia. "You were great," he said. "I don't know what we'd have done without you. I just about smashed the car when I looked back and saw the baby on your lap all limp and not crying." His Adam's apple bobbed for a moment while he tried to continue. "She wasn't breathing, was she?"

"No, she wasn't," Julia admitted.

"That's just how our first baby looked—" a sob tore through David's throat, "and then he died."

Julia swallowed at the emotions building in her own chest. She reached over and touched David's arm. "This one's okay, David. Trust me."

David gave her a long curious look. "I do trust you, Julia. You got her breathing. I don't know how, but you did it. I watched you. You were so calm and efficient, you could have been a doctor."

Julia found a need to lighten the mood—and change the subject. "I guess that explains our wild-hare ride. You were supposed to be watching the road, David."

David settled back, laughing. "I guess I was a little shook up, huh?"

"Yeah, just a little." Julia glanced over at a small side table. It held cookies under a glass dome, Styrofoam cups, and a coffee machine with a glowing red light. "I smell coffee," she said, getting to her feet. "How about a cup?"

"Sounds like a good idea. I take mine black" David said.

"Do you have a name picked out for the baby?" Julia asked, handing him a steaming brew, and sitting down across from him with her own cup.

"Yeah, I guess it will be Marisa Marie. Carrie got to name it if it was a girl. I had Duke picked out for a boy's name. I guess she'll be glad it was a girl," David said, grinning.

A doctor wearing stained scrubs came into the room. Julia recognized Margaret Jenson's smiling face. Julia and David both came to their feet.

"You the father?" she asked David.

"Yes, ma'am," David chirped proudly.

"Well, I guess I don't have to tell you, you have a fine six pound, three ounce baby girl."

"Everything's okay?"

"Better than okay. They're both doing great."
Margaret looked past David, her face brightening. "Sounds
like you're the one responsible," she said to Julia. "Carrie
couldn't stop singing your praises." She reached out a
hand. "Nice work Doctor Morgan."

CHAPTER THIRTEEN

"Dirk doesn't know, does he?"

David had waited until after they'd visited Carrie in her room and left to allow her to rest while they went for a cup of coffee in the cafeteria. Julia knew by the look on his face when Margaret called her Doctor Morgan that it was only a matter of time until he brought it up.

"No," she answered.

David shook his head. "Damn, do you have any idea how much he hates lying?"

"I didn't lie to him."

"Yeah, well, I didn't lie to him when I failed to tell him about Gloria's abortion, but he was ready to bust my head open when he found out everyone knew and nobody told him."

Julia sighed. "I had my reasons, David. It's a part of my personal life I left in Minneapolis."

David gave her a long look. "Are you saying you did something unethical that you're running away from?"

"Oh, no," Julia said, shaking her head. "Nothing like that. It was personal. I wanted to come and I didn't think he'd hire me if he knew."

"You're probably right. Did you know Doctor Jenson in Minneapolis?"

Julia couldn't meet his eyes. "No, I met her when I came to visit the hospital on my day off."

David shook his head. "Help me out here. I'm trying to understand this. You left a practice in Minneapolis—for personal reasons, and drove an hour to visit a hospital in Denver where you didn't know anyone. If I had to make a guess, I'd say you were scooping out the job situation."

A quick flush rode up her face. "I—"

"Which is exactly why you couldn't tell Dirk the truth in the first place. He'd have known you were temporary and you're right, he wouldn't have hired you."

Julia didn't have any defense. He was right on target. She could explain about Katie, but that still didn't excuse her. "I don't know what to say—"

"Please, you don't owe me any explanations." He rubbed work-calloused hands over his weary face. "I should have known in the car. You were so…competent, the stethoscope, your mannerism. The way you took charge."

"I'm sorry. I—"

"My God, Julia, don't be sorry. You saved our baby's life. Had you not been a doctor, she would have died. My only problem is Dirk. You've been so great with his kids. He's come to depend on you, and he trusts you. I don't know how I can keep this from him."

Julia's heart took a dive. She knew this was coming. "I wouldn't ask you to," she whispered. "If he's angry enough to want me to leave, I guess I'll just go."

"I don't see what that would accomplish except leave him without a caretaker for his kids. But I know him; he's damn stubborn about some things."

Julia smiled a sad smile. "He's been through some rough times."

David nodded. "I know, and he's been good to me. I owe him my loyalty, but there's no doubt in my mind, I owe you for my daughter's life." He stared into his empty coffee cup for a moment. "There's a saying about killing the messenger bringing bad news. I'll be damned if I do and damned if I don't. At least if I don't tell him you'll still be there." He looked up at her, smiling. "He won't hear it from me—or Carrie. I'll let you decide if and when you want to clue him in, but don't expect him to take it quietly."

* * * *

David decided to stay in Denver with Carrie while Julia took the suburban home. She did two things before she left the hospital. She called Katie, and started the process to get her Colorado license. It was only a matter of time until she had to tell Dirk the truth. It would be far worse if he found out on his own, and she fully believed what David said about Dirk's reaction to her deceit. She wanted to be prepared.

From Katie, who'd made it a point to date one of Geno's confidants, Julia had learned that Geno had financial problems. In view of his newly acquired gambling vice, his parents weren't happy about his spending habits or his divorce, and were cutting him off, demanding he repair his relationship with Julia and straighten up his act.

Julia could only shake her head. The man made more money in one month than most people made in a year. He liked to swing with the upper crust though, and no matter how much he made, he always spent more. Now without her to manage their money, he was on his own. It was a relief not to have to worry about Geno and his spending habits anymore.

What she did have to worry about was Dirk finding out about her medical degree. She wasn't ready to leave the ranch. The kids meant more to her than she cared to admit, which was something she hadn't bargained for when she'd accepted the position as nanny. Even crabby old Gus seemed to be coming around.

* * * *

Jason, Christa, and even Megan, were excited about the new baby, and the following Saturday, when Dirk left for Denver to pick up the happy couple and tiny Marisa Marie, Julia could hardly contain the children. She, however, was still on edge. She trusted David when he'd promised not to mention her MD status, but Dirk already knew Julia had delivered the baby in the backseat of the car. The first thing Dirk did when Julia got home was give her a giant bear hug proclaiming her a heroine. As long as nobody went into detail about the delivery, she hoped it would all blow over.

"Are you a grandma now?" Christa asked during lunch.

Julia laughed. "Why would you think that?"

"'Cause you maked the baby come."

"I didn't make the baby come." Julia explained, "I just helped it along."

Megan rolled her eyes. "You have to be a mother to be a grandma, silly. Julia's not a mother."

Megan's simple explanation stung. Julia wandered if she'd ever get past that empty feeling when the subject of mothers came up. She decided it was time to change the subject, but before she could think of a way, Christa spoke up again.

"You can be my mother, Anna," she said innocently.

"You already have a mother," Megan barked.

The ringing doorbell saved Julia from the conversation. Before Julia could rise from her chair, Megan leaped up and ran to the door, swinging it open wide. It was Deputy Sanford.

Julia's heart sank. She approached the door preparing for battle, wishing Dirk were there.

"Dirk home?" he asked, looking past Megan to Julia.

"No!" Megan answered. She would have swung the door shut in his face if he hadn't put a hand out to stay it.

"Why don't you go play with your dolls," Sanford told Megan. "I need to talk to your nanny."

"She's not my nanny and I don't play with dolls." Megan gave him a scathing look and stormed back to the kitchen.

"Testy little brat," Sanford grumbled.

Julia gave him a condescending glare. "If you have other business here besides antagonizing children, I suggest you come back later. Dirk will be home in a couple of hours."

Sanford maneuvered his chaw from one cheek to the other, glaring at her. "Much as I enjoy harassing that boy, I don't feel like driving all the way out here again."

Out of the corner of her eye, Julia saw Mack standing in the doorway of the barn with a pitchfork in his hand. "It's all of eight miles," Julia retorted, hoping Sanford would leave before Mack involved himself.

"You're trespassing on private property," Gus said coming around the corner of the house.

"I'm the sheriff," Sanford snarled.

"Deputy Sheriff," Gus corrected.

"I have business with Dirk."

"Then do like the lady said and come back when Dirk is here."

"This is important." Sanford bit out. "It's about his ex-wife."

"He doesn't have an ex-wife," Gus commented dryly.

"Fine! You just tell him she's been found. I'll be back later this afternoon. And I might just be bringing handcuffs."

Sanford spun around, stalked to his car, and wasted no time spraying gravel over the yard.

Julia looked at Gus. "Do you think we should have gotten more information from him?"

"I seriously doubt he'd have given us more. Obviously he has a bombshell he wants to drop in Dirks lap. I just hope she ain't coming back. Dirk will do her bodily harm if she tries to take those kids away from him."

"What do you think he meant by the handcuffs comment?"

"It's just a scare tactic. The asshole is bluffing."

"I hope you're right. Maybe Dirk can find out what's happening by calling someone besides Sanford."

Charlie Mack strode up to them, pitchfork in hand. "What did dungface want?" he asked.

When Gus explained the details of Sanford's visit, Mack let out with a string of obscenities. Turning to Julia, he said, "Sorry ma'am, but that man brings out the worst in me."

Julia smiled. "He has that effect on me too."

* * * *

When Dirk returned with the Masters family around four o'clock, Julia, who'd been keeping a nervous vigil by the front window, was relieved to see Gus intercept Dirk before he could come to the house. At least she wouldn't have to tell him about Sanford's visit. She gave herself a mental shrug, realizing she'd forgotten all about her medical secret. Finding out what was going on with Gloria would overshadow any other thoughts Dirk had.

She met Dirk in the kitchen where he gave her a grim smile.

"Hell of a mess," he replied. "Where are the kids?"

"The twins are upstairs playing in their room. Megan went out to the stable a while ago."

"Did they hear anything Sanford had to say?"

She shook her head. "No, thank goodness. Megan answered the door and would have slammed it in his face if he'd let her."

Dirk grinned. "She's a smart kid."

Relieved to see Dirk smile, Julia laughed. "Yeah, I wish I'd have the nerve to do that."

"After listening to David and Carrie brag about you all the way home, I'd guess you have plenty of nerve."

Julia's heart did a jump-start as she waited for him to go on, but he just squeezed her arm and walked past her toward his office.

"I have to go make some calls and find out what's going on. Maybe I can avoid another visit from the distinguished a-hole deputy."

Seated at his desk, Dirk looked up the number to the Danango Sheriff's department. His prayers were granted when Sheriff Richard Gunderson answered. "Rick? Dirk Travis here. How you doing?"

"Not too good," Rick said. "My gout's acting up again. That's why I had to send Sanford out there. Sorry about that, I know how you feel about him, but I had no other choice. That's not the kind of news I like to give over the phone."

Dirk's heart rate accelerated. "Well, I guess you're going to have to tell me over the phone anyway. I wasn't here and all he'd tell Dad was that Gloria had been found— oh, and he'd be returning with handcuffs."

Gunderson swore. "He had no call to say that. At this point you're just a suspect—"

"A suspect to what?" Dirk ground out, not liking where this was going.

"Some hikers up in Clear Creek found a body early this morning. Sanford identified it as your wife, but since it's been a while, they'll still check dental records to confirm it."

Dirk's heart leaped to his throat. A freight train packed with emotions raced through his brain. His first thought, *now she can't take the kids away from me*, his second thought, *how would he tell them, especially Megan*. "What happed to her?" he managed to ask.

"Don't know yet. There'll be an autopsy, but just between you, me, and the fencepost, it looked like strangulation. We can't do autopsies here so we had to send her to Denver."

"I'd sure like to know how Sanford identified her after all this time. She's been missing nearly three months."

Gunderson was silent for an uncomfortably long moment. "Well, now, Dirk. That's the interesting part. She hasn't been dead all that long. My guess is about three weeks. Plus she was wearing a piece of jewelry you described when Sanford was out there questioning you. You said she never took it off."

"The black and white ying-yang?" Dirk asked.

"That's the one."

Dirk swallowed hard, trying to absorb the realization that Gloria was dead. Anger suddenly rode him. "Where the hell has she been all this time?"

"Damned if I know. I'm hoping to find out. I can make the arrangements if you want to see her."

Dirk tasted bile in his throat, his stomach churning. "No, that won't be necessary. I have three kids here who are going to need me."

"Yeah, I guess it's going to be rough on them. It's a good thing they have you."

And Julia, he thought. "What about Carl Edwards, the guy who was with her?"

"No sign of him or the car. We put out an APB on him—and the vehicle. It was registered to Edwards, so we know the plate numbers."

Megan's father. "I want to give fair warning that Megan stays here with me," Dirk said.

"Did you ever adopt her?"

"No, but I will. Just as soon as I can get the papers going."

"Gonna be mighty tough for a single man to get custody of her. How old is she now, about thirteen?"

"Eleven,"

A loud sigh came through the receiver. "You best get yourself a lawyer on that issue. As far as your wife's death—or murder, if it comes to that, you'll likely be questioned. If you want a lawyer present there that's up to you, of course. But considering what happened last time I'd recommend it."

"Just make sure it isn't Sanford questioning me, and I don't think I need to tell you why."

"I'll do what I can, Dirk."

Dirk hung up and called Brad Denton, the lawyer who'd managed to get the appeal to get Dirk out of prison. After explaining the situation with Gloria, he asked Brad to start custody proceedings on Megan. Brad wasn't any more encouraging than Gunderson had been.

Dirk hung up the phone, swearing to spend every dime he had if necessary, but he wasn't going to let Megan go. She'd been through too much already.

Thinking about Megan made Dirk's stomach churn. He had to tell her about Gloria. He also had to tell Jason and Christa, but it was Megan who concerned him the most. The other two were young—and they had Julia. Thank God for Julia. She was so perfect. What would he do if she left him? He didn't even want to think about it.

Wearily, he pushed out of his chair. He'd tell his father and Julia first. They needed to be prepared, since he didn't know what Megan's reaction would be.

He found Gus waiting for him at the kitchen table.

"Any more coffee left?" Dirk asked, indicating the giant mug cradled in his father's fingers.

Gus nodded. "I just made a full pot."

Dirk filled a cup and sat down just as Julia walked through the door. "Pour yourself some coffee and have a seat," he said. "You both need to hear this."

Julia shook her head regarding the coffee and sat down.

"Where's Megan?" Dirk asked.

"She went outside after her piano lesson about an hour ago." Julia said. "I haven't seen her since."

"Most likely in the stables," Gus supplied.

Dirk sighed. "They found Gloria's body up in Clear Creek," he said. "There'll be an autopsy, but Sheriff Gunderson guessed she died of strangulation."

"Oh, my God," Julia gasped. "You mean she was murdered?"

"Yeah, it looks that way."

"What about her car and the fellow she was with?" Gus asked.

"No sign of him, and apparently, it was his car."

Tears glistened in Julia's eyes. "How are you going to tell the kids?"

Dirk ran a hand through his hair. "I was hoping you had some ideas. I'm not too worried about the twins. It's Megan who concerns me. How do you tell an eleven-year-old her mother is dead?"

A sharp cry from the stairs had them all three turning toward it. Megan stared at them wide eyed. She made a dash for the front door, and was through it before Dirk came to his feet.

CHAPTER FOURTEEN

"Megan!" Dirk called, running after the fleeing girl. Both Julia and Gus where close at his heals.

Megan disappeared through the barn doors. Inside they heard her climbing the sheer stairs to the hayloft. "I know where she's headed," he called over his shoulder. "The barn cat had a litter of kittens two weeks ago." Just as he'd said, he found her behind a bale, a mewling kitten in each hand pressed to her face, covering her eyes.

Dirk slumped down to his knees in front of her. "Megan, honey, I'm sorry. You shouldn't have heard about your mother that way. I don't know what to say—"

"It doesn't matter," she rasped, refusing to look at him. "I hate her. I'm glad she's dead."

When Julia sank down beside Dirk, he acknowledged her with a look of utter helplessness. At the same, Gus arrived, all but collapsing on a bale, breathing heavily, clutching his chest, his face drained of color.

"Dad? Are you okay?" he asked.

Gus nodded as his trembling hands searched his vest pockets. Dirk jumped up, rushed to his father's side and quickly located the bottle of pills he needed. Dirk shook one out and placed it in his father's hand. Gus put the pill under his tongue to dissolve.

Megan peeked out from behind the kittens. She leaped

to her feet, dropped the kittens in Julia's lap, and was beside Gus in an instant. "Grandpa?"

"Gus put an arm around her, a grimacing smile on his face. "I'm all right, Meggiebug. Don't you worry about me."

Tears fill Megan's green eyes before she pressed her face into his shoulder. "I'm sorry I made you run Grandpa."

Julia picked up the kittens, touching their soft fur to her lips, and watched with medical alertness as the color came back to Gus's face and his breathing slowed. With the help of the nitro he seemed to be coming out of it. His attention turned to comforting Megan.

Julia's heart went out to her, knowing all too well the pain she suffered. Julia knew what it was like to lose a parent you had a love/hate relationship with. In many ways it left you more bereft than losing the parent who'd been able to openly show affection. Megan's struggle to find love from her mother was over, but coming to terms with that fact would take some time, possibly a long time. Pressure welled up in Julia's throat.

"He's all right now," Dirk assured Megan. "You and I need to talk."

Megan nodded, tears sliding down her face. "I knew she wasn't coming back. I just knew it. She just went away and left me. What's going to happen to me now?"

Dirk gripped her arms so she had to face him. "Nothing's going to happen to you, Megan. You're staying right here at the ranch where you belong."

"But I'm not your kid. Jason and Christa are, but I don't belong to anybody any more."

"You belong to me," Dirk said.

"What if that Carl guy comes back?"

"I've already talked to my lawyer. I promise, nobody's going to take you away."

Dirk reached out and pulled Megan into his arms. Over the top of her head his moist eyes met with Julia's. In his expression she saw a frightening truth—he didn't know if he'd legally be able to keep his promise. Plus, she knew if Carl Edwards showed up and demanded custody of Megan, Dirk could have an impossible fight on his hands—if Edwards truly was Megan's father.

Julia returned the kittens to their mother. "I need to get back to the house," Julia whispered, touching Dirk on the shoulder.

Dirk nodded. "We still have to tell Jason and Christa."

"They won't care," Megan mumbled. "They have Julia now."

They have Julia now.

Julia didn't miss the troubled look Gus passed to his son. The sweet hay smell and coziness of the loft suddenly closed in on her. Her stomach shifted as she got to her feet and made her way down the steep steps that had been much easier climbing up than down. Her mind protested, *I'm the nanny, not the mother*, but her heart said something else entirely.

For an educated woman, who'd taken five child psychology courses, how could she ever have thought of this as a vacation?

At the house, she went to the twins' room and sat with them while they practiced writing numbers until Dirk came a short while later.

"How's Megan?" Julia asked.

Dirk shrugged. "Fine, I hope. It's hard to tell with her. I don't believe for one minute she hated her mother. I guess she'll just have to work through it. She stayed with Dad. They're good for each other."

"And how is Gus?"

"Okay for now. His doctor told him months ago he needed to come in for a checkup, but he keeps putting it off. "Dirk sighed. "One of these days he'll have an attack, and he won't come out of it." He looked at Jason and Christa, obviously dreading what he had to tell them. Pulling a larger chair up to their little table, he looked with interest at the work they were doing.

Jason held up his worksheet. "See Dad, I can make fives. They're real hard, but Anna teached me how."

"I like to make eights," Christa said, maneuvering her pencil to finish a perfect row of eights."

Dirk complimented them on their work, looked at Julia, and shook his head. He was struggling, but she knew he was the one who had to do it.

"Listen guys," Dirk said. "I have to tell you something about your mother."

Jason looked up, but Christa continued to make eights.

"Your mother...your mother had an...accident."

"Is she hurt?" Jason asked.

"I'm afraid so. She won't be coming home."

"Can we go see her?"

Dirk drew a deep breath. "Jason, do you know what it means to die?"

Jason nodded. "Sure, we had a hamster that died. We put him in a box and buried him in the park."

"And when our fish died," Christa supplied eagerly. "We flushed it in the toilet."

Julia glanced at Dirk, wondering how he was going to get around that. She was surprised to see a hint of a smile on his face. "That's because fish like to be in water," he said. "What I'm trying to tell you is, you can't see your mother anymore because she died."

"That's okay," Christa said. "Anna can be our mommy."

"No she can't," Jason argued. "Megan said you could only have one mother."

"She's not here," Christa insisted tearfully.

"Megan said she's coming back to get us."

Dirk reached over and pulled Jason on his lap. "No son, I'm sorry, but your mother can't come to get you because she died. I'm here for you. I'll always be here."

Hearing the emotion in Dirk's voice endeared him to Julia like nothing else could have. As much as he disliked

Gloria, he was able to set his anger aside when explaining her death to his children.

* * * *

In the days that followed, Dirk, for the kids' sake, decided to hold a small memorial for Gloria in Danango. He didn't call any of his family. His mother was still on her cruise and his sister working undercover. He did call Gloria's sister, Connie and her agent, Tom Payton. As he'd expected, neither one was interested in showing up. Payton at least thanked him for calling; Connie on the other hand made another pitch to hit him up for the money Gloria owed her.

If Gloria had any friends, he didn't know about them, neither did he care. He just wanted to get it over with. Gloria's autopsy did indeed prove the cause of death was strangulation. It was her own scarf wrapped around her neck. No sign had been found of Carl Edwards or his car.

Dirk had been glad when Megan asked if she could do a small collage of her mother's pictures. He wasn't happy to see one of them was their wedding photo. Gloria looked resplendent in the seventeen hundred dollar white gown he'd bought, but the grinning button-nosed two-year-old he held in his arms easily upstaged the bride—at least to Dirk's discerning eye.

Dirk asked Julia to come help care for Jason and Christa. They'd mutually agreed to mingle separately so as not to appear as a couple, thereby squelching possible rumors. That was a moot point when Melody Dupree waltzed in wearing a slinky black satin dress, making her stand out like a hooker in a convent. Her attendance, however, was of no great concern to Dirk, since Danango was a small community, and everyone knew Gloria had left him over two years ago. Fortunately, Melody, after offering condolences, chatted for a few minutes about her new colt then had the good sense to mingle elsewhere.

Of course, Rosa and most of her large family made an appearance. It amazed Dirk how they all clustered around

Julia as though she were some kind of celebrity. Apparently she and Rosa had become fast friends.

Megan gravitated toward Gus who, along with Charlie Mack, kept a low profile while David and Carrie eagerly showed off their new addition.

He could have done without Sanford and his son, Matt, lurking outside the little chapel. At least they had the decency not to come inside, or approach him.

He wasn't surprised to see Mayor Paul Chatterley and his wife, Francesca. She was pasted to him like a Star Trek cling-on. The man had already announced his plan to run for the senate, and Chatterley rarely missed an opportunity to spend a day shaking hands and patting babies on the head, even if his timing was inappropriate.

When Sheriff Gunderson called Dirk aside to let him know he'd have to come out and question everyone at the ranch, just as a formality, Dirk made a mental note to remove Gus's Smith and Wesson from the house.

* * * *

After the kids were in bed and the house quiet, Dirk found Julia in the kitchen, putting a filter in the coffeepot. "You want some?" she asked.

Dirk snorted. "Forget the coffee, I need a beer." He opened the refrigerator. "How about you?"

Julia hadn't had a beer since she was sixteen. Geno thought it beneath his station to drink beer, so he didn't allow it in the house. "Beer sounds good," she said, snapping the lid back on the coffee grounds. "I'd like it in a glass though."

Dirk grabbed two Miller Golden Drafts, and Julia followed him outside to the porch where he dropped into a chair, releasing a sigh that sounded like it had been building all day. He popped the top on both cans sliding one, along with a glass, across the table to her.

He took a long swallow, set the can down with his fingers wrapped around it.

"Lord, I feel like such a hypocrite," he said, staring out at the darkening forest.

Julia didn't have to ask him what he was talking about. She filled her glass and took a sip of the cold brew, shuddering as the first sting hit her. "You did what you had to do—for the kids."

"I know, but it still doesn't sit well with me. I like to lay things out as they are, but it probably wasn't necessary. I doubt any person there could have said a kind word about Gloria. She just wasn't an affable person unless it benefited her in some way."

"The pastor did a fine job."

"Yeah, good thing he kept it short. How long could he talk about her skill at the piano and the three great kids she had—no thanks to her," he added through clenched teeth.

Julia was reminded of her father's funeral. The Minister asked her to give a eulogy like she had for her mother three months earlier. She'd refused for the same reason Dirk couldn't speak about Gloria—she'd had nothing good to say about him. One of his drinking buddies had done it instead, extolling about what a *great husband and father* Elias Morgan had been. Julia had to clamp one hand on Katie's knee to keep her still, and the other over her own mouth to stifle the nausea.

"Thanks for coming today," Dirk said, breaking off her thoughts.

Julia hoped he wouldn't ask about all the time she spent with Rosa and her family, who seemed determine to plague her with medical questions. She had somehow spun a web that wasn't going away. "I was happy to help out," she said. "Especially with Christa not wanting to leave my side."

"Yeah, I noticed."

Of course he'd noticed. She had the feeling Dirk was aware of her every move. All afternoon, he kept looking her way, catching her eye. At one point while Melody chatted up a storm in his ear, he'd looked over her shoulder at Julia and she was certain he'd winked. An unsolicited flush had settled over her cheeks so much that Rosa asked if she was feeling okay.

Dirk ran a hand through his dark hair. "I need to spend a little more time with them—especially now." He was thoughtful for a moment then a smile appeared. "I was happy to see Megan laughing and chatting with Trish and all her girly buddies today. It's been nearly three months since she's seen Gloria; I think she'll be just fine. Plus Jason didn't seem to have a problem being clingy. He was having a wonderful time running around with the little friends he made."

"Kids need to be around other kids their own age." Julia said.

"I'm starting to realize that. I've been rethinking the home schooling thing, maybe I should get Jason and Christa involved in a preschool program even if it's only a couple of days a week. There's probably something right here in Danango."

After Julia nodded her agreement and offered to do the driving, they settled into a comfortable silence. Julia contemplated something Rosa's niece had told her. The abbreviated clinic in Danango was in serious need of help. Maybe if the twins went to preschool she could use that time to get involved, possibly as a volunteer.

Dirk downed the last of his beer, his thoughts running deep. He was now, officially a free man, a widower. The word left a sour taste in his mouth. Interestingly enough, it was Melody who'd pointed that out today. Up until then he hadn't given it much thought. He hadn't remained celibate when Gloria left and Melody had become a convenience. A convenience he'd given up when his children came home. It had been nearly three months since he'd been with a woman—far too long.

He watched Julia take a sip of her beer and lick at the foam. Her tongue slid over her lips as though savoring the taste. She closed her eyes, laying her head back on the chair, while her fingers played with a wayward curl.

Dirk crushed his beer can between his hands, attempting to get a rein on his thoughts. He was growing hard...and it wasn't from thinking about Melody Dupree.

CHAPTER FIFTEEN

Even though Dirk knew it was standard policy to question every person even remotely involved in a murder case, it still irritated him when Rick Gunderson spent Friday morning at the ranch grilling his employees, his father, his nanny, and even Megan. The one placating element was Gunderson showing up rather than Sanford.

At eleven thirty, Gunderson, hobbling with a noticeable limp, approached Dirk for the second time. Dirk, working out his aggression cleaning stalls, stopped to lean on his pitchfork while the sheriff flipped through his notes.

"It seems to me," Gunderson said, "nobody around here cared too much for your wife."

Dirk grunted. "You knew her. Did you like her?"

"Well, you got me there," Gunderson replied, chuckling.

"Gloria was a master alienator." Dirk kicked a chunk of manure from his boot. "Now that you have a list of people on the *Rocking T* who didn't like her, I hope you're planning to look farther than this ranch for your answers. What's the story on Edwards?"

"No sign of him."

"How the hell can a person just disappear?"

Gunderson scratched his balding head. "Pretty easy if you're hiding out—or dead. I was hoping you could give me some information on him"

Dirk snorted. "I never saw the man until the day Gloria dropped the kids off."

"It's in the record that Megan said he was her father."

"Yeah, well, that's what she was told. I'm not so sure I believe it."

Gunderson's brows rose. "You have a valid reason to say that?"

"No, but I was married to the woman for six years. She never mentioned a man named Edwards."

"Well, he's our prime suspect, but I still have to investigate other avenues."

"Let me ask you, Rick—am I a suspect?"

Gunderson's gaunt face took on a serious frown. "Until this thing is solved everybody's a suspect. Close as they can tell, Gloria died exactly three weeks ago today between nine p.m. and one a.m. Her body was found forty-five minutes from here. The math would work, but since it was before your nanny arrived, I doubt you're the type of man who'd leave his kids at home alone while he goes out to hunt down and murder his wife...but on the other hand—"

Dirk stabbed his pitchfork into the hard ground at his feet. "I have a fucking record," he finished for Gunderson.

* * * *

Saturday morning at breakfast, Dirk looked around at his kids and realized they were being too well behaved. Even Julia was more quiet than usual. It seemed an aura of gloom hung over the house. Between the memorial and Gunderson's visit, it had him in its grip too.

"Who wants to go riding today?" he asked.

Jason and Megan gave a synchronized, "I do."

Christa, on the other hand pulled a pout. "I'm afraid to ride by myself."

Dirk gave her reassuring smile. "You can ride with me, honey bun."

"Is Anna going too?" she asked.

"I don't know," Dirk said looking at Julia. "How about it Julia? I think you've ridden enough to handle Seminole—unless you want to ride with Christa and me? We'd probably have to take Black Lightening though—to carry all three of us."

Julia laughed at the wide-eyed look on Christa's face. "That won't be necessary. I think I can manage by myself. David even supervised while I saddled her yesterday."

"Where are we going to go?" Megan asked.

Dirk reached over to refill Christa's juice glass. "There're some good trails in Pike. We could ride to the river, maybe go for a swim."

Jason threw his arms up with a cheer, spilling his milk. Megan, grumbling at his clumsiness, rushed to get a dishrag. Dirk sat back enjoying the normalcy of it all. He glanced at Julia, and they shared a smile that told him she read his mind.

Within an hour they had a lunch packed along with swimsuits and towels. Gus came out to the barn to help Mack round up the horses and with only a bit of prompting from Dirk, Gus rounded up a horse for himself as well.

Their little entourage was just about ready to leave when a white Mercedes pulled into the yard.

"This, we didn't need," Dirk mumbled to Julia.

Melody, squeezed into a pair of red spandex pants and a cleavage baring top, stepped out of her car, "It looks like I'm just in time. I was hoping to go for a ride."

Talk about a day going from honey to road apples. Dirk gritted his teeth, but saw no tactful way to tell her she couldn't go. One of the reasons she kept her horses at the *Rocking T* was because she had unlimited riding privileges. He'd been looking forward to spending the day with his kids—and Julia. Gus coming wasn't a problem, but Melody? Hoping to dissuade her, he explained it was a family outing and his kids would take all his attention. She'd be on her own. Plus they'd have to go at a slow pace.

Melody gave him a red-lipped smile. "Oh, that's okay, Dirk, honey. I was looking for a chance to get to know your kids better anyway. I promise not to be in the way."

Dirk had a hard time hiding his irritation as he asked Mack to saddle one of her horses. Mack rolling his eyes didn't help matters, and neither did Megan's open glare. With a silent curse, he vowed to see that they all had a good time in spite of this slight inconvenience. It was going to be an interesting day.

Julia shook her head at this new turn of events. Gus coming along was disconcerting enough. If she hadn't really been looking forward to this ride she might have opted to stay home. Plus Dirk might need her to help with the kids, she reminded herself. So what if his girlfriend came along?

She gave the cinch on her saddle a vicious yank.

"Good job," Dirk said, coming up behind her. "That's the way to tighten it down." He supervised while she did the loop and snapped the strap in place like David had shown her. Dirk smiled at her perfect execution. "We'll make a cowgirl out of you yet. We really need to get you some boots. Those sneakers aren't made for stirrups. By the way, since Gus is going, I'm having Jason ride with him. Jason's doing okay in the corral, but it's a little different when you get out in the woods. We'll keep the pace slow, so you and Megan should be all right."

When Dirk moved away, Megan came up to Julia, leading her pony. "At least we can saddle our own horses," she snickered, indicating Mack getting Melody's horse ready.

But she might ruin one of her perfect red claws. Julia reminded herself she was an adult and bit back the nasty retort. "Well, Megan, she's a customer and entitled to special treatment."

Megan snorted. "I'd like to give her a special treatment."

Julia hid her smile and said nothing.

Before they left, Dirk gave instructions on the order in which they would ride. He wanted the experienced riders alternating with the inexperienced. Megan rode behind him followed by Gus and Jason, next came Julia, with Melody bringing up the rear.

If Melody was unhappy with the arrangement she didn't show it.

They rode toward the southwest and the Pike national Forest. The ranch nested so near the outskirts it only took fifteen minutes to enter the dense woods. A wide shaded path wound easily through the enormous lodge pole pines. The only sounds came from the horses as they plodded over the soft needle bed covering the ground. Julia breathed with surprising pleasure the earthy smell of the forest. Pungent pine and fragrant undergrowth, along with the birds and small animals complaining of the human invasion gave her a feeling of intense exhilaration.

The deeper into the forest they rode, the more enchanted her mood. Not even Melody's presence could dampen her spirit. Plus, she was a part of a family outing enjoying an experience like nothing she'd ever had before. Seminole felt good beneath her and even the smell of the animals invigorated her. She leaned forward and rubbed the rust colored animal's neck, speaking to her in a soothing voice, wanting the horse to know what a fantastic time she was having.

Occasionally, Dirk would stop to point out an osprey nest, or eagle soaring overhead. They passed a small clearing where they spotted a doe with two spotted fawns. The animals showed interest in the entourage but continued grazing undisturbed. She saw Gus lean forward and stretch his arm out to make sure Jason saw them.

After the clearing, the path widened, and Julia was surprised when Melody urged her mount up to ride beside her.

"Isn't it beautiful in here," Melody said.

Julia nodded. "It is. I've never experienced anything like it."

Melody soft laughter filled the air. "I know. I just love riding. Being so close to the forest is why I like to keep my horses out here. I know Dirk didn't really want me along today," she said, her voice low, "but I came out to ride, and it's not much fun doing it alone."

Julia had the feeling Melody was truly trying to be friendly. "Like you said, you wanted to get to know his kids."

Melody laughed. "He knows that's a lie, but he let me come anyway. He's a nice guy, Julia. You're so lucky."

"I'm the nanny. How does that make me lucky?"

Melody slowed up to wind around a tree in the path then urged her mount up beside Julia again. "The way he looks at you. The way his face softens when he's talking to you. I'd give anything to have him look at me like that. It'll never happen."

"You're imagining things. Our relationship is strictly business."

Melody shrugged. "Maybe for now. I've had my horses out here for over five years now, so I've known him a long time. You can trust me on this—the woman he falls in love with is going to have to love his kids as much as he does. After Gloria disappeared I thought I had a chance with him—until the kids came back." She laughed. "I'm the first one to admit I'm not the mothering kind."

"Sadly, it seems Gloria wasn't either," Julia said.

They rode in silence for a few minutes until Melody suddenly blurted out, "You know I was there the night Dirk had the fight with Marcus Sanford."

Julia was shocked. "I didn't realize."

"Well, I was and I'm here to tell you Dirk slugged the wrong man."

Julia had the feeling she was getting into a gossip session, but curiosity got the best of her. "Why do you say that?"

Melody took a deep breath and glanced forward obviously to make sure the others were far enough ahead so they couldn't hear. "Gloria was messing around with somebody besides Marcus that night. I saw her follow him into the barn."

"Who?"

"I can't tell you, but I can tell you the man has a lot to lose if he's found out."

"Oh, my gosh. Maybe that's something the sheriff should know? I mean with the murder case going on."

Melody rolled her eyes. "Well, that doesn't mean this person is involved. I think they're still looking for the guy who was with her when they dropped the kids off. Besides, if Dirk found out I knew about this and didn't tell him, I'd really be in his doghouse. If there's one thing he hates, its secrets."

Julia's heart rate kicked up a notch, and Melody continued talking without pause. "I suppose it's understandable after being married to the secret queen of the universe. I don't know what he ever saw in her. Of course, he wouldn't have looked twice at me back then, I was still living with my husband. By the time I divorced the two-timing bastard, Dirk was married to Gloria and she was pregnant."

Melody laughed. "Man, I saw her in her last month of pregnancy, carrying twins she was as big as a house and ornery as a pole cat. I always imagine women getting soft and melancholy toward the end, but not her. Dirk waited on her hand and foot."

Julia couldn't stop the wave of grief that overwhelmed her. If Geno had half of Dirk's compassion she'd be nearing her delivery time about now. Maybe she'd be as big as a house, but she wouldn't have cared. Being pregnant with your first child was a special time in a woman's life, and she was cheated out of the experience...by Geno.

Julia wasn't aware she'd tightened up on reins until Seminole started to balk. The little mare thrashed her head as her front feet came off the ground.

"Loosen up on the reins, Julia, you're holding them too tight!"

Melody's warning came too late. Julia started sliding backward, still clutching the reins and causing the horse to rear higher. Melody pressed her own horse toward Seminole, reached and gripped the reins below the bit, taking control of the confused animal and preventing it from rearing over on top of Julia.

Even in her panicked state, Julia realized what Melody had done.

Julia tumbled over the back of the horse slamming with a lung-jarring thud on the ground. Still gasping to get her breath back, she saw Dirk hover over her, concern etched in his face. He lifted her upper body seemingly at a loss as to what to do.

"Julia? Are you hurt? Talk to me, sweetheart."

Only in her mind was Julia able to scream, *don't move the patient until you know what the injuries are.* Why was he calling her sweetheart?

On the verge of blacking out, her lungs finally filled. She sat up greedily gasping air, waving a hand in front of her face. "A…minute…need to…breathe." She wanted to tell him to stop squeezing her so tight.

Christa stood sobbing beside her. "Is Anna going to die?"

Melody who'd come down on spandex knees put an arm around Christa. "No, honey, Anna's not going to die. She just got the wind knocked out of her. She needs to catch her breath."

"What happened, Melody?" Dirk asked, a hint of accusation in his voice.

"My own…fault." Julia managed to say.

"I'm not sure," Melody said. "We were just talking

and it seemed like all of a sudden she started pulling back on the reins. She pulled harder and Seminole tried to rear.

Christa tugged free of Melody and flew into Julia, throwing thin arms around her.

"I'm okay," Julia said, holding the terrified girl, smoothing her hair. She looked at Dirk. "It was my own fault. We were talking and I wasn't paying attention. If it hadn't been for Melody's quick thinking, Seminole would have landed on top of me." Sitting there in Dirk's arms was causing her breath to shorten again. "I think I'm over the worst of it. I can get up now."

Dirk pried Christa away and helped Julia to her feet. He brushed the leaves and dust from her, at the same time feeling her body for injuries.

"You're sure you're not hurt anywhere?"

Julia managed a weak smile. "Just my pride. Sorry to be such a nuisance."

Dirk threw his arms around her and pulled her against his body. "God, Julia, don't ever give me a scare like that again. My old heart can't take it."

"I'm fine, really I am." Julia mumbled into his chest, wishing there weren't five other people watching.

Dirt finally set her back. "Do you want to ride with me? Melody can take Christa."

The thought of riding with her body pressed to Dirk was enough to make a quick decision. "No way—if I don't get back on now, I may never trust myself to do it again."

Dirk gave her a relaxed smile. "Good girl. Come on I'll help you mount. We're only a mile from the swimming hole, you can rest there."

When he had her safely back on board, he glanced up at both her and Melody.

"What in the world were you guys talking about that had you so distracted?"

CHAPTER SIXTEEN

"Just girl talk," Julia said with a quick glance at Melody.

Dirk gave each of them a quizzical look before he picked up Christa and headed back to his horse.

"If I said something to upset you," Melody said when Dirk was safely out of earshot, "I'm really sorry."

"No, it's not your fault, and thank you for grabbing Seminole. You likely saved me from a far worse fate." She rubbed her backside and forced a laugh. "I thought Mack was kidding when he warned me not to jerk back on the reins like I did. I have a feeling I'll pay more attention to what I'm doing in the future."

They stopped at a spot where the river separated leaving one section little more than a bubbling brook. Dirk was beside her in an instant to help her dismount. "Are you sure you don't need to see a doctor?" he asked.

Julia, far too aware of his nearness for comfort, shook her head. "No. No. I'm fine. I might have a few bruises, but—"

"You want me to check them?"

Julia stared for a moment into his startling gray eyes wondering if she imagined the sexual undertone in his question. The thought of his hands roaming over her body brought her female senses to disconcerting awareness. She had the bizarre urge to rub her pelvis up against him. She moved away from him before she embarrassed herself. If she'd had the nerve she might even have cooed. *Maybe later.*

Instead she declined his offer and said, "Let's check if the food survived the trip. I'm getting hungry." She was hungry, but not for food. She was hardly naïve, and yet the feelings he stirred in her were new and unexpected.

Together, they set the ham and cheese sandwiches, chips, and pickles out on a large flat, blanket-covered, rock while Megan and the twins went to explore the riverbank.

"You guys stay where I can see you," Dirk called. "Don't get wet before you have your swimsuits on."

"This sure is a lovely spot," Melody said, sitting down on a stretch of grass. "Too bad I didn't bring a suit."

"Water's too cold for swimming anyway," Gus mumbled, finding his own perch on a jutting rock. "It's melted snow coming straight down from the mountains."

Julia stretched her back looking up at the snow-covered peaks in the distance. "It's awesome and the air is so fresh," she said, breathing deeply of the earthy pine smell. "I went skiing up there once," she added wistfully. *In another life—with Geno before they were married.* One of his friends owned a lodge at Breckinridge.

"Did you ski often?" Dirk asked, handing out the kids' swimwear.

"No, just that one time," Julia said. After the wedding he never asked her to go along again, though he went a couple of times a year. She actually encouraged him since she was happier at home when he was gone. Being away from him now made her realize just how miserable she'd been.

"Maybe we should swim before we eat?" Dirk asked Julia. "Unless you're too hungry."

"No. That's a good idea," she replied, tucking the sandwiches back in their cold container. "Let's get our suits on."

"Boys to the left, girls to the right." Dirk said, taking Jason with him into the woods.

Megan, towing Christa, followed Julia, going around the rocks on the right side. When they emerged a few minutes later, Dirk and Jason were already waiting. Julia did a double take when she saw Dirk in his swim trunks. His broad hair studded chest and muscular arms gave him a devilishly handsome look—or was it the lock of dark hair falling over his forehead and the silver glint in his eyes as he watched her come toward him?

For some reason, she glanced at Melody and found the woman grinning, her eyebrows raised as if to say, *I told you so*. Julia had a sudden urge to submerge her face in the water to cool it off.

Jason put his foot in the shallow water. "It's not so cold, Grandpa."

Dirk pointed to the left. "Over there is a little eddy formed by the rocks. There's not much current, but it's probably too deep for Jason and Christa. You guys stay here where Grandpa can see you. Megan, you can still swim, right?"

"Of course I can swim. Didn't we come here before? When I was little?"

"We sure did, honey. In fact I've been coming here since I was your age."

Gus made a harrumphing sound. "Not with me you didn't. I always knew you rascals where up to no good when you rode off into the woods and came back with your hair all wet."

Dirk laughed. "Well, I guess now you know."

Christa squealed with delight when Dirk picked her up and carried her into the water. He set her down where she was only knee deep.

"Is it too cold?" he asked.

Christa shivered. "No, come on, Jason, it's fun."

Jason splashed out to her and threw himself into the

shallow water. Megan charged in after him, while Julia stood on the bank dipping a toe.

"You want me to carry you out here too?" Dirk asked, that wicked glint still in his eye.

He was too quick for her. Before she realized what was happening, she was in his arms and a moment later dropped into the icy rock pool. From the shore the pool, formed by boulders falling into the river, appeared to be about fifteen feet long, twelve feet wide, and only about three or four feet deep. The depth surprised her almost as much as the numbing coldness. She came up gasping, never having touched bottom.

She heard the kid's laughter even before she saw Dirk standing on the rocks holding a hand out to her, his self-satisfied grin stretching the length of his face.

When she reached for the proffered hand, she grasped her other hand around his wrist, braced both her feet on the rock, and yanked him into the water on top of her. They went under together. When they came up, his arm encircled her waist. While he was still trying to catch his breath, she wriggled free of his grip, splashed water in his face, and using his shoulders as leverage, submerged him again. He was still struggling for air by the time she'd swum to the other end and climbed out on the rocks.

That's when she heard something she hadn't ever expected to hear. Gus was laughing, loud and hard.

Dirk heard it too. It had been a long time.

He shook the water from his eyes and looked around for Julia. She sat on the far rock with her feet dangling in the water. Apparently she anticipated his intentions because she jerked her feet out of the water and pulled them out of his reach. Her undiluted smile did an odd number on his heart and, in spite of the cold water, his body responded in turn.

When he swam toward her, she laughed down at him from the safety of the rocks.

"What? You don't trust me?" he asked.

She flipped wet hair back. "I could have drowned. You didn't even ask me if I could swim."

In one easy fluid motion, he hiked himself up on the rock beside her. "You told me in your letter you were on a swim team. I was just showing you how much I trust you." He saw something flicker in her eyes, like she was surprised he remembered. "I made Dad laugh though, that was worth it all."

Julia gave him a devilish look. "I don't think he laughed until I pulled you in."

"I think you're right," Dirk admitted, chuckling. Her wanted to kiss her so bad he ached. One glance toward shore reminded him they still had an audience. Even Melody seemed to be amused, which surprised him. Maybe he'd underestimated the woman.

"Let's swim a few laps before we eat," he said to Julia. She eyed him suspiciously. "I'll behave, I promise."

He could have sworn she looked disappointed.

* * * *

That night in the solitary loneliness of his bed, Dirk reflected on the events of the day.

The kids sure had a great time. Christa fell asleep in his arms on the ride home. Gus seemed happier than Dirk had seen him since his mother left. Which reminded him, he still hadn't made contact with her. Melody had been on her best behavior.

And Julia...he experienced an odd ache in his chest. She'd make a good wife and wonderful mother. It was a thought he couldn't entertain until the thing with Gloria was resolved. Where the hell was Edwards anyway? Dirk had already made up his mind he'd rather kill the man than let him take Megan away. Thoughts like that certainly wouldn't win any sympathy from the sheriff.

His mind drifted back to Julia and he decided it was a good thing they didn't have opportunity to spend time alone together. He was the one, after all, who'd insisted their relationship remain strictly business. Of course, she'd readily agreed. He wasn't sure when his interest in her turned from business to something entirely different.

He was still disturbed by the mystery surrounding her. He knew she was divorced, though not how long, and she'd had a miscarriage of twins. At one point she'd mentioned a sister. She also had contact with a psychiatrist in Minneapolis—the person who'd sent the application to him, which in itself he found strange. Though she appeared to have no physical ailments, she'd researched hospitals and clinics in Denver. Her name popped up nowhere on the Internet.

* * * *

Julia expected the day after frolicking in the water to be awkward at best. Instead, she and Dirk seemed to have slipped into a smooth camaraderie. She found his teasing nature at breakfast, usually directed toward her through the children, to be endearing and fun. She couldn't recall ever having that in her stale life except with Katie.

The ringing phone brought Julia out of her musings. Megan charged up to answer it, and called "It's for me" as she took the cordless handset to the laundry room for privacy.

"Wow, big surprise," Dirk said, laughing. His hand snaked out with lightening speed to stop Jason from racing after her. "Stay and finish your pancakes, son. If she wants you to know what she's talking about, she'll tell you."

Jason slumped back in his chair. "No, she won't. She never tells us. It's just girly, girly stuff anyway."

"Then you don't need to hear it," Dirk said getting up to retrieve the coffeepot. He brought it back to the table and filled his cup. "Julia?"

Julia pushed her cup toward him. "Sure, thanks."

As he poured, he leaned into her, his large hand settling on her shoulder as if for balance. Heat shot through her like a fireball. She couldn't see Dirk's face to determine if it was an intentional thing, but she was glad he couldn't see hers either. Her hand shook when she poured cream in her coffee after he went back to the stove with the pot.

When he sat back down he smiled at her. "So...Julia...it's your day off. You have big plans?"

Julia hadn't even thought about it. Spending day and night with Dirk and the kids had become so natural; she didn't know what to do without them. She gave a quick laugh and rubbed her backside. "I can tell you it won't include horseback riding for a couple of days."

"A little sore are you?"

"Nothing that won't be back to normal in a few days. I...guess I could just laze around the house, maybe write some letters."

"Oh, now that sounds exciting." Still grinning, he looked at the twins "What about you, guys? What would you like to do today?"

"Can we go to a movie?" Christa asked.

"Yeah," Jason piped up. "I want to see the one with big explosions."

Dirk snorted. "Son, by the time you're old enough to see Bruce Willis, he'll be in a nursing home."

Julia tried to hide a grin, but Dirk caught it. He winked at her. "Isn't that right, Anna?"

Her heart rate spiked. She was saved answering when Megan charged back in the room holding a hand over the phone.

"Guess what?" Megan said in a whispered shriek. "Mona's mom wants me to come for a sleepover tonight. Okay?"

"Both mom and dad there? No boys?" Dirk asked.

Megan rolled her eyes. "Of course, everyone knows your rules.

Dirk grinned. "Good. Then no problem."

Megan put the phone back to her ear, turned to the side, and started talking rapidly. After a few minutes, she swiveled around to look at Dirk, again holding her hand over the receiver, her youthful mouth drawn into a frown.

"Mona has a brother who's six and two little sisters. They're three and five. They want Jason and Christa to come too."

Dirk studied her for a moment. "Are you okay with that, Megan?"

Megan stared back open mouthed as though she couldn't believe Dirk was actually asking if she minded. She suddenly smiled and shrugged. "Sure, they have a big house."

Dirk looked at the wide-eyed twins. "How about it, you guys wanna go?"

They leaped from their seats and started jumping up and down, shrieking.

Dirk looked a Julia. "You think that means they want to go?"

Julia laughed. "Either that or they need to go to the bathroom real bad."

"There's your answer," he said to Megan.

"Okay, the brats are coming," Megan grunted into the phone, though the undertone of her voice implied she didn't mind at all. Seconds later they both raced to their rooms to pack their Pajama's and favorite toys even though it was hours before they would leave.

Megan walked after them shaking her head. "I better go up and make sure they don't take all the junk in their room. By the way, they're making hotdogs on the grill so we should be there around fiveish."

Julia's heart swelled. All her life she'd longed for a loving, happy family. Realistically this wasn't her family, but just being able to share and observe had her throat tightening.

Dirk reached over and cupped a large hand over Julia's smaller one. "Thank you," he said.

His touch sent rivers of sparks shooting through her veins. She felt as though she should pull away, but it was the last thing she wanted to do. Confused, she looked into his surprisingly misty gray eyes. "For what?"

"You do realize what things were like here before you came?"

"I didn't—"

"Oh, yes, you did," he corrected before she could finish. "You brought harmony to this house, Julia. I appreciate you more than you'll ever know." He gave her hand a firm squeeze and released it.

Apparently finished with being serious, his mischievous twinkle once again lit up his eyes. "Well, Ma, looks like it's going to be just you and me tonight. What would you like to do? After you get your letter writing out of the way, of course."

CHAPTER SEVENTEEN

After dropping the kids off at Mona's house and declining an offer to stay for hot dogs, Dirk suggested they drive up to Breckinridge for supper. Julia was surprised to learn it was actually closer than Denver, although, as Dirk explained, with the road winding through the mountains and Hoosier Pass it took nearly as long to get there.

As they gained altitude, Julia admired the way Dirk maneuvered Gloria's SUV around the tight curves. He'd explained they'd taken her car instead of his pickup because it handled better in mountain driving.

Julia shifted in her seat, trying to keep her above-the-knee skirt from riding up. The sleeveless black sheath was clingier than she preferred, but it was the only non-nanny outfit she'd brought with her. Katie had been the one who had packed it for her. Her strappy sandals were impractical and most definitely not nanny-like, but she loved them. When she finally gave up trying to control her skirt on every turn, she threw her black sweater over her legs and could have sworn Dirk looked away to hide a grin. She'd brought the sweater because Dirk mentioned it might be cool where they were going. Though they were just employee and employer going out for dinner, it was the closest thing to a date she'd had in months. Watching Dirk's capable hands on the wheel took her mind to wondering about the time he'd kissed her, holding her with those same tender hands.

"That's Mount Lincoln," he said, pointing off to the left. "It's over fourteen thousand feet."

Julia leaned over to look out his side window at the snow-capped peak. "Everyplace I've seen in this state is beautiful. Actually breathtaking." She braced her feet and reached for the doorframe as they came to a sharp turn.

"You scared?" he asked. "Am I driving too fast?"

Julia gave a shaky laugh. "Just a little, and no. I'm just not used to mountains. We barely have large hills in Minnesota."

"You did say you've been up here skiing."

"Well, just once, but we flew in a friend's private plane. I would have to say that flying over in a tiny 150 Piper is a whole lot scarier than driving though." *Especially with Geno at the controls.* "Don't mind me, I'm fine. Holding on is just instinct."

He reached over and covered her fingers gripping the center console with his hand giving her a light squeeze. "The Hoosier Pass is coming up. It's just a few more miles after that. I hope you aren't sorry you came."

"Heavens no. It's beautiful up here."

The mere touch of his fingers did peculiar things to Julia's stomach, and the rest of her body responded in kind. She was beginning to think her lightheadedness had nothing to do with the altitude, and she wondered what her feelings were toward this man. She couldn't remember ever becoming flustered by a simple touch. When he moved his hand back to the wheel she felt an odd sense of loss.

Fifteen minutes later he stopped in front of the Chalet Elaina. Nestled into a rock wall, it rose at least three stories and was constructed entirely of mammoth golden logs. Giant pillars supported the wide covered veranda that swept around the front to encompass both sides. Their sign advertised juicy porterhouse steaks, tender ribs, chicken to melt in your mouth, and suites with vibrating beds.

"In the winter this place is hopping," Dirk said, helping her out of the car. "It's more down-to-earth than classy, but they have terrific food." His eyes flicked over her appreciatively. "Did I tell you how ravishing you look?"

Julia gave a flustered laugh as a hot flush raced to her cheeks. "No, I don't believe anyone has ever described me as ravishing. I'm more the acceptable basic type."

Dirk took her arm to direct her up the steps. "What? You were married to a blind man. Or is he just your basic idiot."

"No, I—"

He slipped an arm around her waist and pulled her aside as three rowdy young men burst from the door. All three turned to look Julia up and down. One gave a low whistle as they passed by.

Another said, "Man, I gotta find me one of those."

Dirk laughed. "Go find your own, this one's taken."

After the three had clomped down the steps, Dirk leaned into Julia. "See what I mean—ravishing."

"They were drunk," she replied, a little surprised at how lightly he took someone else ogling his 'date'. Most men she knew responded with jealous anger. Of course, she wasn't really a date.

"Yeah," he said, putting pressure on her waist to usher her inside as he held the door open. "They were drunk, but they weren't blind."

Inside, a waiter directed them to a corner booth. Except for a small group of people celebrating a birthday, and three individual couples sitting in secluded alcoves, the dining area was pretty much empty. Julia decided it was large enough to hold a convention, and it was easy to imagine it in the winter during skiing season.

A handful of people took up one end of the pine bar. It had quaint rustic stools, and nested in one cozy corner separated from the dining area by a small dance floor. The

Dixie Chicks belted out a tune from a jukebox standing on a stage large enough to hold a live band.

"Can I get you something from the bar?" the waiter, who identified himself as Bruce, asked as he handed them each a menu.

Dirk glanced at Julia. "Wine maybe?"

Julia nodded. "Sure, a glass of Chardonnay if you have it."

"Make that two glasses," Dirk said.

"How about a bottle?" the waiter suggested. "Won't cost much more."

Dirk snickered. "I have to drive back down this mountain tonight, so I reckon not." He looked at Julia. "Unless you can drink it."

"One glass will be enough. I have to ride back with you."

Bruce bobbed his bushy eyebrows. "Rooms are quite inexpensive this time of year."

"Thanks," Dirk said. "We'll keep that in mind."

After Bruce left, Julia unfolded the short menu. "It's been absolutely ages since I had ribs. I think that's what I'd like to have."

"Go for it. I'm never one to pass up a steak." He set his menu aside. "Do you think he gets a commission for renting a room?"

Julia gave an easy laugh. "I wouldn't be surprised. I imagine tips are hard to come by when it's this slow."

"We don't have to pick the kids up until eleven."

Her head shot up from the dessert list, thinking she'd either heard wrong or misunderstood his meaning. Dirk was staring down at the pictures on the back of the menu. Bruce showing up with the wine spared her from commenting, but it did nothing for the sudden rush to her system.

Bruce handed off the wine glasses and pulled out his notepad to take their orders. When he left a moment later Dirk raised his glass to Julia.

"I'm glad you're here with me, Julia. Thanks for coming."

Julia held up her own glass, smiling. "It's been a long time since I've done anything like this. Thanks for asking me."

They touched glasses and Julia took a sip, savoring the pungent wine on her tongue before she let it slide down her throat. It was sharp and sweet at the same time, and raced like wildfire to her head.

"It's been a while for me too," Dirk said. "In fact, since the kids came I've pretty much stuck close to home. As much as I love having them with me, it's nice to get a night off."

"I imagine most parents would agree with that. Plus, you work awfully hard."

"I love it though. I enjoy what I do and I wouldn't want to be anywhere else. How about you? Being a nanny isn't very challenging."

Julia laughed. "Are you kidding? I never dreamed two four-year-olds could be so…demanding."

"The ranch is real secluded. Don't you miss the city and the life you had before you came here?"

Julia's heart quickened. He was giving her the opening she needed. She could tell him the truth, tell him about her life in Minnesota, about her practice and about Geno. Maybe he'd understand. Maybe. But if he wouldn't, she didn't want to spoil the evening. She shrugged. "I… miss my sister."

"Why don't you invite her for a visit?"

Julia's heart did a little happy dance at the thought. "That's a wonderful idea."

* * * *

One thing Dirk knew for certain. He wanted to make love to Julia more than he'd ever wanted to make love to a woman in his life. So much that he had a difficult time concentrating on anything else. Just watching her lick the barbeque sauce off her fingers and listening to her moans of delight all but sent him through the roof. The thought was a bad idea, and the act would be an even worse idea. They had both insisted their relationship remain business only—and that certainly meant platonic in his book.

It wasn't just that she was beautiful and looked like a hot babe in the little black number she wore. It was more than lust. He'd known that for some time now. He didn't just want sex with her—he wanted...more. Would he shock those sexy little sandals off her feet if he told her he wanted to make love with her?

"...don't you just love Elvis?"

Dirk wasn't even aware that the music had changed and two couples from the bar had walked out on the dance floor. Julia was eyeing them as they moved to Presley's *Love Me Tender.*"

"Would you like to dance," he asked, almost hoping she'd say no.

She hesitated a moment. "Yeah, sure. I'd like that."

Not exactly leaping into his arms, he thought.

He stood up and held out his hand. She took it and he led her to the dance floor where she slipped into his arms like a well-worn glove. It only seemed natural for him to pull her against his body.

Something magical happened when their bodies came together. She pressed into him, placing her head in the curve of his shoulder. He laid the side of his face on top of her head breathing in the sweet scent of roses—roses and woman. His woman. All his life, it seemed, he'd been waiting for this one moment. They had stepped over the threshold into the Land of Oz, and there was no turning back. She slipped her arms around his neck, easing her body closer and he knew without a doubt she felt it too.

Their bodies barely moved to the music. He had no idea if the song was even playing anymore, or if the other dancers had left.

He nuzzled his face close to her ear. "Lord, Julia, I'm

not sure what just happened here. I'm charting new
territory. What do we do now?"

Julia raised her head to look into his eyes. Her limbs
were Jell-O and her female parts were charging full speed
into overdrive. She wanted to kiss him, to climb inside him,
but something in the back of her mind warned her that this
wasn't the place. "I don't know," she whispered. "But I
want you so bad I ache with it."

Dirk's breath was hot and labored against her cheek.
"Will you hate me tomorrow if I suggest we get a room?"

She gave a throaty laugh. "I'll hate you if you don't.
Bruce needs the commission."

He drew back, chuckling. "Thanks, I needed that right
now. Come on."

He grasped her hand, went back to the table and
picked up her sweater and handbag. He released her long
enough to fumble in his wallet and throw a hundred dollar
bill on the table. With his arm around her shoulders and her
arm around his back, they moved like Siamese twins, past
the bar to the check-in counter. Julia suspected everyone in
the room was watching them, but for once in her life she
was going to be spontaneous and she wasn't going to worry
about what anyone else thought.

It took an interminable ten minutes to check-in. Before
they left with keys in hand, Dirk reminded the clerk that
Bruce recommended the room and to be sure he got his
commission. Heady from the wine she'd drunk, Julia stifled
a giggle as they all but raced each other like teenagers up
the wide stairs to the second floor.

At the door, not wanting to be separated from Dirk
even for a moment, she leaned against his back encircling
his waist with her arms while he struggled to work the key
card. When he finally got the little green light to come on,
Dirk opened the room, pulled her inside and kicked the
bulky pine door shut behind him.

Their lips met in a wild crashing frenzy. Julia tore at his clothes trying to reach his skin, barely conscious of the cool air on her own flesh as her dress, assisted by his eager hands, hiked up to her waist. Those buttons that didn't give willingly under her trembling fingers popped free of their bindings.

Her mouth opened to devour his kisses, sensations crowding her brain. She was on fire, driven by a passion more urgent than anything she'd ever experienced in her life.

Finally his shirt pushed off his shoulders and her racing hands sought the taut muscles on his broad back, his solid arms, his firm chest.

He dropped his arms long enough to shake free of the shirt and when his hands came back up, the remains of her dress came with them. She gave a whimpered protest when their lips had to part long enough for him to pull the stretchy fabric over her head.

His warm hands touched the sensitive skin on her bare back, and a moment later, her lacy black bra dropped to the floor. When her black panties followed, and she'd kicked free of them, he lifted her in his arms and carried her to the bed.

It took him only seconds to shed the rest of his clothes and join her.

"You are so beautiful," Dirk said before his lips came down to take her in another hungry kiss. Julia couldn't get enough of running her hands over his solid shoulders, his arms, digging her fingers in his dark curly hair, moving her mouth to mate with his kisses.

"I love feeling you," she managed to say. "You're so strong, so muscular, your body is—" She cried out with pleasure when his mouth moved to her breast. "Please don't tease me... I need you...inside me."

"I know, honey, I need you too. I've needed you so long." Instead of entering her, he slid to the side and touched her where the heat was building her need. He found the tiny nub, and began rubbing it as his mouth sucked at her breast. He pushed his leg between her knees and held her down as she cried out in release.

She panted, drawing deep gulps of air. "I want more, Dirk. I want to feel you inside me." He gasped when she reached down and circled her fingers around his rigid shaft. "Please…now," she pleaded.

"Oh, honey, I want you too. You are so wet, so ready for me. But honest to God, sweetheart, I didn't plan this"

"It's okay," she said. "I didn't either."

"You don't understand. I didn't bring protection. I could make you pregnant."

"You won't. I had a depo shot…after my miscarriage… I won't conceive."

He paused for only a second to absorb what she'd said. He rolled on top of her and positioned himself between her legs. With his erection poised at the opening of her heat, he paused, took her face between his hands and stared down into her eyes.

"I think I'm falling in love with you, Julia."

His raspy whisper came just before he claimed her mouth again, entering her at the same time. He moved slowly at first, quickly building to a starving urgency. Julia matched his thrusts with a fury of her own. She moaned, climaxing again only moments before he gave a roaring shudder. His body collapsed on top of her, his seed propelling with driving force inside her.

Dirk rolled to his side pulling her with him, reluctant to break the contact between them. "Sweetheart, you've done me in," he said, chuckling.

She nuzzled his neck. "I think it's the other way around. I'm exhausted. I've never…"

"Never what?" he asked when she stopped talking.

"Never climaxed twice in one night."

Dirk lifted her chin until he could look in her emerald green eyes. "Are you serious?"

She nodded instead of answering.

He kissed her, tasting her with undue tenderness. "Honey, it's not even fully dark yet. You're going to do it more than twice before the night is over—and that's a promise."

She gave a soft chuckle. "You can't do that again until you have a few hours to regenerate."

He grabbed her buttocks and pressed his rigid erection against her. "Wanna bet?"

"You can go again?"

"Julia, I've been wanting you since the day you walked into my house and talked Jason out of the bathroom."

"You made it clear, our arrangement would be business only—and I agreed."

"Well, I guess we both lied."

It seemed like a good time to come clean with him, tell him the truth about her medical practice. Before she could think of a way to bring it up he interrupted her thoughts.

"By the way, you said you had a depo shot. I'm not sure exactly what that is, but I'm guessing it's a form of birth control?"

"Yes, it is. I requested it after my miscarriage. It's good for over three months."

"That was a difficult time for you, wasn't it?"

Tears stung her eyes. "Yes."

"You'd probably rather not talk about it, right?"

She smiled and reached up to run a hand through his hair. "I'd rather get back to that promise you made."

"I can see you're going to be a tough customer. Come here." Planting his lips firmly over hers, he pulled her on top of him, entering her at the same time. She took control from there, moving with him, matching his stride. Within minutes she fell on top of his chest, sighing with satisfaction, and laughing with pleasure.

"You're such a stud," she said.

Dirk pulled her to his side, nestling her in the curve of

his arm. "Honey, what kind of a man were you married to anyway?"

"A very selfish one. Either that or I just didn't turn him on."

"The man was an idiot is all I can say. You are the most perfect woman I've ever known. How could any man let you go?"

"He didn't let me go. I let him go."

"His loss, my gain. I meant what I said Julia. I'm in love with you."

Julia's heart raced. She wanted to say she loved him too, but she wasn't ready to take that step. "I'm not sure what to say, Dirk. I care for you—a lot. But I've only been divorced a few months. I don't know if I'm ready to love again. He—damaged my heart."

Dirk pushed a strand of hair from her face and traced a finger along her jaw. "I'll wait for it to mend. I can't promise anything more right now anyway until this thing with Gloria is settled. Let's just go slow. I'll even keep my hands off of you in front of the kids. Now come to me my passionate little flower, we're going to take a shower together and then I'm going to pretend I'm a bee and drink from your honey cup."

Julia threw her head back and laughed. "I can't believe you said that."

Dirks chest bounced with his own laughter. "I can't either."

CHAPTER EIGHTEEN

Julia had a hard time concentrating on Megan's piano lessons. More than once she felt herself grinning, and had to hide it fast before her student noticed and wondered what was making her so giddy.

Sex. That's what she was smiling about. Not just sex, but great, mind boggling, fun—and fulfilling—sex. She'd never known you could actually laugh and have fun while making love. Other than a brief affair she'd had during med school, Geno was her only example, and he was too concerned about taking care of himself to see to her needs.

Lovemaking with Dirk, she realized, could be addicting. They'd decided to come home last night after all, since they weren't ready to announce to everyone at the ranch that Dirk was keeping his nanny out until the wee hours of the morning. They made it home by midnight and she spent the rest of the night in his king-size bed doing very little sleeping.

"Julia?"

Heat flooded Julia's face when she realized Megan had been talking to her.

"I'm sorry, honey. What were you saying?"

Megan gave her a long measuring look. "I asked if you wanted to finish with Dueling Banjos."

Yes, great. That would get her mind off the other thing. "Sure, that's a fun piece, and terrific finger exercise." She fished through the music sheets until she found it and spread it out in front of them.

They went through it the third time with flawless precision and looked up to find they had an audience. Both Dirk and Gus gave them a round of applause and praise from the kitchen doorway.

Megan giggled, then stood up to do an elegant bow.

* * * *

The next two nights, Dirk went to her room after he made sure the twins were sleeping. It was a test of will for him to keep his hands off her during the day, but they'd mutually agreed it was the right thing to do. He'd already had odd looks from both Mack and David when they caught him whistling while mucking out stalls.

Thursday morning when Gus walked out to the road to get the mail, he went straight to the barn and handed Dirk, among other things, a letter hand addressed to Julia. It had a two days prior Denver postmark and a return address for Sandra Westerly with a Denver address.

"You worry too much," Dirk said, laughing at his dad's furrowed brow.

He found Julia in the yard trying to keep his giggling twins sprinkling water on the flowers instead of each other. Those two clearly adored her. And God, he loved the way her mouth widened showing brilliant white teeth when she laughed. Her smile could light up the sky on the cloudiest day.

Lord, he had to watch himself before he started spouting poetry.

When he handed her the letter, her smile faded. She turned it over, studying the envelope, then dodging a spray from the hose, folded it in half and stuffed it in the back pocket of her jeans. Seemingly unconcerned, she warned Jason he was going to do reading penance if he got her wet.

Well, he thought, so much for finding out what the letter was about. It really was none of his business anyway.

Having great sex with the lady didn't give him the right to pry into her personal life. Did it?

A dust cloud trailing a car coming down the road drew his attention from Julia. He recognized Gunderson's patrol car. He gave Julia a disparaging look then purposely strode toward the barn to direct the car away from the twins.

The sheriff wore a non-committal look as he eased his bulk out of the car. "Morning, Dirk. How's it going?"

Dirk shrugged. "Okay. What's up, Rick?"

Gunderson scratched the back of his neck. "Well, it seems we found Edward's car."

"And Edwards—?"

"Yup, he was in it, or at least what was left of him. A high caliber bullet near took his head off."

Dirk ran a hand through his hair. "Jesus, do you know what happened?"

"Kinda looks like suicide. We found a note on the seat beside him."

"What did it say?"

Gunderson shrugged. "Not much. Said he killed Gloria, he was sorry, and he loved her. That's about it."

Dirk's heart rate accelerated. He stared at the sheriff trying to absorb the magnitude of what the man was saying. "He admitted killing her?"

"That's what the note said."

It seemed too good to be true. "You sound like you have doubts?"

"Well, there are a few things that don't add up, but that's just speculation. I won't know anything more until the boys from Denver have a look."

"Where?" Dirk asked. "Where was the car?"

"Heavy woods. About three miles from where Gloria's body was found. For your information, dental records confirmed it was her."

Dirk drew in a long, slow breath and blew it out in a huff. "What a goddamn mess. Where were they all this time? Why were they hanging around here?"

"Hopefully, they'll find something in the car that'll give us a clue to both those questions. Sure would clear things up easy like if it turned out to be just as it appears. We can close the case and put it all to rest."

"Yeah. I guess that does seem a little too pat."

"No sense making something of it until we have a reason. For now, that's all we have. I'll keep you posted."

"I appreciate that, Rick. Thanks."

Gunderson worked his pained leg back into the car, closed the door, and rolled the window down. "You be sure and let me know if you think of anything that might help us out on this."

Dirk leaned against the window frame. "You can bank on that. I want this thing solved as much as you do, probably more. Before you go I'd like to ask if you can you get a DNA sample from Edwards? I want to give Megan the option of knowing if he's really her father."

Gunderson nodded. "I'll see what I can do."

* * * *

After Julia had the kids settled at the table to eat their lunch, she pulled the strange letter from her pocket. The only thing she knew for sure is it wasn't Katie's handwriting. It was a one-page hand written sheet.

Ms. Julia Morgan,

It has come to my attention that you've shown interest in helping the people of Danango. As you probably know, the clinic here is only open two days a month, and we're extremely shorthanded. I was wondering if you might be interested in doing some volunteer work on the days we're open, even if it's just answering phones, or helping with paperwork.

You could meet me at the clinic to discuss it Friday evening about seven o'clock. If you can't make it then, I'll also be there Saturday morning between ten and noon.

Respectfully,
Sandra Westerly

Julia flipped the paper over looking for a phone number. The back was blank. It was posted in Denver two days ago. She found it odd that the woman hadn't given a contact number. Well, at least she'd given Julia two time periods to work with.

How ironic. It was actually something she'd been thinking of doing. Obviously, Sandra Westerly had no idea Julia was a doctor since she hadn't asked her to work in a medical capacity. That meant she hadn't received her information from Margaret Jensen.

Likely it was someone in Rosa's family. Twice earlier in the week Rosa had fielded calls to Julia. On Monday it was Rosa's niece, wanting a prescription for cough medicine. Julia explained she couldn't write prescriptions and recommended an over the counter medication. The next day, Rosa's neighbor cut his hand and asked Julia if she would come in and stitch it up. She had to tell him to drive to Denver to get treatment.

She hated turning these people down and wondered if she could do anything to persuade the powers that be to keep the clinic open at least during the week.

That prompted her decision to meet with Sandra Westerly tomorrow night. Afterwards she would sit down and tell Dirk the truth—about everything. Her medical practice, Geno, even her sister and her father. If he truly loved her, he would understand. Then they could make love until they were both exhausted as they had the night before.

Julia laughed out loud, feeling her face and her body heat up at her own thoughts. After spending four nights in Dirk's arms she had become a wanton hussy. Geno would be appalled. After making love with Dirk multiple times in one night, she was certain her husband had used her for casual sex, and saved the wild side of him for his girlfriends.

Anger surged through her, anger with Geno and with herself for being so naïve. She vowed never to be any mans fool again. She already knew Dirk was unlike Geno—or her father. Katie was right. Elias Morgan treated his wife and daughters like property, taking and using, giving nothing but heartache in return.

Knowing she only had one more day until she bared her soul to Dirk, when he came to her that night she welcomed him into her body, into her heart.

* * * *

For four nights, Dirk had taken pleasure in making love to Julia, watching her come apart in his arms, collapsing in a soft, sexy bundle afterwards. On this particular night it was he who came apart. She became the aggressor, skillfully draining the energy out of him. By the time she'd finished, he was plucked, drawn, and utterly happy.

Dirk believed the carefree spirit Julia displayed was due to relief that Edwards had been found, and the possibility of Gloria's murder solved. Not wanting to alarm her, he didn't mention Gunderson's reservations. After all, in his own words he'd said his doubts were merely speculation. Maybe Edward's did kill Gloria, taking Dirk off the hook, and putting an end to the travesty in his life. All he had to do was legalize custody of Megan, and start living the family life he'd always dreamed of having. A man and woman getting married, raising their kids, and sitting on the back porch growing old together.

He cradled Julia in his arms, and kissed her sleepy eyelids. She smelled of lilacs, like sweet musky woman.

"Are you tired?" he asked.

"Mmmm," she purred, snuggling into his shoulder.

"Are you satisfied?"

She chuckled. "You are a superb lover. I'd have to be real greedy to want anything more."

"Does that mean you want me to leave so you can go to sleep?"

Her arms around him tightened and she raised up to flick her tongue over his nipple.

He rolled over, pinning her beneath him. "You are a tempting little minx, but one of us has to see that you get some sleep." He feathered her face with kisses, ending up with the smiling curve of her mouth. "Goodnight my sweet, I'll see you in the morning."

* * * *

When Gunderson's car came up the drive again, Dirk watched the cloud of dust approaching like a bad omen. Beside him, Mack spit on the dry ground and swore.

"Them son-a-bitches just don't give up do they."

"As long as it's not Sanford," Dirk grunted.

"I thought they had everything solved when they found Edwards?"

"Well, maybe that's what he's here to tell me."

"Uh-huh… Right. In your wet dreams, buddy. They never give you a tax payers visit to share good news."

Dick hoped Mack was wrong.

He stepped through the rails to meet the car while Mack made a dash for the barn.

"Sorry to bother you again," Gunderson said, getting out of his car.

"No problem as long as you're bringing news I want to hear. Like Edward's note was legit."

Gunderson gave a rueful smile. "Don't know about that, but—"

The sheriff's hesitation made the skin across Dirk's back itch. "But what?"

"The steering wheel was void of fingerprints. Seems strange for a man to tidy up by wiping down the steering wheel before he puts a gun to his head and blows his brains out."

"Well, shit. Where does that leave the investigation?"

"It means I need to ask you a few more questions. I'd like to remind you, it's your legal right to tell me to take a flying leap into a pile of horse dung if you want."

Dirk clenched his teeth and shrugged. "Go ahead, I have nothing to hide."

Gunderson smiled. "Good, I was hoping you'd say that. See…the thing is…and correct me if I'm wrong, you were sending your wife money even though you weren't divorced and didn't have a legal obligation to?"

"She had my kids. That's obligation enough for me."

"I realize that. I just needed to hear you say it, and I need to know how much you gave her, and how often."

Dirk stared at him a moment. "Where are you going with this?"

"I'd rather you answer my questions first."

"Fine. I sent her two thousand a month."

Gunderson's brow's rose. "That seems generous enough. Starting when?"

"After I got out of prison. I wasn't too worried about it until then, since she cleaned out my bank account when she left."

"How much was that?"

"She made a withdrawal for around six thousand dollars."

Gunderson made a whistling sound "Musta made you mad, huh?"

"That doesn't even come close to describing how I felt. And it wasn't for the money—it was for taking my kids. Now, I hate to sound like a lawyer, but I hope you're planning to tell me where this line of questioning is going."

"I guess you deserve that. It seems she was renting a pretty fancy place in New York."

"Yeah, it was nice. I was there."

"Did she tell you it cost three thousand a month?"

"No, she didn't mention that, but considering New York, it seems logical. She must have been making a bundle playing concerts."

"Well, that's just the thing, her agent said she was making a little money here and there, but nothing steady, and nothing close to enough to pay that high rent and live too. Did she ever ask you for more money?"

Dirk snorted. "All the time. Instead of money, I sent clothes for the kids, gift cards to grocery stores, and even McDonalds certificates."

Gunderson chuckled. "You're one clever dude, Dirk. I'll bet you even tore the tags off the clothes so she couldn't return them."

"You know I did, it worked. Megan said they never went hungry—although she did complain about my taste in clothes. When Gloria brought the kids home, the only clothes that came with them were ones I sent."

"You sent clothes for Megan too? She's not even your kid."

Dirk gave Gunderson a hard look. "As far as I'm concerned she became *my kid* when I married her mother."

Gunderson blew out a huff of air. "Dirk, you have a short fuse, and it doesn't seem to take much to light it."

"Only when it comes to my kids."

"What about your wife?"

"I got over caring about her while I sat in that hell hole. Not because I blamed her for what I did—I have my own mind. You're well aware of my feelings there...so why don't you quit flappin' your jaw, Rick, and tell me why you really came out here."

"Yeah. Sorry, Dirk, I just had to feel you out a little first. Gloria had to be getting extra cash from somebody and apparently it wasn't you."

"How much cash?"

"Can't be sure. There were a few unexplained deposits—a couple of thousand here and there. The interesting thing is she paid her rent in cold cash every month. Her disgruntled landlord was real eager to supply that information since Gloria just all of a sudden quit paying her rent. You think she might have been dealing drugs?"

Dirk shook his head. "I find that hard to believe. She didn't do drugs. She didn't even drink. Said it messed up her mind and she couldn't play piano. I called her regularly, she never sounded stoned. From what I know, a lot of people who deal, also use."

"I tend to agree with you there. Plus, I think she came back here for something. It coincided with the stop of her cash flow. Then she ended up murdered. We're missing something"

Dirk stared off toward the mountains at the clouds rolling in. Looked like it could rain. They needed rain. It was too damn dry. The pastures were starting to turn brown.

He just wanted this whole mess with Gloria to go away. Why would anyone kill her? She didn't have many friends, but nobody hated her enough to kill her—other than him, of course. Her money flow stopped, so she came back to Colorado to start it up again then she ended up dead. Seemed like whoever was giving her money didn't want to pay any more, and she was here to squeeze that person. That sounded like—

"Blackmail. She must have been blackmailing somebody."

Gunderson's bushy brows rose, his eyes widened. "By golly, you might have something there. But who and why?"

"Find the who, and you'll probably find the why, and her killer."

* * * *

Julia got in the SUV and headed for Danango just as it started to rain. She put her wipers on to clear the large scattered drops from her windshield, noticing the sky overhead growing darker by the minute. She'd told Dirk that coming from Minnesota driving in rain didn't concern her, besides she was only driving eight miles to Danango. He'd still didn't like the idea of her going alone, offered to go with her while Rosa stayed with the kids. Julia declined his offer, she hadn't told him why she was leaving; only that she needed a couple of hours by herself. She suspected he knew it had something to do with the letter she'd received, but he had no good reason to stop her, though he made it clear he wasn't happy about it.

After the intimacy they'd enjoyed she had a bad feeling about keeping secrets from him. She looked forward to coming home after her meeting with Sandra Westerly and baring her soul to him. It had gone on long enough. If he truly loved her, he'd understand. *Understand she'd taken the position as nanny under false pretenses with full intention of applying for a medical position in Denver the first chance she got.* Was it too much to ask?

The clinic was dark except for a small interior security light. The rain, though steady, had turned in to a slow drizzle. Only one car, a newer Lincoln Continental, was parked in the far end of the lot. Sandra must be a doctor to afford a vehicle like that. If so, Julia wondered why she hadn't signed her name with the M.D. attached. Of course, there were lots of fields in the medical industry that paid well without an M.D. in the title.

Julia parked beside the Lincoln and got out, smiling. At the same time Sandra opened her door, got out, and hurried around her car. The woman had long black hair and a large floppy hat that she held close to her face against the rain.

Not until she was two feet away did Julia recognize the face. Before she realized what was happening, something akin to a bee sting pricked her arm. Julia's legs buckled, rain pelted her face, and the sky closed in on her like a black shroud.

CHAPTER NINETEEN

Dirk stood at the window behind the piano, staring out at the rain until nine o'clock, it was time to put the kids to bed. Forcing aside a pang of alarm, he trudged up the steps, got Jason and Christa tucked in, read them a story, kissed them both good-night and went back downstairs to continue standing vigil at the window.

Where was she? Did she slip off the road? Have a car accident?

At ten he called Rosa. He explained his worry about Julia, and asked Rosa if she had any idea where Julia could be. Rosa seemed to take a long moment to answer.

"Sometimes she helps people," Rosa said finally.

"Helps who?"

Again she hesitated.

"It's all right Rosa. I'm just worried about her. She said she'd be home by eight-thirty. It's pouring out there. Please tell me what you know."

"My family. Sometimes Julia helps my family."

Dirk swallowed at the lump in his throat. That would be like Julia to come to the aide of anyone in need. "Rosa, could you call your family members and see if anyone knows where she is?"

"Yes. Yes. I do that and call you back."

"Do you know who Sandra Westerly is?"

"No. I do not know of her."

Dirk thanked her, hung up, and called Gus to ask him to come over and stay with the kids. Gus was there in five minutes.

"What's up," he asked, shaking rain out of his coat.

"Julia went in to Danango at six-thirty. She said she'd only be gone two hours. I'm concerned and thought I'd drive in and see if I can find her."

"You're gonna have a hard time seeing anything until this rain lets up."

"I know, but she might have slipped in the ditch and got stuck."

He didn't like the look his father gave him and he wasn't in a mood to hear any lectures. As he started walking out the door the phone rang. He picked it up before the second ring.

It was Rosa. No one she knew had seen Julia tonight. He made a mental note to find out just exactly what kind of help Julia had been giving Rosa's family. In the meantime, he jumped in his truck and headed for Danango.

By the time he got home, two and a half hours later, the rain had all but stopped. He had literally driven every street in town, and found no sign of her white SUV. With a heavy heart he checked the garage. It was empty.

Rubbing a weary hand over his face he walked in the house, praying that she'd called. Gus drug himself up off the sofa, shaking his head.

After his father left, Dirk sat down at the kitchen table and dropped his head in his hands. He hadn't had much sleep the last few nights, he was wrung out, frustrated, angry, and scared. Maybe he should just go to bed and try not to worry. Maybe she'd be home by morning.

Or maybe she left like Gloria did.

He got to his feet, swearing under his breath at his wayward thoughts. There's no way she'd do that. Especially after what they'd shared together the last five days.

She promised she'd never leave without telling him. Something horrible had happened—he could feel it.

In his office, he got out a Denver phone book. There were six Westerlys listed, but no Sandra. Hell, it could be under her husband's name for all he knew. He glanced at the clock. It was after 1 A.M. If he called anybody now, they'd think he was a crackpot. He considered calling Gunderson, but abandoned that thought in a hurry. Instead he went up to his room hoping to get some sleep so he could continue his search fresh in the morning.

She better be home by then or there would be hell to pay.

Who was he kidding? If he wanted to be truly honest with himself, he didn't care where she was, or what she was doing just as long as she was safe.

That's when a thought hit him that could have chilled him in a hundred degree heat. A killer out there. Certainly Gloria and Carl Edwards were isolated incidences. Gloria had likely been involved in a blackmailing scheme, what if Julia knew something. Had she given him a strange look when he'd mentioned the blackmail aspect?

Sleep eluded him as his mind paced through every possible scenario.

None of them were pretty.

* * * *

Julia woke up with a throbbing pain in her head. It hurt to try to think.

She smelled coffee.

With considerable effort, she managed to bring a hand up to massage her temples. A dull jingling sound played with her senses. Sharp stabs entered her head with the light when she opened her eyes. Something heavy circled her hand; no it was manacled around her wrist. When she raised her arm to examine it a chain drug along. Not a real heavy chain, the kind you'd use to restrain a large dog. Confusion fogged her brain. She had to get home, Dirk would be worried. She had to call Melody...ask her to tell

Dirk about the man in the barn. Coffee would help clear her head.

She recalled a really bad dream. It was raining, a woman stepped out of a car...walking toward her...long hair...a big hat...couldn't think...had to sleep.

* * * *

Dirk sat at the kitchen table drinking black coffee, waiting for Rosa. She was already a half hour late. He planned to question her in depth about who Julia helped—and why.

He'd already called every Westerly in the phone book. No one knew of a Sandra—at least that's what they yelled in his car—no one was happy to hear his voice that early on a Saturday morning.

Saturday.

Rosa wasn't coming.

Dirk ran a frustrated hand over his beard stubbled face. He'd already heard the kids rumbling around upstairs. He had to make breakfast. What would he tell them?

Where the hell was she?

Gus came in the door with Mack at his heels.

"Any word?" Gus asked.

Dirk shook his head, looked up, and watched his father help himself to the coffee. Concern etched the old man's face. Could it be that Julia had gotten to him too?

"Tell me what you want me to do, and I'll do it." Mack volunteered.

Dirk stared at his loyal hired hand a moment, thinking. "Drive in to Danango, check every street, every driveway. I did it last night, but it was dark and raining. A white Land Rover shouldn't be hard to spot. On the way to town, check the ditches on both sides of the road. If you can't see clearly, get out of your truck and look. If that doesn't work, talk to people, anyone but the sheriff at this point.

Mack made a face. "No need to worry about that on my count."

"I hear you. You find out anything at all suspicious, call me. If the phone is busy, call David. Have either of you talked to him this morning?"

Gus answered. "Yeah. Carrie said to send the kids over. She'll make them breakfast—and they can stay as long as you need them to. She thinks Megan will be happy to help take care of Marisa."

As though summoned, David came in the door. "Any news?" He looked around at the solemn group. "Guess not. Carrie sent me over to get the kids. Anything I can do?"

"Thanks, but I reckon Carrie will need your help," Dirk said.

Mack filled a cup of coffee and headed for the door. "Well, I already ate. I'm outta here."

"Wait," Dirk said. "When you talk to people, see if anyone knows a Sandra Westerly. Julia got a letter from her yesterday."

When Mack left, Gus took a seat across from Dirk. "You think that letter might have something to do with her disappearing?"

Dirk shook his head. "I don't know. I just don't want to miss anything. It had a return address on it, but I don't remember what it was. Twenty-First Street or something."

"Eight-oh-nine, Twenty-First Avenue South," Gus supplied.

Dirk's gaze shot toward his father. "You remembered that?"

Gus shrugged, a slight grin curving his mouth. "It's a long walk from the mailbox."

"I don't suppose you were able to see through the envelope?"

"It was thin, one sheet of paper, hand written."

"That really should piss me off," Dirk grumbled.

"Yeah, and if I'd been able to read it, you'd probably jump across the table and kiss me."

Dirk dropped his head in his hands, covering a slight laugh. "Shit, you're probably right. I'll check the address out." He released a deep sigh. "If you think of anything else, let me know. I have some calls to make in my office." The first one was going to be to Julia's psychiatrist.

He did one other thing first. He went into Julia's room. He tried to avoid looking at the neatly made bed, the jeans she'd worn the day before laying across a chair, the half glass of water on the nightstand. In the bathroom was her toothbrush, toothpaste, makeup kit. If she came back, he was violating her personal space.

If she came back.

A tight band closed around his throat making it hard to breathe. Why was this happening to him? Why now? He loved her, dammit. If she was all right, why didn't she call? Because she couldn't, or because she didn't want to? Had he pushed her too far by saying he loved her?

Her things were everywhere. He took solace in that. She wouldn't just leave without taking her clothes.

He checked the closet and found the sexy clinging dress she'd worn the night they drove to Breckenridge. He fingered the stretchy material, remembering his eagerness to get it off of her; she was just as anxious to help shed his clothes. His vision clouded as he studied the other clothes, neatly hung on separate hangers. There weren't many. He recalled her wearing nearly everything there at one time or another.

He picked up the suitcase on the floor—something in it. He swung it to the bed, zipped it open and found a matching smaller suitcase in side. He opened that one and found it empty.

He looked back in the closet. Something was missing. The smaller old-fashioned boxy overnight case she'd taken with her when she left with David and Carrie.

He made another quick search of the closet. Shoes— the strappy saddles, sneakers, a pair of black dress pumps, and one other pair of cream-colored flats. On the upper shelf he found a couple of folded shopping bags, one from a toy store in Denver, another from a music kiosk.

Where was the overnight bag?

He went through the rest of the room, under the bed, drawers, back to the bathroom, anyplace large enough to hold that case.

He finally stood up and looked around. Why would she have taken that with her? Was she planning to stay overnight? She'd left through the garage door so he hadn't seen her leave. He spotted the jeans lying over the chair, picked them up and went through the pockets.

In the hip pocket he found the envelope she'd received in the mail. With shaking hands he pulled it out.

It was empty.

That meant she had taken the letter with her, and her leaving likely had something to do with the contents. After one more hurried search for the overnight case, he left the room and went to his office.

After booting up his computer, he pulled out Julia's original application and compared the handwriting from Sandra's envelope. No match. Not even close. The writing on the envelope was more boxy, scribbled, actually making it tricky to read at first glance. The letters were thick, like the writer had pressed hard with the pen. He picked up his own pen and wrote the name on his pad. His handwriting was similar. The letter could have been addressed by a man. That was a long shot.

He pulled up Map Quest and entered the address—no match. The address was likely bogus—dead end.

Sandra Westerly probably didn't exist, so it was nobody Julia knew—not good.

What could have been in that letter, from somebody she didn't know, to make Julia pack an overnight bag and leave?

He dialed the number he'd saved for Katie Benson. An answering machine picked up announcing the office was closed on Saturday. It gave a number to call in case of an emergency. He jotted the number down then dialed information and asked for Katie's number. It was unlisted—no surprise there. Telling the operator it was an emergency proved futile.

Biting back his frustration, he dialed the emergency number he'd gotten from the machine. A live person from a mental health clinic answered the phone

"I need to speak with Katie Benson," he said.

"She's not here. Are you a patient?" He got the feeling if he said no he would be directed to a psychiatrist on call. "Yes," he lied. "I need to speak to her as quickly as possible."

"What is your name please?"

He decided he might have better luck giving his real name. After all, Katie Benson, author of Julia's application, was well aware who he was.

"Dirk Travis."

"Mr. Travis, are you sure you can't talk to someone on call here?"

"Yes, I'm sure. I need to talk to Ms. Benson."

"What is the number where you can be reached, please?"

Dirk rattled off the number.

"That's an out of town number," she said. "Mr. Travis, I'm sorry but I have to ask—are you suicidal?"

Dirk wondered if he'd get to talk to Katie Benson quicker if he said yes. He could also find an ambulance at his doorstep.

"No, I'm not suicidal, but this could be a matter of life and death," he nearly choked on the words. "Could you please have Ms. Benson call me immediately?"

She must have sensed the trauma in his voice. "She has a pager. Please stay by your phone."

When Dirk disconnected, he stared down at his shaking hands. Jesus, what was happening to him? He needed a break. He had to eat something.

He got up, stretched his back, tucked the cordless receiver in his pocket, and headed for the kitchen. The house was empty. At least he didn't have to explain to the kids were Anna was. He was sure, for a while, they'd be too enamored with the new baby to realize Julia wasn't home.

He popped a couple of pieces of bread in the toaster. When they came up, he took the browned slices back to his office without bothering to put anything on them.

He'd taken one bite when the phone rang.

He plucked the receiver out of his pocket like a drowning man grabbing a lifeline. "Hello, Dirk here."

"Dirk, it's Katie Benson." Her voice had a tone of alarm that disturbed him. Now that he had her on the line he wasn't sure what to say"

"Ms. Benson, I—I'm kind of grasping at straws here, but I need to ask some questions about Julia Morgan. I understand she's one of your patients."

"She's not a patient, Dirk. Is she okay?"

Not a patient? That stopped him cold. "No, she's not okay. She's missing."

"Oh my God. When? How long?"

"Since yesterday. If she's not your patient, who are you? I know you filled out her application papers. Before I tell you any more I need some straight answers, Ms. Benson."

"Call me Katie. She's my sister. Where is she?"

"Lord I wish I knew. She left yesterday around six-thirty. She said she'd be gone a couple of hours. It was raining. I have people out looking for her but—"

"Is there any particular reason she left?" Katie asked.

"I don't know. She didn't say, but Thursday she got a letter from a Sandra Westerly, postmarked in Denver."

"What did the letter say?"

"I didn't read it. Do you know the woman?"

A heavy sigh came through the phone. "I never heard of her."

"Well, that makes sense. I checked the name and address out in Denver and neither seems to exist."

"Dirk, sit down and take a deep breath. You sound like you're ready to collapse. I have to make a phone call and I'll call you back in a couple of minutes. Don't worry, we'll find her. Stay by the phone."

Katie hung up before he could comment. *How did she know he was standing up?* He dropped into his chair and stared at his dry toast in distaste. Maybe he was ready to collapse. The stress was getting to him.

Her sister. Katie was a psychiatrist and was Julia's sister. It shocked him to realize how little he knew about his elusive nanny. Hopefully, Katie knew something about Julia that would tell him where she was.

He had one other call to make. He punched in the Los Angeles number then laid his head back on the chair waiting for Bella Travis to pick up. When she finally answered on the fourth ring, he sat up told her who he was and, for the first time in life said, "Mom, I need you."

She shocked him, saying okay, before he even told her why. After a brief explanation, he summed it up by telling her he needed someone to look after the twins for a couple of days. Again she surprised him by sounding excited. "I'll be there on the first flight out of here. It sounds like you're busy, so I'll have your father pick me up."

"Thanks so much, mom. You want me to call dad and tell him?"

She gave a sweet lilting laugh. "And take all my fun away? Not on your life."

"Charlie Mack can pick you up if Dad refuses to do it."

"Trust me, son, he'll be there. By the way, he's been keeping me up to date on what's been going on at the ranch."

As soon as Dirk hung up, and before he had time to fully comprehend his mother's last statement, the phone still in his hand rang.

"Yeah, Dirk here."

It was Mack.

"No sign of her car," Mack said. "But there's a shiny new Lincoln Continental in the clinic parking lot, and nobody seems to know who it belongs to. It may not mean anything, but that's a pretty expensive car to be abandoned in this neighborhood.

"There's nobody at the clinic?"

"Nope. Closed up tighter than a duck's ass. You want me to break into the car?"

"Not just yet. Call me back in twenty minutes and I'll let you know. What's the license number?"

Mack gave him the number and hung up, promising to call back.

Dirk took a bite of crusty bread, starting to get his appetite back. He'd just swallowed the second bite when the phone rang again.

It was Katie. "This may or may not be good news," she said, "but I'm pretty sure I know where she is."

"Is she all right?"

"I hope so. Geno, her ex-husband took a leave from work. He told coworkers Julia had agreed to go on a little getaway with him, and they were going to try to patch things up between them."

Dirk's heart slammed with alarming force into his chest. He couldn't breathe. Katie's voice broke through his shock.

"Dirk? Are you still with me?"

"Yes. Yes, I'm here. Sorry that news just took me by surprise. I didn't realize she was planning to get back together with her ex."

Katie gave a bitter laugh. "Believe me, she isn't. Geno Campanili is a devious man. He's covering his bases by passing that information around work. The good news is I'm sure I know where he took her. His buddy has a ski lodge near Breckinridge."

"Would he hurt her?"

Katie took too long to answer. "God, I hope not. She

keeps telling me he's not violent, but I've always had my doubts about that."

"Tell me how to get to the lodge, I'll go get her."

"I was there once a few years back, I think I can find it as long as I go in daylight hours, but I'd never be able to give directions. It's near the top of the Banger ski slope, and extremely isolated. Geno's pretty thick with Randy, the owner, so I'm reluctant to ask him for a map, he might just tip Geno off. If you can pick me up at the Denver airport, we can head straight out from there."

Dirk would have preferred to go immediately, but he couldn't see that he had a choice. "Yes, okay. When?"

"There's a flight leaving here at one-thirty. I'll call you from the airport with the ETA. We have a one-hour time difference and the flight takes two hour. I have to race if I'm going to make it. And Dirk?"

"Yeah?"

"Do you have a gun?"

"Yeah."

"Bring it. I can't take mine since I won't have time to check luggage. Do you have a cell phone?"

"No, you can't get a signal out here, so I never bothered getting one."

"Then see if you can find Julia's so I can contact you when I get to the airport in Denver. I doubt she's carrying it with her since I cautioned her not to use it.

"It's there, I saw it."

"Good. I'll wear red and I'll call you in about an hour."

Five minutes later, Mack called. "Okay boss. The car was rented by a Geno Campanili, four days ago in Denver."

"How the hell did you find that out?"

"You don't want to know."

CHAPTER TWENTY

Fully awake now, Julia sat up in the bed and pulled on the chain. It was long, probably twenty feet, just enough to reach the bathroom. She leaned over and saw it was padlocked to the massive wooden bedpost. By the looks of it, she may as well be chained to a tree.

The pain in her head had settled to a managing throb. Coffee. Coffee would take care of it.

She tried to pry her hand loose from the shackle, but it was just tight enough not to cut off her circulation. Beneath it, an ace bandage circled her wrist. Likely, she assumed, to prevent any telltale marks.

Her head shot up when she heard a movement from the doorway.

"Good morning. Want some coffee?"

Julia glared into the laughing, amber eyes of Geno Campanili.

"Have you lost your mind, Geno? What do you think you're doing?"

"I'm having a little tête-à-tête with my wife."

"Ex-wife. There are laws against kidnapping, Geno."

"Did I force you to come here?"

"Just let me go, and I'll forget I ever saw you." She threw the covers aside and swung her feet out of the bed, looking down she noticed they were bare. A long cotton nightgown shrouded her body. At the same time she realized she was naked underneath. Anger surged through her.

"Where are my clothes?" she hissed.

"In the other room. You want some coffee?"

"I want my clothes and this thing—" she held up her hand, "taken off my wrist."

"My, my, you've become feisty. You used to be such a sweet little thing. What happened to you?"

"You, Geno, you happened to me."

"Now, honey, seriously. I didn't bring you here to fight. I'll get your coffee."

When he left the room, she yanked as hard as she could on her tether. It was useless. While the chain was lightweight, it was impossible to break free without a tool—or a key. She got up and walked to the bathroom, dragging the chain behind her. It had more than enough leeway to do what she had to do, even take a shower if she'd been so inclined. In fact, she could do anything but close and lock the door.

When she came back out she found Geno lounging in a fat-cushioned log chair. A delicious smelling cup of coffee waited for her on the nightstand.

She sat back down on the bed, massaging her chained wrist. "My employer will be looking for me, you know."

"No, he won't. You wrote him a nice letter explaining you wanted a week or two off to try reconciling with your ex-husband. Don't you remember? You mailed it at the post office in Danango, last night. He should have it by tomorrow."

Julia's heartbeat accelerated along with her anger. She couldn't even begin to imagine Dirk's fury. Would he believe she'd written it?

"There won't be any reconciliation."

Geno shrugged. "Doesn't matter. As long as you're pregnant by the time you leave here you can do whatever you want."

She stared at him, dumbfounded. "You intend to rape me until I'm pregnant?"

Geno laughed. "Have I ever raped you?"

"Well, there's not much chance of me getting pregnant."

"You could be pregnant already."

She swallowed, gaping at him, confused.

He got up and walked out of the room talking over his shoulder. "You know, sexually, you're about as exciting unconscious as you are wide awake."

Julia stared after him, forcing herself to breathe. He couldn't have. She'd know. Wouldn't she? Obviously he knew about the trust her father set up. Apparently he didn't know about the depovera shot. If she hadn't been so furious, she might have laughed.

She glared at the cup of coffee, wanting it badly, but knowing it was likely laced with sleeping powder, so he could... God, she was in the middle of a nightmare.

Her breathing grew heavy with anger. She picked up the coffee cup and heaved it across the room where it shattered against the far wall.

She walked toward the door but the chain stopped her two feet from it. She looked back to survey her prison. The bulky rustic dresser, chest and nightstand along with the chairs were made out of the same heavy log design as the bed. She realized she remembered this place. It was Randy's ski lodge.

She'd been here before—with Geno.

Since she couldn't see him she called out. "You're wasting your time. Geno, I can't get pregnant. I had a depo shot, you fool."

"Are you talking about the one you requested in the hospital?" He called from somewhere in the other room."

"Yes."

His laughter filled the lodge. "Honey, you can't believe everything you read."

Julia leaned against the wall, trying to comprehend. "She read the chart herself. She'd had a depovera shot. *Can't believe everything you read.* Certainly he had the power to fake her records, but why?

"Why would you bother faking that?" she asked.

He came back in the room, walking past her, chewing on a piece of toast, slathered with orange marmalade. He sat down and licked the marmalade off his fingers. "I didn't know you were going to divorce me, sweetheart. I wanted you pregnant again. I figured if you thought you were safe, you wouldn't bother with birth control. My question is why did you ask for a depo shot in the first place?"

"Isn't that obvious? I wanted to make sure I wouldn't have another pregnancy by you."

"You just couldn't stand to see me get what was rightfully mine, could you?"

Julia walked back, and collapsed on the bed. "I guess that means you know about Daddy's trust."

Geno gave an evil laugh. "I don't know what horrible thing you did to him after your mother died, but the old bastard didn't want his darling daughters to have anything. He couldn't stomach leaving it to charity either. You should be glad I got involved, otherwise there's no telling what he might have done with it. Of course, he didn't know he was going to drop over from an aneurysm seven months later.

Julia felt her stomach lurch. She closed her eyes, attempting to control the mounting nausea. Right now she couldn't decide whom she loathed more, Geno or her father. "What do mean you got involved?" She didn't want to ask, but she had to know.

Geno gave a laugh she had come to detest. "My dear, I helped him write it up. Have you read it closely—the fine print? It gives the father of your child a third, you a third, and the kid a third, controlled by the father of course. I don't even have to raise the kid."

Julia's nightmare became more horrific be the minute. Unwanted tears stung her eyes. "Then why were you so angry when I got pregnant?"

"Angry? Just how do you think you got pregnant?"

Julia rubbed her brow. Her headache was returning big time.

"You replace my pills with placebo then acted angry so you had an excuse to screw around?"

"Something like that. Actually, I didn't want you to know how excited I was. It did piss me off when there were two of them though, that meant they each got a quarter, leaving me with only a fourth."

"You did something to me that night, so I'd abort, didn't you?"

"How evil do you think I am? They were my babies. I did everything in my power to keep you from losing them. It was your fault you miscarried. You messed everything up. Twins usually come early, they would have been born by now. I need that money Julia. Even a fourth is a good sum. You left me with a pile of bills."

They were his bills, but what was the use of arguing with a misguided reprobate. She wanted to hurt him. Physically. Mentally. She had taken an oath to heal, to help people, but she wanted him to suffer pain as intense as she had when she lost her babies. "How do you know I'm not pregnant already—by somebody else?"

Again that hateful laugh. "We haven't even been divorced three months. You're a frigid fucking prude. It took me eight months to charm those god-awful cotton underpants off of you. I'm a pro."

She glared at him while he slurped marmalade off his toast. "You're an ass, Geno. That's what you are." She didn't dare tell him she could indeed be pregnant. If he even suspected, he'd make her abort. Besides, if he got angry enough, there's no telling what he'd do. "How long do you intend to keep me here?"

"As long as it takes. Shouldn't be more than a few days. You see, being a doctor gives me access to your medical records. You should be in heat right about now, and as soon as that little test turns blue, you're free to go. I know you won't get rid of it. It's just not in you to kill a baby."

"No, but I could kill its father."

Geno snorted. "You're a pathetic wimp, Julia. Those are your own father's words. Now. Katie, at least, she's got some spunk. I'd give my left nut to get her ass in my hands. I'll bet a hundred bucks she's not wearing fricking cotton."

"You're such an arrogant jerk, I don't know why I ever married you."

His smile vanished, he got to his feet and moved toward her, like a cat stalking a mouse. Bile rose to her throat and her stomach clenched. She could tell by the gratification in his eyes how much he enjoyed her fear.

He grabbed her by the upper arms and pulled her to her feet. He brought her face to within inches of his. "You married me because you wanted the best. When I operate I hold the power of life and death in my hands. I can perform miracles!"

* * * *

On the way to Denver to pick up Katie, Dirk stopped at a Wal-Mart. He wanted a picture of Julia in case they had to ask anyone about her. He took his camera in and asked the photo department to develop the pictures. He'd only taken twelve, including those of Star's filly.

"I'm sorry, sir," the pimply-faced clerk said, talking around a wad of gum, "there are fifty-eight pictures in here. It's going to take at least an hour."

He didn't have an hour. "I only took twelve," he insisted, checking his watch, trying to temper his frustration."

The clerk popped her gum. "Well then somebody else must have taken some."

"I didn't see any others."

She grinned. "Maybe you don't know a lot about digitals. Even if you delete pictures sometimes they stay on the card until you copy over them. If you want copies of them all, it's gonna take an hour, maybe longer."

Dirk plowed a hand through his already mussed hair. Most likely they were of the kids when they were little. "Fine. Print them all. I'll pay in advance and you can send them to me."

"Can do." She handed him a photo envelope and a pen. "Just fill this out, name, address, phone number."

"Can you print out just one picture while I'm doing this? The third one—of the twelve I took."

She pointed to his left. "You can do it on that little machine over there."

"I've never used that thing and I'm in a hurry. Could you please do it for me?"

She shrugged. "Sure, no problem. It'll take me couple of minutes to download your chip anyway. I'll give it back so you can use your camera."

By the time Dirk had the envelope filled out, she'd rung up his bill and handed him a four by six glossy of Julia, smelling a flower held by Christa.

Dirk stared at the photo for a long moment. He brushed at his eyes with the back of his hand. She was so beautiful. Her face reflected an aura of sweet innocence.

If Geno Campanili harmed one finger on her body he was a dead man.

An hour later, Dirk got his first look as Katie Benson as she walked through security, toting a bright fuchsia overnight bag. Even if she hadn't worn red, he'd have known her. Not that she looked anything like Julia, plus being shorter by at least two inches, she walked swiftly with the same air of confidence he'd perceived when talking with her on the phone. Any lady who asked him to bring his gun had her head screwed on straight—at least he hoped she did. And what a head she had. It was mobbed by a halo of riotous brown curls. Besides the red t-shirt, she wore white jeans and sneakers, and carried a woven handbag large enough to house a VW. He wasn't surprised to see every male she passed turn for a second look.

Apparently she recognized him too because she walked straight toward him. Her hand stretched to greet him.

"Hi, you must be Dirk."

He smiled. "You're Katie Benson, the elusive sister. I wish we were meeting under different circumstances."

"Trust me, so do I. My sister is the world to me. If that arrogant monster has laid one finger on her he'll have hell to pay."

"I'll help you send him there, Katie. The car's in the parking garage. You want me to take your bag?"

She gave him a sidelong glance. "You'd actually pull this pink bag for me?"

Dirk shrugged. "I don't know why not? I'll even carry your gunny sack bag if you like."

Katie made a sound like she'd just eaten something really tasty. She grinned. "Thanks, but I can manage it."

When they reached his truck, he hefted her bag in the back and held the door for her. She gave him a raised eyebrow look.

As he made his way out of the parking lot, she glanced at her watch. "You know the way?" she asked.

"I can get us to Breckinridge, but you'll have to direct from there."

"Pray to God I can find it. How do you think we are for time? Will we make it in daylight."

"Shouldn't take more than two and a half hours. As long as we don't get held up at the Eisenhower tunnel we should get there by six-thirty. Doesn't get dark until almost nine."

Katie blew a huff of air that rearranged the curls on her bangs. "I'm glad you're driving, I need to relax. I've been riding on an adrenaline rush since you called this morning. Just give me a few minutes. Then we can talk."

Katie laid her head back, but Dirk got the feeling she wasn't sleeping. He'd told her on the phone about finding Geno's car in Danango, solidifying the idea that he grabbed Julia and took her to Breckinridge. He still had too many questions crowding his mind. He allowed Katie ten minutes to rest.

"Just how dangerous is Geno Campanili?" he asked.

Katie took a deep, shaky breath and sat up. "I'm not sure. I'm going with the feeling that he won't hurt her. He wants to reconcile with her, but his intentions are anything but honorable. How much do you know about Julia?"

Dirk made a snorting sound. "Enough to fill a thimble. She's been pretty close-mouthed about her life. I know she's divorced and had a miscarriage of twins. Beyond that, nothing, except—" he stopped himself. He wasn't ready to tell Katie that he'd fallen in love with his nanny. "Maybe you could fill in some blanks."

"Except what?" she asked.

Katie Benson was a sharp as her sister.

"Just some…personal things."

She studied him while he made the turn onto Interstate seventy. It made him uncomfortable. His hands clenched on the steering wheel.

"Okay," she said, drawing the word out. "I guess that doesn't have anything to do with finding her."

Dirk gave her a sullen glare. "Quit reading my mind while I'm driving. It makes me edgy."

Katie laughed. "Sorry, hazard of the trade. I'm getting the feeling that you really care about Julia. Trust me, Dirk, I'm not knocking it. In fact it was my idea she come here."

"Is that why you filled out her application and sent the references?"

Katie grimaced. "Oops."

Dirk smiled. He liked this woman. "You want to tell me about that?"

"No, but I will. Julia was depressed after her

miscarriage. She divorced Geno right afterwards. I think she blamed him for the miscarriage."

"He caused her to miscarry?"

Katie shook her head. "I don't know. She's awfully quiet when it comes to Geno. I suspected he was abusing her, if not physically, certainly emotionally. I think she was embarrassed to admit it—even to me. That's not uncommon, even for highly educated people."

"I am going to kill him."

"Step to the back of the line."

Dirk swerved when a PT Cruiser suddenly cut over in front of him, narrowly missing his right fender. He swore, and Katie gripped the dash. It reminded him of Julia.

"I see you have idiot drivers in Colorado too. Not very bright when you're maneuvering mountain passes."

"The last thing I need now is an accident. I already have to push the speed limit to make it in time."

"You won't hear me complaining."

After a few minutes he realized she never did explain why she faxed the nanny application."

"Why did *you* decide she needed to take a nanny position in Colorado?"

He didn't like the way she took time to think about her answer. He got the feeling she was deciding how much to tell him.

"Well," she started. "They worked together and Geno was her superior. After she divorced him, he made it impossible for her to stay on. It just added to her depression. By chance, I had a layover in Denver—the firm I work for has an office here—I glanced though a paper, found your ad, and figured it was a good way to get Julia back to work, and far away from Geno."

"What kind of work did they do?"

Katie's gaze flicked over him. She turned to stare back out the window. "Geno is a surgeon, one of the most skilled and highly acclaimed in the country. Julia worked at the same hospital. If you need to know more, you'll have to ask her."

"I had a feeling she worked in the medical field, or teaching. She's so good with the kids. And," he added smiling, "she delivered my employees' baby on the way to the hospital. They believe it might have died if she hadn't been there."

"That's Julia. She's good at everything she does. Did you ever get her to ride a horse?"

Dirk spent the next half hour telling Katie about Julia's accomplishments and some of the things going on in his life.

They approached the Eisenhower tunnel, and due to construction inside, had to wait fifteen agonizing minutes for a pilot car. From there it took only fifteen minutes to make the turn going south on state highway nine.

* * * *

As Julia stared out the window at the sun, a large red ball hovering over the treetops, tears flooded her eyes. Geno had given her an ultimatum—eat the food laced with sleeping powder, or take another shot in the arm. Her choice. The shot would put her out twice as long, and she'd wake up with an extreme headache again.

Anger simmered deep in her gut. He expected her to comply without argument as she's always done—to keep the peace. She stared at the plate of cold eggs and her anger came to a boil. She'd already exhausted every possible way to free herself from the chain, her only option as she saw it was to barricade herself in the bathroom. She might starve, but that was better than being abused by Geno. The bathroom door was built of heavy lumber. It would take some effort to break it down.

She made yet one more search of the drawers that she could reach, looking for a weapon of some sort, and once again came up empty. Geno had been quite thorough; going so far as to remove the lamp from the nightstand. She found nothing solid to wrap her fingers around. He'd even given her a spoon instead of a fork to eat with.

The chance of her being rescued was slim. Nobody knew where she was, and tomorrow, when Dirk received Geno's letter, if in fact the letter existed, Dirk would be so angry the last thing he'd want to do was find her—if he believed Geno.

She heard Geno moving around in the next room, and knew she didn't have much time. Heart pounding, she grabbed the blanket and a pillow from the bed threw them in the bathroom and as an afterthought, took the toast and the spoon from her plate. She was extremely hungry, and figured he hadn't bothered drugging the toast—as long as she scrapped the marmalade from it.

In the bathroom she pushed the door shut as far as the chain would allow, sat on the blanket and braced her back against the door using the pillow for a cushion. When she tried to eat, her stomach didn't welcome the dry toast. After only two bites she set it aside.

"Julia?"

The sound of Geno's voice from the other side of the door ripped like a knife through her. She stuck out her feet to wedge them against the stool. It was a good fit. He would have a hard time pushing the door open with her body and legs braced against it.

"Julia, come out. It's time for you to eat."

"Go away," she said, trying to keep her voice from quaking.

"Julia, Julia. What's become of you? I don't know this belligerent person you've turned into. I don't like it!" He finished with a vile curse and a fist hitting the plank above her head.

A sudden thud jerked the door behind her as he obviously threw his shoulder against it. Thankfully she was able to hold it shut. Then he became incensed, swearing loudly, ramming the door repeatedly. She knew by the slur of his words he'd been drinking.

All of a sudden it was quiet. She envisioned him searching for a wood-chopping axe, and knew it was only a matter of time. Anger couldn't stop the frightened tears from clouding her eyes. He wouldn't kill her, at least not intentionally. He needed her alive—and pregnant—to get his hands on her money. If he marked her up in any way his plan of saying she'd come willingly wouldn't ring true.

He seemed to be gone a long time. What if he just drove away and left her? How long would it take for somebody to find her? No, he had a mission—he wouldn't leave until he'd done his evil deed.

She thought about Dirk, Christa, and Jason. Her tears flowed in earnest, Christa would be asking for her. They'd all think she let them down, even Megan. She reached for a scrap of toilet paper to blow her nose, and that's when Geno struck again.

The door moved behind her, not a lot, but enough for him to wedge the flat end of a 2x4 in the gap. She heard a rattling sound and realized he was pulling on her chain. Before she could wrap it around something, her hand was drawn up to the gap in the door.

Panic seized her as she tried to pull her hand back to no avail. A sharp prick punctured the soft flesh between her thumb and index finger. He released the chain and she brought her hand up to rub at the pain. A small dot of blood smeared onto her fingers.

He'd given her a shot.

His evil laugher came through the door like a villain in an old horror movie. The man was deranged. Expecting instant darkness as before, she was surprised when it didn't happen.

"What did you give me, you bastard?"

"Julia, sweetheart, such language coming from your pretty little mouth. You really need to get away from that backwoods hick farmer. Your father would wash your mouth out in the toilet."

Nausea rolled up in Julia's stomach. Why had she ever told Geno about that? "What kind of shot did you give me?" she asked again.

"Have you been reading your medical journals? Are you familiar with Renobazel?"

A small sound escaped her throat. Renobazel was a test drug for Parkinson's patients. It worked to bring them temporarily out of their condition but the side effects were horrendous. They went into intermittent bouts of deep sleep and Schizophrenia that became increasingly worse with each dose. It never made it out of the test labs. She could only guess where Geno got his hands on it.

Already she felt the numbing effects.

Her last thoughts were of Dirk. Surely he wouldn't want anything to do with her after Geno finished what he had started. She put her hands over her belly, praying she was already pregnant—with Dirk's baby. Fortunately, Geno didn't suspect she might already have had sex. If she'd felt like laughing, she could have found humor in that.

The thought couldn't stop her wrenching sobs as she buried her face in the pillow and let her grief pour out.

Tomorrow Dirk would get the letter Geno had written. She envisioned him tearing it to shreds in a rage.

How could she blame him. She'd made a promise not to leave without talking to him first. As far as he knew, she'd broken her promise and behaved exactly like Gloria and his mother.

* * * *

They both kept a wary eye on the sun while Katie watched for signs directing them to the ski area. It was well marked and they found it easily enough. Directly after that turn she had him take another right. Multiple roads turned off going into private homes along the slopes. They made several wrong choices and each time ended up back where they started.

Dirk tried to stay calm. Following her instructions, then returning to the main road repeatedly while the sun stole their daylight.

"There!" she cried suddenly. "That's the turn. I'd forgotten about that little bridge. It's about three miles to the top. Where's your gun."

"In a case, under your seat. How much do you know about guns?"

"Enough," she said, plunking the case from beneath the seat. "I go to a shooting range once a week. I tried to talk Julia into going with me, but she wouldn't go."

Within seconds, she had the gun out, inspected it, found the safety, then flicked it on and off. "A 38 Smith and Wesson? It's a good gun. I'm surprised you're allowed to own this."

"I'm not. There, I see Julia's white Land Rover!"

CHAPTER TWENTY ONE

Dirk cut his lights and stopped about twenty yards from the house. He stretched out his hand. "Give me the gun."

"You could get into trouble. Let me keep it. I know how to use it.

"Fine," Dirk said. "If we have to shoot him, I'll give it back to you." In the growing darkness, Dirk saw the hint of a smile on her lips as she placed the weapon in his waiting fingers. "We're keeping a positive attitude, that's good, right?"

Katie reached for the door handle. "Yeah, that's good. A plan is good too. What's your plan?"

Dirk looked up at the two-story log home. In the center of the perimeter a solar yard light flickered on and off, moments away from generating to full solar. In the house, two rooms appeared to have lights on.

"This place is built like a fortress," Katie commented.

"Has to be," Dirk explained. "They get a lot of snow up here. Let's see if we can look in the windows. Maybe we can locate where they are inside, and make sure he's alone with her."

"I hadn't thought of that."

"Exactly why I have the gun. We don't know what we're facing here, Katie. Maybe you should wait in the car."

"Maybe we should knock on the door and yell trick or treat when he answers."

"Might not be a bad idea." Dirk opened his door, careful not to make a sound while Katie followed suit. He walked the twenty yards to the house keeping in the shadow of the trees as much as he could. They made it up to the side of the house only to find the windows were too high to look in.

"Cup your hand and lift me up," Katie whispered. "I'll take a peek."

Dirk stuck the gun in his belt, and did as she asked.

She stared in the window a moment. "Okay, let me down." Back on the ground, she said, "He's in there alone—sitting at a desk at the far side of the room. He has a half empty bottle of what looks like Scotch in front of him. Let's go around to where the other light is on."

She hurried around the house without waiting for a reply. Dirk followed since it seemed like a good idea. At the next room the light coming through was dimmer—like a night-light. He hefted her up again, gave her a minute then brought her back down.

"Julia's there." Katie said

Dirk noticed the sparkle of tears glistening in her eyes. He felt a tightening in his own throat as she brushed at her eyes.

"She's in bed and it looks like she's sleeping," Katie said, a hitch in her voice. "Should I knock on the window?"

"No, Geno could hear. The last thing we want is to alert him. If he suspected even for a minute it's you or me out here, he'd go straight to Julia's room. It's time for trick or treat. Let's check the door, maybe we'll get lucky. Do you know if he owns a gun?" Dirk asked as they stole around to the front staying close to the building.

Katie shrugged. "Not that I'm aware of, but it wouldn't surprise me if he did. I didn't notice one on the desk where he was sitting though."

The massive front door, built like a bunker fortress, was locked. Dirk was certain not even a shot from his 38 would loosen the fortified deadbolt. He motioned for Katie to go around to the side where they could talk.

Katie rubbed her arms against the cold. "Maybe we could break a window in back and climb it."

"I'd thought about that, but it's tough to muffle the sound of breaking glass. Plus, I'd have to push you in first and I don't like that thought at all. The front door is still our best option."

"How about I bang on the door and yell fire!

Dirk gave Katie a long look. "You know, that could just work. It's dry and we're surrounded by trees—forest fires are always a threat up here. But if he answers the door waving a gun, I want you to dive out of the way and I'll take him down. Understand?"

"Got it. Honestly, it would be awfully gutsy to answer the door to a park ranger with a weapon in your hand."

"Alcohol has a way of making a man act foolhardy. I'm an expert on that subject. Let's go get our girl."

Katie raised her hand to knock, and paused. "What park service?"

"Pike," he whispered. "This is the Pike National forest, hold your hand over the peephole, he'd spot that hair of yours from a mile away."

Katie gave Dirk a look that promised to question him on that comment later. She put one hand over the eye and with the other gripped the large brass knocker, and pounded it hard, three times.

"Hello, is anyone home?"

She pounded again, more rapidly.

"Yeah. Whata ya want?"

"I'm from the Pike forestry service. We have a forest fire threatening your home. We have to ask you to evacuate immediately."

No answer from inside.

"Sir. Did you hear me?" Katie yelled.

"Yeah. Yeah. I heard you. I'll leave shortly."

Katie glanced at Dirk, then talked again to Geno. "Maybe you don't understand how quickly this fire is approaching. If you'll come out you can see the flames from here."

Dirk's heart rate accelerated to overdrive when the lock turned with a resounding click. He motioned to Katie. "The door opens outward. Get behind it." She complied when the door cracked open.

It was barely an inch, but it was enough.

Dirk gripped the door and flung it open, forcing a surprised Geno back and struggling to remain on his feet.

Geno stared like a deer into headlights into the barrel of Dirk's 38. "What the fu—who the hell are you?"

"The man who's going to beat you to within an inch of your life if you make one wrong move."

Geno looked past Dirk to the open doorway. "Katie? What are you doing here?"

"What have you done to her, Geno?"

"Nothing, she's in the bedroom sleeping." He looked back at Dirk. "What the hell is this all about?"

As Katie disappeared into the bedroom, Dirk gave Geno a shove backwards. Geno stumbled, caught himself on the desk, and stepped around it to collapse into the chair.

"Keep your hands on the desk where I can see them," Dirk warned.

Geno gave Dirk a murderous glare. "Who do you think you are anyway, busting into a man's house? Do you know who I am? Who you're dealing with?"

"Yeah. I know who you are, Geno Campanili. You're a no-good scum sucking son-of -a-bitch."

Geno laughed. "Oh. That's real original. You must be Dirk Travis, country hick, ex-con. Where's your permit to carry that gun, Travis? Seems to me that's a violation of your parole."

Katie came in the room in time to hear. "Don't worry about the gun, Geno. It belongs to me. Right now you're lucky it's in Dirk's hands instead of mine." She looked at Dirk. "Julia won't wake up. She's breathing fine, but she's drugged on something." She turned on Geno with a look to freeze steel. "What did you give her?"

"I didn't give her anything. She took a sleeping pill about an hour ago and went to bed."

"Why is she chained to the bed?" Katie ground out through clenched teeth.

Geno downed the last of his Scotch, and shrugged. "She sleepwalks, and since it's so isolated up here, she wanted to make sure she didn't walk outside in the middle of the night."

"You're a lying bastard," Dirk spat. "She doesn't sleep walk."

Geno smiled. "Well that just means you haven't slept with her. Ask Katie."

Dirk looked to Katie to deny it.

"She hasn't walked in her sleep since she was a child. Where's the key?"

Geno motioned to an ashtray on the desk. "Right there, where she asked me to put it."

Katie gave him a scathing look as she fished through the keys. "Which one?" Her question held a threatening bite to it.

"The small one with the leather strap."

"And her clothes?'

Geno nodded to a chair. "Right there where she left them."

Katie grabbed the key and the clothes before heading back to the bedroom.

Geno called after her. "She's here of her own free will, Katie. She wrote a letter asking me to come and get her. Said she was tired of living on a godforsaken ranch with this uncouth cowboy."

Dirk's jaw worked as his hand tightened its grip on the gun. "Why the letter from Sandra Westerly?" Dirk asked.

Geno's mouth turned down as he concentrated on refilling his glass. "That was just to set up the meeting place so you wouldn't know about it. She detested you, you know. Did you seriously think an educated woman with a doctorate in pediatrics would be willing to give up a successful career to baby-sit your brats?"

Dirk blinked a couple of times trying to wrap his mind around Geno's words. Julia a pediatrician? A doctor? Suddenly things started falling in place. Julia *helping* members of Rosa's family, David praising her skill at delivering and saving the life of his baby, and her adeptness at handling his own children. The first week she was there she looked up websites on hospitals and clinics in Denver…looking for employment? Was he the only one too blind to see what was right in front of his nose?

Dirk didn't want to hear anymore. The man was actually starting to make sense. However, he owed it to Julia to listen to her side before he passed judgment. He gave himself a mental shake. "I don't know why you did this to her, but I'm going to find out as soon as she wakes up. I might just put a bullet through your worthless hide and see if you have the skills to operate yourself back to life."

Geno threw his had back and laughed. "You better talk to Julia before you pull that trigger. I never met an ex-con so anxious to get back to prison. You must have enjoyed all that backstabbing you got in there."

Dirk had no idea how Geno knew so much about him, but then prison records were open to the curious public.

Katie appeared at the bedroom door, her face etched with concern. "She seems to have woken up, but she just stares at me like she doesn't know who I am. I can't get her up by myself. We might have to carry her out to the car. You'll have to do it." She turned on Geno. "What did you give her?"

The semblance of a grin twisted Geno's lips. "You know, Katie, she really hated your interference in her life.

We'd probably still be married if you had stayed away. I heard you at the hospital accusing me of whatever. Like I wanted to get rid of her babies. That was total nonsense, but you just couldn't keep your nose out of it."

Katie walked over to Dirk. "I'll take the gun while you go in and get Julia. I got some of her clothes on her, but left her nightgown on for warmth."

"You sure you can manage?" Dirk asked.

Katie glowered at Geno. "Oh, I'll be just fine. Geno and I have a few things to settle. Go get Julia."

Geno's eyes widened when Katie took the gun from Dirk and pointed it at Geno's chest. He backed his chair until it bumped into the wall behind him. "Katie, dammit, don't be a fool. You'll go to jail if you pull that trigger."

"For killing a kidnapper? For ridding the world of a menace to society? I don't think so. I'd probably get a medal."

"I didn't kidnap her!"

Satisfied that Katie had Geno backed in a corner, Dirk went into the bedroom. Seeing Julia laying on the bed, eyes closed, not moving, he swallowed hard and walked up to her. He touched the warm skin on her throat feeling for her pulse, relieved to find it strong.

He shook her, trying to wake her up. "Julia. Julia, can you hear me?"

Her eyes opened but didn't seem to focus on anything. She mumbled something he couldn't quite make out. It sounded like *must call Melody*. What she meant by that, if he'd heard right, he didn't have a clue.

In the other room, he heard Geno pleading for his life. He appeared far more distressed now that Katie held the gun. Katie's hatred was likely justified and long standing, and Geno was obviously aware of it. Dirk wouldn't have been surprised if Katie did pull the trigger. When he spotted the chain on the floor, he hoped she would.

He got Julia wrapped in a blanket, picked her up and carried her out.

"I'll put her in the truck and come back," he told Katie, not even sparing a glance at Geno. "Kill him if he gets out of line. Save us the trouble of hauling him back to the sheriff."

As he walked out the door, he heard Geno ask to use the bathroom and Katie's reply, "Piss in your pants for all I care."

Julia mumbled unintelligibly while Dirk positioned her in his truck, tucking the blanket around her and making sure her head lay straight. Thankfully he was able to lay the seat back just far enough so she didn't pitch forward. In spite of the blanket, her body convulsed with shivers. He closed the door and walked around to the other side, started the vehicle and turned the heater on full blast. He then leaned across the seat to give her a quick kiss.

"You're going to be fine, sweetheart. It's just about over."

She opened her eyes and reached up to touch his face. Her hand fell short and she stared past him toward the lights of the house.

Dirk hurried back inside, intending to chain Geno securely, and then let Katie drive Julia back while he took Geno in with the Land Rover.

Just as he opened the cabin door, Julia started screaming from the truck.

Katie charged toward him. "What's wrong?" she asked, looking past him. Neither one of them saw Geno coming. He crashed into Katie, taking both her and Dirk with him across the short porch and to the bottom of the three steps. Geno was the first one to his feet and he had the gun in his hand. He got up running. Dirk untangled himself from Katie and charged after Geno, who swung his hand around firing off a wild shot behind him.

Dirk dropped to the ground unhurt, but when he got up and saw where Geno was headed, his racing heart nearly took him back to his knees. Geno had reached the pickup and was inside. It only took him seconds to have the already running truck in gear. The F250 shot forward, heading straight for Dirk.

As Dirk dove to the side, Geno wheeled the truck around, spraying gravel in his wake, and roared down the road into the darkness. He obviously hadn't taken time to find the light switch.

Dirk raced after the disappearing truck calling out her name.

"Julia! Julia!"

CHAPTER TWENTY TWO

Dirk ran until he collapsed to his knees, breathing so heavily that his lungs were close to bursting. He never got within fifty feet of the pickup.

She was gone—with Geno. He'd let Geno take her. He was driving on a mountain road with no lights, too drunk to walk, and Julia strapped in beside him. Helplessness raged inside of him.

Bright lights suddenly appeared at his back.

"Get in," Katie yelled. "We'll catch them."

With renewed energy, Dirk sprang to his feet and hurried around to the passenger side of Julia's SUV. Katie spun out in the loose gravel before he had the door closed.

Still struggling to breathe, Dirk was thankful it was Katie behind the wheel—until he looked over and saw the tears streaming down her face.

"It's my fault," she sobbed, swiping a hand over her eyes. "I shouldn't have taken my eyes off of him. It's just that…when Julia screamed."

"It's not your fault, Katie, it's mine. I left the truck running with the keys in it for Chris' sake. How convenient for the bastard."

"I should have shot him," she said, braking at the bridge just before the T in the road.

"They went to the right. Let's just get her back. It's our luck he left the keys in this car."

Katie took the corner to the right, decreasing her speed only enough to keep the vehicle on the road. "He didn't. I saw them in the ashtray when I took the chain key. I didn't think he'd own keys with a pink Rabbit's foot."

"You're a smart lady—there they are!"

"My God, he's driving in these curves without lights. Is he crazy?"

"No, he's drunk. Probably too damn drunk to operate the light switch."

"That's an alarming thought," Katie whispered.

"Yeah. Maybe we should keep our distance so he doesn't—God, he just disappeared on the curve."

Katie made a frantic sound. "He went over the side." She reached over grabbing Dirk's wrist as she brought the Land Rover to a sliding stop on the curve where all they could see was the tops of trees in the headlights, and darkness below.

Dirk slammed his hand against the glove box. When it flipped open, he reached in and grabbed a flashlight.

"Maybe you better stay here," he said, leaping out the door. Stopped by a five-foot drop at the edge of the road, he shined the flashlight down into the trees.

Katie appeared at his side, her fingers digging into his arm, her breath coming out in short rasps. "I don't see the truck. Did she have a seatbelt on?"

"Yeah. There!" He pointed to a gap in the trees below. "It must have gone though there. Stay here!"

Scrambling down the embankment, he started plowing his way through the brush. With a closer look, he could see a path of double tracks going down a sharp incline.

He heard Katie making her way behind him. "Can you see anything?"

He couldn't answer. His heart pounding in his chest stole his breath. About twenty feet below, the back end of his new F250 Super Duty was tilted high in the air exposing its underbelly, the wheels on the passenger side three feet off the ground. It had swiveled to the side, enough to see the front end wrapped around a partially sheared tree.

Beside him, Katie muffled a scream.

Dirk gave Katie a quick glance before he continued down. He didn't bother telling her to stay put.

The putrid steam of the hissing radiator assailed his senses as he climbed up the side of the tilted vehicle, being careful of the broken glass. With a hopeful prayer he peered inside, conscious of Katie's gasping sobs behind him.

Geno's head was pushed through the windshield, his chest crushed by the steering wheel post. Blood trailed from a wide gash in his face where his right eye hung from a gaping socket.

On the passenger side, the force of the motor had pushed the dashboard to within inches of the seat. Julia's blanket lay wedged in the gap.

Dirk stared down at Katie. "She's not here."

"What?"

Dirk jumped down from the truck. "She's not there."

Katie opened her mouth to speak, but no words came out. She looked around, rubbing her arms against the chill of the night. "How? If she had her seatbelt on... Did she fall out?"

"No, I put her seat belt on myself. She must have jumped out when we heard her scream. Let's get back to the cabin."

She hesitated. "What about Geno?"

"We got our wish. He's dead."

He grabbed Katie's hand and tugged her up the hill. The sheer effort of the steep climb kept them speechless until they reached the top.

"You want me to drive?" Dirk asked.

She tossed him the keys and jumped in the car. "We have to hurry. It's really getting cold out here. I put her shoes and slacks on, but other than that, all she's wearing is a lightweight nightgown."

It took less than ten minutes for them to get back to the cabin.

"I'll start looking in the woods where the truck was parked," Dirk said. "You check the cabin in case she got cold and went inside."

Katie nodded. "I'll look, but I can tell you she'd stay out and freeze to death before she'd go back in thinking Geno was there."

"Look anyway, and then come back out. See if you can find another flashlight," Dirk called, charging for the woods.

Beyond the narrow beam of his flashlight and the glow from the solar yard light, he met with total darkness.

"Julia! Julia! Where are you? It's Dirk. Answer me, Julia."

He stopped and listened, heard nothing. About twenty feet away, he spotted a large outcropping of boulders. He moved toward it thinking it might be a place she'd go to hide. In the distance he saw another light and heard Katie calling, too. That meant she hadn't found Julia in the house as he'd hoped.

She had to be here.

He walked around the rocks, shining the light as he went, alternating between calling her name and listening. A scrap of pale blue fabric hanging over a rock above his head caught his attention—Julia's nightgown.

He scrambled up the rocks, calling her name. "Julia?"

She huddled scrunched between the rocks lying in a fetal position. "Over here, Katie," he called as he went to his knees, gathering Julia in his arms. She struck out at him. "It's okay, honey, its Dirk." She stopped struggling and pressed her body against him. She was trembling from the cold.

"Geno?" she asked, her voice shaky and hoarse.

Dirk could hear Katie coming at a run, likely following the direction of his light.

"Geno's dead. He'll never bother you again."

Katie climbed up beside him and put her arms around her sister. "Oh, my God, honey. I've been so worried about you." To Dirk she said, "We better get her in the house. I'm cold and I've only been out here a few minutes."

Dirk agreed, and together they got her off the rocks. Dirk handed Katie his flashlight, picked Julia up, and followed as Katie led the way through the trees.

Inside, they put Julia to bed and started rubbing warmth back in her limbs. The cold must have brought her fully out of the drugs because she seemed to be alert and awake, but she couldn't stop shivering.

"Where is Geno?" she asked again.

Katie answered. "Geno's dead. He escaped with Dirk's truck and crashed it in the trees up the road." Her voice hiccupped. "We thought you were in the truck with him. I've never been so scared in my life. Are you okay?"

Julia managed a timid smile. She reached up and touched Katie's face. "I think so. I'm so happy to see you. What are you doing in Colorado?"

Katie looked up at Dirk and they shared a shaky laugh. "It's a long story. Would you like something hot to drink?"

"Yes, please," Julia said. "Coffee would be good. I can't seem to wake up."

Katie squeezed Dirk's arm. "I'll go make coffee. We could probably all use some. In the meantime I'll figure out how to light the gas fireplace. Why don't you crawl in bed with her and try to warm her up?"

Dirk sent a questioning look after Katie as she left the room, then wasted no time slipping his shoes off and crawling under the covers with Julia.

He pulled her against him, covering as much of her body as he could without smothering her. It only took a couple of minutes for her shaking to slow to intermittent shivers. When she didn't say anything, he took the cue from her and just held her, cradling her, rubbing where her skin felt cool. The events of the last hour, the last day, played over in his mind as he imagined all the things that could have gone wrong. He still didn't understand why Geno took her, what he'd hoped to accomplish. They'd have to wait until Julia was ready to talk about it. At the moment though, he didn't care. She was in his arms, and she was safe.

He closed his eyes and gave thanks.

Tomorrow he'd have to call the local authorities and explain what happened, and why Gus's gun would likely be found in Dirk's demolished truck with a dead man.

CHAPTER TWENTY THREE

Katie sat in the back with Julia while Dirk drove the long, nearly two hour trek home. Julia oscillated between hysteria and normalcy, with intermittent bouts of sleep that came on very suddenly.

During one period when Julia seemed rational, she told Katie about the drug Geno had given her. She was able to describe the effects of Renobasil and convince Katie that she didn't need to see a doctor. The behavior would subside and disappear within six hours.

Each time Katie asked Julia why Geno took her, she got a closed look on her face and stared out the window until she fell asleep. She was keeping something from them.

Dirk gripped the steering wheel, wishing it were Geno Campanili's neck he was squeezing. He felt cheated out of the chance to kill the rat himself. It wouldn't have been a good idea for a man with a prison record though. Maybe he did have an irrepressible temper like the judge suggested. He thought about it a moment and decided it wasn't true. If he were indeed unable to control himself, Geno would have died right there at the cabin two seconds after Dirk laid eyes on the chain in the bedroom.

He looked in the rearview mirror and saw that Julia slept peacefully with her head on Katie's shoulder. He got the feeling either one would do anything for the other, which explained why Katie sent the nanny application to Dirk.

Julia had lost her job due to Geno's influence and Katie wanted to help get her away from him. He even understood why they'd withheld the information about her medical status. Obviously they knew he wouldn't have hired Julia if he'd known she was just coming to the ranch until she found work in the medical field. It didn't take a fancy degree to come up with that deduction.

It all boiled down to one thing. Their relationship was over. Now that she had nothing more to fear, Julia would return to Minneapolis and reestablish the practice she already had there.

He was glad Julia's ordeal had come to an end, but that didn't appease the sense of betrayal gnawing at him. *If she had just told him the truth.* Surely after they'd made love she could have trusted him enough to tell him. Did he love her? He pushed the answer from his mind and concentrated on other things.

Gloria.

He wouldn't feel free until her killer was caught and he was no longer a suspect. Blackmail seemed the most likely option.

Who was it, and what could she possibly be holding over this person? Was it something that happened while he was in prison? The way Gunderson explained it, she was getting a hefty sum on an irregular basis. That probably meant she had to keep prodding the person for cash. Apparently she'd prodded once too often.

They were passing through Danango when Julia woke up again. Katie asked her one more time why Geno planned this whole thing. Did he really expect her to reconcile with him? Dirk watched Julia's face in the mirror. With help of the glowing lights in town, he could see the shine in her eyes as they clouded with tears, but she didn't answer.

Then he heard Katie say, "Did it have anything to do with the trust fund?"

Julia dropped her face in her hands and nodded.

What trust fund? He wanted to ask, but he didn't. He wanted them to tell him about it, but they didn't do that either. Instead they started whispering. Dirk wanted to swear, which he did—internally.

When he pulled up to his house ten minutes later, he was surprised to see lights on in the kitchen. He hit the garage door opener and drove in, shut the motor off, and turned to look at the girls. Julia was awake but seemed to be staring into space. Could be she was just tired.

Helping Julia out of the car, he took both her and Katie the few steps down the hall to Julia's room. There he left Julia in Katie's capable hands and went up the five steps to the main part of the house to investigate the light in the kitchen.

Dirk found both his parents sitting at the table at one-thirty in the morning drinking coffee, a half empty pint of brandy on the table between them. He looked from one to the other, expecting…he didn't know what he expected.

His mother jumped up and hugged him. "Dirk, sweetie, I'm so glad you're home. I've been worried. I heard you talking, is Julia home?"

He looked at Gus who had the same question written in his expression.

"She's home. She's okay. Her sister is with her. It's been one hell of a night. If you have any of the coffee left, I'll sit down and tell you about it."

"You look like hell, son," Gus said, getting up to get the coffee pot. "You want any of this stuff in it?" He held up the brandy bottle.

Dirk gave each of them a raised eyebrow look. "Something going on here I should know about?"

Gus chortled. "Nope, nothing you need to know about. All you need to know is if you want brandy in your coffee."

Dropping into a chair, Dirk said, "Yeah, heavy on the brandy."

He had just finished giving them a shortened version of what went on up on the *hill*—as their family had always called the ski area—when Katie walked in.

After making introductions, Dirk motioned her to a chair.

"Want some coffee?" Gus asked.

Katie gave a sigh so heavy it might have been drawn from her toes. "Oh, that would be wonderful."

"How about sweetener?" Gus held up the brandy bottle with a half-inch of liquid still remaining.

Katie stared at him a moment then laughed. "Sure why not, but go easy on it."

"I don't know about you," Dirk said. "For some reason I'm really hungry."

"I'm starved," Katie said, laughing again. "The last thing I had to eat was stale pretzels on the plane."

She had a nice easy laugh, Dirk thought, like Julia had after she'd been at the ranch a while. "I'll see what we have."

When he started to get to his feet, Bella Travis put a firm hand on his shoulder. "I know my way around this kitchen. What would you like?" She looked at Katie. "An omelet?"

"Yes. Wonderful. Thank you, Mrs. Travis."

"Please...call me Bella."

"Do you think Julia might eat something?" Dirk asked Katie.

"I'm sure she would. I'll take something in to her. I was planning to stay in the room with her, anyway. I don't want to leave her alone until I'm sure the affects of that drug are worn off."

"Good idea. Since Mom's staying in my room, I'll bunk in the office—that's the room across from Julia—then I can spell you so you can get a little rest too."

"I won't be needing your room, Dirk," Bella said, pulling cheese and eggs out of the refrigerator.

"It's the most comfortable bed in the house, mom."

"Now that you're back," Gus said. "She doesn't need to sleep here in the house."

Dirk stared at the back of her head while she searched for a pan. His gaze swiveled to his father. *His* eyes were on Bella's bent over backside.

* * * *

Julia awoke with a start. She sat up in the bed frantically searching her surroundings. A soft light glowed from the bathroom. Her bathroom…in her own room…at the ranch.

She lifted her arm—the chain was gone. Katie was asleep in the chair beside the bed. The clock read 3:00 AM.

She smelled food. The enticing aroma came from a foil-covered plate on the nightstand. She put her hand on it—still warm. Wasting no time, she swung her legs out of bed, tore the tin foil off, picked up the fork supplied for her, and started to shovel the delicious omelet in her mouth. After seeing Geno's drug-laced eggs, she'd thought she'd never eat them again.

She must have made a purring sound because Katie opened her eyes.

Julia smiled. "Thank you so much for the food. I really was hungry."

Katie smothered a yawn. "Don't thank me, Dirk's mom made it."

"Dirk's mother is here?"

"Uh huh. She came to help out with the kids while Dirk and I looked for you."

"That reminds me. I meant to ask… How did you find me?"

Katie explained about Dirk calling her, her quick flight, and their desperate trip to Breckinridge.

"He believed I didn't just desert them?"

"Oh, yes, that man is stuck on you, honey."

"I wonder how he knew about you?"

Katie laughed. "He didn't really. He thought I was

your psychiatrist. He also knew I'd filled out your application."

Julia put a hand to her mouth. "Oh no… I wonder if he knows—"

"That you're a doctor? I'm afraid so, Geno told him. He made up some cockamamie story about you asking him to come because you were tired of living in hick country."

"Dirk believed him?"

"Of course not. Well, not about you asking Geno to come and get you, but as far as your practice is concerned." Katie shrugged. "I'm only guessing, but Geno was pretty convincing on that part."

"Dirk wasn't angry?"

"Honey, he was far too busy to be angry,"

Julia rubbed a hand over her forehead, saw the bandage around her arm where the chain had been. She ripped it off, cursing Geno Campanili to hell.

Katie got up, sat down beside her sister, and put an arm around her. "It's over; Geno will never bother you again. You can come back to Minneapolis if you want to, and take up where you left off."

Katie's head shot up. "What was that?"

Julia's heartbeat quickened. "I didn't hear anything."

Katie got up and went to the door. "It sounds like scratching noises."

Julia charged to her feet, grabbed the bedpost to steady herself, and then went past Katie to fling the door open. Just as she thought, Christa was scrunched on the floor.

"Anna, you're home!"

Julia bent down and picked the tearful little girl up. "Yes, I'm home, sweetie. Anna just had some things to do. Would you like to sleep with me?"

Christa threw her arms around Julia, nodding in her neck. When she carried her back to the bed and sat her down, Christa turned to stare at Katie. "Who are you?"

Katie grinned. "I'm Anna's sister, Katie. Where is your brother?"

"Sleeping."

"Well," Katie said. "Why don't we all lie down and get some sleep."

Julia and Katie laid down with Christa between them. After a few minutes, when Christa's breathing slowed, Katie spoke in a whisper. "Welcome back, Julia."

Julia knew she meant *welcome back to the drug-free world.* "Thank you. It's good to be back."

Julia didn't sleep. Too much was swirling through her mind. Dirk knew the truth. He knew she'd come to the ranch under false pretenses. He may not have been angry in the flurry of the night, but tomorrow would dawn to a normal day. How would he feel then? And now his mother was there, he probably didn't need a nanny anymore.

Worst of all, how could she tell him about what Geno had done to her? What about the fake depo shot?

What if she actually ended up being pregnant?

Who's baby would she have?

* * * *

Dirk couldn't sleep. He'd decided to stay in his office to be near Julia and Katie if they needed him. After peeking in their room and finding them both asleep with Christa between them, he decided they would be all right. Julia appeared to be sleeping peacefully. The drugs must have had run their course and worn off.

Watching his daughter with the Anna she adored brought a lump to his throat. He worried about how his family would react if Julia left.

At first light he'd have to call Gunderson, maybe go back up on the hill with him. He didn't know if Gunderson had jurisdiction up there, but Katie would need her things. Everything she'd brought with her was in that truck.

A boatload of questions plagued him. Why did Julia keep insisting she had to call Melody, and what about that damn trust fund that prompted Geno to kidnap his ex-wife?

Dirk wanted to be angry with Julia for withholding her

MD status, but he couldn't seem to hold that anger. The thought of loosing her worried him more.

Keeping up with this line of thought would drive him stir crazy.

Trudging up the stairs to his son's room, he sat on the edge of Jason's twin bed and brushed the rust colored curls back from his sleeping face. Love for his children was the one constant in his life. Something that wouldn't change— wouldn't go away. Lying down on the little bed, he cradled his son in his arms and went to sleep.

CHAPTER TWENTY FOUR

A soft, small hand patted Dirk's stubbled face.

"Daddy, can I ride Champ today?"

Not, *Why are you sleeping in my bed?* or, *Where is Anna?* but, *Can I ride Champ today?*

Smiling, Dirk bent over and kissed his son on the forehead, "Jason, I have a lot to do, but if there's any way I can take you riding, I will. If I can't, maybe grandpa will—if he's not too busy with grandma," he muttered.

"I like grandmamma. She baked cookies, and teached Pickles how to sit, and guess what? She kissed Grandpapa on the lips."

"No kidding?" Dirk asked, as shocked at that revelation as Jason apparently was. "Wonders never cease," he said, swinging to a sitting position. He encouraged Jason to go back to sleep and headed to his empty room intent on taking a badly needed shower and change of clothes. Knowing where his mother was sleeping left a medley of questions in his already clogged brain.

Twenty minutes later, he found Rosa, and the welcoming smell of strong coffee in the kitchen. She bombarded him with questions about Julia and was visibly relieved when he told her Julia was home, safe and sound. Then she went on to tell him exactly how Julia had been helping her relatives.

Still absorbing that information, he grabbed a cup of coffee and headed for his office. Pausing at Julia's door, he listened for any sign of activity inside, but all was quiet. But then, it was barely after seven-thirty. He wondered how early Rick Gunderson got up.

When the sheriff answered on the second ring, the first thing Dirk did was ask if he had jurisdiction at Breckenridge,

"Heck yes," Gunderson assured him. "As the crow flies it's only twenty-five miles. What's up, Dirk? I heard your man was in town asking about Julia."

Dirk groaned. "Yeah, it's about Julia. I hope you're sitting down, this is going to take a while."

He started from the beginning, telling an abbreviated version of the story, leaving out the part concerning the Smith & Wesson. That information, he decided, could wait. Dirk agreed to meet him in town in forty-five minutes and they'd drive up to the site together. Dirk dreaded the trip, but it had to be done, and soon, before somebody else spotted the truck.

On his way out, he stopped and knocked on Julia's door. He couldn't just leave without telling them where he was headed.

Katie came to the door wearing the same rumpled clothes she'd had on the day before. She smiled. "Good morning, Dirk."

Dirk wasn't sure why, but he felt a little awkward. He looked past her and saw Christa still asleep in the big bed. "How's Julia?" he asked.

"Good, I think... She's in the shower. She's feeling a little sheepish about coming out and facing everyone."

"I can imagine. Well, at least I'll be out of her hair. I'm on my way to take the sheriff out to the truck." He gave her a once over. "I'll bring your things back with me."

Katie breathed a sigh of relief. "Thank you, I really appreciate it. My purse with all my credit cards is in there.

Not to mention my clothes. I can wear something of Julia's, but she's a couple of inches taller than I am."

He nodded. "Okay, I'll be going then. I have to take the Land Rover since I don't seem to have a truck anymore." He gave her a small grin.

She smiled back. When he turned to leave, she stopped him. "Dirk?"

"Yeah?"

She reached out and touched his wrist. "From the bottom of my heart, I thank you."

He smiled. "You probably know by now I'd do just about anything for her. Tell her—" Dirk hesitated. He wasn't sure what he wanted to say.

Katie helped him out. "Yeah, I will. Go ahead, and good luck. I don't envy you going back up there. By the way, I'll be hanging around a couple of days if you don't mind."

Dirk smiled. "I was hoping you would. She needs you right now, so plan to stay as long as you like."

"Thanks. I've missed talking to her. Since we were afraid Geno would find her through phone records, I'd warned her not to make any calls from her cell phone, or from the house here. He had countless connections and I knew he could trace my incoming calls. Yet as careful as we were, he still found her. I'm glad it's over."

"Me too, for her sake." He gave her arm a squeeze and left.

Something about what Katie said bothered him, and it wasn't until he was half way in to Danango it struck him. He had called Katie's office after she'd sent that fax warning Julia about GC—Geno Campanili. It was very likely the call that enabled Geno to find Julia. Now, he could pack his bags for yet another guilt trip.

* * * *

Julia came out of the shower feeling clean, but not cleansed. She had no recollection of Geno touching her, but she still couldn't rid herself of the likelihood he had violated her body. Granted she'd had sex with him many times during eight years of marriage, but this was different. His purpose was to inject sperm inside her womb—to impregnate her. The horror of it intensified because she had no idea if he'd succeeded.

He was right about one thing—she could not abort a child even if it turned out to be his. It was at least comforting to know that even if he had made her pregnant, Geno would have no hand in raising the child.

What if it were Dirk's baby? How would he feel about it? How would he feel if it was another man's child? Maybe she would be spared and not be pregnant. Whatever the answer, this time she'd tell him the truth. No more secrets. If she'd leveled with him right away he wouldn't have allowed her to go in to Danango alone that night.

Katie was waiting for Julia when she walked into the bedroom. She found it wasn't difficult to put a smile on her face for her sister.

"How are you feeling?" Katie asked.

Julia shrugged "Good as—used."

"Are you going to tell me about it, Julia?"

Julia took a deep breath, hesitating. "Yes." She glanced at the bed to make sure Christa was still sleeping. "It's something you need to know. Apparently Geno helped our beloved father set up the trust just a few months before he had the aneurysm. We can't touch the trust until we have a baby."

"Yeah, I knew that."

"What I didn't know, and I don't know if you did, the money would be split three ways between the baby, me, and the child's father."

"You've got to be kidding."

"Not according to Geno. I tend to believe it's true because he went to an awful lot of trouble and risk to make me pregnant. He said it didn't matter if we were married or not, and he wouldn't even have to raise the child. He'd still get his cut."

"What an ass," Katie said, shaking her head. "Actually, I can't decide who was the bigger ass—Geno or our so-called father."

"I'm just thankful they're both dead and we don't have to deal with either one ever again. I thought I read all the stipulations on that ridiculous trust. There must be an addendum I didn't see."

"I wonder if the part about us receiving the money if we turn forty without bearing a child is accurate?"

Julia sat down on the bed to brush out her wet hair. "I have no idea."

Katie gave Julia a long, hard look. "Is there a chance you are pregnant—did Geno touch you?"

Julia couldn't look at her sister. Instead, she stared at the wall behind her. "I don't know. He kept me drugged, but—" her voice hitched, "he said he did."

Katie paced the small space by the bed, agitated. "That bastard," she hissed, keeping her voice low. "Right now I wish he was alive so I could kill him." She picked up a pillow and, with one eye on the sleeping child, heaved it across the room. "What are the chances? You were only with him two nights."

"There's something else," Julia whispered.

Katie stopped pacing. "What more can there be?"

"Geno faked the depovera shot I supposedly got in the hospital. There's a chance I... I could have been pregnant before Geno took me."

Katie collapsed into a chair staring open mouthed and wide eyed at her sister. "Dirk?"

* * * *

By the time Dirk dropped Gunderson off at his office, he was tired from lack of sleep and weary to the bone. It had been an exhausting day to put it mildly. Gunderson was unable to walk down the slope to the pickup, so he called a tow truck with a long wench to pull it out. Under the guise of finding his gun, Dirk had insisted he needed to go down and locate Katie's purse and suitcase before the workers arrived.

The sight of the truck turned his stomach, and looking inside, the horrific stench of death and sound of greedy feasting flies, emptied it. He had to pry the passenger side door open to reach Katie's purse wedged between the seat and the exposed motor. Leaning forward he felt around the floorboards beneath Geno's legs until he located the blood-drenched gun, all the while avoiding the gaping eye socket that still haunted him from the night before.

Wasting no time, he climbed into the back and pulled out Katie's suitcase. He opened it, found a plastic bag covering a pair of dress shoes, shook the shoes out and stuck the gun in the bag. He then tucked it beneath the clothes, zipped up the bag and towed it up the hill. Thanking God for small favors. He really didn't want to explain why he was carrying a contraband weapon.

After the tow truck and coroner left, Dirk took Gunderson to the cabin to show him the room where Julia was chained, hopefully putting some validation to his story. Gunderson snapped several pictures with his Polaroid and mentioned he'd still have to talk to both Julia and Katie before he closed the case.

Dirk waited outside while Gunderson walked around the building. On the outside of the porch he stopped to put his fingers in a hole in the railing.

"Did Campanili own a gun?" he asked.

Dirk shook his head. "Not that I know of."

Gunderson gave Dirk a long look before he spoke. "Dirk, for your sake I need you to tell me right now—is there any chance the forensic people are going to find a bullet hole in that body."

Dirk met his questioning gaze head on. "No, no chance. Not because I didn't want to put one there, though."

Gunderson shook his head. "Young man, you're too damned honest for your own good. I'd recommend you don't share that little tidbit with anyone else. Far as I can see, we're done here. Let's go home."

Dirk pulled into the yard to what looked like a party going on by the corral. It appeared everyone on the ranch had turned out for this mystery event. Even Carrie, with a stroller, was there. He also saw Melody's car parked near the barn.

Dirk drove the SUV in the garage, got out and walked toward the crowd. They were so intent on watching the goings on in the corral he didn't think anybody even noticed his arrival.

Gus and Bella were up against the rail cheering, while Julia and Carrie, with Christa, cooing over the baby stroller, were lined up next to them. Beside them, a laughing and clapping Melody.

The center of attraction was Katie attempting to mount Seminole with the help of Charlie Mack. The sound of Julia laughing was like the sweetest music he ever heard. He was glad to see Jason astride Champ, being led by David—and Megan sitting handsomely erect on Victoria, circling the parameter at an easy gallop. That young lady was becoming an excellent horsewoman.

Megan saw him first. She pulled her horse up and waved.

"Dad, come and watch. Katie's going to ride."

Had she called him Dad? He wasn't sure with all the commotion going on.

All eyes turned to acknowledge him, some questioning, some just glad to see him home. After the day he'd had it was like walking on stage with all his favorite people in the audience.

Christa racing toward him, arms outstretched, capped his pleasure. "Daddy, Daddy. Come and see Katie ride. I held the bottle for Marisa and Megan's riding really fast."

Laughing, Dirk swung her up in his arms. "You, my dear, are talking really fast."

He kissed her on the forehead glancing over the top of her head toward Julia. She was obviously taking pains not to look his way. He knew he had to talk to her. Already he suspected she planned to be on the next plane back to Minneapolis with Katie. Geno was dead, her reason for abandoning her life gone with him. Would the few nights they'd spent together make a difference? He doubted it.

She had a career, an obligation to follow the path she'd spent years training for.

How could he blame her?

By all rights he should be furious with her for coming to care for his children under false pretenses, knowing she wouldn't be staying. During her first week she'd already checked out the local hospitals laying the groundwork for her departure. It was inevitable she would leave. It had been her plan all along.

She wouldn't stay because a backwoods rancher said he loved her. No wonder she never said the words back to him.

He noted the adoration in her face as she watched her sister. They obviously cared very deeply for each other. She suddenly turned to look at him her expression unreadable. After only a brief moment, she gave him a small smile and turned her attention back to Katie. He had the odd feeling he'd been replaced.

Christa squirmed to the ground and grabbed his hand. "Daddy, come see Marisa. She's so tiny and cute. Carrie let me hold her." She tugged him toward the stroller.

He stooped down on his haunches and made the appropriate cooing sounds to the baby, his gaze straying back to Julia. He was sure she'd been watching him but she turned away again so quickly he thought he might have imagined it.

Well she'd have to face him sooner or later and it might as well be sooner, he decided. He asked Christa to stay and keep an eye on the baby while he went to talk to Anna.

In the corral, Katie rode around in a circle tethered to a rope held by Mack. As Dirk approached Julia he heard her warn Katie not to pull back on the reins too tight.

Dirk laughed. "I guess you're a quick study." When she turned to smile at him he resisted the urge to put his arms around her.

Obviously comfortable with a safe subject Julia laughed. "Katie always was the courageous one." Silence hung between them a moment before she spoke. "Did everything go alright today?"

Dirk gave a short nod. "Yeah, I'll fill you in later." He hesitated before adding, "We have a few other things to discuss too."

Julia looked at him. "I really am sorry for everything, Dirk."

Dirk shrugged. "It's not your fault your ex was a psycho jerk."

"That's not what I'm talking about. I know I kept vital information from you—"

"Are you talking about a little matter of an MD?"

Tears swam in her beautiful eyes. "I was planning to tell you when I got home that night."

Dirk was aware that all eyes had turned in their direction. "We can talk about it when we have a little more privacy," he said.

Julia, too, noticed the attention they were receiving. Dirk looked bone weary and at the same time so damn sexy she wanted nothing more than to throw her arms around him and suggest they retire to the bedroom, but the intimacy they'd shared had been replaced by an uncomfortable shadow.

She wondered if he knew Geno had likely molested her and also wondered how he would feel about it. That combined with the knowledge she'd withheld information from him, she suspected he was going to ask her to leave.

She'd had some conversations with Bella Travis, and it seemed Bella missed her grandkids and was talking about moving back to the ranch. Would Dirk still need a nanny with his mother willing to step into the position?

Julia decided to venture into a safe area.

"You need to speak to Melody," she said, keeping her voice low enough so only he could hear.

Dirk frowned. "Melody? Why? What's she doing here anyway?"

"She's here because I asked her to come. She came only a half hour ago, so I haven't had a chance to talk to her, but she has some information about Gloria that might be important."

"Like what?"

Julia glanced at Melody and nodded. The woman left her position at the rail and walked toward them.

"Did Julia tell you why I'm here?" Melody asked.

Dirk nodded. "Yeah, some. Let's give it a few minutes and go talk in my office. I'd just as soon not everybody get a whiff of what we're discussing."

Before Melody could comment, Bella approached them.

Forty-five minutes later, Dirk ushered both Julia and Melody into his office. He sat the women on the sofa and rolled his desk chair up to face them

"Now, who's going to tell me what's going on between the two of you that's so all fired important?"

Melody fidgeted with the snaps on her blouse.

"Go ahead," Julia prompted. "You need to tell him."

Melody looked like she'd rather be anyplace else than where she was. "Well," she said, clearing her throat. "That day we went riding I mentioned to Julia I thought you had popped the wrong man when you slugged Mark Sanford."

Dirk passed a suspicious look between the women. "Okay," he said, drawing out the word. "You have my attention, keep talking."

Tears glistened in Melody's eyes. "This is hard for me, Dirk, because I know how you hate it when people keep things from you, and then you went to jail and I just didn't want to make any more problems for you. Now Julia thinks it might be important in Gloria's murder case."

Dirk sent Julia a piercing look. "You're right. I do have a problem with people keeping secrets from me. Comes from living with a lying, cheating wife, I guess. Now are you going to tell me what this is all about?"

Melody nodded. "That night you had the fight with Mark, I saw Gloria follow a man into the barn. It wasn't Mark."

"Who the hell was it?"

CHAPTER TWENTY FIVE

"I'm not sure," Melody blurted. "It was dark."

Dirks face darkened. "Well, then there wouldn't be any point in telling me, would there? Who do you think it was?"

"It looked like… Raymond Sanford, Mark's father."

Dirk leaned back in his chair and rolled his eyes. "That's fucking ridiculous! Even Gloria had more class than to crawl into the sack with that reprobate."

Melody shrank back against the sofa. "I didn't say it was him, I said it looked like him. I only saw him from the back. I just know it wasn't Mark. This man was shorter and heavier and he wore a dark shirt like I saw Sanford wearing earlier."

"Hell, half the men there were probably wearing black."

Julia had stayed silent up to this point. "It proves Gloria was involved with someone else. We just have to figure out who it was."

"There were at least eighty people at that party, maybe more."

"But half were women," Melody supplied.

"Now we just have to eliminate those who wore light colored shirts." Julia said.

Dirk shook his head, swearing. "Hell, I don't even remember what I was wearing. I do know Mark had on a yellow shirt, and it looked damned good covered with blood."

Melody grimaced. "Red and yellow, well that definitely eliminates Mark."

Dirk gave her an incredulous look. "You know, Melody, if I was in a better frame of mind that would be funny."

"Maybe we should all lighten up," Julia said, looking directly at Dirk.

Dirk gave her a look back that suggested he battled a war with his emotions, and let out a long, audible breath. "Good idea." Turning back to Melody, he said, "Okay, tell me again exactly what you saw—in detail."

Melody visibly relaxed, forced a weak smile. "It was just starting to get dark, and I was sitting on the back porch drinking a glass of wine talking to Paul Chatterley—for a would-be congressman he's an obnoxious flirt, by the way. Anyway, I got bored when a couple of his cronies joined us and they started talking politics. That's when I noticed this man go into the barn. I guess at the time I figured it was Sanford since it was his place and the man looked like him from the back. Then about five minutes later Gloria went in—"

"They didn't go together?" Dirk asked.

"No. I assumed at the time they were being discreet."

Julia smiled. "Well that eliminates this Chatterley fellow and all his friends if Melody remembers who they were."

"Oh, I remember all right," Melody said. "But they all wore suits. The man going in the barn definitely wasn't wearing a suit."

"Sanford likes hobnobbing with the bigwigs," Dirk said. "I need a beer." He got up and went to the tiny refrigerator behind his desk. He brought back three bottles of Miller light, opened them, and handed one to each of the women. He took a deep, long swallow and motioned Melody to continue.

Julia stared at the cold bottle, but didn't drink it. "How far is the house from the barn?" she asked.

Melody shrugged. "I'd say about fifty yards or so."

"Then, just for the record, are you sure the woman was Gloria?"

Melody laughed. "Yeah, I'm sure. She had on this white strapless chiffon number you could have spotted from a mile. It flowed around her like a cloud."

"That little *number* set me back four hundred dollars," Dirk ground out, snorting.

"How long were they in there?" Julia asked, ignoring Dirk's comment about the dress.

Melody started peeling the label from her beer and took a small sip. "I don't know. It was at least ten minutes because that's when the dinner bell rang and Chatterley suddenly remembered he had a wife to escort and left to find her. Everybody else, including me, headed for the buffet line."

Dirk leaned back in his chair and took another swig of beer. "You never did see them come out of the barn?"

"I'm afraid not."

"Well, let's do a little recap," he said. "You saw Sanford, or somebody else, go into the barn. Gloria followed a few minutes later, they were both in there at least ten minutes and you didn't see anyone come out."

Melody looked a little sheepish when she nodded. "I guess it isn't much, huh?"

"But it could be," Julia said quickly. "Somebody killed Gloria and there are no suspects. Dirk, you're theory is she was blackmailing someone, and Melody, you originally said the man in the barn had a lot to lose by being exposed—"

"That's when I believed it was Sanford. I'm not so sure anymore."

Dirk sat forward in his chair rolling his empty bottle between his hands. "Let's just assume it was Sanford for a moment. He does have a lot to lose. Gunderson is retiring and Sanford has had his eye on the sheriff's position for a long time. A scandal like that could definitely put a crimp in his plans. How do we prove anything?"

"They could subpoena his bank records," Melody offered.

Dirk shook his head. "Not without probable cause. I don't think seeing him go into his own barn would do it. I also don't think he had the kind of money Gloria was obviously getting. His wife did, but I can't see her putting out a dime to save his sorry ass."

"Who else at the party had a lot of money and a lot to lose?" Julia asked.

Melody laughed. "That's easy. Chatterley."

"And probably half his political friends," Dirk added. "They were all on the porch with you. I think we're forgetting something. Even if Gloria had an affair with Raymond Sanford—which I seriously question—or with anyone else, she would need some concrete proof to hold over their head."

"Like an audio or videotape," Julia said.

"Or a photograph," Melody's back straightened, eyes wide. "Did Gloria have a camera with her that night?"

He gave a derisive snort. "I have no idea. I didn't see her using it, and I can't imagine Gloria with Sanford. She sure as hell wouldn't want the event immortalized on film."

"Even if the man wasn't Sanford," Julia reasoned. "How could she take a photo of herself?"

"Did it have a remote?" Melody asked.

Dirk shook his head. "Not that I'm aware of. Besides the man went into the barn first. Can you see him standing around waiting while she sets up the camera to get a picture to blackmail him? Even Sanford's not that stupid."

Melody released a sigh. "That pretty much makes it a dead-end."

"I'm sorry," Julia said. "I really thought it was a lead."

"I guess I might as well go," Melody said, getting to her feet. "I want to be home before dark."

Dirk stood and reached for her half empty beer bottle. "Maybe you shouldn't mention this to anyone. What if we're missing something and that man really is a killer? It wouldn't be a good idea for him to know you saw him go into the barn with Gloria."

Melody grimaced. "Ooh, I never thought of that. I may have mentioned it to a couple of friends, but that was a long time ago."

"Like before we had a killer on the loose?" Dirk asked.

Watching the other woman shut the door behind her, Julia would have liked to get up and leave with Melody, but she and Dirk had to talk.

Dirk sat back in his chair saying nothing, watching her.

It made her uncomfortable. She got up and walked behind him to set her untouched beer on his desk.

"How are you feeling?" he asked without turning around to look at her.

She walked over to stare out the window and noticed the flowers needed watering. "Almost back to normal. I don't think there are any lasting effects to the drugs he gave me." She walked back and sat down on the sofa. "How did things go today?" she asked.

Dirk shrugged. "All right, I guess. The sheriff will want a statement from both you and Katie, but he said it was just a formality. I told him everything I knew and he seemed satisfied."

Julia smiled. "You have a lot of integrity, and he knows it."

Silence hung for another moment.

"Did he hurt you, Julia?"

"Nothing that won't heal. The ordeal was more mentally abusive than physical."

"You want to see a doctor—" Dirk swore before the last word left his mouth. "Sorry, I forgot for a moment there you *are* a doctor."

"I know I should have told you," she said. "I was afraid you wouldn't hire me if I had."

"Damn straight, I wouldn't have. It's obvious you never intended to stay. You were researching hospitals and clinics the first week you got here. I checked the computer after you used it."

"You were spying on me?"

"You might say that. You were too nice, too perfect, and you were so close-mouthed about your past. I was suspicious. Don't be blaming me—I had my children to protect. As it turns out, I was right to be wary. You used me and my family to get away from your ex-husband."

Julia internally cringed from the hurt and anger flashing in his eyes. She blinked at the tears threatening her composure. "I have no defense. Everything you're saying is accurate. I know it's too little too late, but I was planning to tell you the truth when I got back from Danango that night. The letter Geno sent implied I could work as a volunteer part time at the clinic. I thought maybe I could still take care of the kids and do that too."

"Well, I'm sure that's changed now with Geno dead. You're free to go back to Minneapolis and resume your career."

Julia swallowed at the lump in her throat. She had used him and the kids, but she hadn't bargained on how much she'd come to care for them and the ranch. Leaving wouldn't be easy.

What if she was pregnant? He'd never forgive her if she kept that from him.

Dirk must have noticed her internal struggle. "Don't worry about the kids. They got over their mother. They can get over you. Mom seems more than willing to pitch in until I can hire someone else."

Unable to speak past the pain in her chest, Julia nodded. His tone was so bitter, she wondered if he was including himself in that statement. *He got over Gloria. He could get over her.* It seemed she'd already been dismissed. She stood up and forced her feet toward the door.

"By the way," Dirk said, stopping her. "I made the call that helped Geno find you. When you got the fax from Katie, I recognized her handwriting and realized she was the one who'd filled out your application. I was curious enough to call the number at the top of the fax. When the secretary answered, I discovered Katie was a psychiatrist, and since I didn't have a clue she was your sister, I assumed she was your doctor."

Julia turned to face him. "It's not your fault. It's mine for not leveling with you." Once more she turned to leave and he stopped her.

"Julia? I'm not sorry you came."

She gave him a tremulous smile. "In spite of what I put you through, I'm not either."

* * * *

Julia and Katie had an appointment with Gunderson at one-thirty the next day to give their statements. Dirk drove them in to Danango and asked if they wanted him to wait in the car. Both women declined his offer.

Inside, after introductions were made, Gunderson motioned them to sit down and flipped his recorder on. He asked to speak to Katie first and informed her she had the right to have a lawyer present and she assured him it wasn't necessary. He asked the other two not to speak while Katie was talking. When Katie finished her account of what happened, Gunderson thanked her and switched the recorder off.

"Thank you Ms. Benson, your story collaborates with Dirk's exactly. There's just one thing missing." He sat back in his chair and crossed his arms over his chest. His gaze moved from Katie to Dirk. "Off the record, tell me about the gun."

"I have a license to carry," Katie said.

Gunderson gave her a questioning look. "Then it was yours?"

Dirk spoke before she could answer. "It's registered to Gus," he said.

"I asked him to bring it," Katie said.

Gunderson smiled. "It's off the record, Ms. Benson, you don't have to defend him."

"I'm just telling you the truth. I knew Geno could be dangerous."

"All right, just one more question, actually, two more, and for my amusement why don't you both answer at the same time. How many shots were fired?"

"One," they said in unison.

"Who fired it?"

"Geno," they answered together.

Gunderson grinned. "Well done. I'm not going to ask, Dirk, but I'll assume you've returned the gun to your father." He turned to Julia. "I asked Katie to speak first hoping to give you a little time to relax. Would you trade seats with your sister?"

Julia did as he asked while he reminded the other two not to speak while the recorder was on. Julia told her story, what she remembered of it. Since she wasn't sure Geno had molested her, she omitted that part."

"If I understand you right, you were pretty well drugged up through the whole ordeal?" Gunderson said.

Julia nodded. "Yes. I don't even recall Katie and Dirk coming to rescue me, or the ride home."

"There's just one thing I don't understand. Your ex-husband was a successful man, why would he jeopardize his career to abduct a woman who obviously wanted nothing to do with him?"

Julia took a deep breath. She knew this would come up and it was the main reason she wanted Dirk there. He had to know it all. She glanced at her sister looking for reassurance. Katie smile and nodded. It gave Julia the strength to go on.

"My father put my inheritance in a trust fund. The only way I could get it before I turned forty was to have a baby. The money would then be split between the child, the father of the child, and myself. It specified I didn't have to be married to the father or even live with him. He also wasn't required to have a hand in raising the child. Not too surprising, Geno helped our father write it up just a few months before he died."

Gunderson stared at her for a long moment after she stopped talking. "Julia, I don't want to put words in your mouth, so please explain exactly what Geno Campanili hoped to accomplish by abducting you."

Julia felt tears stinging her eyes as she turned her gaze to Dirk. "He wanted to make me pregnant."

Dirk came to his feet and Gunderson put up a quick hand, motioning him to silence. He pointed to the chair Dirk had vacated and Dirk reluctantly dropped into it looking fit to wrestle an angry bull.

Gunderson turned back to Julia. "Since you were only with him a little over twenty-four hours, I think we can safely assume he didn't accomplish his goal. Since Geno Campanili is dead I see no reason to go into it further." Gunderson pressed the off button on the recorder. "I for one am glad the man's in hell where he belongs. Sorry to put you through this, Julia, but it was necessary. I should be able to wrap this up without having to release all the details."

Julia let out a tormented sigh. "I'd appreciate that."

"One more thing. Even though Geno is dead, you should probably have a physical examination."

"I believe I have the right to refuse to have that done," Julia said.

Gunderson nodded. "Yes, you do, but we do require a blood sample."

Julia reached into her purse and pulled out a small vial. "I have it right here. It's labeled and dated. My sister can vouch that it's mine."

Gunderson accepted the vial, staring at her in surprise. "You've done this before?" he asked.

"Not for myself, but I've had to do it for at least three of my patients. I suspected you'd ask for it. I'll take care of the exam myself when I get back to Minneapolis."

After casting a quick glance at Dirk, Gunderson turned back to Julia. "I'll have these typed up and then either give you a call to come in and sign them, or I'll stop out at the ranch."

Dirk ushered the women out the door then turned to Gunderson. "Thanks, Rick."

Gunderson nodded. "You're a good man, Dirk. Take care of that woman. She been through a tough time with that asshole she was married to."

"I'll see to it. By the way, where is my truck? I have some personal items in there I need—like some insurance papers and a camera."

Gunderson shrugged. "It's right outside town at Dewey's towing. This is pretty much an open and shut case, I'll let him know you're coming, so just take what you need. The truck's totaled though, I can tell you that."

"Yeah, figured as much. Also, I may have come up with a theory on Gloria's death. It might be a long shot but… How about I stop in tomorrow when I get my stuff from the truck and we can talk. Right now I want to get Julia home."

"Sure thing. We're dead-ended, so any ideas you have can't hurt."

When Dirk got out to the Land Rover, the women were in the back seat together. He sat behind the wheel feeling a bit like a chauffeur, but he set his feelings aside knowing Katie was looking after her sister. They'd been talking, but the minute he got in, they both clammed up.

"Can we stop at the mercantile?" Katie asked. "I need to pick up a couple of things."

While Katie went inside, Dirk waited in the car with Julia in uncomfortable silence. He glanced in the rearview mirror a couple of times, but she just stared out the side window. He wanted to ask her if Geno had touched her sexually, so he could somehow let her know it wasn't an issue for him.

What did it matter? She'd be gone in the next few days, and he'd likely never see her again. He couldn't help think about her father though. The man must have been a first class bastard to put such outlandish stipulations on his daughters' trust funds.

Katie came back with a small brown bag in her hand—probably some feminine products she needed.

They were halfway home when the silence started irritating him. He got the feeling they were hiding something from him, and by the time they pulled into the yard, he was certain of it. He sat in the car, stewing for some time after they went inside, and when he finally got out, he went to the barn instead of the house. His nerves were cutting a sharp edge, he didn't want to do or say anything he might be sorry for.

Being around animals had a way of calming him. When he entered Star's stall the prize mare nuzzled his arm looking for a handout. He rubbed her forehead, smiling. "Sometimes I think you're the only female around here I can trust."

"She's beautiful, isn't she?"

He turned at the sound of Julia's voice. "Yes, she is," he said, trying to ignore the thumping dance in his chest. It made him feel vulnerable and it wasn't a feeling he was used to. He didn't like it.

"I need to talk to you," she said.

He walked up to her, but kept the railing between them, unsure if he could trust himself alone with her. Whatever she was going to tell him took a lot of courage on her part. He admired her for that, and waited. Hell, he could wait all day. Just looking at her, smelling the lavender scent of her hair as she pushed it back from her face gave him pleasure beyond reason.

"I asked you to be present when I gave my statement today because I wanted you to hear everything, but there are a couple of details I couldn't bring myself to say out loud to the sheriff." She met his gaze full on and continued. "I don't know if Geno molested me or not. He said he did…at least twice while I was out, but I have no way of knowing. Since his reason for bringing me there was to impregnate me, I have to believe he did."

The tears rushing down her face did him in. He came through the gate and had her in his arms before he'd even realized he'd moved. She held him like she never intended to let go, sobbing in his shoulder.

He smoothed a hand over her hair, breathing in the smell of her as though it were the oxygen he needed for life. She felt so right leaning into him, allowing him to comfort her. He wanted to bury himself inside her sweet warmth and take her right there in the barn, he even went so far as to consider coaxing her up to the hayloft, but he was concerned she might not be ready. She'd been through so much. Right now she needed comfort, not a horny interlude.

He continued to stroke her hair, pushing it back from her face as she had done a few minutes earlier. "It's okay, honey. Whatever he did wasn't your fault. The man was deranged. He's gone. He can never hurt you again. Just be thankful you had that depo shot."

"Dirk, I—"

Before she could finish what she was about to say, he heard Jason's chattering voice and Gus's response. They were on the way to the barn to visit the kittens.

With a reluctant sigh, Dirk separated himself from Julia, but not before he brushed his lips over her cheek and tasted the salt of her tears.

CHAPTER TWENTY SIX

Julia had brushed the dampness from her face, and by the time Gus entered the barn, she was rubbing Star between the ears. Jason burst in behind Gus like a whirlwind. He barely spared a quick hello to Julia and Dirk before charging for the steps. Dirk questioned his father about climbing to the loft, and the older man thumped his chest and grinned.

When she had come into the barn she'd planned to tell him everything, but the memory of his erection pressed against her just moments ago gave her second thoughts. What if she told him she might be carrying his child and he made it impossible for her to leave? She needed some time to think, to sort out her feelings for him, to decide what to do with her career—and to get past the trauma of what Geno had done to her.

Besides, if she wasn't pregnant it was a moot point.

"Do you know when you're going to leave?" he asked, apparently not realizing she'd been about to bare her soul to him.

She nodded. "We have reservations for Friday morning."

Dirk watched her slumped shoulders as she walked back to the house. She'd been through a lot. Not just in the last week, but he could only imagine what her life had been like being married to Geno, and even before that, with her father. Dirk suspected the trust fund was just a scratch on the surface of that man's character.

As much as he wanted to beg her to stay, he couldn't do it. This was probably the first time in her life she was free to do and go wherever she wanted. He wouldn't take that away from her. She'd have melted in his arms if he'd kissed her just moments ago, but he wasn't going to influence her decisions by making love to her. He wanted her to stay—but he also wanted her to be sure, and not regret it later. Four more days. Maybe she'd change her mind on her own.

* * * *

Due to a mare going into labor the next morning, Dirk didn't make it into the towing lot until almost closing. Dewey McDonald wore faded coveralls in serious need of a washing, and he wasn't the most organized person in the world, but he knew exactly where to find Dirk's truck.

"It's a cryin' shame about yer pickup," he said as he led Dirk through a graveyard of metallic remains to a fenced off area behind his shop. "I'm a Ford man myself, but all I get to drive is junkers I pull from my pile an' fix up. There she is. I have to keep 'er in lock up till I get the go ahead from Gunderson. It's just like they brought it in. I ain't touched nothin', 'specially since I knew it were yours. I'll just wait right here for you to get what you need. Rich give me orders not to let anyone near it unless they have permission."

Dirk's stomach knotted as he approached what was left of his F250. A vision of Geno hunched over the wheel flashed through his mind as he wrenched open the cubbyhole door to get his camera and the papers inside. The camera was missing. He checked the floorboards, but found nothing except a pair of pliers and a couple of screwdrivers.

"Has anyone else been here?" he asked.

Dewey scratched his unshaven face. "Just an insurance man. All he did was walk around it and shake his head. I coulda told him over the phone it was totaled."

"You didn't see a camera?"

"Nope, like I said, I ain't touched it. I guess it coulda fallen out up at the sight. That was one nasty crash."

Dirk examined the cubby door noticing pry marks on it. He didn't doubt Dewey's word, but the door had not opened on its own. "Just the sheriff and the insurance man? Nobody else?"

"Nope. Except for Ray, of course."

"Sanford was here?"

"Yup. Not mor'n a couple of hours after it came in. Didn't think anything of it, him bein' the sheriff's deputy an' all."

Dirk took his papers and tools, thanked Dewey, and left. He headed straight for Gunderson's office, hoping to find him hanging around, but no such luck—the office was closed. Not surprising, since it was already after six. No sense bothering him at home, Melody's information would likely amount to nothing anyway.

With Sanford on his mind, he decided to drive by the deputy's house. He was sure the thieving bastard took the camera and there probably wasn't a thing he could do about it, but it pissed him off enough to make him want to go by and give him hell. The Sanford house, the one his wife inherited from her father, was in the upper crust neighborhood, a block from the Chatterley mansion. No one was home and it probably wasn't a good idea to confront a man with a badge. He'd may as well wait and report the theft to Gunderson in the morning.

At home he found his entire family, along with Katie, crowded in the sitting room while Julia and Megan performed Dueling Banjos on the piano. The sight brought an unexpected lump to his throat. They'd waited supper for him.

* * * *

Dirk stood in the doorway of the barn watching Gunderson's patrol car coming up the road. It was barely after nine in the morning. The sheriff was either in a hurry to get his papers signed, or he couldn't wait to hear what Dirk had to tell him about Gloria.

Gunderson pulled up in front of the barn and rolled his window down without getting out of his car. "H'llo Dirk. Looks like you're up and at 'em this morning."

Dirk shrugged. "There's never a lack of work to do around here. Sorry I missed you last night; I didn't finish out at Dewey's until after six."

"Yeah, I talked to Dewey. He said you'd been there. Why don't you sit in the car with me so we can talk."

Dirk splashed the last contents of his coffee on the ground, set the empty cup on the rail, and got in the passenger side of the patrol car.

"Okay," Gunderson said, not wasting any time. "What did you want to tell me about Gloria?"

An odd sensation crept up Dirk's spine. Why did he have the feeling Gunderson had something entirely different on his mind. *Well, I can play this little game*, he thought. "The night I had the fight with Mark Sanford, someone saw Gloria follow a man into the barn. The man wasn't Mark."

Gunderson grunted. "Who was it?"

"This person wasn't sure, but suspected it was Mark's old man."

"Who is this *person* we're talking about?"

"Wants to remain anonymous," Dirk said. "Besides, it's insignificant. If we're going with the theory that Gloria was blackmailing someone... I don't know. Like I said, it was a long shot."

"Where did you go last night after you left Dewey's?"

Dirk gave himself a mental shake, wondering where this was going. "I went home."

"You went straight home?"

"What the hell are you getting at Rick?"

"Answer the question and I'll tell you. Or tell me you'd rather speak to a lawyer first."

"No, I don't want a fucking lawyer. What's going on?"

Gunderson stared at him for a long minute. "Somebody saw you drive by Sanford's house last night."

"The bastard stole my camera. After I went by your office, and found it closed, I drove by Sanford's house because I was pissed."

"Did you stop?"

"If somebody saw me drive by they'd know I didn't stop. The asshole has a fucking badge, what did you expect I'd do?"

Gunderson reached into the back seat and pulled out a brown envelope. He extracted a plastic bag and held it up. "Does this look like your camera?"

Dirk stared from the camera to Gunderson's face. A tight knot formed in his stomach. "What's going on Rick?"

"Ray Sanford is dead."

Dirk's mind went blank. "What? How?"

"Somebody put a bullet through his head."

"Well, shit," was all Dirk could think to say. "There goes the theory that he was the one Gloria was blackmailing."

"You said your informant wasn't sure it was Sanford going in the barn with Gloria."

Dirk shook his head slowly, trying to think. "Where did you find the camera?"

"On the floor by Ray's body. I can almost guarantee you it wasn't suicide. If you check out the camera you'll see it was crushed, and the photo card is missing."

"Dammit, Dewey said Sanford was nosing around my truck. I suspected right away he was the one who took it. I thought he was just stealing it."

"I think there's more to it than that."

"Obviously."

"It was your camera. What the hell was on it?"

"It belonged to Gloria. When Rosa found it under the mattress about a month ago, everything on it had been erased."

"Well crap. Looks like yet another dead end."

"Not necessarily," Dirk replied. "The reason the camera was in the truck was because I took it to a Wal-Mart in Denver when I picked Katie up. I had taken some photos of Julia with the kids and I thought I might need one for ID. I only took about ten pictures, but the clerk said there were over sixty images, so it would take an hour. I didn't have time to wait so I prepaid and asked her to send them."

Gunderson's face lit up. "And?"

"They haven't come yet. I don't think Gloria had her camera with her that night, so I didn't expect to find anything more than pictures of the kids."

"Well, hell, who says whatever we're looking for was taken that night? Somebody took the time to pull the digital card out. I'd be real interested to see what you have. How long did they say it would take until you get them?"

Dirk shook his head. "I have no idea. I had a lot of other thinks to worry about at the time. It was on Saturday and today is Wednesday. I'd guess today or tomorrow for sure."

"Can I ask you not to open them until we can do it together?"

"Now why is that?" Dirk questioned.

"For your protection as much as anything. As long as you have nothing to hide."

"Hell, no, I don't."

Gunderson gave him a toothy smile. "Good then, let's work together on this. I'm short a deputy."

"No big loss there," Dirk mumbled, getting out of the car.

"What time does your mail come?"

"Between two and three."

"I'll be talking to you then."

If Gus thought it strange when Dirk suddenly wanted to get the mail himself, he didn't say. He just gave his son a curious look. "Fine."

Dirk was at the mailbox waiting when the mail truck pulled up. The driver, one of Rosa's nephews, greeted Dirk and handed over a short stack of letters and ads that clearly eliminated a package from Wal-Mart.

After thanking him, Dirk asked if he could pick up his own mail in the morning before it left on the route.

"Sure thing, "Manuel said. "I'll leave it at the post office if you like. That way you can get it by eight-thirty. You expecting something special?"

"Yeah, you might say that. Thanks."

Dirk walked back, called Gunderson and told him he'd come by his office by nine if the package was there. When he hung up the phone, Bella was sitting at the kitchen table waiting for him.

She gestured to a chair beside her. "Have a seat, son, we've hardly had a chance to talk with all the commotion going on."

Dirk sat down, smiling. "Where is everybody?"

"The girls are all over at Carrie's. Christa wanted to see the baby. Jason is with Gus—he adores his grandpa."

"Yeah, he does. Listen Mom, I want you to know how much I appreciate you helping me out here."

"It was hardly an imposition. You'll never know how happy I was you called. Frankly, I wasn't sure I was welcome." At the sight of Dirk's surprised face, she held up a hand. "I know I deserted you, and I'm sorry. I'd like a chance to make up for it with my grandchildren. I hardly know them. I'd like to remedy that."

"How does Gus feel about it?"

Bella's laughter was quick, almost a giggle. "He likes it just fine."

"Well, it's sure fine with me. I can use the help, with Julia leaving."

"I can't believe you're letting that woman go. She's a jewel."

Dirk averted his gaze. He got up to check the coffee pot, poured himself a cup and sat back down. "I don't want her to leave, but she has a career to go back to. She's a doctor. I can't ask her to stay; it has to be her decision."

"That girl is crazy about you."

"Yeah, well, I like her too, but sometimes that isn't enough."

* * * *

Dirk walked into the post office at exactly eight-thirty. Manuel called out a greeting from behind a stack of shelves, and said it would take just a few more minutes for them to finish sorting.

Dirk paced back and forth while perusing the pictures on the wall and varieties of stamps available until Manuel came up to the counter with a handful of mail.

"Here you go," Manuel said. "Sure is some excitement around here lately, ain't it? First your ex-wife and that fella with her, and now Deputy Sanford. Lot's going on for a small town. Makes a fella wonder if it's safe to walk the streets. Sorry about your ex by the way. I didn't make it to the memorial, but they said it was real nice."

Dirk didn't bother mentioning that Gloria wasn't his ex. He just murmured his thanks and hurried out to the Land Rover to go through the mail.

It was there. On the bottom of the pile. A thick photo package. He really wanted to rip it open, but what the hell, he didn't have anything to hide. He started the SUV, jerked it in gear, and headed for the sheriff's office, hoping Gunderson would be there early.

Gunderson's patrol car was parked out front. He hurried into the office, package in hand.

The sheriff greeted him with a grin. "All right. Let's hope we have something there." He got up and locked the front door while Dirk took a seat at a side table.

When Dirk started opening the sticky flap, Gunderson cautioned him that the pictures should be kept in order. Dirk nodded and pulled out the inner envelope, noticing his hands were shaking. Truthfully, he didn't expect to find anything helpful. He handed the envelope to Gunderson.

Gunderson carefully removed the photos, and starting at the top, began flipping through them, handing each one to Dirk as he went. There were numerous shots of Jason and Christa as babies, of Megan holding them, and even a couple of him holding them. The sheriff was flipping through them at a fast rate, but Dirk couldn't help but pause to look at the cherubic faces of his twins. Why hadn't he seen any of these? Why had she deleted them? Rosa had found the camera after Gloria left for New York, so the photos were of the kids when they were still quite small. He was going through the ones where they'd started walking just before he went to prison, when Gunderson made a hissing sound.

Dirk looked up. "You find something?"

Gunderson handed over a photo. "Take a look."

It was a dark haired woman in a red dress walking into the barn. "Who is it?" Dirk asked.

Gunderson handed Dirk the next photo. It was a picture of Raymond Sanford in a heated embrace with the same woman, her dress shoved up to her waist. Only the side of her face was visible.

Dirk shook his head. He couldn't tell who it was. "Are there any more?"

Gunderson flipped through the next couple of photos. "Nope. That's it."

"Hell, who is it?"

"I don't know, but I have a hunch if we can figure it out, we'll know who your wife was blackmailing. Who was wearing a red dress like that?"

Dirk stared at the picture, trying to think. Finally he shook his head. "Damned if I remember."

"Well, shit. Somebody must know?"

Dirk's head shot up. "Melody Dupree. She notices clothes. She'd know."

Gunderson reached over to his desk, grabbed the cordless phone, and pushed it toward Dirk.

Dirk dialed Melody's number. It rang four times before she picked up. She answered with a cheery hello.

"Melody, it's Dirk."

"Hi sweetie. What's on your mind? Sex?"

Dirk laughed. "No, not this time. I'm sitting here with Gunderson and we're going over a few things. I was wondering if you remembered who was wearing a red dress the night of Sanford's party."

"Hmmm, what kind of red dress?"

Dirk looked at the picture. "I'd have to say sort of figure hugging. Maybe stretchy."

"Why do you want to know? Do you have a new lead?"

"I don't have time to explain now, but it's important."

"Well..." Melody hesitated, obviously thinking. "Sharon Berkley had a red dress, not necessarily slinky though."

"Sharon's blonde. I'm looking for someone with dark hair."

"Geez, picky yet. Let me think a minute... Oh wait, I know." She gave a silky laugh. "What's it worth to you?"

"Melody!"

"Okay. Okay. Have you ever heard the expression 'two squirrels fighting to get out of a gunnysack'? Trust me, some woman should not wear spandex."

He knew she was playing him because he wouldn't tell her what was going on. "Cut the crap, Melody. I'm not in the mood."

"So what's new there?"

When she finally put a name to her little antics, Dirk gave her a curt thanks, promised to call her later, and hung up the phone. He turned to stare at Gunderson in disbelief.

CHAPTER TWENTY SEVEN

"What did she say?" Gunderson asked.

Dirk shook his head. "We may still be on the wrong track. Melody said Francesca Chatterley had a tight red dress on. Maybe there was someone else Melody doesn't remember."

Gunderson blew a stream of air through his teeth. "Maybe not."

"You don't seriously believe Paul Chatterley's wife would have an affair with the likes of Ray Sanford?"

Gunderson took another look at the photo then sighed. You're too young to remember this, but Ray and Francesca dated in high school.

"Crimony, you've got to be kidding."

"Not only am I not kidding, but they were pretty hot and heavy back then. Problem was they both wanted something the other didn't have—money. They parted ways, and when Francesca married Chatterley, Ray pursued Ramona Melendez—"

"Daughter of Ramon Melendez, founder of Danango," Dirk supplied. "Which is how Sanford got his big spread and the house in town."

"You got it. It's no secret she keeps him on tight purse strings."

"You think Francesca and Sanford have been having a thing going for—what—thirty-some years?"

Gunderson shook his head. "I seriously doubt that. Chatterley isn't one to share his wife with anyone, especially since he's planning to run for the senate this fall. A scandal would ruin any chance he had of getting elected. Which brings us to Gloria, and this photograph."

Dirk picked up the two photos again. "I guess we're thinking along the same lines here. Paul Chatterley had the most to lose, and the money to pay Gloria off."

Their eyes met in silent agreement.

"What do we do now?" Dirk asked.

Gunderson rubbed his hands over his face in a weary gesture. "We need to think this thing out. First of all, who killed Ray Sanford? If it was Paul, why do it now?"

Dirk nodded. "Yeah. I can't see him suddenly going into a jealous rage after all this time. We're still missing something. Whoever killed Gloria and Edwards had an accomplice. Their bodies were several miles apart. Somebody needed to drive one of the vehicles."

"Yup, that's my thought," Gunderson concurred. "I don't think we have enough evidence to arrest him. These photos aren't proof of anything except that Ray and Francesca had a little tryst."

A number of ideas rolled around in Dirk's head. Being a lawyer, Chatterley had a vast understanding of the law. He wouldn't be prone to making foolish mistakes…but if the pictures got him to react once, they might work again.

"Wire me," Dirk said. "I'll approach Chatterley with the pictures and see if I can get him to admit he was being blackmailed."

Gunderson scratched the short beard on his chin and shook his head. "Sounds too dangerous. If he is our killer, he already has three murders under his belt. One more isn't going to faze him."

"Yeah, and in the meantime we have a killer walking around loose. The whole town is scared."

It took over an hour for Dirk to convince Gunderson that going after Chatterley before the police were involved was the best way to trap him—possibly the only way. Once Chatterley knew he was a viable suspect, he'd start lawyering up on them, and with his connections and no direct proof, he'd be untouchable. If Dirk went to him with the photos, Chatterley would have no way of knowing the police were already involved.

Gunderson didn't have the type of equipment they had in larger stations. He was able to hook Dirk up with a recorder and a mike, but didn't have the remote needed to listen in on their conversation.

* * * *

A few minutes before noon, Dirk walked up to Chatterley's sprawling residence and rapped the lion's head knocker several times. As he waited for someone to answer the door, he went over what he planned to say. He'd show the photo to Chatterley and ask if he'd seen them before. Dirk was certain he could tell the truth by the man's eyes. Dirk would then tell him he knew about the blackmailing scheme.

After a few minutes, Dirk hit the knocker again, harder this time. Glancing to the left, he double-checked the open garage door. When he'd approached the house he'd seen two cars parked inside, Francesca's candy-apple red Corvette convertible and her husband's Escalade 4x4 beside it.

Somebody had to be home.

He shot a glimpse back to the trees by the gated entrance where he knew Gunderson was stationed, shrugged and tried the door. It was unlocked. He pushed it open and looked inside. The house was as lavish inside as outside. Everything appeared neat and tidy, no sign of anything amiss. He stepped inside the large foyer wondering if walking through an unlocked door was breaking and entering. He left the door open thinking that might make a difference. A large archway gave him a view of the elaborate kitchen and dining room, on the other side a formal sitting room.

"Anybody home?" he called out.

From a partially open set of French doors off the dining room he heard a muffled "Go away."

He debated only a moment before entering the elaborate office. A mammoth mahogany desk scrolled with intricate detail dominated a corner of the room. Large leather bound books lined the wall. Behind the desk sat Paul Chatterley, a drink in his hand, a nearly empty bottle of expensive Chivas Scotch in front of him.

He acknowledged Dirk with bleary red eyes. "What the hell you want, Travis?"

Dirk kept his distance, staying near the door, contemplating the man's inebriated state. It took him only a moment to decide it might work to his advantage.

He walked forward and flipped the pictures on the desk in front of Chatterley. "I know Gloria was blackmailing you, and I thought you might like to have these back."

Chatterley picked up the prints and stared at them a moment before he suddenly crumpled them in his hand and flung them into a wastebasket at his side.

"You are so full of shit, Travis. Sit down and have a drink." He reached behind his chair and pulled a highball glass off a shelf. He filled it half full, shoved it toward Dirk, and then refilled his own glass.

Not sure what else to do, Dirk picked up the glass and sat down in one of the two leather side chairs. Things were not going as he'd expected. He could have sworn when Chatterley looked at those photos, he was seeing them for the first time. His best move was to let the man talk. Drinking men loved to talk.

He took a small sip of the smooth Chevas and waited.

"You're a good man, Travis. I wish you'd have let me represent you when that asshole, Sanford took you to court. I can promise you one thing—you'd never have spent so much as one night in jail."

That statement made Dirk wonder if Chatterley knew his wife and Ray had dated thirty years earlier. Chatterley came from Denver, but Danango was a small town.

"I really loved that woman," Chatterley murmured, probably more to himself than to Dirk. "I would have given her anything. I gave her more money than she knew what to do with—I didn't even ask how she spent it, but it wasn't enough to keep her from—"

Dirk waited for him to go on, but he seemed to be lost in thought. He shifted in his seat and spilled some of his drink out on the carpet beside his chair, then pretended to have another sip.

When Chatterley remained quietly staring at the far wall, Dirk prompted him. "Did you pay Gloria off to protect Francesca?" he asked.

Chatterley's puffy eyes swiveled back to focus on Dirk. Suddenly he threw his head back and laughed. "Do I look stupid? If she'd tried to blackmail me, I'd have made sure she never saw the outside of a jail again, even if it had cost me the election. I have a good law practice; I can live without being in the senate if it had come to that."

Dirk resisted the urge to drain his drink, and wetted his lips enough to make it look like he was drinking.

Chatterley sat back and looked Dirk straight in the eye. "I told you I'd have done anything for Francie, but that's not quite true—I wouldn't have killed for her. I'm an honorable man, Dirk. I would have made a good senator."

Dirk was starting to believe him. "Then why ruin it all by killing Sanford?"

Chatterley's gaze turned brittle. He gave Dirk a quick once-over then smiled. "Why don't you take your wire off, Travis, and lay it on the desk so you don't miss anything?"

Even drunk, Paul Chatterley was no fool. Dirk reached beneath his belt, unthreaded the wire receiver, and placed the recorder on the desk in front of him.

"Is it still on?"

Dirk nodded. "Yeah, want me to turn it off?"

"No, leave it. I have nothing to hide at this point."

Something about the chill in his voice disturbed Dirk. He took a serious swallow of his drink and sat back, waiting. Chatterley obviously had more to say.

The wanna-be senator stared blankly at the picture of his wife occupying a sacred spot on his desk. Moisture brightened his eyes as he picked it up. "I wouldn't have killed for her, but I would have given up the senate race. If only she'd come to me. But no, she went to that bastard instead. They schemed and plotted behind my back, taking care of things in their own ignorant way." He flung the framed photo against the far wall where it shattered into jagged fragments.

His gaze swiveled back to Dirk. "Do you have any idea what it's like to love a woman who can make your heart bleed without making a wound?"

Dirk had an answer, but he kept it to himself. He released a deep internal sigh as he put the pieces together in his mind. Gloria was blackmailing Francesca, and when Gloria came back to Colorado, probably to get more money, Francesca went to Sanford and the two of them murdered Gloria and Edwards. Apparently Francesca knew her husband would give up the senate race for her, and that was likely the last thing she wanted.

Up to this point Chatterley hadn't said one thing that incriminated him, but he also hadn't explained what happened to Sanford either. He glanced at the recorder's blinking red light.

"When did you find this all out?" Dirk asked.

"An hour before Ray Sanford's brains hit the wall." Chatterley said with a sneer that brought chills to Dirks spine

Dirk's hand squeezed around the empty highball glass. *Was that a confession? Not exactly.* He wanted to ask who killed Sanford, but he also didn't want Chatterley to clam up in the face of a direct question. Dirk was certain that if he could keep the man talking he'd inadvertently explain what happened.

"How did you learn the truth?" he asked.

Chatterley sat forward and leaned his elbows on the desk. "Love is an amazing thing," he said dryly. "I'd just come back from a meeting in Denver. The phone was ringing as I walked in the house, and by the time I picked it up, Francie had already answered upstairs. It was Sanford. He was all excited about this camera he found in your truck—Gloria's camera. They went on to talk about how much they loved each other and when I'd be going back to Denver so they could get together again. As I listened, I had to choke down the bile in my throat to keep from heaving."

Dirk wondered why Chatterley talked so openly in front of a recorder. The obvious answer was Chatterley didn't plan to allow that evidence to leave the room. Dirk was debating whether or not to grab the recorder and make a run for it when Chatterley pulled a gun out of his desk drawer. Adrenalin pounded like a drum in Dirk's head. He hit the floor in front of the desk a split second before the roar of the 45-caliber weapon reverberated throughout the room. The next thing Dirk heard was Chatterley's chair overturning and his body falling with a sickening thud to the floor.

He was still trying to catch his breath when Gunderson charged through the door, his gun drawn. He stopped dead, swearing profusely, when he spotted Dirk on the floor.

"Are you all right, son?"

Still breathless, Dirk nodded. "Yeah, I think so." While Dirk got to his feet, Gunderson made his way around the desk.

"What the hell happened here?" Gunderson asked.

Gripping the edge of the desk, Dirk shook his head. His mouth felt dry. "He was talking and all of a sudden he had a gun in his hand. I dove for the floor before he fired it, but I guess I wasn't his target."

"Thank God for that. Where's Francesca? Her car's in the garage?"

Dirk came up beside the sheriff and looked down at what was left of Chatterley's head. His stomach lurched. It was the second gruesome sight he'd seen in less than a week. "I don't know. I haven't seen her."

"Well, if she's in the house, the shot would have brought her in here." Gunderson nodded toward the desk. "What's with the recorder?"

Dirk walked away from the sight behind the desk. "He was on to me. I took it out and offered to turn it off, but he said to leave it on."

"Did he confess?"

"Not exactly. It seemed strange he had no inhibitions about talking in front of the recorder. It appears he'd planned on ending his life all along. I don't understand though. He didn't actually admit to any wrongdoing. Why did he give up so easily?"

"Did you find out anything?"

"Oh, yeah, it was Francesca being blackmailed and she sought out Ray Sanford to help do the dirty work. It's all on there."

Gunderson stuck his gun back in its black leather holster, walked over to the recorder, hit rewind then play. The tape was somewhat muffled until Dirk had set it out on the desk. From that point it was loud and clear.

"I guess we better find Francesca. Looks like she's the only one left to arrest."

They found her in the master bedroom laid out in the bed in a pool of blood.

Dirk stared at the broken body of Paul Chatterley's beloved wife. "That's why he gave up. As much as he loved her, he couldn't deal with her loving Ray Sanford. He didn't exactly confess to killing Sanford, but he sort of admitted to seeing him die. I'd make a bet the same gun killed all three of them."

CHAPTER TWENTY EIGHT

After reporting to Melody as he'd promised, Dirk put the twins to bed, then called his family and employees together to tell them what had transpired. He relayed his own relief that Gloria's saga was finally put to rest. The only tears came from Megan, who sat in the protective cradle of her grandmother's arms.

* * * *

Charlie Mack was going to drive Julia and Katie to the airport since Dirk had opted out. Julia knew why, and she felt awful about it, but she knew she had to leave, had to go back and find out if she still had a life and a practice in Minnesota.

She had already said her goodbyes to the kids, which was difficult even though she'd spent the last few days preparing them. But she still had some unfinished business with Dirk. She couldn't leave without telling him she could be pregnant.

The light was on in his office when she knocked. He called out to say the door was open, and when she entered, she found him facing the window, staring out into the darkness.

"I need to talk to you," she said to his back.

He swiveled around and motioned to the chair in front of his desk. Julia noticed the dark circles under his eyes and hoped his sleeplessness was from the ordeal he'd been through with Chatterley, rather than her leaving.

She ignored his request to sit down. "I have something I need to tell you," she said, swallowing at the thickness building in her throat.

"Unless you find it necessary to stand over me while you talk, would you please sit? Otherwise my mother's manner book would require me to stand too—and frankly I don't have the energy."

Julia wrapped her arms around her body and sat down at the edge of the chair. "Sorry, it's just that this is difficult for me."

His brows rose. "Sounds serious."

"It could be."

"Well, after everything that's happened this week, I don't think anything you say would surprise me—unless you're going to tell me you're staying in Colorado after all."

She mentally flinched at his words, but summoned her courage to go on. "I know I should have mentioned this in the barn the other day, but I kept hoping…things would…be resolved before I left."

Dirk steepled his hands in front of him and waited for her to go on.

"After I had my miscarriage, I had requested a depo shot. It seems Geno found out about it, gave me a placebo, and falsified the report because he wanted me pregnant again right away. At the time he didn't know I'd be filing for divorce."

It only took a split second for Dirk's eyes to widen. "If I understand you correctly, that means you could be pregnant."

"Yes." Her answer was little more than a hoarse whisper.

His gaze slid to her belly as though he might see some evidence.

"I'm sorry I didn't tell you sooner… I just—"

"And if you are," he continued, "the child could be mine...or Geno's."

She nodded, blinking back tears, telling herself she wasn't going to cry. None of this was her fault, and she was tired of shouldering the blame for the actions of other people, namely Geno and her father.

He leaned back in his chair staring at her for a moment. "By all rights I guess I should be angry at you for not telling me sooner, but I've been sitting here doing a little soul searching of my own. I've come to the realization that what other people say and do isn't always about me. Sometimes they need to do what is right for them." He smiled. "I know you kept your professional status from me because you thought I wouldn't hire you. On the other hand, I didn't mention in my ad that I was an ex-con. Who would have come to work for me? I also feel you didn't tell me about the possible pregnancy because you believed I would put pressure on you to stay. Am I right so far?"

She nodded.

He sat forward placing his arms on the desk. "Among other obvious reasons, Gloria left because I was too rigid. I'm not going to make that same mistake with you. Don't get me wrong—I love you and I want you to stay, but not if you're going to regret it a couple of years down the road and start wishing for your old life back. I hope you get my drift there. If you choose to stay or come back later, it has to be until death do us part. A lot of women wouldn't be happy here, but it's my home, and ranching is pretty much all I know."

"I understand," Julia murmured.

"There's something else you should understand. I'd love your child; I don't care if the baby is Geno's. I'd love it because it's yours, and I'm willing to send support money. Plus, rest assured, I have no intention of putting a claim on any of your trust fund."

Julia brushed her hand across her eyes. "Thank you."

"Will you do me the kindness of letting me know if you are pregnant so that I don't have to spend the rest of my life wondering?"

"Of course."

She stood up to leave. Just being in the same room with him was making her heart ache, she wanted him so much. He was right though. What if she stayed and then regretted her decision? There'd be no going back. She'd hurt him as surely as Gloria and his mother had.

"One more thing," he said. "You did a great job preparing Jason and Christa—and you did it without leaving them with false promises. I hope someday you do have children because you'd make a wonderful mother."

She thanked him, smiling. "I did promise to write to Megan. I hope that's all right."

"Certainly, I know she'll appreciate it."

"Okay, then, I guess I'd better get some sleep. We have an early flight." She was glad he didn't hold out his hand to shake. Touching him would not have been a good idea.

"I won't be there to see you off in the morning, so I'll say goodbye now, Julia. I hope everything goes well for you in Minnesota."

"Goodbye, Dirk" She could barely get the words past her constricted throat.

When she turned to flee from the room, his voice stopped her at the door.

"Julia, if you came to my room just for tonight, I wouldn't turn you away."

Her heart rate did an instant triple time. "I can't."

Julia hurried out the door and pulled it shut behind her. She leaned against it and allowed her silent tears to flow. *I can't, my love, because if I'd spent the night in your arms, I'd be unable to leave.*

CHAPTER TWENTY NINE

Two weeks after she returned home to resume her old life, County Med called to offer her position back. She should have been elated, but somehow she couldn't summon the enthusiasm she should have had. It's what she wanted, wasn't it? Her medical practice without interference from Geno?

It was what she wanted—before Colorado.

She agreed to meet some former co-workers for lunch at the hospital cafeteria, thinking it might cheer her up and get her back in the mood to practice again. The lunch turned out to be a gab session with her fielding details about her deceased ex-husband. It seemed they were more interested in hearing about him than what she'd been doing the last month and a half.

The only person wanting to know about her was an attractive, energetic anesthesiologist. When he asked her to go out to dinner, she wished she could get excited about it and go, but after Dirk, other men paled in comparison. She declined his offer, and was glad he didn't persist after she turned him down.

Afterwards, she did go shopping for sheet music to send to Megan. From there she went home and wrote Megan a letter. Mostly she asked about the twins and told Megan to watch for a birthday gift coming in the mail. She hoped the snow globe would arrive in time. Though it pained her, she didn't ask about Dirk.

As much as she loved Dirk, she couldn't give up medicine to live on the ranch. The calls she had from Rosa's family had made Julia realize her need to use her skills. Being handicapped without a license had torn her apart, in addition to the illegality, she'd been unable to write needed prescriptions, and because of the poverty level, she couldn't refer anyone to other doctors—they wouldn't have gone. Telling a person in pain to wait two weeks until a doctor came to town was unconscionable and archaic.

Thinking about Dirk and the pathetic excuse for a clinic in Danango depressed her. As usual, when she needed cheering up, she picked up the phone to call Katie.

However, instead of dialing, she sat with the phone in her hand thinking. Katie would just tell her, "If you don't like how your life is going—get off your behind and do something about it."

Julia decided it was time to take charge of her own life—and she knew just where to start.

She dialed information for Denver.

* * * *

A few days later, Julia knew she was pregnant. If she'd had any doubts about wanting to have a baby, they were quickly dissolved. It surprised her to realize how thrilled she really was.

Thoughts of Geno put a bit of a damper on her elation, but she told herself it didn't matter. Geno was dead. In all likelihood, Dirk was the father. They'd made sweet, wonderful love many times during that week.

She missed him. She missed Jason, and Christa, and Megan. She even missed Gus. But it was Dirk her arms ached for each night she crawled into her bed, a bed that seemed too big and too cold for one person. She longed for his touch, for his kisses. She missed sitting out on the deck together and watching the sun go down. She missed the way he made her laugh.

The ringing phone pulled her from her musings.

It was Katie. "How did the test come out?"

Julia laughed at her overzealous sister. "You don't beat around the bush do you, sis?"

"No! You better tell me before I come over there and start shaking you."

"I'm officially pregnant, Katie."

"Are you happy about it?"

Julia smiled. "I'm very happy. I just have to figure out how to tell Dirk."

Katie's soft chuckle came over the line. "You just call him up and say 'hi honey, you're going to be a father'."

"I wish it was that simple," Julia said.

"I'll be done here in about an hour. I'll pick up a bottle of non-alcoholic champagne and Chinese take-out, and we'll celebrate. You can tell me how your plans for the clinic are coming along. See ya."

The phone went dead. That was Katie.

While waiting for Katie, Julia walked down to her condo lobby to pick up her mail. She found a letter from Megan. Julia tore it open and started reading even before she got back to her apartment.

Dear Julia,

Thank you for the Simon and Garfunckle music. I know they're really old, but I still love to play their songs. I've been practicing every day just like when you were here. Also, the snow globe came. It's twice as big as the one I had and it's even more beautiful. Thank you so much. I've been watering the flowers. They look really nice.

School starts next week. Grandma and I went to Denver on a shopping trip. It was so much fun and she knows a lot about clothes just like you do. Jason and Christa will go to pre-school three days a week. The bus will come right to the ranch and pick us up.

I guess I should tell you that Dirk is pretty miserable. Some days he forgets to shave and grandma keeps telling him to eat. The morning you left, he took off on Black Lightening and didn't come home until suppertime. We were all worried, but granddad said he'd be okay. Mack said it's good for Black Lightening to be getting a lot of exercise. Charlie Mack really likes Katie by the way.

We all had to write letters to the judge because Dirk is filing papers to adopt me. Do you think he'd mind if I'd start calling him Dad?

I miss you very much.

Love,
Megan

Julia looked up from the letter, tears stinging her eyes. Her emotions were on a seesaw ride. She wanted Dirk to be happy—so why was she glad to know he wasn't? She put a hand on her belly willing it to be Dirk's child growing inside her.

When the doorbell started its incessant ringing, she glanced at the clock, thinking Katie must have finished early. Not wanting her sister to see her sadness, she brushed away her tears and forced a smile on her face.

She swung the door open to face Dirk.

"Oh my God!" She stood frozen with the doorknob in one hand, the other pressed over her mouth.

"Does that mean I can come in?" he asked.

She had to force herself to keep from throwing her arms around him. "What—what are you doing here?"

"I heard they had good pizza in Minnesota."

She laughed and stepped back. "I'm sorry, come in. You just really surprised me."

He walked passed her. "I'm surprising myself by being here."

"Is everything alright at home?"

"If by *home* you mean the ranch. Yes, everything is fine except that its heartbeat is missing."

She stopped resisting and flew into his arms, pressing her face into his neck. He held her a long moment before they stepped apart.

"How are you feeling?" he asked glancing at her mid-section.

"I feel good and I just found out today I'm pregnant." She was unable to keep the excitement out of her voice.

He smiled. "You sound happy about it."

"I am. I'm very happy—and I'm even happier to see you. I just got a letter from Megan, she brought me up to date on what's been happening."

Dirk made a snorting sound. "I suppose she mentioned I've been doing a lot of riding."

Laughter bubbled out of her. "She did say something about Black Lightning getting quite a bit of exercise."

"Yeah. Well—"

"I'm happy to see you Dirk, but I'm curious. Why exactly are you here?"

He stuck his hands in his pockets and shrugged. "I've been doing a lot more than just riding, Julia, I've been thinking. I only need one more year of school to become a licensed veterinarian. I've specialized in large animals, but it wouldn't take much to get up to speed on dogs and cats." He offered her a sudden arresting smile. "I hear they have a lot of pets in Minneapolis."

Julia's heart started racing at the speed of light. "Are you saying you'd be willing to give up the ranch and move here?"

He nodded. "That's what I'm saying, Julia. With Mack's help, David is willing to take over for me. I love you, and I can't function without you. I need you, you're in my blood, and you're in my heart. I'm willing to do whatever it takes to be with you—if you'll have me."

She again threw herself at him, kissing his face, his eyes, his mouth, his cheeks. "I love you too," she managed to say between kisses. "I've missed you and the kids so much I can't think most of the time."

"Does that mean you'll marry me, Julia?"

"Yes, yes, yes."

He picked her up and swung her around. "It'll take me a year to start holding up my end, but I have enough cash set aside to get a house big enough for all of us."

"Julia, are you home? Your door was open—Oh my—"

Dirk set Julia down grinning at her sister. "Hello, Katie. You can be the first to congratulate us."

Katie's gaze moved back and forth between the two of them. "What exactly are we celebrating?" she asked.

Julia hugged her sister and told her how Dirk had agreed to go to school and move for her.

Katie set her packages down, smiling "I guess that means you didn't get around to telling him your news yet."

"She sure did," Dirk said. "I guess you know we're going to have a baby."

Katie, eyebrows arching, looked at Julia. "You haven't mentioned anything about you-know-what, have you?"

"I didn't get a chance."

Dirk frowned, his razor sharp look zeroing in first on Katie then Julia. "Is somebody going to tell me about *you-know-what*?"

Julia's smile broadened as she shot her sister a mischievous look. "Do you suppose I should tell him?"

Katie glanced at Dirk. "Only if you want to live to breathe another day."

"I got my license to practice medicine in Colorado, and I've been working on funding to expand the clinic in Danango and keep it open five days a week. I'm asking for two doctors with alternating shifts, an RN and a receptionist. I'm also hoping for different specialists to volunteer their time once a month."

Dirk stared at her. "You really think that's possible?"

"Yes, I do."

Katie laughed. "Trust me, Dirk, when this lady sets her mind to something she's awfully persuasive."

"There certainly is a need for it. Will you be able to get the funding?"

"I already have most of it—from some unbelievable donors."

One side of Dirk's mouth kicked up into a disarming grin that had a way of making Julia melt. "If it'll keep me from tending to gerbils and hamsters I'll volunteer labor, and rebuild that clinic myself."

"You might have to put up with me once in a while," Katie said. "I'm working on transferring to Denver."

Dirk groaned. "I'm not sure Colorado is big enough to handle the two of you, but I do have an employee who'd like to hear that."

Katie laughed. "He already has. I'm leaving now because I think the two of you have a lot of catching up to do. If you manage to get around to eating, there's Kung Pao Chicken in those bags on the table. See ya later."

After Katie left, Dirk took Julia in his arms. "She's right, you know. We do have a lot of catching up to do."

Julia slipped her arms around his neck and pressed her body against him. "What did you have in mind?"

"Sex."

"You want to eat Kung Pao chicken first?"

"Maybe on our fiftieth wedding anniversary, I'd answer 'yes' to that—but maybe not."

EPILOGUE

"Nice place you have here."

Julia looked up at her husband, and smiled. She got up from behind her desk and came around it to plant a warm kiss on his lips. Then she bent to the bundle on his arm and gave her six-month-old son a kiss. She was ever amazed at how soft a baby's skin was.

Jaymes Michael Travis waved his chubby arms at her, gurgling. She plucked the wriggling infant from her husband and nuzzled his neck. "I love you, Jaymes, just as much as I love your daddy." She turned to Dirk. "What brings you into town, honey?"

Dirk gave her the lopsided grin that had a way of turning her to mush. "Thought you might need a little help getting ready for the open house tomorrow. Mom and Dad took the twins to Taco Town and then they're going trick or treating. Jaymes insisted he'd rather see you than get candy."

Julia laughed. "Talking already is he?"

"Only to me. He whispers in my ear."

"Does that come with slobber?"

Dirk grinned. "Usually, yes. Are you ready for the big day?"

Julia looked around at the new Paul Chatterley Clinic. Some people were shocked at the name, but since the Chatterley family donated seventy-five percent of the funds to build it, she'd been able to make it twice the size she'd planned. The three Chatterley sisters wanted their brother remembered for all the good works he'd done, rather than murdering two people. No one in town had known of all the charities and non-profit organizations Paul Chatterley had supported over the years.

"Do you think some people won't come here because we used Chatterley's name?"

Dirk put an arm around his concerned wife's shoulders. "Not a chance, sweetheart. Not with you running it. You had these people won over before you even built the clinic. Did I ever tell you how many calls for medical help we got after you left?"

"That reminds me, you know what I heard today? Ramona Melendez Sanford is running for mayor. She's going to speak at the opening tomorrow."

Dirk's brow shot up. "Now isn't that a fine turn of events. I'll bet a hundred bucks you had something to do with that."

Smiling, Julia bet over and whispered something in her son's ear. To her husband she said, "You'll have to ask your son about that."

About the Author

Born and raised on a North Dakota farm, Jannifer started writing at the age of twelve, creating novels by memory while walking home from a one-room schoolhouse. After moving to Minnesota she began serious writing in 1974 while working full time. She has since retired and spends summers in Minnesota and migrates with the birds to Yuma, Arizona for the winter.

When she's not writing, she's sewing for craft shows, painting rocks, and pursuing her favorite pastime—traveling the world on a cruise ship. And, last but not least, spending valuable time with her incredibly awesome family.

She is currently working on her sixth novel, Blood Crystal.

Learn more at: www.janniferhoffman.com

A Perfect Escape by Maddie James

A changed identity. A secluded beach. A sniper…

Megan Thomas is running for her life. From Chicago, from the mob, from her husband. She runs to the only place she feels safe—a sccluded cottage on an east coast barrier island.

Smyth Parker is running from life. From work, from society, from a jealous ex-wife—his only consolation the solitude of Newport Island. He doesn't need to anyone to screw up that plan. And he sure as hell doesn't need to complicate it with Megan Thomas.

But when Megan fears she's been found, she runs to the only safe place she knows, and straight into the arms of the one person who might be able to help, Smyth. Her escape might yet still be perfect.
Or is it?

$6.50 e-book
$15.99 Print

Brilliant Disguise by JL Wilson

An undercover FBI agent in a tiny Iowa town finds you can't hide anything from a woman who's determined to find out the truth...

Nick Baxter, an undercover FBI agent, thinks his BRILLIANT DISGUISE will fool the hicks in New Providence, Iowa. They won't suspect he's there investigating widow Shannon Delgardie, under suspicion of treason. What Nick doesn't know is that everybody in town is conspiring to protect her and investigate him in return.

Shannon needs help. The men her late husband blackmailed are closing in and the FBI might be involved. When Nick approaches her, can she trust him? With the aid of computer hackers and hair stylists, she uncovers the truth, finding a love she never expected in a tiny Iowa town.

$6.50 e-book
$15.99 Print

Project Seduction by Tatiana March

Project Manager: Georgina Coleman, VP at Pacific Bank, 28 years old. Brilliant and determined, but lacking in social skills.

Project background: Transfer from London to San Diego allows Georgina to shed her dowdy image and get a life.

Project objective: Seduce a man and lose her virginity.

Timeline: Seven weeks, starting from the completion of Project Flowchart.

Target: Georgina's downstairs neighbor, a surly cop named Rick Matisse.

Complication: Rick's 12-year-old daughter Angelina, who thinks Georgina would be the perfect girlfriend to keep Dad on his toes.

Distraction: Money laundering investigation which requires Georgina to mingle with a bunch of Colombian thugs who believe that every woman should be owned by a man.

Project evaluation: A project can go wrong despite successful completion, if Project Manager fails to plan for how to deal with the Target after project closure.

$6.50 e-book
$14.99 Print

Find Resplendence Titles at the following retailers:

Resplendence Publishing:

www.resplendencepublishing.com

Amazon.com:

www.amazon.com

Target.com:

www.target.com

Fictionwise:

www.fictionwise.com

All Romance Ebooks

www.allromanceebooks.com

Mobipocket:

www.mobipocket.com